SHADOW
TAG
PERDITION GAMES

By L.E. Fraser

Also by L.E. Fraser

Shadow Tag, Perdition Games

Frozen Statues, Perdition Games

Red Rover, Perdition Games

Skully, Perdition Games

Simon Says, Perdition Games

"The world is a dangerous place to live; not because of the people who are evil, but because of the people who don't do anything about it." —Albert Einstein

PROLOGUE

ANNALISE COULD FEEL his eyes on her, the way a rabbit senses a stalking predator. As she tried to hurry across the icy sidewalk, the skin at the back of her neck prickled. Intuition was screaming at her that the drone was above her again. She froze and searched the midnight sky. Piercing needles of freezing rain pelted her face. She couldn't distinguish anything through the storm, but low visibility didn't guarantee her safety. She'd read that drones could be equipped with thermal vision cameras. It didn't need to see her. It could pick up her heat formation, record her movements, and send her GPS coordinates to him. He could be hidden anywhere—peering into a monitor and plotting where to intercept her.

Shivering, Annalise dropped her gaze to scrutinize the large park that surrounded the winding residential street. Eerie shadows moved in and out of the spaces between the dense treeline. Early April branches snapped under the violent wind, and gunshot cracks echoed through the night. Tension sliced through her chest and her breath caught in her throat.

The last words Robbie had ever spoken to her rang in her ears: "*Love you?*" he had scoffed. "*You're a bully—a small and vacuous person. I detest everything about you."* Hate had contorted his face into an ugly mask. *"You're an entitled bitch, and you'll pay for the appalling things you do to people. Everyone would be better off if you were dead."*

She wouldn't be out here alone—trying to catch a bus like a loser, no less—if it weren't for Denise. Her so-called friend had coerced her into staying at the bar when she knew Annalise was broke and couldn't afford an Uber. Angry tears mixed with the frosty rain hammering her face. She wouldn't be in this predicament if it weren't for Denise, who had insisted on buying bottomless Bellinis. It had all been show, so everyone could watch in awe when Denise had presented her black American Express card to the bartender. Fat girls were such attention-seekers.

The warm afterglow of the alcohol had dulled Annalise's paranoia for a few blessed hours. She'd been flippant and alluring in her skin-tight black skirt, sexy fringed jacket, and gorgeous suede sandals. As usual, everyone had flocked around her, eager to join her elite circle of friends. It had been great, except now she was out here alone and vulnerable to attack.

As she picked her way across black ice that coated the sidewalk, Annalise mulled over another enraging incident. At a party last week, someone had asked about her ex-fiancé. Denise had interrupted the private conversation, claiming Robbie hadn't stolen anything and Annalise had made it all up. Everyone had treated her as if she were unhinged for using social media to accuse the cheating prick of maxing out her credit cards and emptying her bank accounts. The posts should have incited disgust toward him and a flood of sympathy for her. The friends she'd handpicked as her worshiping entourage should have rushed to offer financial aid. Because of Denise, and her big mouth, Annalise's plan had backfired and making rent had required selling half her belongings on Kijiji. That was after a pawnshop owner had announced that the three-carat diamond engagement ring, nestled in an iconic blue Tiffany box, was paste. The box was a nice touch, he'd told her sardonically. Denise had had the audacity to laugh, as if the ugly creep was a shoo-in to win the next Canadian Comedy Award.

Hail the size of golf balls was now plummeting from the heavens, and her anger toward Denise shifted into high gear. If the heifer didn't appreciate how lucky she was to be included, she'd expel Denise from the group. Annalise managed multiple social media accounts for large corporations around the Greater Toronto Area. She was skilled in the nuances of engagement, and her personal accounts also had a ton of followers. Making Denise's life miserable would be a cakewalk, and she'd enjoy every second of publicly humiliating the traitorous bitch.

She suddenly heard a noise behind her and stopped under a streetlight's weak circle of light to listen. It sounded like the roar of an engine. Her fear rushed back and she spun around, gasping when she saw a large truck speeding toward her. The vehicle swerved toward the sidewalk and a set of headlights blinded her. She uttered a strangled whimper and lifted her arms across her face, cringing at the terrifying sound of squealing brakes. A volcanic spew of ice water soaked her and her eyes snapped open. Choking back tears, she wiped muddy water off her face and stood trembling on the sidewalk, staring helplessly as the truck reversed and rolled to a stop beside her.

The passenger window rolled down. "Hey, sorry about that. I couldn't stop," a man said. "It's nasty out. You want a ride?"

Water dripped from her soaked blouse and she clumsily tried to shield her breasts with her arms. "Like you have a hope of getting with me, take a look in the mirror, asshole."

He grunted something and again drove through the large puddle beside the sidewalk. The truck's spinning tires drenched her bare legs with another shower of frigid water.

"Too old. It can't be one of his friends," she whispered, but she didn't know for sure. She'd never bothered to meet her ex-fiancé's friends and wouldn't recognize a threat until it was too late.

Robbie's harassment had started with juvenile annoyances. He had called late at night and muttered threats, he'd hurled eggs at her house, he'd called the cops and made noise complaints—just irritating pranks that illustrated his immaturity. Then, about a month ago, things changed. On two cloudless days, Annalise had detected a drone above her. It flew too high for her to identify anything about it, but a primitive instinct had warned her it was stalking her. Last week, she'd come home and someone had been in her house. There wasn't any evidence of an intruder, but she knew someone had invaded her home and poked around her private belongings. That's when she started to take his threats seriously. She knew he didn't have the money to buy a drone or the technical skills to operate it. The only thing that made sense was that someone was helping Robbie exact his revenge, and Annalise didn't know how far that person would take the game.

From behind her, she heard the grumble of an approaching bus. She quickened her pace towards the bus stop but knew she'd never make it in time. Turning seductively, she waved her arm and gave the bus driver a good view of her naked breasts pressing against her rain-soaked blouse.

The bus lumbered by, leaving a plume of exhaust fumes in its wake. She stared after it in shock. Seething, she plotted the best course of action. A tear-soaked email to Toronto Transit, describing her fear and misery during a brutal ice storm, would work. After she sent it, she'd manipulate social media to provoke community outrage for the transit driver's reckless endangerment of a woman. By this time next week, the asshole would be unemployed. But that didn't solve her immediate problem. She had to get home. Her ex and his friends could be out there, following the drone, and waiting for an opportunity to grab her. To do what, Annalise didn't know, but she didn't intend to find out.

Taylor Creek Park was to her left. If she took the large city park, she'd cut the walking distance to her house in half. But she'd have to venture off the park's lit main path and navigate a steep hill that cut up to her road. It wasn't the safest route in the pitch dark, and it wouldn't be possible to climb in her heels. She'd tucked Prada flats into her shoulder bag in case the group went dancing after dinner. The inclement weather would ruin them, but at least she wouldn't snap an ankle. She unzipped her bag and dug around to find the shoes.

Balancing on first one foot and then the other, she changed shoes. Her feet were completely soaked now, but she was past caring. Once she'd packed her heels into her oversized Coach bag, she put her phone on voice command. If she saw anyone suspicious, she'd scream *911* and her cell would connect to emergency services. Gripping the phone in one hand and her canister of pepper spray in the other, Annalise scuttled into the park.

Her eyes scanned the fringe of trees that crowded against the cement path. Ice-encrusted branches extended into the inky sky like skeletal arms scraping free from a grave. Did he anticipate she'd use the park route? They'd often taken this shortcut when they were together. A chill slithered down her spine. She couldn't see through the shadows cast by the trees. She wouldn't hear footsteps over the white noise from the rain. A flight sensation consumed her and she ran blindly, expecting to feel a hand against her back at any moment. Her pepper spray fell from her hand but she kept running through the park, too terrified to even stop and catch her breath.

The hill—there's the hill. Just a few more minutes to the safety of the street.

She dashed off the path, her shoes skidding on the frozen grass of the slope. Whimpering in terror, she scrambled up the steep incline to the sidewalk and stood panting beneath a streetlight.

"You're fine," she whispered. "Everything's fine."

Her clawing fear receded and her heartrate slowed. Now she was in her own neighbourhood, she felt safe and continued toward her house, fuming at Denise and plotting her revenge. As Annalise passed a small public school, there was movement in her peripheral vision. She turned around, clutching her thin jacket against her chest.

"Help a veteran?" a voice snarled from beneath a dark hooded coat.

Terror and panic coalesced into rage. "If your free disability doesn't pay for your booze, get a job like the rest of us," she yelled.

The vagrant skulked back into the shadows and Annalise hurried to her house, disgusted and angry that she had to deal with dirty homeless people in her own neighbourhood.

Inside her front hall, she stripped off her wet clothes and dropped them in a soggy pile on the wood floor. Shivering, she trudged up a circular staircase to the second level. The two-bedroom semi was narrow and the living space was small, but the iron banister on the upstairs landing was unique and the western light was wonderful. She didn't want to move, but if she couldn't make rent next month, she wouldn't have a choice. The daunting process of finding an affordable rental in Toronto loomed over her like an executioner's axe. There was no option but to ask her mother for another loan. With the earlier time difference on the Pacific coast, it was eleven o'clock in Vancouver. She hoped her mom was still awake. Annalise could care less about dragging her out of bed, but it would be easier to manipulate her if she were in a good mood.

She stood under a hot shower for ten minutes, turning off the water when she thought she heard something in the hallway. She listened for a minute, but the house was silent. The sound must have come from the other side of the Victorian semi. She toweled off and pulled on a pair of warm leggings and a plaid flannel nightshirt. Admiring her reflection in the full-length mirror, Annalise thought she looked remarkably cute given the harrowing experience she'd just suffered. It all seemed so silly now but she'd play it up on social media. Her followers loved drama. Downstairs, she curled up on her leather sofa, steeling herself for *another* lecture from her mom.

It took seven rings before her mother's sleep-slurred voice answered. After Annalise assured her that she wasn't critically ill, the conversation went south fast.

"Why on earth did you allow that man access to your finances?" her mother asked.

"I didn't," Annalise said impatiently. "He hacked into my accounts. I told you all this."

"I'm concerned about what you're posting on social media," her mother said. "Your politically incorrect statements about the less fortunate are upsetting."

"It's called engagement," she snapped. "You don't understand how social media works."

"I understand that it's dangerous to make offensive remarks online to anonymous people," her mother retorted. "You're a twenty-two-year-old woman living alone."

"No one's going to attack me because of something I posted," she said with an exaggerated sigh.

"Did you really need to make all those disparaging comments about that barista?" her mother asked with disapproval.

"The whore seduced my fiancé," Annalise shouted.

"You don't know that," her mother calmly insisted. "And even if they are involved, the names you called her crossed a line."

It was infuriating that her mother wasn't on her side. She still couldn't believe that Robbie had left her for a one-legged coffee server. Her mom should be showering her with sympathy, not attacking her for getting some well-deserved revenge.

"I want you to come home," her mother stated. "You're making poor decisions and putting yourself at risk. You're going to lose your clients."

Here her mom *might* have a point. Last week, a marketing company had cancelled her contract because they objected to the content she had posted on her personal social media.

"Look, spring is beautiful in Vancouver," her mother continued. "I'll email you plane tickets for tomorrow. Come home and we'll figure everything out together."

A free holiday wasn't a bad idea, Annalise conceded. She could work from Vancouver just as easily as Toronto. By the time she returned, maybe immigration would have followed up on her anonymous tip and Canada would have shipped her loser ex back to the States.

"A mini-vacay sounds awesome," she agreed.

"Fabulous. I'll see you tomorrow, darling."

Annalise disconnected the call and cranked up the stereo. The noise would piss off her neighbour but she could care less. She opened Facebook and Instagram. Maybe a YouTube video would be best to influence the masses. She looked cute enough to get a lot of engagement. She could weep a bit. Hey, maybe she could feign concern for the one-legged bitch and pretend to warn the twat about Robbie by using *#metoo* to garner tons of sympathy. Tapping her foot to her favourite heavy metal band, Annalise deliberated over a narrative that would put her in the best light.

Her head snapped against the sofa back. She couldn't breathe and dropped her phone. Her hands flew to her neck. She felt her fingers clawing at coarse fibres. Gagging, she tried to force a finger between her throat and a thick rope.

Annalise's bulging eyes glimpsed a shadow silhouetted outside the sheer living room drapes. It had to be her neighbour arriving to complain about the music. He'd witness her attack and call the cops.

Desperate to hang on, she bucked against the sofa and fumbled at the rope. The sofa tipped backwards, crashing onto the hardwood floor. Her shoulder hit the circular staircase. Dazed, she felt her body lift off the ground. Her body rose metre by metre and the noose tighten against her neck. Her feet jerked uncontrollably as she swayed helplessly above her living room floor.

Below her, a figure sauntered into her sightline. A long black coat covered his body and a hood shadowed his face. Annalise gurgled, her vision blurring and doubling as she fought for air.

"I am your shadow," a voice said. "I see inside the darkest part of you. I am the omnipotent judge and executioner of the unworthy. For the atrocities you commit against the innocent, you're sentenced to death."

The last thing Annalise saw before she surrendered to the encroaching darkness was a hand reaching for her phone.

CHAPTER ONE

SAM

SAM MCNAMARA LINGERED outside an attractively renovated four-storey brick building from the eighteen hundreds. The clear July sky was a vivid blue, but she'd have preferred rain today. It was too hot for business attire, and she hoped her deodorant would stand up to the heat and stress. It had been nine years since she'd suffered a job interview, back when she was twenty-five and had joined Toronto Police Services. There was a lot of murky water under that blown-up bridge. Two years later, the media had drawn and quartered her after she'd shot a gang-banger who'd killed her partner in cold blood. It had been a righteous shooting. If she hadn't fired, he would have killed her, too, but he had been just fifteen. The ensuing scandal had closed the door on her dream of following in her father's footsteps and honouring his illustrious police career. The public believed doctors could save psychopathic adolescents, and so she had given the pandering upper echelon of the police force what they wanted: her resignation.

Did she still believe mental health experts could save all the broken children? She shaded her eyes against the brilliant sun and gazed up at the private psychiatric hospital. Over the past five years, while operating a successful private investigation agency, she'd worked hard to earn a PhD in clinical psychology. Her thesis had centred on the detection of pre-existing psychiatric disorders in children. After everything she'd encountered over the past year, the only thing Sam knew for sure was that evil existed in human form and it didn't discriminate when it came to age.

She wandered down the street, killing time until her interview. Outside a quaint bistro, she saw a uniformed veteran sitting in a wheelchair with a cardboard sign around his neck—*I lost my leg to an IED. I don't do drug & I'm hungry. Please help.* People were giving him a wide berth as they walked past. One woman, Sam noticed with disgust, scowled at the soldier and muttered something under her breath. The insensitive behaviour reminded her of a bumper sticker with a sentiment she loved: 'If you can't stand behind our troops, feel free to stand in front of them'. If she'd had one in her pocket, she'd have given it to the woman. People's ungrateful entitlement worried her sometimes.

Sam went into the restaurant and bought a coffee and a sandwich. Outside, she handed both to the man and dropped a ten-dollar bill into the hat he held.

"Thank you for your service," she said. "I should have asked how you take your coffee." She gave him some packets of sugar, a few creamers, and a stir stick.

"God bless you," he replied, and eagerly unwrapped the sandwich.

There was still ten minutes before her interview. She didn't want one of her prospective employers to catch her loitering around the front entrance, so she ventured down a narrow opening between the west side of the clinic and a neighbouring structure. A metre into the mouth of the alley, the modern stone façade stopped. Grubby old cellar windows dotted the aged brick at ankle height. The historic building had once housed one of Toronto's first department stores. It had changed hands multiple times over the past century, until Serenity Clinic had saved the derelict structure from demolition five years ago. She'd read that it had taken over two years to refurbish it into a functioning private hospital. Admiring the back ambulance bay, Sam couldn't imagine what the price tag had been for such a massive renovation. No wonder they'd neglected a useless stone cellar.

She swiped fawn-coloured dog hair off her black dress pants and checked her watch. It was time to go in. She needed this clinical practicum to complete her doctoral degree. That required wooing the two pioneering neuropsychiatrists who had rejected public health care and opened Serenity Clinic, a private inpatient facility. A bit of an anomaly in Canada, but an aging population had crippled the health care system. Mental health services lacked funding. Families faced daunting waitlists and minimal options when seeking help for an array of adolescent addictions and disorders. Serenity Clinic provided an alternative, and Sam desperately hoped to be part of what they were achieving. This was a coveted internship, and she didn't want to blow her opportunity.

In the lobby, a security guard took her name and asked her to have a seat. A few minutes later, a tall, dark-haired woman in her early-thirties marched up and shook Sam's hand. She was unremarkable in appearance, other than the difference in colouration of her eyes—the right was blue and the left was brown.

"Sam McNamara? Ophelia, head psychiatric nurse. I'll take you up to Dr. Armstrong's office."

Sam followed her through two sets of keycard-locked doors, and they continued down a long white corridor with a seamless, poured floor in a mosaic of teal and seafoam. Ophelia chattered endlessly about the clinic, the renovations, and the patients.

Annoyed by the stream of inane babble, Sam stopped walking and interrupted the woman's complaints about black mould in the cellar. "Wow. This is gorgeous."

She admired the stunning figurative watercolour of three women. Her best friend had finally recognized her dream and was studying at the Ontario College of Art. As a show of support, Sam had grown better at appreciating art.

"Is it an original Guity Novin?" she asked.

Ophelia's shoulders tensed. "Dr. Beauregard's a collector. He lends us some of his private collection." Her lips pursed together and her nose crinkled. "He has a Picasso etching in his office," she stated with undisguised disapproval. "He likes nice things." She unlocked a heavy stairwell door, letting it swing closed behind her.

Sam caught the door just before it smashed into her face. "There are about sixty residential patients, is that right?" Sam asked.

"Fifty-four, mostly in recovery from drugs, alcohol, eating disorders, and self-harming. We can accommodate seventy-five inpatients, but that includes the ten beds in the lockdown unit. We have five patients there now, including the one they want you to work with."

"They want me to work with a specific patient?" Sam asked with a frown. "Why?"

Ophelia stopped abruptly and Sam plowed into her back, grabbing the bannister a second before they both tumbled down the stairs.

The nurse spun around, glaring at Sam. "I shouldn't have said that. Don't mention it, especially to Dr. Beauregard."

Something strange in the woman's mismatched eyes unnerved Sam. "No worries. But can you tell me anything about this patient?"

Ophelia unlocked the fourth-floor stairwell door, shoving it so hard it bounced against the cement wall. "No. It's not my place." She practically jogged down the corridor.

Sam trotted after her, feeling flustered and irritated. Neither emotion was optimum when trying to impress a prospective employer. She straightened her jacket as she came up beside Ophelia, then jerked in surprise when the nurse grasped her shoulder. Hard.

"Not a word about what I said." She hissed the words into Sam's face, spraying her cheek with spittle. Then, as if nothing at all had happened, Ophelia flung open the office door. "Dr. Emily Armstrong, Ms. Sam McNamara, a clinical practicum candidate."

Sam reached up and wiped her cheek, cringing in disgust.

The doctor glanced up from her computer screen. "Thank you, Ophelia."

Dr. Armstrong was an attractive woman in her mid-fifties, tall and thin with shoulder-length black hair that framed her oval face. A neatly trimmed fringe fell just above her large hazel eyes.

She picked up a blue file folder from her desk and motioned toward a cozy seating arrangement under a large corner window. "Sam, please have a seat." Dr. Armstrong sat on a small sofa and dropped the file onto a teak coffee table. "Can we offer you coffee?"

Eager to see the last of Ophelia, Sam shook her head. "I'm fine, thanks." She sat in a sand-coloured armchair and placed her leather satchel on the table beside the thick blue folder.

Dr. Armstrong smiled at the nurse. "Thank you," she repeated.

Ophelia backed out of the office, closing the door behind her, and Sam experienced a clairvoyant certainty that the peculiar woman was eavesdropping just outside it.

"You attended my seminar last year on bi-polar disorder," Dr. Armstrong said. "We spoke after the lecture and you exhibited enthusiasm about our work here."

Sam laughed. "Well, I'm not surprised you remember me. I accosted you. I don't like to let opportunities slip away."

Dr. Armstrong crossed her legs and smoothed her lab coat over her charcoal dress. "Your letters of reference are impressive. Dr. Roger Peterson is a highly regarded psychiatrist," she said. "You assisted in his murder acquittal a few years back, yes?"

That sounded bad, as if Sam had strong-armed Roger into writing a glowing recommendation because he wasn't wasting away in prison. They'd been friends since childhood. She needed to correct the misunderstanding.

Before she could respond, Dr. Armstrong continued. "Let me speak frankly. I didn't invite you here because of your application," she said. "I'm in need of your assistance. In exchange, I'm prepared to offer you the clinical practicum you need to complete your PhD."

Stunned, Sam leaned back in her chair. "I don't understand."

"You graduated from Queen's University with a double major in criminology and psychology. When you were twenty-one, a drunk driver killed your father. You moved home and did your masters at University of Toronto. Your GPA for your undergraduate and graduate work was above average but not within the top five percent of your class."

Sam was about to defend her respectable 4.0 GPA, but Dr. Armstrong didn't give her the chance.

"You joined Toronto Police Service at twenty-five, left two years later, and opened your private investigation agency," she recited from memory. "You and your fiancé, Reece Hash, run it together with one employee, Elijah Watson. Reece recently completed law school and is articling at the Crown attorney's office."

Sam studied her silently, annoyed but not entirely surprised by the intense research the doctor had clearly done. She wanted to add context to some of the dispassionate remarks but felt it prudent to let Dr. Armstrong finish uninterrupted.

"Regardless of your arduous study schedules, you've managed to work multiple cases," Dr. Armstrong said. "At the inception of your career, you were instrumental in apprehending Incubus, the serial killer who murdered your sister. Last year, you solved the Frozen Statues case. I'm fascinated by your knack for attracting antisocial personalities."

Sam wondered if her aptitude for drawing psychopaths to her was the neuropsychiatrist's motivation for the interview. That was depressing.

Dr. Armstrong leaned forward, and her tone became more intimate. "But I want to talk about Bueton Sanctuary. Specifically, I want to talk about Mussani."

Sam sucked in her breath. Bueton Sanctuary was the cult she had exposed almost five years earlier, and Mussani had been its leader. Seventy-two people had died. It had been Sam's first real case—a missing sixteen-year-old girl who had been discovered living among the cult members. She and Reece had met during that case, when he was an inspector with the Ontario Provincial Police detachment in the town of Uthisca.

"Dr. Armstrong, why do you want to talk about Mussani?" Sam asked, not bothering to hide her suspicion.

"Call me Emily. Everyone does," Dr. Armstrong said warmly. "Is Mussani truly dead?"

"He fell from the Bunda cliffs in Australia." Sam removed her suit jacket and folded it over the arm of her chair.

"Ah, but authorities never recovered his body. You were there, yes?"

Sam nodded. "I witnessed him fall."

He hadn't actually fallen, but Sam would never admit that truth. It had taken her and Reece six months to track the socio-pathic mass murderer. Reece had left the OPP after the Bueton massacre. She harboured no regrets for what had transpired on that cliff, but it had taken her law-enforcing, moral fiancé a long time to reconcile what had happened.

"How sure are you he's dead?" Emily asked.

"Very," Sam answered. "You mind telling me what this is about?"

Emily slid the blue folder across the table. "Fadiya Basha is a seventeen-year-old patient who presents with severe erotomanic delusional disorder. I believe you can help her, which is why I'm offering you the internship here."

Sam scanned the patient file. "She survived Bueton."

Emily nodded. "Authorities found her hiding in a generator shed. She was twelve."

"That can't be," Sam said softly. "There were no survivors."

"Fadiya's parents are very wealthy. They went to great lengths to protect her identity," Emily said. "Their daughter disappeared eight months prior to the massacre. They were staying at a lake house in Uthisca. Her brother, Aazar, took Fadiya to the train station to visit their aunt in Hamilton, and that was the last anyone saw of her for months. Evidently, she'd gotten off the train and ran away to Bueton."

Sam thought back to the case. The women of the cult had run a shop in town that the male followers had used as a front to recruit young girls for their leader. Fadiya could have heard about Bueton there. She shuddered. If the girl had been at Bueton for over six months, Mussani would have initiated her. The ceremony had been a degenerate ritual of sexual assault, in the guise of their Messiah cleansing the victim prior to transcendence.

A light went on in Sam's head. "Patients with erotomanic delusions believe someone is in love with them. Fadiya believes Mussani is alive," she guessed. "She thinks they're in love." Her stomach roiled.

"It's a bit more complicated. Fadiya believes Mussani visits her at night. Here in the clinic. In the lockdown unit," Emily said. "You lived at Bueton, yes?"

"I was inside the gates for a short time during my investigation."

Sam studied the picture in Fadiya's file. She was a beautiful girl with enormous eyes the colour of warm chocolate. They were soulful eyes that mirrored the pain the girl had endured and the horrors she'd witnessed.

"I don't recognize her," Sam said unable to look away from the photo. "It's doubtful she even knew I was there."

Emily leaned forward, her eyes intense. "But you know more about the cult than anyone left alive. You have the information required to challenge her convictions and convince her to renounce the cult's ideologies."

"You want me to act as a thought reform consultant? I'm not a cult expert," Sam said. "Other than my inside knowledge of Bueton, why come to me?"

Emily licked her lips and reached for a crystal pitcher. She poured each of them a glass of water, picked hers up, and sipped it, studying Sam over the rim. "Two reasons. The first is to deprogram the cult's brainwashing. I recognize the negative connotation with the term 'deprograming', but Fadiya didn't leave the cult willingly."

Sam had no familiarity with deprograming, other than knowing it was an extreme and sometimes violent method of intervention. It had nothing to do with her field of study as a psychologist.

"And the second reason?" she asked.

"That's highly confidential. If you're willing to accept the internship today, I'll confide in you."

Sam's distrust ramped up to high gear. She wanted the position but she wasn't negotiating blind. "Look, Emily, I don't know what's going on here, but I suspect it hasn't much to do with a clinical internship. If you need my help, you have to tell me the truth. All of it."

Dr. Armstrong took another sip of water and regarded her coolly for a moment, considering.

"Fadiya is pregnant."

"And..." Sam prompted.

Emily dropped her eyes. "She's in a lockdown unit with no patient fraternization and supervised visitation. The entrance to her room is under twenty-four-seven surveillance. There's no indication on our security footage of any unauthorized personnel accessing her room. She's legally incapable of giving consent."

"Someone raped her," Sam stated.

Emily nodded. "Over the past four months, Fadiya's condition has deteriorated. She's rarely lucid. Her regression baffles me. But every time she's aware, she insists that Mussani comes to her."

Sam contemplated various scenarios. "The most obvious explanation is that whoever raped her told her he was Mussani. It would play into her delusion and keep her quiet."

Sam refrained from pointing out the other logical conclusion: that Fadiya's rapist was someone inside the clinic with access to the girl's private case notes.

"That's my guess," Emily agreed. "But she's only eight weeks pregnant and her insistence that Mussani visits her began four months ago. If our supposition is correct, it means this person has been impersonating Mussani and assaulting her repeatedly over the past four months."

"How many male employees have access to the lockdown unit?" Sam asked.

"My partner, Dr. Beauregard, one psychologist, two nurses, and five security officers. Once apprised of this... this horrific crime, all nine volunteered to do a DNA test. A prenatal paternity test last week proved that none of them fathered Fadiya's baby. I need to know who did." She sipped from her glass of water and dropped her eyes. "My hope is to identify the father before I'm forced to disclose the pregnancy to the family." Emily looked up and held Sam's gaze. "Can you help?"

Disappointment flooded over Sam. Emily Armstrong, a highly respected expert in her field, didn't want her as a clinical psychologist. She wanted her as a private investigator.

"You want me to investigate the rape," Sam stated flatly.

"In part, yes," Emily said. "But the salient need is to help this girl. Three years ago, the Ontario court ruled Fadiya mentally incompetent. Last year, her parents entrusted her to my care. The family situation is complicate, but it's imperative that the federal court overturn the incompetency ruling." Emily took Sam's hand and held it tightly between her own. "I've dedicated my life to studying severe psychiatric disorders and improving quality of life. Given the fact that Fadiya is pregnant and a victim of foul play, I genuinely believe you're her only hope. If you can challenge the brainwashing and convince her to relinquish her beliefs, we can begin trauma work to help her heal from what happened at Bueton."

Sam extracted her hand. "And she can identify her rapist." She picked up her satchel and stood, reaching for her suit jacket. "An unknown security breach that led to the rape of an underage patient by an unidentified subject will provoke a Ministry of Health investigation," she said. "Health advocates who object to private hospitals in a public health system will use it as leverage to demand the closure of your clinic. That's really what this is about."

Emily's eyes widened. "Of course not! It's about the violation of a vulnerable girl I promised to protect." She stood and faced Sam. "Yes, I'm asking you to use your investigation skills, but I'm offering you a legitimate clinical practicum. Much of psychology is investigative. You have experience in both disciplines."

"What you're asking is for me to go undercover and lie to a patient, possibly damaging her in the process." Sam struggled to keep her voice level. "In exchange, you'll sign off on a bogus internship, and I'll receive my PhD under duplicitous circumstances." She laughed bitterly. "No thanks."

"The practicum is genuine, I promise," Emily argued. "Regardless of the outcome of the investigation, my expectations around your clinical performance here will be identical to those regarding any other intern. My mentorship will be identical to what I offer any other intern. Should you not meet my expectations, I will not provide you with a favourable review. I'm not proposing anything deceitful."

Sam stood with one hand on the doorknob, deliberating. On the one hand, she desperately wanted to learn under the talented neuropsychiatrist. On the other hand, she felt manipulated. Yes, Emily had shaken her confidence by admitting that she hadn't earned the spot based on her academic achievements. But was her disappointment making her cynical, clouding her judgment? Sam gave her head a figurative shake. A sexual predator was raping a teenage girl, whom doctors might have misdiagnosed with a mental illness she didn't have. That illness had been the court's justification for suspending her legal right to make decisions regarding every aspect of her life. Did anything else matter?

"I'll take a look into the security breach," Sam said. "If we can recover even a partial frame of the obstructed data, you may be able to identify the rapist."

"Will you think about the internship?" Emily asked. "Maybe meet Fadiya?"

Sam opened her wallet and found one of Eli's cards. "I'll brief our IT expert and he'll expect your call. Introduce him to your security specialist and they'll sort out the system access details."

Emily took the card. "I've handled this dreadfully," she said with a frown. "I'm so sorry. I hope you'll consider me as your mentor. It would be an honour to help you complete your PhD."

"Why?" Sam demanded.

Emily smiled, "I believe you possess the inherent ability to intuitively understand people's unconscious needs. You proved me right this morning."

"How?" Sam asked.

"Life has a way of stripping people's dignity," Emily said. "I was outside the bistro this morning and watched you. You saw a way to give that veteran what he truly longed for."

"I gave him a sandwich," Sam said.

Emily shook her head. "No. You acknowledged how much he'd sacrificed. You gave him gratitude."

Sam stepped into the hallway. "Have your security person contact Eli." She turned back to face Emily, struggling to keep her disappointment at bay. "Thanks for meeting with me."

"Please consider working with me," Emily said softly. "Please help Fadiya. You may be her only hope."

CHAPTER TWO

REECE

REECE PULLED INTO his reserved parking space at the back of a converted warehouse in Corktown where he shared a thousand-square-foot loft space with Sam. At least a faint hint of colour still painted the western horizon. These days, it was unusual for him to get home until well after sunset.

He turned off his Honda and sat quietly in the car, reviewing the multiple tasks on his to-do list that he'd failed to accomplish. He hadn't checked-in with Eli on the office renovations, and he'd promised Sam that she wouldn't have to be involved. His promise was why she'd reluctantly agreed to the massive project. Sam didn't like change, even positive change, but Reece couldn't stand another freezing winter in their dilapidated, miniature office in Little Italy. Not that he'd have an opportunity to visit it. Especially not now, since his articling principal had given him an odious, time-sucking task.

He popped the sedan's trunk and circled the car to retrieve two large file boxes. Closing the trunk with his elbow, he trudged to the building's back entrance, trying to balance the heavy boxes in one arm so he could negotiate the security lock with the other. They were on the top floor of a thirty-thousand-square-foot warehouse with eighteen-foot ceilings, but he wasn't going to risk the unreliable elevator. Reece plodded up the stairs and shuffled down a long corridor to the front of the converted warehouse. The wide hallway was suffocating. Scorching July sun had flooded in all day from the three-storey glass front of the building. He hoped Sam had surrendered to practicality and had put on the air conditioning. She disliked AC, but between the floor-to-ceiling windows and multiple skylights, the loft would be sweltering tonight.

A quiet evening with Sam—with any luck in air-conditioned comfort—was just what Reece needed. He considered various dinner options and settled on Thai coconut chicken curry. He'd grind his own garam masala and make ghee. Cooking always lowered his stress. After dinner, he'd share with Sam the horrible conflict he felt over his new assignment.

Outside their front door, his heart dropped. Voices—one male and two female. The last thing Reece felt like was entertaining. He hoped it wasn't Sam's best friend, Lisa Stipelli, and her husband Jim. Reece enjoyed Jim's company, but at only thirty-nine, Jim was Toronto's most prominent criminal attorney, while Reece was a forty-year-old articling student. The fact Reece had risen to the impressive rank of inspector with the provincial police, didn't assuage his sense of failure tonight. If he hadn't dropped out of law school to pursue law enforcement, he wouldn't be a middle-aged articling student. Maybe he should have accepted the Toronto Police Services' offer and joined their homicide squad. Inside that chaotic bullpen, working with the blue brethren, was where he'd felt at home. Instead, he now faced the loathsome task of betraying colleagues he respected. He kicked one of the damn file boxes.

Childish, sure, but it made him feel better. He took a deep breath, plastered a smile on his face, and flung open the door.

A flash of fawn zoomed across his peripheral vision and a solid mass plowed into his legs, knocking him off balance. The boxes flew from his flailing arms, and file folders scattered across the glossy hemlock floor. As he fumbled to grab a box, sharp teeth nipped at his scrambling fingers.

"Pepin escaped his puppy crate. Again," Sam said from the gourmet kitchen.

Reece squatted to pat the French bulldog. "You have to latch it," he said in Pepin's defence.

She adjusted the heat under one of the six burners on their Viking gas range. "Locking that thing requires a PhD in robotic engineering. Besides, it wouldn't matter. He's Houdini."

Reece caught a note of distaste in her voice. He'd bought her the puppy after Brandy, her golden retriever, had died. It had seemed like a great idea at the time, something to help her deal with her crushing grief. Now, though, he was having second thoughts. Sam was kind to the puppy, but he sensed a growing dislike for the chubby little firecracker.

"He ate one of your slippers." She chuckled maliciously.

"Not the Mukluks! I love those." Reece sighed and turned to their employee, Eli, who stood impatiently by the large kitchen island. "How's everything going with the renovations?"

"It is not good. It is very bad. Removing the wall between the two office spaces is a problem. It is load bearing. We must have an engineered support beam. It will be costly. There is a problem with the flooring, and—"

"Forget I asked." Reece groaned, tugging off his tie, and rolling up the sleeves of his white dress shirt.

Eli, who had Asperger's, had reported this spew of bad news with his usual lack of expression. But Reece had learned to read nuances in the young man's body language that precipitated a meltdown. Right now, Eli's rigid stance, twitching index finger, and roaming eyes suggested he was a heartbeat from freaking out. They could deal with the reno glitches after dinner.

"You're cooking," Reece said to Sam, careful to inject enthusiasm into his tone. Sam was a terrible cook.

"My dad's chili." She held out a wooden spoon.

He tentatively licked it and tried not to gag on the overpowering salt.

"Yummy," he murmured. When she wasn't looking, he'd try to sneak in some lime and fat to neutralize the salt. "How was the interview?"

She turned her back and rinsed the spoon. "She offered me the clinical practicum, but there are strings."

"Strings?"

"Yup, and I consider them unethical." She nodded her chin at Eli, who was watching the two of them uneasily, waiting to hear all about it. "We'll talk about it later," she said calmly, then turned back to Reece. "Any chance of bread sticks?"

"Sure."

"The ones with cheese inside?" She wrapped her arms around his waist and leaned in to whisper in his ear. "If I pretend I don't notice, will you fix the salt in my chili?"

He laughed and kissed her. "Pour me a glass of wine, please." He pulled out a mixing bowl and began assembling the ingredients.

"What's this?"

Reece turned to see Danny, Eli's sister, rummaging around the spilled file boxes.

"My boss asked me to audit police due diligence in those closed sudden-death cases." He swallowed his disdain. "She ordered me to question every ruling and to investigate discreetly."

"Ouch." Sam handed him a glass of red wine. "How do you feel about sneaking around examining the proficiency of officers you respect?"

Leave it to Sam to cut straight to the heart of the problem, he thought wryly.

"Not good, but I don't have a choice. I'm her articling student." He set aside his yeast to bubble. "Gretchen claims she received an anonymous tip that over the past three years, a serial killer has hidden murders as suicides, accidental mishaps, and natural deaths."

"Hmm… So, we can rule out a subject who achieves pleasure from showcasing extreme violence." Sam paused in thought. "Cops and coroners misjudging cause of death might satisfy abnormal gratification." She picked up one of the files. "The question is how we figure out which ones are possible homicides." She flipped through the folder she held. "Studying victimology will be helpful. There might be a profile pattern."

"Why didn't your boss turn this so-called tip over to the cops?" Danny asked. "Shouldn't homicide investigate?"

Sam looked up with a frown. "Good question."

Reece finished grating the smoked cheddar and took a sip of his wine, appreciating the vibrant plum note on his palate. "She wouldn't tell me. She wants the audit to stay off Toronto Police Services' radar," he said with a grimace.

"Maybe Gretchen wants to validate the tip prior to proceeding through usual channels," Sam suggested but her green eyes looked doubtful.

"I can't figure out her agenda. I guess it's above my paygrade," Reece said, trying to curb his bitterness. He mixed the dough and turned it onto the counter to knead.

Gretchen had told him there would be 'dire consequences' should he breach her trust by disclosing any aspect of his assignment to anyone employed by or associated with the police department. Reece didn't know what was going on, but the lack of transparency didn't sit well with him.

"We will help you investigate these files," Eli announced. He placed a box on the dining room table beside the ladder staircase that led to the elevated bedroom loft.

Reece finished kneading the bread dough and set it into the proofing oven, wiping down the Carrera marble countertop. None of his team was associated with the police department, but Reece suddenly felt uncomfortable sharing what he had. If a Crown attorney terminated his articling position with cause—especially due to breach of confidentiality—that would end his law career before it had gotten off the ground.

"Look, I appreciate it, but involving outsiders is against protocol," Reece stated, wishing he'd kept his mouth shut and had spoken to Sam in private.

Danny turned from the eighteen-foot-high windows across the long south wall. "Then don't tell anyone," she retorted, and crossed the large open space to the table. "For a smart man, you can be remarkably stupid." She opened her laptop, which she never went anywhere without, and stared with disgust at the boxes of files. "Any chance your office joined the twenty-first century and you have this in electronic form?"

He opened his laptop bag and pulled out a hard drive. Danny had a PhD in computer engineering and a master's in computer science. She was a world-renowned white-hat hacker on the deep web. She was also a hermit with an off-putting personality who lived with her brother and had an unhealthy distrust of everyone else. She'd grudgingly accepted Sam and Reece into her inner circle, but that had only been because of her brother's devotion to them. Danny could break any encryption and access any system. Although she was just twenty-five, experts considered her a prodigy and she had collaborated with multiple government agencies during the year Reece had known her. She never spoke of her highly confidential projects. Might as well be hanged for a sheep as for a lamb, Reece thought resignedly. He'd intended on soliciting Sam's help with the psychological profiling, which also broke procedure, so he might as well have Danny on board too.

With a twinge of guilt, Reece handed her the portable hard drive.

"I'll design a database and code an algorithm to manipulate the data to search for commonalities in the cases," she said. "You old folks can hunt through mountains of paper." She snickered and attached the drive to her computer.

Sam took his hand. "I know how uncomfortable this assignment makes you," she said sympathetically. "Maybe the tip is bogus. It's possible that the original officers and detectives didn't miss anything." She patted the pile of folders. "Every one of these could be legitimate accidents, suicides, and natural deaths."

"That would be brilliant," Reece said. "Fingers crossed you're right."

"Annalise Huang, a social media consultant," Eli read. "Investigators ruled her death as a suicide three months ago. She hanged herself from her staircase after a breakup."

Danny snorted in contempt. "I hate that 'gotta-have-a-man' type of woman. Who kills herself over a douche-bag?"

Eli ignored her. "According to Mrs. Huang, her daughter's ex-fiancé financially ruined her and was stalking her with a drone." He scrolled through his cell phone, rubbing the six-centimetre scar across the right side of his face. "Annalise posted her suicide note on Facebook. That was after she posted a ton of things about her ex." He passed his phone to Reece. His sleeve rode up and he quickly tugged it down to cover the puckered cigarette burns on his forearm.

Reece scrolled down and read a string of slanderous posts. "Wow, putting all this online seems unstable."

"You can't judge someone's mental stability based on reactionary behaviour after a hurtful breakup." Sam took the file from Eli and read. "Hmm... her mother adamantly argued that her daughter was not suicidal. She was flying home to Vancouver the next day. Phone records confirmed they'd spoken less than an hour prior to Annalise's death." She flipped the file around to show Reece. "Mom's a therapist." She raised an eyebrow at him.

"And aren't you the one who said that therapists often have the most messed-up kids?" Reece ran his fingers through his thick black hair and tempered his tone. "Sorry, I sound defensive but I read that file and the cops couldn't find anyone who saw this alleged drone," he said. "And they did a thorough investigation, even confirming her ex's iron-clad alibi." He pointed at a line in a statement report. "Her friend, Denise, was with Annalise earlier that night and told police she was depressed."

Sam shrugged. "Her other friends denied that. They referred to Annalise as self-important. One described her as a 'quintessential mean-girl'." She paused. "The drone *is* weird, Reece. It's a handy tool for a stalker. Let's put this one in the investigate pile."

They'd just started, and already Reece felt like a traitor, nitpicking at an accomplished officer's investigative prowess.

"Why does this one have a green sticker on it?" Danny asked.

"I vetted it and there's a suicide motive," Reece said. "The woman ran down a pregnant mother and two toddlers in a grocery store parking lot. The heel of her flip-flop doubled back and she couldn't pull her foot off the accelerator. One of the toddlers died at the scene, the other sustained permanent brain damage, and the baby died ten hours after an emergency C-section."

Danny highlighted one line in the middle of the electronic file on her screen. "Did you see this?"

With growing dread, Reece read the notation. Prior to her alleged suicide, the woman had filed a legal appeal, stating that a ten-year licence suspension was unreasonable punishment.

Sam read over his shoulder. "She killed two children, left the third with acquired brain injury, and she considered a licence suspension too harsh?"

"My point exactly," Danny said. "What's the likelihood of someone with no remorse killing herself?"

"Not good." Sam closed the file. "It's not surprising that the investigators missed a note buried in a pile of court documents."

Reece disagreed. Death investigations followed rigid procedures to eliminate the risk of reaching erroneous conclusions. This was a careless oversight by a detective with too high a caseload.

Sam plopped down another file in a separate pile. "This one is natural causes. Cause of death was a pulmonary embolism."

Danny made an odd growling noise in the back of her throat.

Sam rolled her eyes at Reece and then scrutinized Danny. "Out with it. That growl always means you have something to say."

"Potassium chloride," Danny mumbled.

"What about it?" Reece was certain he didn't want to know.

"Leaves no trace and presents as pulmonary embolism," she said. "Buy potassium chloride pills in the vitamin aisle of any drugstore, compound a high concentration into a liquid, pick an obscured site, and inject your victim intravenously. Easy-breezy." Without shifting her eyes from the code on her screen, she reached for another file.

"Danny has been studying medicine as a hobby," Eli announced proudly.

"Fantastic." Reece wondered why anyone would read *Gray's Anatomy* for recreational purposes.

"My main interest is bioinformatics," Danny said. "But George Church's lectures on genetics are interesting so I'm studying that, too. I'm enjoying all the Harvard classes."

"Harvard?" Sam asked, looking as confused as Reece felt.

"Danny is very smart," Eli said.

"But Harvard is in Boston and you're in Toronto," Sam said. "How does that work?"

"Some of the courses are online with edX," Danny said. "For others, I have to get a bit creative to access the professors' lectures and course materials."

Reece scowled at her. "You're hacking, breaching the professors' privacy, and stealing material other students pay a fortune for. You're breaking the law."

"Knowledge should be shared," she answered heatedly. "If I don't want the stupid piece of paper, what's the difference?"

"You're stealing," he retorted. "There's no moral ambiguity around it."

Danny glared at him, her eyes narrowing behind her thick spectacles. "Society is drifting back to an eighteenth-century class system where your family's socioeconomic position impacts your educational opportunities. Harvard and MIT hire brilliant professors and researchers, yet they deny the masses access to the knowledge. How is that moral?"

"If you don't like the system, work within the law to change it," Reece countered, realizing too late that he sounded like a bourgeois prig.

"Both of you take a breath." Sam turned to Reece. "You're cranky because you don't want to admit that some of these files require a closer look. There are inconsistencies that the first responders failed to examine."

Feeling ashamed by his outburst, Reece laid his hand gently on Danny's shoulder, feeling her tense under his touch. "I was out of line. If you're still willing to help, I'd appreciate it. Your algorithm idea is good."

"Yeah, it is," she mumbled, clearly not mollified by his apology.

Reece sighed and gazed at the boxes of files. If even one of these sudden-death cases was a homicide, he had a responsibility to uncover the truth. There was no moral ambiguity around that, either. But the Crown attorney's office investigating closed cases would incite rampant suspicion in the police department. He'd be the target of that suspicion. Reece saw no scenario in which the blue brethren wouldn't brand him a traitor. He'd feel the same in their shoes.

A backstabbing turncoat was exactly what he was. He wished he'd never gone back to law school.

CHAPTER THREE

SAM

SAM LEAPED OFF the Queen East streetcar at Yonge. A two-hour workout and an advanced Muay Thai fighting class had energized her, and she headed south at a fast walk. The closer she got to Toronto waterfront, the trickier it was to navigate around a mass of confused summer tourists. The scorching July sun beat down, and sweat dribbled between her small breasts as she wove around jostling pedestrians. She was boiling hot and parched by the time she arrived at Eli's stunning high-rise condominium.

Sam strolled to a tinted-glass door beside a gold placard that read *Executive Entrance*. Before she hit the buzzer, the door magically swung open. She grinned and walked into an empty marble lobby with four private elevators and a curved reception desk artfully designed with backlit frosted glass and swirls of glossy stainless steel.

A uniformed concierge waved at her from behind the modern desk that discreetly hid multiple security monitors. "Caught you on the street cam," Gerald said with a smile. "Here to see his royal highness?"

She laughed and pulled her wallet from the back pocket of her jeans. "I've got a keycard for his elevator around here somewhere." She found the black card and waved it triumphantly.

Gerald beckoned her over and walked around the security desk to join her. "Can I bend your ear for a sec, Sam?"

She registered the slight holster bulge under the ex-cop's left arm. "Sure. What's up?" At five-foot-three and less than a hundred and twenty pounds, she felt like a dwarf beside the giant man.

"Any word on Elijah's father?" Gerald's eyes were dark. "I'm worried about Danny." He leaned closer and lowered his voice. "I've seen a couple of men hanging around. Not the type I'd associate with a con, but one of them was carrying."

Eli's biological father was responsible for the brutal scars that marred his face and arm. The man's hatred toward his only child was a reflection of his obsession with Eli's mother, a woman who had escaped the clutches of her abusive husband. A month after she fled with her eight-year-old son, an unknown shooter had gunned her down during a convenience store robbery.

Authorities had moved Eli from Montreal to London, Ontario and hidden him in foster care. A year later, Quebec police had arrested his father for armed robbery. The deranged man was now serving a twenty-year sentence in a federal maximum-security penitentiary, but his incarceration hadn't prevented him from finding Eli. A few years ago, in an attempt to extort money from his son, he had sent a thug to threaten Danny. Eli had relocated them from London to a high security Toronto penthouse. Their foster parents were overseas with Doctors Without Borders and Eli didn't worry about them too much, but he lived in constant fear for his sister.

His motivation for being a private investigator rose from his burning need to implicate his biological father in his mother's murder. Sam and Reece were doing everything they could to help, but they knew it wouldn't solve Eli's problem. So long as the man lived, everyone his son loved was at risk.

"The board denied parole again," Sam told Gerald. "But next July, he'll have served his time and then he'll be out, unless we can find evidence to convict him of murder."

"A twenty-year-old cold case, good luck," Gerald said bitterly.

There wasn't much to say to that.

He held her eyes. "Maybe an inmate will shank him and solve Eli's problem permanently."

Gerald wasn't wrong on that either, but she ignored the veiled threat. "Eli hired private security for Danny," she said. "That's probably who you've seen. He should have brought you up to speed. Talk to him."

Gerald nodded. "I'll do that. Appreciate the chat, Sam."

He turned back to his monitors and she crossed the lobby to the private elevators. She flashed the card at the reader and the doors slid open.

At the fifty-fifth floor, the doors automatically opened and Sam stepped into a modest hundred-and-fifty-square-foot space with maple hardwood floors, white walls, pot lights in the ceiling, and a window with a fabulous view of Lake Ontario. She descended a curved maple staircase to the three-thousand-foot open-concept, living space. Every exterior wall was glass. The unobstructed, panoramic views of Lake Ontario and downtown Toronto were breathtaking.

Danny sat at a module desk that looked like it belonged at NASA. Surrounding her was a video wall comprising nine 4K UHD monitors. She'd added three since Sam's last visit. Danny's fingers flew across a keyboard, and code flashed on the multiple screens at lightning speed.

"Eli's in the pool," she said without shifting her eyes from the wall.

Sam grunted an acknowledgement, skirted a restored, autographed 1979 KISS pinball machine, and went through a set of sliding glass doors that accessed a garden terrace with three-directional views. The city's landmark CN Tower appeared close enough to touch. Fifty-five storeys in the air, there was a nice breeze that ruffled her short strawberry-blonde curls. She circled the exterior of the penthouse to the swimming pool.

Eli had opened all the solarium's exterior glass walls, which weatherproofed the pool and hot tub for year-round use. He was lounging in a giant rubber ducky that floated serenely on the crystal-blue saltwater.

"Must be nice to be idle and wealthy," Sam teased. She stripped off her sneakers and socks and sat on the edge of the pool, dangling her feet in the cool water. "Any regrets?" she asked

He didn't say anything for a minute. When he spoke, his voice was more stilted than usual. "I developed the video game and enhanced graphics for people's enjoyment," he said. "Microsoft reaches more people. Selling them the rights and innovative graphic code was the correct decision."

She splashed water at him as he floated by her. "But it was your baby."

He kicked his feet to move his duck away from her reach. "You are wrong. The horse ranch for kids with autism and Asperger's is my baby." He paused. "No, that is not right, either. My philanthropic foundation is my baby. Since it operates the camp, it is the same thing."

Eli had purchased the two hundred acres that had once been Bueton Sanctuary in Uthisca. They had demolished all reminders of the cult and had turned the wooded, lakefront property into a beautiful summer camp. It was Eli's pride and joy. It didn't bother him that seventy-two people had perished on the land, or that Mussani had buried an additional twelve women in the woods. Eli was too pragmatic to believe in restless spirits.

Sam bathed her arms with pool water, inhaling the aromatic scent from the surrounding garden. "That clinical practicum I interviewed for—there's a patient who survived Bueton."

"There were no survivors. They are lying," Eli said.

"Reece checked with a buddy at the OPP last night. Authorities did find Fadiya Basha alive in the aftermath," she said. "She's seventeen now and suffers delusional disorder. Fadiya believes Bueton still exists."

"Bring her to the ranch," Eli said matter-of-factly. "She will see it does not."

Actually, that was a good idea, Sam thought. If she accepted the internship, she probably couldn't get permission to remove the girl from the hospital, but perhaps she could show her some pictures. It could aid in dissolving her fantasy. Accepting Emily Armstrong's offer was ethically ambiguous, but if it served to help Fadiya, Sam could reconcile the subterfuge. The university wouldn't. They'd have plenty to say about using a psychology internship as a means to investigate undercover. The price could be her PhD.

"I forgot to tell you that someone from Serenity Clinic will be reaching out to you," Sam said.

Eli jumped off the yellow duck and climbed out of the pool, refusing to look at her. "You did not tell me," he stated. "I was unprepared when I received the call. I do not like to be unprepared." Eli marched out of the solarium, arms glued to his side.

That explained his weirder-than-usual behaviour: he was annoyed with her. Sam followed him through the patio doors that led into the penthouse.

He ignored her, and she changed tack. Eli didn't process negative emotion well, and his feelings might be hurt, which was harder for him to deal with than anger. Moving straight to business to distract him was her best option.

"We need to know who accessed a room," she said. Understanding how much Eli wanted to be a respected private investigator, she added a bit of manipulation. "I told them if anyone could recover missing data, it would be you."

"You are wrong," he retorted, clearly unimpressed by her flattery. "I tried. It is above my technical expertise." Eli towelled his brown hair into damp spikes across his head. His hazel eyes darted around the ceiling. "I did not want to involve Danny without your permission." He pursed together his lips and opened a sub-zero freezer. "Would you like a snack?"

"Just water," Sam said, hiding her smile. Eli always offered refreshments. A social grace his foster mother had taught him. "Can we ask Danny?"

He opened a frozen Jamaican patty and fussed around to position it in the microwave. As he waited for his treat to heat up, he grabbed a Mountain Dew and handed her a bottle of water without looking at her. They waited in silence for the microwave to ding.

Patty and soda in hand, Eli marched across the penthouse to Danny's workstation.

"Get away from me with that cat food in a mitten," Danny snarled.

Eli ignored her. "Can you tell us if there is missing data from CCTV footage?"

Behind her oversized glasses, she rolled her grey eyes. "Duh. Gee whiz, like I could give 'er a try, eh?"

"I will access the clinic's server."

She spun around and clamped her hand around his wrist. "Don't even think about putting that can of soda on my workstation. Give me your phone. That hospital dude gave you unrestricted access to the backend, right?"

Eli's eyes narrowed. "It is confidential."

"Give it." She waggled her fingers. "I'll resist the urge to post the credentials online."

He handed it over and she glanced at his screen. Swivelling her chair to face her monitors, she began typing. The monitors on the video wall spun through images.

Sam leaned over her shoulder. "First, I want to know if anyone had unauthorized access to the lockdown unit over the past four months. There should be a list of keycards programmed to enter the unit."

"There is." Danny brought up a page of employee pictures. "So, you want to eliminate all these people?"

"Yeah."

Video flipped across three monitors. Code flashed by on the other six.

"No abnormalities in the card-reader data," she said after a few minutes. "I can run facial recognition software, eliminate the authorized folks, and ask the system to pull unrecognized images. It would tell us if anyone snuck in using a cloned card or piggy-backed on authorized personnel entry. It'll take time to run it."

"Is there anything you can do faster?" Sam asked. "I'm only interested in unauthorized male access, but the camera that points to room 319 didn't record anything."

Danny swivelled back to her keyboard. "There's probably data obfuscation."

"She is checking whether there are erased or concealed files on the data stream from that camera," Eli explained.

Sam had no idea how they would find missing data in a ton of video files, but Danny and Eli were unfazed. More importantly, Eli had relaxed now he was in his element. Sam didn't enjoy having the quirky young man upset with her.

After half an hour, Danny sat up straight and turned to face Sam. "Okay, there's lots of advanced obfuscation. Someone was definitely inside the system messing around. From what I can tell, it happens about once a week, always after midnight. I can break the encryption, but I need time."

"Will that recover the missing files?" Sam asked.

Danny shrugged. "I can get some of it, for sure, but whoever did this has mad skills. No malware or remote access tools embedded in any of the system files."

"Someone with internal access to the security system and advanced IT capabilities did this," Eli said.

"Hacking chops, yes," Danny said. "Access, not necessarily. There's an escape hatch on their mainframe, like a virtual backdoor. It's well hidden but not undetectable when you know what you're looking for."

"Why are they hiding activity only outside that room?" Eli asked.

"That's Fadiya Basha's room," Sam explained. "She's mysteriously eight weeks pregnant. She's delusional and under supervised care. There's no opportunity for her to commingle with anyone."

Danny's lips thinned and the colour drained from her round face. "What's the matter with you?" she snarled. "She's unable to give consent to *commingle* with anyone. Some douche-bag raped her." She shoved her blunt cut black hair behind her ears. "If it happened two months ago, why go back four months?"

"Fadiya's delusions worsened four months ago." Sam turned to Eli, noticing that he stood frozen rigid, his eyes darting aimlessly, and his lips moving silently. "That's when she began to claim that Mussani was visit—"

"Hospital personnel have violated her for four months?" Eli's voice had risen to a shriek by the end of his question. His arm twitched at his side.

Sam tried to head off an imminent meltdown and pointed at the employee pictures. "No, all those men underwent voluntary

DNA tests. Fadiya's physician did a non-invasive prenatal paternity test, and none of them fathered the baby."

With her back turned to Eli, Danny muttered, "There are a lot of sickos out there." Her tone was hard and without expression. "They'd pay big bucks to get their freak on and rape a teenage girl in a hospital."

"That is sex slavery," Eli yelled. He began to pace in a circle, flapping his arms wildly. "Prostitution!" he shouted.

Sam jerked at his high-pitched screech, watching helplessly as his agitation escalated.

Danny stood with a sigh and walked over to her brother. "What is the square root of fifteen-hundred-forty?"

"Human trafficking!" Eli's face was crimson and spittle flew from his lips. He hit his forehead, dodging Danny's attempts to restrain his arm. The circle he stomped around grew tighter. "That is what happened to Danny. Her mother sold her. She was seven. They locked her up. Men used her. Police did not rescue her until she was ten. Perverts! Pedophiles! Degen—"

Danny slapped him across the face so hard that Eli's head whipped to the side and he stumbled back. The scar on his face was a white slash against his red cheek. He dropped to the floor and sat on his butt with his legs splayed. He stared up at his sister, a look of utter shock in his wide hazel eyes.

Danny stood above him, wringing her hands. Tears streamed down her sheet-white face but she didn't make a sound. Her entire body trembled.

"I should not have told," Eli whispered. "This is bad. This is not good. This is very bad. I promised I would never tell." He snapped a thick black elastic he always wore around his wrist. It cracked against his bare skin and Sam winced.

She had known that something awful had happened to Danny. She'd recognized the signs of complex trauma—the agoraphobia, the paranoia, the wall of contempt that Danny wore as a shield to avoid relationships. Sam had never imagined anything as awful as this. She wanted to reach out and offer comfort, but her instinct warned her to remain distant. Their relationship was still tentative and unstable. Danny's defence mechanism over this spontaneous revelation could be to sever all contact with Sam. Avoidance was denial's best friend.

After a minute of tense silence, Danny turned on her heels and ran to the bedroom wing. In the distance, a door slammed.

Eli manically snapped the elastic, the repetitive flicking an indication of his sensory overload.

"Give Danny a bit of time," Sam said. "I'm sure—"

"Leave." Eli stretched out the elastic and snapped it again, flinching as it slapped against a ring of red welts.

Knowing that anything she tried to do right now would make it worse, Sam mutely climbed the stairs to the elevator and pressed the button to summon the car. Danny would forgive Eli for his breach of confidence. They shared a peculiar codependent relationship. What worried Sam was the possibility that Danny might transfer blame to her. If that happened, Eli might enable his sister's avoidance technique and leave their employment, but Sam had no option but to cross that bridge if they came to it.

During the ride to ground level, she tried to focus on work and considered Eli's words. Human trafficking was a rash conclusion in the case of Fadiya Basha. That didn't make it impossible. The only way she could figure out what was going on at that hospital was to work from the inside.

She just had to decide if she were willing to risk her PhD in the process.

CHAPTER FOUR

REECE

THE FRONT DOOR banged against Reece's beloved antique church altar. It had taken him months to restore the piece and it was one of his prize possessions. Sam stalked into the kitchen with a stormy expression.

She scowled at the array of pots on the stove. "I thought we were ordering pizza."

He handed over his glass of cold wine. She looked like she could use it. "I'm making salmon Wellington, Gordon Ramsey's recipe."

She took a large gulp of wine. "I was in the mood for pizza, not fancy."

It was odd for her to be contentious over something as silly as dinner. He took off his chef's apron, circled the island, and wrapped his arms around her. "It'll keep until tomorrow." She laid her head against his chest and hugged him tightly.

Given her mood, Reece decided against sharing his bad news. He'd forgotten to close the barn doors that led to their walk-in closet and spa bathroom. While he'd enjoyed a long steam shower, Pepin had pulled Sam's leather jacket off a hanger. By the time Reece had discovered the puppy, there was a sizable hole chewed in the sleeve. He'd taken it to a tailor who was unsure whether the damage was mendable. Reece figured he'd wait for the outcome before confessing.

"Where's the dog?" she asked suspiciously, as if she could read his mind.

"Sleeping. I took him for a run earlier."

In the beginning, Pepin had bounded over to welcome her every time she returned home. Now he ignored her. Reece couldn't identify the barrier that prevented Sam from bonding with Pepin. He wished she'd talk to him. He'd learned the hard way that ignoring feelings never worked. The only way to strip their power over you was to face them.

She took her wine into the living space and flopped onto the contemporary leather sofa. "Everything's a big mess," she muttered, putting her glass on an onyx side table. "Danny's going to shut down emotionally and never speak to either of us again. Eli will probably quit."

Reece sat beside her. "It can't be that bad."

After she told him what had happened at the penthouse, they sat quietly, watching the early evening light sparkling against the glossy grey floors.

"That explains a lot," Reece said finally. "About Danny's personality, I mean. It's why she's so guarded and closed. How do we handle it?"

"We don't," Sam said. "Acknowledging it will guarantee she'll pull away from us. We need to pretend Eli never blurted out her secret." She sighed and sat up, reaching for her wine. "It's enabling, I know. Our silence gives her permission to avoid it. But forcing her to talk would be worse." She passed him her wine glass.

Reece took a sip and tried to imagine the horrors Danny had suffered. It was so vile he couldn't process it. "Her own mother sold her into sex slavery," he said with a shudder. "How does anyone recover from something like that?"

"Many don't," Sam said sadly. "That level of betrayal and years of physical trauma at such a young age are the stuff of nightmares." She took back the wine and sipped. "Why are people so awful? Sometimes I fear humanity is extinct."

"The weird thing is, I spoke with—".

Sam interrupted him. "The other problem is the internship." She put down her wine glass in frustration. "Fadiya is a victim of sexual assault. I can't identify the rapist unless I'm inside. But I'm morally conflicted about using the clinical practicum as a vehicle to investigate."

"Can you help Fadiya?" Reece asked. "Clinically, I mean."

She shrugged. "I don't know. If I make a therapeutic error, it could have devastating results." She frowned and ran her fingers through her short curls. "I'm angry at Emily Armstrong for putting me in this situation. Not a great foundation for learning."

He put his hand on her cheek and turned her face toward him. "Why don't you meet Fadiya and then decide."

Sam's phone rang and she lifted her butt from the sofa to pull it from her back pocket. "My mother," she said with a groan. "No doubt about the wedding *again*."

She picked up and listened for a few minutes. "Mother, we aren't doing that. We said small, remember?" She pinched the bridge of her nose. "No ice sculptures, no five-hundred guests whom Reece and I have never met, no orchestra playing music we don't like, no strangling haute-couture dresses, and absolutely no indigestible cuisine concocted from disgusting exotic ingredients."

Reece returned to the kitchen, noting with distaste that Sam's voice had risen. He didn't hear his fiancée's parting comment, but the tone was unpleasant. She marched into the kitchen and stalked over to the kitchen island.

"Mother is planning *everything*," she told him. "Don't start in on me about her early-onset Alzheimer's. Since they got back from that experimental clinic in Sweden, Grace is doing fantastic."

With a twinge of regret, Reece covered his puff pastry in plastic wrap and put it in the fridge with his salmon. It would have been delicious.

"She's doing better because planning the wedding makes her happy," he said logically.

"Do you want to get hitched at their palatial estate on Millionaires' Row with all Mother's snobbish society friends?"

"Not especially," he admitted. "But it's just one day. It wouldn't kill us to suffer through it. Your mother and stepfather are all the family we have."

Sam smirked at him. "She wants doves. A whole flock of them."

Reece hated birds. It was irrational, he knew, but just thinking about nasty birds soaring over his head as he recited his vows made him itchy and anxious.

"I need your thoughts and professional advice on something," he said, deliberately ending the topic.

She sat on a bar stool at the island and reached for the open bottle of wine. "I'm sorry. All I've done since I walked through the door is talk about me. What's going on?"

"Danny's algorithm pulled numerous files from the database she generated for my sudden-death cases. It's flagged an interesting commonality," he said.

Sam frowned. "When did you talk to her?"

"Just before you got home. That's what I was trying to tell you earlier," he said and held up his hand. "Before you ask, she seemed fine with me." He handed her a flyer for her favourite pizza joint. "A number of cases had multiple statement reports that described the victims as extremely rude and unpleasant people."

Sam looked over the take-out menu. "Examples?"

"Neighbours described a man who fell down his cellar stairs and broke his neck as vulgar and uncivil. A month earlier, he threw a tire-deflation spike strip across his corner lot to stop kids from cutting across his lawn on their bikes. A child fell onto the spikes and lost his eye." Reece sipped his wine. "Then there was a suicide ruling in a shooting. The man's wife has cerebral palsy, and neighbours claimed he frequently degraded her in public. They also stated that she often had black eyes and bruises."

"I suppose the hanging victim we started with was there," Sam said. "Annalise Huang, right? Her friends told police she was an entitled 'mean-girl.'"

"Yup, and the woman involved in vehicular manslaughter, who appealed the 'harshness' of her licence suspension after killing the toddler and baby."

Sam reached for her phone. "Give me a sec while I order," she said. "I spent hours at the gym. I earned a sausage pizza."

"Get a medium veggie, too," Reece said.

He waited until she'd placed the order before he continued. "I also found a second drone sighting. Harold Taylor, the wife-abuser, had complained to police about a drone following him."

"Just like Annalise. Any more drone references?" she asked.

"Danny's searching all the records now. Thoughts?" he asked.

"I stand by my original opinion that the drone is suspicious," she said. "If there are only two, it could be a coincidence. Any victim similarities?"

"The victims I'm taking a closer look at are different ages, genders, and ethnicity," he said. "Of the five suicides the algorithm flagged, all statement records noted family disbelief," he told her. "None of the victims was depressed, none had a history of mental health issues, and none had suffered a loss or disappointment. They appear to have killed themselves for no reason."

"Suicide is complicated," she said dismissively. "Often there are no obvious indicators."

"I suppose, but I can't shake the certainty that this anonymous tip Gretchen received is legit. There could be homicides hidden as suicides, accidental mishaps, and natural causes. This could date back years."

"If one person murdered all these victims, you're looking at a serial," Sam said. "There must be a commonality that attracted the killer," she said. "What about geographical?"

"The ones I researched didn't live anywhere near each other. As far as work, I don't know," he admitted. "But two were retired."

"Don't discount retirees," Sam said. "They could volunteer, shop nearby, or frequent a restaurant in your vicinity."

"It can't be random, right?" he asked.

"Selection can appear random but it typically isn't," she said. "The killer has a vision of an ideal victim, such as a physical characteristic or specific quality. You ruled out the obvious—gender, age, race, education—but they all share some commonality recognizable to the killer."

"Could *specific quality* be conduct?" Reece asked tentatively.

"I suppose," she said. "Antisocial personalities seek to feel superior to their victim and see vulnerability in their target."

"So behaviour could be the trigger?" he asked again.

She studied him. "You think you know what attracts the killer."

Reece hesitated. He felt foolish putting his outlandish thought into words. He figured he might as well gauge Sam's reaction to his wild theory before he voiced it to his boss.

"I think the trigger is rude and entitled people," he stated. "I believe the killer encounters behaviour that puts the person on his radar."

Aloud it sounded more preposterous that it did in his head, and he saw justifiable doubt on Sam's face. To her credit, she didn't laugh.

"Nearly three-million people live in Toronto. Not to mention tourists, and business and entertainment visitors," she said with skepticism. "We're a friendly city but there are some real assholes out there. You're talking about a gigantic pool of potential victims."

"I think it's a *specific* type of rudeness," he said. "But I'm stuck on how to identify it."

"You need to speak to the victims' family, friends, and co-workers," Sam said. "How does the drone figure into this, if it does at all?"

"Surveillance?" Reece suggested.

"Serial killers are cautious and won't make a selection without a high probability of success," she admitted hesitantly. "I suppose a killer could use a drone to learn the victims' routines to choose the best abduction location."

That wasn't Reece's theory. He believed the killer used the drone to monitor the victims' behaviour to ensure it fit a profile. He'd never heard of any serial killer being so particular about that sort of thing.

"I'd like to interview Harold Taylor's wife, the man who complained about a drone," Reece said.

The doorbell rang and Sam got up to pay the pizza delivery. "Can you do that without permission from the Crown attorney's office?" she asked.

"No," he admitted. "I'll have to share my unsubstantiated suspicions and see if Gretchen authorizes me to proceed."

Sam didn't respond until she'd closed the door and put their pizzas on the kitchen island. "Well, she's the one who asked you to follow-up on the tip." She picked up his tablet and scrolled through his notes. "Any idea why Gretchen's anonymous informant had her look at these cases?"

His boss hadn't disclosed anything to him about the nature of the tip. Working in the dark was frustrating, but maybe she'd be more transparent once he outlined what he'd uncovered.

Sam opened the greasy lid of a pizza box and pulled apart a slice, separating a string of cheese with her finger.

Reece grabbed plates from the cupboard and handed her one. "Let's say one person did kill these people. Is there any other psychological profile—other than a psychopath—that would commit multiple homicides?" he asked.

She scrolled through his notes again and ate her slice of pizza. After a few minutes, she put down his iPad. "I understand why the 'serial killer' label is bothering you. I don't see a control or superiority aspect. Cause of death in all of these was too quick and clean." She reached for a second slice and popped a chunk of sausage in her mouth. "We need more intel on the victims. If your hunch is right, I need to understand what repetitive conduct attracts the killer before I can judge."

"It's going to be difficult to sell Gretchen," Reece said bleakly. "I wish I had more than just my gut to go in with."

Sam handed him a slice of veggie pizza. "Trust your instincts. They've never let you down in the past."

That wasn't true. A murderous sociopath had run a cult right under his nose in Uthisca, and Reece hadn't a clue that Bueton Sanctuary was anything but a religious retreat.

"If Gretchen denies your request to interview the families, you have an alternative," Sam said. "Open the investigation under the agency."

Her suggestion shocked him. "If my boss orders me to drop it and I use my private business to continue to investigate, I'm in breach of trust," he said.

She shrugged. "If you believe you're onto something and Gretchen disagrees, a killer could continue to hunt. Are you okay with that?" She picked up both pizza boxes and took them into the living space. "You don't always have to do everything by the book."

"I do," he retorted. "I'm an articling student and a Crown attorney is my principal. I'm obligated to abide by her directive."

She put the boxes on the coffee table. "Sorry I suggested it," she said with a sigh. "The best advice I can give you is to trust your instincts."

He sensed her frustration with his rigid morality. "Thanks for listening. I needed to hear that." He squeezed her fingers. "Let's find something stupid to watch on the idiot-box." She smiled at him knowingly, and reached for the remote.

Sam's broadminded philosophies had always been in direct opposition to Reece's rigid principles. His inability to see the grey in ethical issues had caused problems in the past. Now, they both respected each other's boundaries and agreed to disagree before an argument ensued.

He returned to the kitchen to grab the half bottle of wine from the island. His thoughts raced around a hamster's wheel. His skin tingled, the way it used to when he was an inspector with the provincial police and knew he was onto something. His gut was screaming at him that Toronto citizens were at risk.

"I know you're out there," he whispered. "I'm coming for you."

CHAPTER FIVE

The Journal

THIS LEATHER JOURNAL fulfills a promise I made to my father. It narrates my family's story. When you finish reading it, you may think what you want about me. I am not seeking forgiveness. Judge me harshly, if it pleases you. Decide that only a monster is capable of what I've done. Then comfort yourself by believing I'm an evolutionary anomaly. Lie to yourself if you want. But when I dwindle away like the grey mist that hangs above the bayou at dawn, some likeminded soul will materialize from the dissipating vapour. We protect the innocent. We are your shadows. We see inside the darkest parts of you. We are the omnipotent judges and executioners of the unworthy.

Call me Blu, as everyone in my childhood home of Louisiana did. I inherited my father's coarse black hair and stature, but my eyes—a deep cobalt blue—are unique to me. Blu was a name my mother claimed suited me because the clear Louisiana sky owned my soul.

My mother spoke with a cultured drawl, round and soft with a hint of aristocrat. As with everything about her, the accent was bogus, but I didn't realize that fact until I was in high school and our lives had disintegrated into dust. I can't recall how I discovered that my mother hailed from a small town in Ontario, in Canada, and not from Georgia as she claimed. It wasn't from my father's lips. He was a southern gentleman, so he paid no heed to her trivial mendacity.

Mom's contrived lilting intonation drew attention to my father's heavy Cajun accent. When people saw them together, Dad with his thick curly hair and knotted muscles and Mom with her silvery blonde tresses and elfin features, they often wondered what a genteel woman saw in such an uncultured man. One could easily imagine Dad shirtless and braced on the deck of a sea-soaked fishing trawler, while Mom sipped tea from Wedgewood china in an elegant drawing room. Not that she ever did that. My mother was a brilliant thespian who wove her life's tapestry from satin threads of lies.

She claimed her provenance traced back to the founding father of the colony of Georgia and that her ancestors had been plantation owners in Savannah. She'd eloquently declare to fascinated guests that the vice president of the Confederacy had once sat upon a fragile chair with an unravelling needlework cushion that perched at the head of our dining table. Sometimes she'd offer me the slightest of smiles. You see, we'd found that ugly old chair on the side of a road in Iberia Parish. It was a reject from an estate sale—an item so undesirable that no one had offered a single dollar to possess it. I had just turned seven on the day I helped her load it into our pickup truck. Although I didn't know the truth about her then, I understood her whimsical imagination and knew she'd knit a colourful anecdote about the chair's history. What I could not see back then was that those harmless fantasies were evolving into her reality and precipitating her descent into madness.

My father meticulously repaired the delicate chair and refinished the wood. He left the worn needlepoint cushion intact because Mom said that the neglected appearance added authenticity to the story of its origin—a story that didn't hold even a whisper of truth. When she ultimately came to believe that her family had indeed passed down that homely chair through the generations, my father listened with rapt attention and never contradicted the woman he adored.

When I was ten, Mom took me to East Gaston Street in historic Savannah to an elegant mansion where she claimed she'd lived as a child. On that sweltering day in August, the air was laden with oppressive humidity that threatened to drown you every time you took a shallow breath. Gnarled black branches of an ancient oak tree stretched across the sidewalk, and I swatted at the leaves that fluttered through the blistering air. My hair was too long, and it stuck in soggy clumps against the nape of my neck. Sweat gathered along the itchy collar of my button-down shirt. The sharp edge of a brown belt that I'd cinched around my baggy shorts chafed the slick skin of my hipbones. I didn't know what had possessed my mother to drag me to Savannah, and all I wanted was to go home to my sister, Pearl.

The estate had a low brick fence topped with ornate wrought iron, which my mother stopped in front of as she gestured grandly at the enormous house and grounds. Her joviality and antics began to draw unwelcome attention. I was mortified. She pranced like a dressage horse across the sidewalk, pirouetting and waving her arms above her head. Women stared with disapproval as Mom pontificated on her childhood in the Georgian jewel with its antebellum architecture. Brash comments and snickers floated around us like the rotten leaves of the old oak tree. I averted my eyes, cringing as each hateful word assaulted me. Suddenly, something fleeting crossed my mother's face, as if a deep pain afflicted her. Her gaiety ebbed and her gaze dropped to the sidewalk. A tear dripped onto the silk bodice of her outdated dress.

An ephemeral beam of maturity showed me the truth that day: her fantasies protected her from the harshness of reality. She needed them to survive, as much as we both needed the humid air we breathed. She needed me to believe, to be her armour against reality. It was a gift I had the power to bestow, a small token to shield her from the scorn of pitiless strangers.

I straightened my shoulders, raised my eyes in defiance, and took my mother's hand. I glared at the privileged women who strolled along the streets of Forsyth Park, and the first worm of hatred toward the entitled burrowed into my brain. Imperious people were a stain on the fabric of humanity.

I told my mother she was dazzling in her seafoam silk dress, with its yards of chiffon that billowed around the perfection of her pale skin. I danced with her on that boiling sidewalk until her laughter drowned out the snide remarks.

I took her to a bench and we sat in the shade of the oak tree. With nothing awry to gawk at now, people strolled by without paying us any mind. My mother's melodic voice serenaded me with fanciful stories, and I willingly followed her down the rabbit hole. She may never have resided within the walls of that estate or been born into an aristocratic family, but my mother owned the lie. Sitting ladylike on the bench, she was a vision that had stepped from the pages of a history book to stir my imagination. I could so easily envision Old Savannah's finest arriving for a ball hosted for the most sought-after debutante in Georgia. It was what she longed to believe, and my acceptance was the key to her happiness.

On that day in Savannah when I was ten, I began my metamorphosis into an intuitive chameleon, able to hide my true self and transform into what people desired me to be. My mother was a gifted prevaricator, and under her unsuspecting tutelage, I honed what would become an essential survival skill.

When a man appeared at the front door to the house, my mother called to him and, together, we charmed him into inviting us inside. He had recently acquired the estate, and it delighted him to learn about his home's illustrious past from a previous resident. We stayed for an hour and had tea at a poolside garden. Every childhood memory Mom recounted to the enchanted Yankee rang with truth. But even if he grew to suspect her of fraud, it didn't matter. Few men were impervious to my mother's beauty. Her huge eyes were aqua, the colour of the Gulf of Mexico when the sun hits it just right. Her complexion and hair were so pale that she resembled an ethereal fairy. God had graced her with an aquiline nose and plump lips that were a natural shade of rose. She'd been a dancer in her youth, and her lithe body moved in fluid motions that resembled choreography. There wasn't a man in the world immune to my mother's beauty.

Except for my paternal grandfather, that is.

My father was born in the South, but not from old money. His kin hailed from Lafayette and were nouveau riche, which is often worse in terms of intolerance. His father, my grandfather, was a southern chauvinist who hung his Confederate flags with pride, drank mint juleps dark with Michter's Bourbon, and exploited the Blacks he employed. Grandfather disowned my dad, his only son, the instant he married Mom. As a misogynist, my grandfather was invulnerable to Mom's beauty and suspicious of her purported genteel charm. My grandfather was acutely aware of the subtleties of deceit, because he was a cruel and dishonest man. As I learned in my teens, Grandfather exercised great resourcefulness in exposing my mother's true background. Tawdry detectives—some employed by the Lafayette Police Department—burrowed into Mom's past like pigs rooting for truffles. My mother hadn't perfected her delicate glass webbing of lies, and it shattered under their determined investigation.

The egg was her revenge. The egg was the catalyst that led to the brutality that eventually destroyed my family.

The last time Grandfather had tolerated Mom in his mansion, she'd lifted his prize possession, a Fabergé egg encased in aquamarine and adorned with emeralds and diamonds. She didn't steal the egg; my mother was much too clever for such a pedestrian act. She simply broke it and left the pieces on the marble floor below its lit pedestal, which an artist had crafted to display its splendour. I imagine that the glittering shards had twinkled like the crystal splinters of the fantasy she had spun to gain approval from a man who was her inferior.

Beaten down and disowned, Dad dropped out of medical school and abandoned a promising career as a surgeon. Perhaps he did it out of spite—it had been my grandfather's aspiration for his son to become a world-renowned surgeon. Perhaps he did it out of a calling to serve his country, because he immediately joined the army as a combat medic.

We lived inside the gates of Fort Polk Army Base in Vernon Parish. Whenever the army deployed my father, it was my responsibility to keep the nosy military wives away from our house. But between school and caring for Pearl, I could not protect my mother. Eventually, there were rumours that she was unfit to care for us. So, my father moved us to an isolated property outside Breaux Bridge in St. Martin Parish, where my mother and Pearl would be safe from prying eyes.

Two limestone walls marked the entrance to a lane with dual tire tracks gouged into the earth. Beyond the wall were twelve acres of land that hugged the banks of the Bayou Teche. The day we arrived, my father slowed to make the turn onto the rutted dirt lane, and I jumped out of the truck's cargo bed and scrambled onto the thick limestone wall. Shading my eyes from the brilliance of the sun, I looked toward the river and my gaze fell on an ancient bald cypress tree draped with Spanish moss. The magnificent tree stretched a hundred feet into the sky, like a sentry protecting the land it watched over. In that moment, I knew with absolute certainty that Mom and Pearl would be safe in this bayou oasis.

We lived in a mobile home for a year, while Dad and I completed our elevated home. We built the hipped-roof cottage from cypress timbers, and the foundation sat on steel pilings to raise the house and safeguard us from flooding. We built my mother a grand staircase that led to a deep porch that surrounded the four sides of the house. Inside was a kitchen at the back, a living room with a limestone fireplace, and two bedrooms on either side of the living space. I slept in a loft with a small window that overlooked the ancient bald cypress tree I had grown to love.

Whenever Dad was stateside, Mom and Pearl would accompany us while we trawled the bayou, pulling up traps laden with crawfish. My mother's sweet voice would float over me as I rebaited netted cylinders with beef melt and returned the traps to the still water. Mom would stretch out in the boat and tell mesmerizing stories of her fantasized childhood in a non-existent palatial estate in Old Savannah.

When we'd arrive home, her long white skirt would float around her legs as she and Pearl stepped into the water to wait for me and my father to pull the small mud boat to shore.

Dad would drape his arm around my shoulders and we'd watch our fairies dance beneath the twisted branches of the cypress tree. The sun would form lustrous halos around their platinum hair, and the twirling edges of their dresses would dry in the last whisper of the day's heat. I'd clap to the beat of their steps and their sultry laughter would float across the breeze as delicate needles dropped from the tree's gnarled branches.

That cypress tree, exquisitely strung with webs of Spanish moss, would come to embody the annihilation of everyone I loved. From beneath its aged branches, I would rise from the ashes of our demise as a ubiquitous avenger of the persecuted.

But I digress. There is so much more you need to know, so much more for you to understand.

CHAPTER SIX

SAM

SAM HAD BEEN waiting in Dr. Armstrong's office for nearly an hour, and security had paged the neuropsychiatrist three times. From the large window, Sam watched two police cruisers pull up to the clinic. Maybe they were bringing in a patient for an involuntary psychiatric assessment. That would explain why Emily was so late for their meeting.

Security had also paged Ophelia, which had been a huge relief. After an hour listening to incessant chatter and gossip, Sam had wanted to gouge her ear out with her pen. The nurse's one-sided rhetoric was an inauspicious start to bridging a positive relationship. Off-putting personality aside, if they were going to work together, Sam had to figure out a way to connect with her.

She dropped a copy of *American Journal of Psychiatry* onto the teak coffee table. Dr. Armstrong's paper on experiential therapy was intriguing. It left Sam battling her conscience again over the proposed internship. The research had cited the high success rates Serenity Clinic had had with non-traditional treatment settings, such as sculpting and rock climbing, for treatment-refractory depression and severe psychological trauma. And Emily had given credit to her former intern and praised his doctoral dissertation. A co-authored paper in the *American Journal of Psychiatry* would launch any psychologist's career and garner instant respect in the industry.

Bored, Sam repositioned a turquoise throw pillow on her armchair. Hues of teal, green, and blue were everywhere. They gave the place a peaceful, oceanic ambience, but the space was a mirror image of reception and lacked personal touches. She wandered around, stopping at a tall bookshelf to snoop for items that might offer a hint about her potential mentor's life. The shelves held nothing but academic textbooks. Emily had hung her medical degrees from the University of Toronto, Western University, and Dalhousie University, but there were no photos on the glass desk or any indication of the woman's family or interests. Sam was returning a Montblanc fountain pen to the desk when Emily breezed into the office, flushed and slightly out of breath.

"I'm so sorry for being late."

"I hope everything's okay," Sam said. "I heard the security calls."

Emily hung her suit jacket across the back of her desk chair. "A patient left last night. It happens." She crossed the room and took a seat on the sand-coloured sofa.

Sam sat on the adjacent armchair. "Was the patient an involuntary admission?"

"At first, yes. The certificate expired a month ago. Based on her willing participation in therapy, I decided against signing a renewal." There was a note of sadness in Emily's voice. "She was free to go, but she was making significant progress. I can't understand what motivated her to leave without telling me."

"Does it happen often?" Sam asked.

Emily shrugged. "It's difficult for teenage patients to be cooped up during the spring and summer months."

"How old was she?"

"Fourteen." Emily plucked a speck of lint off her black pencil skirt.

"Her family must be frantic," Sam said sympathetically.

"This isn't the first time their daughter has run. After a few days, she'll show up," Emily stated brusquely, then changed the subject. "Before we discuss the reason I asked you here, I'm eager to learn what you discovered in the security footage."

When Sam finished updating her, Emily's distressed expression accentuated the crows' feet around her hazel eyes. "Someone inside the hospital tampered with the files," she said softly. "I can't believe anyone who works here would do such a thing."

"Danny found an escape hatch on the server. It's possible an outsider accessed the system that way," Sam said. "How does security handle visitors in the facility?"

"All visitors report to reception, sign in with one piece of picture identification, and receive a dated photo badge," Emily said. "The badge must be worn and visible at all times."

Sam had done all that herself, but the four-storey building spanned nearly a full city block. There had to be multiple access routes. "Could someone bypass reception?"

Emily shook her head. "People can exit through some of the doors without a keycard, but they can't get in. All the exterior doors automatically lock."

"What about police? Where do they bring involuntary admissions?"

"A block to the south, where the parking is. There's an ambulance bay at the rear of the building," Emily replied.

"I imagine it's chaotic when a patient is brought in by force," Sam said. "Is it possible for someone to sneak in unnoticed?"

"I suppose." Emily's frown was skeptical. "But employees are conscientious about patient privacy. If a stranger were roaming the halls, someone would detain the person and notify security." A tic in the corner of her mouth twitched. "If the employee recognized the person, though, their response might be different," she admitted. "We keep circling to the same conclusion. Whoever assaulted Fadiya is known to us." She crossed her legs and wrapped her arms around her thin waist.

Sam disagreed. It was just as likely that the rapist was on the premises visiting a patient. "Once visitors are inside, can they walk around unsupervised?"

"They're supposed to stay in the visitor centre, the restaurants, or the courtyard garden. If they're here for family counselling, they'd be with an employee," Emily said. "But we aren't running a prison, Sam. So long as they weren't in the lockdown unit, which is supervised visitation only, and they had a visitor badge, unescorted guests wouldn't raise any red flags."

"The patient that left last night—how did she get out of the building without anyone noticing?" Sam asked.

"Like I said, there are exits that open from the inside, in compliance with fire laws," Emily said. "We run on a skeleton crew after midnight, so it's possible she left without anyone noticing." She checked her watch. "I'm late for a meeting with Fadiya's mother and brother. That's why I asked you here. Mrs. Basha is eager to meet you."

"Why?" Sam asked.

"She's aware of your connection to Bueton." Emily held up a hand before Sam could respond. "I didn't tell her. She recognized your name from the publicity after the mass murder."

"I'm committed to helping you uncover the security breach, but I haven't decided on the ethics around the practicum," Sam stated honestly.

Emily waved her hand dismissively. "This isn't a ploy to strong-arm you. When facing a life decision, information is empowering. Wouldn't meeting Fadiya and her family help you to decide?"

"Well, yes, but I don't want to mislead them."

Emily stood and walked over to her desk. She repositioned her fountain pen beside a notebook and took her jacket from the back of the chair. "I understand, but please don't worry. They'll accept whatever decision you make." She led Sam into the corridor and locked her office door. "The boardroom is on this level. Did Ophelia give you a full tour?"

"All but the cellar." Sam followed her down a long hallway. "Last time I was here, she said it was off-limits. I understand it was a boiler room in the early nineteen-hundreds."

Emily nodded. "We tabled the mould and coal dust remediation pending an influx of operating capital. My partner, Dr. Beauregard, is in the process of securing new investors." She waved at a tall man who stood outside a closed office door fiddling with a key chain. "Mathias, come and meet Sam McNamara, the clinical practicum candidate I mentioned."

He sauntered over with a confident swagger that screamed *narcissist*. Dr. Beauregard's dark hair was coiffured, his indigo tie matched his eyes, and his black trousers were expensively tailored.

At a few inches over six feet, he was nearly a foot taller than Sam was. He looked down his thin nose at her, with an imperious expression that made her instantly dislike him.

"The investigator," he stated with a sneer of contempt. "I don't approve of Dr. Armstrong's decision. That said, your investigation skills are beyond reproach, and I concede it's her right to choose her own intern, regardless of her motivation. Please don't embarrass our good name."

Sam didn't appreciate his supercilious edict. She bit her tongue on a sharp retort.

He turned to his partner. "I'm late for a meeting with investors. Your tardiness forced me to entertain Mrs. Basha." Without another word, he entered the office outside which they stood and closed the door in their faces.

"Don't mind Mathias," Emily said with a laugh. "He's a product of his Harvard and Oxford education." She continued walking down the hallway, indicating that Sam should follow her. "Prior to joining the private sector, Mathias served with the military. His work overseas with veterans' post-traumatic stress disorder is impressive. We use his techniques to treat pediatric trauma and psychotic symptoms with remarkable success."

"I see," Sam said, not bothering to hide her negative impression of the priggish man.

Emily patted her arm. "Fear not. If you accept my internship, you'll have limited interaction with Mathias. He doesn't treat patients. Without private funds to invest into our venture, securing new investors falls under his purview. His business prowess is a great asset to the clinic."

Sam considered it a blessing he didn't treat patients. His bedside manner was probably as obnoxious as his professional manner was.

Emily opened double doors at the end of the corridor, leaving them slightly ajar. She circled a large oval table and took a seat next to a woman garbed in a traditional Afghan burka. The blue linen cloak encased her entire body. Delicately embroidered flowers surrounded a mesh screen that covered her eyes. The burka worried Sam. If she accepted the practicum, open communication with Fadiya's mother would be instrumental in developing a course of treatment. It would be difficult to converse with Mrs. Basha through the thick facial netting. It would be impossible to read her expressions and body language.

Beside the woman sat an emaciated man, possibly in his midtwenties, with sharp facial features, jet-black hair, and large brown eyes set in a pale face.

Emily introduced Sam to Mrs. Basha and her son, Aazar. The woman held her hand over her heart and nodded but remained silent. The young man smiled and nodded, but didn't offer his hand. Something about him seemed familiar, but Sam couldn't put her finger on what was triggering her memory.

"It is an honour to meet you," Aazar said pleasantly, wheezing between words. "You were inside the Bueton cult. You can help my sister."

"We welcome you to Fadiya's circle of care," Mrs. Basha said in a commanding voice. She turned her head to address Emily. "It is imperative that Fadiya be deemed legally competent. Time is of the essence, Dr. Armstrong. Did you receive my husband's email regarding our family's proposed donation?"

"Yes, thank you. It's very generous," Emily said and colour flushed her cheeks. "I've spoken with the surgeon and understand the urgency to have Fadiya legally able to consent. Sam's experience with Bueton's style of indoctrination can help us attain that goal."

The surgical urgency must be to abort the baby before Islamic law prevented it, Sam realized. It surprised her that Mrs. Basha knew. Emily had specifically said she wasn't disclosing the pregnancy until they were able to identify Fadiya's assailant.

They continued to chat, with Emily updating the family on Fadiya's progress and setbacks. Sam sat silently auditing the exchange and mentally struggling to settle the ethics of becoming involved in Fadiya's case. She could speak informatively about Bueton and use that common ground to bridge trust. She had plenty of experience in working with victims of trauma. She could study deprograming strategies and seek advice from experts in the field. Perhaps she could lead Fadiya into accepting that the cult and its leader were gone. That breakthrough could help Emily to dispel the girl's delusions. Maybe she was underestimating herself. If her knowledge of Bueton could help to reinstate Fadiya's legal rights and return her quality of life, Sam had an obligation to try. Helping people was why she'd studied psychology.

At last, Mrs. Basha and Aazar stood, startling Sam from her inner debate.

"*Jazakallahu Khairan*," Mrs. Basha said to Emily.

"*Wa iyyaakum*," Emily replied.

Sam joined Emily at the door and they watched the mother and son enter the elevator.

"She said, 'May Allah reward you with goodness'," Emily told her. "I responded 'And to you'."

"Does she know about the pregnancy?" Sam asked.

"No. As I told you during our last meeting, I'm waiting to disclose it until we have facts," Emily said.

"Doesn't Islamic law prohibit abortion after a certain number of weeks?" Sam asked.

Emily nodded. "The Hadith permits abortion until the fetus is about four months old. After that, it's deemed a living soul." She closed and locked the boardroom door. "Waiting another few weeks won't hurt. By then, you may have answers."

Sam disagreed, but it wasn't her place to argue. "If it's not an abortion, what surgery does Fadiya need to consent to?"

"Aazar requires a lung lobe transplant. Fadiya is a living-donor match," Emily said. "Since a judge declared her mentally incompetent to provide consent, we need to overturn the verdict quickly or her brother will die."

Sam followed her to the stairwell, feeling her cheeks flush with outrage. They intended on harvesting tissue from their deluded daughter to save their son. She took a calming breath. Could it be that straightforward? Reining in her spinning emotions, Sam considered the situation objectively.

"Do you believe that Fadiya would consent if she were capable of doing so?" she asked.

"She did consent before her condition worsened and she regressed," Emily said.

"Do families of your patients often offer generous donations as incentive?" She'd tried to curb her disapproval but heard it loud and clear.

They travelled down three flights of stairs in silence, with Sam acutely aware that she'd offended the doctor. Emily escorted her through the locked doors that led to the front lobby and they stood together in a secluded alcove.

"Private hospitalization in a predominately public health care system is difficult for many people to understand," Emily said. "Like hospitals in the United States, we rely on private donors and investors to secure operating capital. Otherwise, our residential program fees would be staggering."

"I understand fee-for-service health care models, but I have concerns about private donations to encourage preferential treatment," Sam said.

"Fadiya would receive the same treatment with or without her family's generosity," Emily said curtly. "Do you object to Children's Hospital running the Dream Lottery?"

"That's different," Sam said. "The patients' families aren't gifting the hospital money with the expectation of receiving a higher level of care."

Emily held out her hand for Sam's visitor badge. "That isn't Mrs. Basha's intention. You didn't recognize Aazar, did you?"

Sam shook her head.

"Find out who he is," Emily said stiltedly. "Then you'll understand the urgency." She disappeared through the locked door.

CHAPTER SEVEN

REECE

REECE PARKED IN front of a nondescript brick bungalow. The wood frame grids around the circa-1960 bay window were rotten, and the thin glass appeared fragile enough to crack under a strong breeze. Weeds sprouted from yellow grass, and a broken concrete walkway wound across the neglected yard to three sunken cement stairs that led to a decaying wood porch.

His boss had authorized him to investigate the two drone sightings, so he was starting with Susan Taylor, the wife of the man who'd shot himself with an illegal firearm. Reece glanced around the dilapidated house and his mouth grew dry with dread. He had no answers for the widow, only intrusive questions that would catapult her into more misery over her husband's death.

There was no doorbell, and the storm door was either locked or jammed. Reece rapped on its rusted metal frame. After a minute without any response, he tentatively reached through a tear in the mesh screen and knocked on a rickety front door. From inside, a dog yapped.

He waited another minute to no avail. "Mrs. Taylor? Reece Hash from the Crown attorney's office. We spoke on the phone," he shouted.

The door opened a crack and a short, chubby, grey-haired woman with a thin upper lip peered at him through thick-lensed spectacles.

Reece smiled and held up his identification. "Hi, I'm a bit early. Is this convenient?" He was on time and she had agreed to speak with him, but her suspicious expression implied his arrival was an unpleasant surprise.

She closed the door. He heard the chain unlatch and the door reopened. She unlocked the storm door and stood aside, silently waving him inside. A scruffy Yorkshire terrier sat at her feet, glaring accusingly at Reece.

He entered a musty foyer and followed her uneven gait into a gloomy front room. The house was stifling hot and there was an unpleasant smell. It was a combination of stale cigarette smoke, mouldy carpet, and dirty dog. The only light came from a narrow opening between black velvet drapes. Dust motes danced in the thin sunbeam.

"Detached retina. Light hurts my eyes." She sat in a torn vinyl BarcaLounger and lifted the mangy dog onto her lap. It put its snout between its paws and stared at Reece.

"I'm sorry, Mrs. Taylor. That must be unpleasant." He perched on the edge of a shabby floral sofa across from her, discreetly swiping perspiration from his upper lip and breathing shallowly through his mouth.

"That's life," she replied casually. "Call me Susan. I don't answer to Taylor no more. What do you want to know about Harold?"

"I'm following up on an incident report he filed prior to his suicide," Reece began.

"Right, his *suicide*." She wrapped the word in air quotes. Her right hand was a gnarled claw that trembled with palsy.

"You don't believe he committed suicide?"

"We were married forty-years. Harold was a nasty son-of-a-bitch. He wouldn't take his life and leave me to enjoy the end of mine in peace." She lit a cigarette, blowing smoke out of the corner of her lips. "Besides, Harold was a papist. Suicide is a mortal sin. He took that bullshit serious. Went off to confession for a priest's blessing every time he laid a beating on me. Never understood how that worked. Commit whatever sin you like, trot into the confessional, and skip out absolved. You Catholic?"

"No," Reece answered. "Did you report the abuse?"

"I called the cops and they rushed right over to serve and protect." Her voice dripped with disdain. "Government offered disability benefits and found me what the kids today call a safe space." She cackled and rummaged in a drawer in a table beside her. "Son, you've got a lot to learn about the real world. There ain't no help for women like me. We made our beds." She held out a grubby envelope. "I got an iPhone Harold didn't know about and got pretty good at selfies."

Reece stood and took the envelope. Inside were dozens of photos he assumed were of the woman in front of him. It was hard to tell in some of the pictures. The brutality of her injuries was horrifying. He dropped the envelope on a dusty coffee table but held onto the photos.

"Case you didn't notice, I have cerebral palsy," she said. "Docs figure my mother was a drinker. Fetal alcohol syndrome, they call it. Always had trouble with my eyes and I got osteonecrosis." She lit another cigarette. "Means my bones are dying. I was saving to leave Harold, but I had to give up my job nineteen years ago. Tried to get disability benefits. It went all the way to a tribunal, but the government still denied me."

"Can I take these?" He held up the photos from the envelope she'd given him.

Susan shrugged. "Don't see why not."

He tucked the photos into his shirt pocket. "Harold reported to police that a drone was following him. Do you know anything about that?" Reece asked.

"If it wasn't one conspiracy theory, it was another," Susan said. "Yeah, I heard about the drone."

"Did you see it?"

She shook her head. "Harold told me he was gathering evidence to persecute the operator. Hoped he could sue in civil court and have himself a payday." She gestured behind her. "His office is in the outbuilding. He lived out there when he wasn't itching to hurt me. It's where he died," she said. "Whatever the police left, you're welcome to. I can't get down the hill and haven't been inside since he built himself his palace." She put out her cigarette. "You think someone murdered the old bastard, eh?"

"No, I'm just following up on the drone report," Reece said quickly.

She cackled. "Yeah, and Prince Harry and that pretty wife of his are dropping by for tea tomorrow."

"Can you think of anyone who had an issue with Harold?" Reece asked.

"Everyone who ever met the bastard. He was a bully and preyed on the weak." She studied him pensively, as if deciding whether to say more.

Reece had interrogated many reluctant witnesses over his years as a police inspector. He sensed that Susan had a story to tell. He stayed quiet and waited, knowing she'd eventually fill the silence.

"I had a son." She spoke softly. "Harold wanted me to abort the baby. I wouldn't, so he beat me near gone every day. My boy was born three months early, but he was a fighter. Lived for sixteen days." She wiped her eye with the back of her knuckle. "I reckon lots of men like to hurt women, but Harold's evil ran deeper. He considered people like me a throwback. Believed society should scrub the gene pool." She lowered her eyes with undeserved shame. "That's what he did with my son."

Sensing its mistress's anguish, the dog whined and licked her hand.

"That was a long time ago. I only tell you because it gives you an idea of Harold's personality." She snuggled her Yorkie, kissing the top of its head. "He killed our neighbour's dog last year. Fed it poisoned meat. He picked something slow acting, so the poor animal suffered. Harold stood at the fence with a big grin and watched it die."

"Were the police involved?" Reece asked.

Susan nodded. "Neighbour suspected Harold but the authorities said there wasn't any proof, not that they looked too hard." She laughed bitterly. "But they sure took a hard look at me after the son-of-a-bitch died. Brought in detectives, and they don't do that with suicides."

"They do," Reece assured her. "Especially with gunshot victims. Do you know where Harold got the gun?"

She nodded. "He hung out at a restaurant around here that hires disabled employees. Owner kicked him out because of the sinful things he said and did to those poor folks. He met some street thug there and bought the gun from him," she said. "He told everyone he knew. Harold never had a lick of shame. He kept it out in his palace in a strongbox. Cops took it and good riddance." She reached for a television remote beside her. "Keys to the outbuilding are on a peg by the back door. Latch it on your way out."

Reece thanked her and walked to the rear of the house. A keychain was indeed on a peg beside a rickety screen door. He looked across a neglected backyard. At the base of a sharp decline was a large, detached building in pristine condition. That would be Harold's palace.

"Like I said, help yourself to whatever you want," Susan called from the front room. "Burn it to the ground, if it suits you. You'd be doing me a favour." The television blared, causing Reece to wince at the audio assault.

He locked the door behind him and picked his way through scattered trash to the crest of the steep hill. The July was scorching and sweat dripped from his hairline as he carefully descended. Beneath knee-high grass were uneven stepping-stones. Rather than easing the descent, however, they were a tripping hazard, and Reece kept his eyes glued to the ground as he sidestepped down the sharp incline.

Investigating spouses in sudden-death cases was common, but the cops would have quickly eliminated Susan as the shooter. The feeble woman couldn't negotiate this perilous hill with her health issues. Still, he couldn't help but question the lead detective's due diligence. One short interview with the widow had already left Reece suspecting that Harold's death could be something other than what it seemed.

He reached the outbuilding. The door had two deadbolts and a padlock. Harold was a suspicious man, apparently. Beside the door, a top-of-the-line air conditioner hummed. It said a lot about the man. His medically fragile wife languished in a rundown house without modern conveniences, while Harold enjoyed state-of-the-art climate control in his man-cave.

It took a few minutes to figure out the keys and open the door. The metallic odour of old blood hit him first. Then the rancid stench of feces, urine, and decaying meat crawled across the room and punched him in the face. The seven-hundred-square-foot living room and kitchen buzzed with feasting flies. Gagging, Reece shoved the door open wide and stumbled back, covering his nose with his hand. If someone hadn't had the presence of mind to leave the air conditioner on, the putrefaction would have been much worse. Reece couldn't believe that authorities hadn't contacted Victim Services Toronto. The woman's husband had blown his brains out in this room. Susan had a special need, for God's sake, and obviously required assistance to hire a crime scene clean up company. It was costly, which was probably why she'd ignored the issue, but there were programs available to provide financial assistance. It was irresponsible to leave her unaided with a biohazard risk in her backyard. The insensitivity of the lead detective infuriated Reece.

He still had a crime scene kit in his car, left over from when he'd served with the provincial police. There would be a mask with the protective equipment. Reece trudged back to his car and popped the trunk, rummaging around in a box until he found a half-face respirator mask. He took out a pair of protective goggles, gloves, booties, and a handful of large plastic evidence bags. He didn't have a suit, so he would have to sacrifice his clothes to the cause.

He circled the house to the backyard and trekked down the hill. Outside the building, he donned the booties, mask, goggles, and gloves. He'd move fast, get what he needed, and get out. Reece took a deep breath and stepped into the ghastly room.

A maroon starburst soiled the wall behind an expensive, ergonomic desk chair. Clumps of hair and bone clung to the wall, glued to the dried blood spatter. More blood and brain matter stained the deep-piled beige carpet beneath the chair. Reece averted his eyes from the gruesome death scene and turned his attention to an enormous white board on the adjacent wall. Harold had created an investigation board, complete with red strings linking photos and index cards. Printed in thick black marker on the cards were dates and addresses. In the centre of the white metal board was a blurry, five-by-seven picture of a drone. The logistics made no sense. From what Reece could discern, the web of red string didn't link any commonalities. He pulled at the edges of the heavy board and found that thick screws anchored it to the wall. He stood back again, thinking. It was too large to fit in his car anyway. He'd have to recreate the schematic at the office. Reece took out his phone, snapped numerous photos, and removed all the photos and index cards from the board, tucking them into one of the plastic evidence bags that he'd brought from the car.

Harold's laptop was open on the desk; it, too, was covered in blood spatter. On top of a black metal file cabinet, Reece found a pop-up container of disinfectant wipes. He pulled one free and scrubbed the laptop screen. It took ten sheets before he was able to dislodge the crusted gore. Grimacing, he snapped open a second evidence bag and sealed the contaminated laptop inside the protective plastic. He swatted at a fly that landed on his forearm. His skin crawled and itched as he quickly searched the desk drawers and metal filing cabinets. On top of his other repulsive traits, Harold had had a liking for sadistic pornography. His preference was young girls. Very young. Reece flipped quickly through a stack of Asian snuff magazines; the obscene content made his stomach roil. Eager to get out of the vile place, he took a final look around the two bedrooms and full bath. Satisfied he hadn't missed anything drone-related; he exited the building, stripped off the goggles, mask, and gloves, and locked one of the deadbolts. He tucked the keys behind the central air unit.

Back at his car, he put the wrapped laptop, the bag of photos and index cards, and his protective gear in the trunk and walked back to Susan's house. From the porch, he called Eli.

"Can you do me a favour?" he asked.

"What do you need?"

"Call a crime scene cleaning company and arrange for them to come to the address I just texted you. Sam should have one listed in the agency's contacts. Have them charge us directly. It's the building in the back and I left the keys behind the air conditioner. Ask them not to bother the homeowner."

"I am on it." Eli hung up and Reece knocked on Susan's door.

She answered the door more quickly than she had the first time. "Get what you needed?"

"Yes. I arranged for a company to come and clean Harold's office, and—"

"What? They charge three-hundred dollars an hour," she yelled. "They could have a party down there and I'd be none the wiser." Her curled hand shook and her small eyes filled with tears. "I can't pay the bill. Why would you do this?"

Reece gently grasped her fluttering hand. "I run a private investigation agency with my fiancée," he said. "We know an honest company and you won't be charged."

"I don't take charity." Tears dripped down her face.

Reece squeezed her hand. "It's not." A white lie to comfort the proud woman wouldn't hurt. "The city will reimburse us. You can trust me, Susan."

Her face relaxed. "You're a kind man," she said. "The first one I've ever met. Your fiancée is a lucky woman."

Reece smiled. "Nope, I'm the lucky one." He took one of his PI agency business cards from his pocket and tucked it into her hand. "If you need anything, call me."

She nodded and returned his smile before she shut the door.

He walked back to his car and stood for a moment gazing at the dilapidated house that was at odds with the modern building in the backyard that Harold had occupied.

Reece did not condone murder. It was black and white. There was no grey area. Yet he couldn't silence a niggling voice inside his head.

Society was better off without Harold Taylor in it.

CHAPTER EIGHT

THE JOURNAL

MY MOTHER AND father loved each other with an intensity that reduced everything around them to white noise. Whenever Dad deployed to some war-torn country to save godforsaken women and children from the tyranny of a patriarchal dictatorship, my mother would float weightlessly inside her fantasy world until his return.

When we moved off the Fort Polk army base to that isolated property on the Bayou Teche, the solitude created the perfect backdrop for Mom's imaginings. My sister, Pearl, and I would follow her down the rabbit hole, where our ancestors were southern aristocrats who held balls for Old Savannah grandees and Mom wore gowns spun from the finest Asian silk.

But after 9/11, that rabbit hole warped into a petrifying abyss.

I was thirteen when the planes hit the World Trade Center and over three thousand people perished. A year later—a day after my fourteenth birthday—my father received his orders to ship out to Afghanistan. Before he left, he took me to Lafayette.

"You can't do this alone," he said. "Fourteen is too young."

I straightened my back and put my elbow out the car window. "Done it before. You ever come home to trouble?"

"Blu…" He trailed off with a sigh and didn't speak again until he turned off the main road and onto a lane bordered with towering oak trees.

"This deployment is not like the others," he said sadly. "Pearl and Mom don't understand the significance, but you know why I have to go."

Seared into my brain were the images of New Yorkers stampeding through an apocalyptic tidal wave of blinding smoke as glass and shrapnel lashed their faces. I understood what those animals had done, and I was proud of my father's decision to fight against the horror of terrorism.

"Pearl and Mom are safe with me," I said with a teen's naivety. "Always are."

"Mom is different now. You need help to keep away the authorities." He didn't elaborate but the regret in his voice made me turn to look at him.

"Where are we going? Why did you make me wear this stuff?" I was dressed in my best clothes, which were uncomfortable and itchy in the cloying humidity.

The red roof of a looming brick mansion materialized above the treeline. We continued along the elegant, oak-lined lane to a grand entrance. My father stopped the truck and climbed from the driver's side, waiting for me to join him. "Never tell your mother I brought you here," he muttered hoarsely, refusing to meet my eyes.

We walked up a flight of majestic stone steps flanked by towering white columns. Southern magnolia trees shaded a porch decorated with stylish wicker furniture strategically placed just so. Above each chic seating arrangement, a row of ceiling fans moved in leisurely swishes. Intricately painted ceramic pots, the rims of which came to my chest, flanked an ornate front door with wrought iron fixtures. Vibrant coloured blossoms cascaded down the sides of the urns and the humid air was laden with the scent of sweet olive and roses.

Dad rang an ornamental doorbell and stood at parade rest, a military posture I mimicked. A cold shiver of dread ran down my back.

A butler opened the door and his eyes widened with recognition. He nodded silently, quietly closed the door, and we waited. When a portly man with coiffured grey hair opened the door, he looked my father up and down with no expression. His black serpent eyes skimmed over my face before a mask of contempt fell across his features and he turned away, dismissing me as insignificant. My grandfather spoke just one sentence before shutting the door: "You made your bed. Now lie in it with your Yankee whore and the urchins she spawned."

The ugliness of those words made me feel dirty and worthless. My father's slumped shoulders and the tremble in his hand shamed me. This righteous man had stood meek beneath the steely gaze of an entitled snob who denied his own blood. Hate coiled around my heart and squeezed until it became a palpable ache.

No words could soften my humiliation or my father's shame, so we travelled home in tense silence, driving through the opening in the limestone wall and up the dirt lane to our house. In the yard, my father turned off the truck and stared through the cracked windshield at his wife and daughter. Mom and Pearl were playing under the cypress tree, both of them breathtaking in the coral-tinged light from the setting sun. Their lilting laughter glided on a breeze that drifted off the Teche. They were perfection incarnate. The stranglehold of hate toward my grandfather intensified.

"You're young, but you have depth and stability." My father's wistful expression softened the rigid lines of his profile. "Blood joins us all, and I wish your grandfather was a better man. I have to rely on you to keep our fairies safe." He turned to look at me. "I'll take what money we have from the bank. It'll be enough to keep you going for a year, if you're careful. Never use your mother's bank card. Pay cash. Go into Breaux Bridge only once a month or so. Never go to the same store twice. Mind your business, child. Understand?"

I did. The city was small—only about eight thousand locals. Someone would question why I was frequenting the grocery store alone. My presence would remind them that they hadn't seen my mother in town. That couldn't happen. The Department of Children and Family Services would pay us a visit. It had happened once before. This time, they'd take us away. They would institutionalize my cherished sister, and probably have my mother locked away in an asylum.

"I know what to do," I said. When the cash ran out, we'd live off the bayou. I would never do anything that could put Pearl's happiness at risk.

"Hospitals are enemy territory," he said. "I'll leave three Unit One Packs and some suture kits. Your sutures are better than mine."

My chest swelled with pride. I'd practised on bananas and a piece of denim for hours, until I mastered the half-curved needle. He'd taught me subcutaneous and intravenous injections and airway management. With the supplies in the combat kits, I could provide emergency medical care for my mother and sister so we could avoid inquisitive doctors.

"You're like that deep-rooted cypress tree—strong, resilient, and unwavering," he said pensively. "You have a unique instinct to understand a person's true desire and to give them what they yearn for." His eyes shifted from the tree to me. "Your mother is fragile, Blu, and your sister is special. People don't understand them. Without understanding, cruelty reigns. While I'm gone, people will be your greatest threat."

The high, two-syllable whistle of a Mississippi kite sounded from the bayou. "I can keep them away," I told him. "Done it before." My eyes followed the kite's streamlined silhouette across the sky.

He held my hand between both of his. "You have an old soul, Blu. I wish it didn't have to be like this. I wish there was family to help."

My sister shaded her eyes against the sun and a radiant smile lit her face when she spotted our truck. Pearl was autistic and she rarely spoke. When she did, her eyes would flit across the heavens and her finger would tap the rhythm of her words against the air. My mother claimed that the archangels had wept with joy at her birth and their celestial tears had dripped against her brow, transforming Pearl into a living cherub.

As I watched my sister run toward us, hate toward my grandfather gurgled in the pit of my stomach. Someday, he would not dismiss my family as paltry. Someday, I'd strip away his dignity in the same callous way he had stripped away ours and leave him to die in his burning mansion. Someday, he'd pay for denying my sister.

I climbed from the truck, stripping off my trousers and shirt as I ran to meet Pearl. Clad only in my underwear, I tugged her to the mud boat. Together, we pulled it into the Teche, and I relished the coolness of the water against my heated skin and the sweet sound of her innocent laughter. We caught catfish until a riot of colours from the setting sun painted the Louisiana sky in abstract hues of pink and orange. Mom fried our bounty on an outdoor fire pit and Dad sang Cajun folk songs until the splinter of a new moon climbed high into the molasses sky.

Hours later, I watched from my bedroom window as my parents waltzed beneath our cypress tree. They swayed in perfect synchronization and profound despondency overwhelmed me. I wept as they danced to music only they could hear, dreading his forthcoming absence and fearing that I could not keep the vow I had pledged.

It was a dire premonition that would come true.

Shortly after Dad deployed to Afghanistan, Mom slipped into an impregnable cavern of depression. Without his presence to anchor her to reality, Mom's mind glided into the ethereal mist that cloaked the bayou. A year into my father's tour of duty, her essence had vanished to a place I could not reach. Late at night, I would stare down the road from my bedroom window and rage would rise like a tsunami in my chest. Less than twenty miles away, in his grandiose mansion in Lafayette, my wealthy grandfather smoked cigars and sipped bourbon from a crystal glass, indifferent toward his suffering daughter-in-law and destitute grandchildren.

A year after my father's deployment—just after I'd turned fifteen—the money ran out. Pearl contributed to our survival without understanding her gift. She tended a vegetable garden, and maybe my mother was right and the angels had blessed Pearl because every plant she touched grew hearty. But she refused to eat them because she claimed to hear the vegetables cry out in pain when I pulled them from the earth or cut them from their stems. The bayou was rich with fish but Pearl wouldn't eat the moist white flakes of a catfish or suck the flesh from a crawfish. The only game she'd eat was wild rabbit, never associating the rich meat with the swamp rabbits she'd spy in the eelgrass and beaked tassel weed. But rabbits were hard to hunt in the swamp because of their surprising agility in the water. If I suffered an accident, my sister and mother would be vulnerable to authorities. So, when the cash ran out after the first year, I hunted swamp rats, which tasted similar to wild rabbit.

At night, I'd lie beside Pearl and stroke her smooth cheek, revelling in the pure love that flowed from her being. I'd chant the verses of a Cajun lullaby, and she'd sing the chorus. I would stay by her side with my arm entwined in hers until she was fast asleep. When I was certain she wouldn't wake and follow me, I'd sneak outside with a lightweight Remington. With only the moon for light, I'd wait motionless on the riverbank with my back pressed against the trunk of a black cottonwood tree that towered above me, its branches disappearing into the inky sky. Smoke-coloured fog would drift from the algae-covered water, and the haze would shroud the feathery nexus of eerie Spanish moss in a mystical aura. Hours would pass before I caught a glimpse of the arched brown body and dragging chest of a nutria, the infamous rodent that plagued Louisiana. When the giant swamp rat with its bright orange buckteeth lumbered to shore, trailing its ten-inch tail behind it, I'd exhale and fire. On a good night, I could pick off several and be gone before anyone cared to trace the shots.

I sold each tail to a man with a licence to hunt nutria. Cyril was notorious on the bayou for consorting with lowlifes. Rumour was that he held ties to the New Orleans mob. My father had warned me many times to stay away from the man. It was a promise I could not keep. Cyril was the only person willing to pay for the tails without asking questions. The stipend I received was enough to buy milk for Pearl.

I didn't miss a day of school and was always dressed in clean clothing. The overworked teachers never suspected that I was single-handedly caring for my mentally ill mother and autistic sister.

But someone knew. Someone had lurked behind the veils of Spanish moss that hung from the trees along the Teche, watching us and waiting for his opportunity. Someone had coveted Pearl's beauty and innocence, and ultimately, he pilfered what he viewed as his entitlement.

On the night that altered the trajectory of our lives, I tumbled over Pearl's broken body curled beneath the cypress tree. My gory cache of swamp rats dropped against her side with a wet smack. Hurling them off her, I plunged to my knees and screamed. I wailed at the dark, and at the inhuman beast that had vanished into the night. I cursed a God who had allowed such evil to be done to a child of innocence. My guttural cries, laden with sorrow at my failure to protect her and filled with my vows of retribution, ripped apart the stillness of the night. But there was no one to hear. There was no one to sense a flicker of dread. He had stolen what he craved and had vanished into the mist.

She'd curled her ravaged body into a tight ball and was rocking in the river silt. He'd draped her nightgown around her neck in concertina folds, and I dug her beaten face from the bloodstained pleats. Folds of swollen skin encased her right eye and a savage ring of bruises rose against the delicate skin of her neck. A serrated blade had slashed her forearms in ragged lines. A torn clump of her long platinum hair slithered across the back of my hand to fall beside her trembling shoulder. When I tried to lift her, a river of blood ran down her battered thighs and pooled into black puddles in my palms.

Rage fermented into something darker, something I could not name. I laid her gently back on the ground, then lay beside her and stroked her cheek the way I did each night before she fell asleep. Blood dripped from my fingertips and streaked her flawless ivory skin with ghastly trails of silver-blue in the moonlight. My tears fell against her cherished face, and I felt the inexorable splintering of our childhoods. Desperate to cling to a tiny fragment of our innocence, I sang in a hushed tone.

Oh, the scissortail roost on a telephone pole,
When the evening is old and the bayou is cold.
Then me got a lot of fishing to do.
Tomorrow I'll come back to you.

Rocking her in my arms, I yearned for her to come back to me and sing the lullaby's chorus. She didn't make a sound, but her trembling stilled and her body pushed against mine, seeking the sworn protection that I had failed to deliver. My voice wet with tears, I rocked her and sang.

When the old horned owl in the piney woods yell,
Don't worry, my belle, my sweet Mademoiselle,

'Cause everything's gonna be ca c'est beau, oui,
Tomorrow for you and for me.

Her arms tightened around my neck. I felt the whisper of her breath against my ear and at last heard the sweetness of her voice.

Oh, bayou, my baby, on the bayou tonight.
To a katydid's serenade, my cherie, sleep tight,
And dream of tomorrow when the fishing is through.
I'll fly o'er the bayou to you.

"I'll always fly o'er the bayou to you," I whispered, but I could not finish the oath I had made to her each night since my father's deployment.

My pledge to keep her safe had been a worthless platitude, uttered by a naive child. The angels' punishment for my failure would be swift and merciless.

None of us would survive their wrath.

CHAPTER NINE

Sam

SAM HAD MANY issues around the office renovation. The primary one was that without a functioning office, her loft was the substitute. Every time she arrived home, Eli was there. Where he went, his sister followed. Sam wanted to talk to Eli about Aazar Basha, so she should have been pleased to see him. She wasn't. Especially since he was sitting on the floor playing with Pepin. In her opinion, if Eli wasn't going to work, he might as well go home.

Danny was ensconced at the weathered ebony dining table, typing on a laptop. She lifted her head and nodded a silent greeting at Sam. Evidentially, she'd forgiven her brother for spilling her secret. As Sam had predicted, Danny's method of coping with her brother's breach of trust was to pretend it had never happened.

Sam dropped her keys and phone on the ugly church altar that Reece loved. She kept hoping to come home one night and find it had magically disappeared, but no such luck. Someone had dumped a plastic shopping bag on the floor beside it. Annoyed, Sam untied it and gasped when a putrid stench hit her.

"My God, what is that smell?" She clamped her hand over her mouth and opened the bag fully with the toe of her sneaker. It contained jeans and a stained white T-shirt. The clothes Reece had been wearing this morning.

"That is the smell of death." Eli threw a stuffed pig across the room, much to the delight of Pepin, who chased after it.

"Where's Reece?" Sam looked around frantically but he wasn't in the loft.

"Relax." Danny stood and stretched her back. "He's in the shower." Crinkling her pug nose, she strode over and crouched to re-tie the bag. Then she stood with the ties pinched between her fingers and opened the door. "I'll take it out to the trash chute. No way will he ever wear those jeans again." She sniggered and stepped into the hallway. "I think that grey clump stuck on the leg is a chunk of rotting brain."

Sam felt like she'd stepped into an alternate universe. "Whose brain?"

Reece descended the ladder staircase from the bedroom loft. "Harold Taylor's," he answered.

Sam stood on her tiptoes and wrapped her arms around his neck, inhaling the familiar scent of citrus soap. The relief of finding him in one piece turned her legs to jelly. As he stroked her back, the terrified butterflies in her stomach calmed.

He took her hand and led her into the kitchen. "My day calls for scotch on the rocks. Anyone want a drink?" he asked, as Danny returned, shut the front door, and went into the kitchen to wash her hands.

"I'll take a beer," Danny said, wiping her hands on a dishcloth.

"I would like a Mountain Dew." Eli hurled the stuffed pig again, and Pepin raced across the grey hemlock floor after it, skidding on the glossy surface. His sharp toenails were probably scratching her expensive floor.

"Stop doing that!" Sam instantly regretted her peevish tone.

Eli's face froze. He extracted a treat from the bag beside him and stiffly held it out. The puppy dropped the pig, gently took the chicken strip from Eli's hand, and trotted into the built-in crate tucked beneath the kitchen's stone countertop to enjoy his snack.

Brandy's crate, Sam thought with a twinge of resentment. She glared at the puppy as he circled twice before lying down with the treat—Brandy's favourite variety, no less—propped between his front paws. Pepin had his own crate, and he shouldn't be stealing Brandy's bed. She crouched, intending to shoo the puppy out, and spied a new blanket tucked around Brandy's electric cooling pad. A new purple elephant lay beside a new ceramic water fountain. Sam's cheeks heated with indignation. Pepin was making himself at home in Brandy's crate because Reece had fixed it up for him.

"Unbelievable," she muttered, outraged that Reece had commandeered the last reminders of her beloved golden retriever.

"You are in a bad mood. Again," Eli stated, accepting a can of soda from Reece.

Sam stood and reined in her anger. "I'm not always cranky."

"Yeah, you are." Danny shoved her glasses up the bridge of her nose. She stared meaningfully at Pepin in Brandy's luxury crate and then lifted her eyes knowingly to Sam's face.

"That's just because of the conundrum over her clinical practicum," Reece said to Danny. He handed Sam a glass of wine and kissed her.

"If you say so," Danny mumbled.

Reece sipped his scotch and debriefed them on his interview with Susan Taylor.

When he finished speaking, Sam thought in silence for a moment. "That poor woman. She endured forty years of psychological and physical abuse, and her husband essentially murdered their child," she said with disgust. "Shouldn't the detective have taken a look at the neighbour whose dog Harold killed?"

"If he did, it wasn't in the file I received. I'll dig deeper." Reece turned to Danny. "Did you find any drone pictures on Harold's hard drive?"

"I had to weed through disgusting kiddie porn, but I found a few," she stated grimly. "The pervert wasn't a good photographer. I need to enhance some of the better shots. No operator name or contact details on the drone that I can see."

"That is illegal." Eli hovered over her shoulder, peering at the photo Danny was in the process of enhancing. "Oh. It is a Vanguard." His hazel eyes twinkled with excitement. "It is a long-range surveillance drone. It has a 1080p visual feed through a dual-antenna setup and a dual camera with a thermal detection mode," he recited. "LAN offers real-time IP data transfer, and there is a Bluetooth connection for radiometric calibration to a cellphone."

Eli's massive source of trivial information didn't surprise Sam any longer. "Drones can't fly long, right?"

"You are wrong. This one can remain airborne for over ninety minutes," Eli said.

"How far is the range?" Reece asked.

"Around thirty-five kilometres," Eli answered. "It has an antenna tracker."

"A stalker's wet dream," Danny muttered.

"A rich stalker," Eli said. "These cost over forty-five thousand dollars. The Vanguard is one of the most expensive consumer options."

"How do you know so much about it?" Sam asked suspiciously.

"I would like to purchase one," Eli said.

She laughed. "Of course you would."

"It would be useful for investigations," he stated primly. "Particularly insurance fraud cases."

"What would be useful is for you to take your driver's test and get a licence," Reece said. "Transport Canada has strict laws around drones. You can only fly it during the day, there's a maximum height restriction, and you have to see your drone at all times. We may as well watch the subject ourselves. From a car," he added pointedly.

Danny grunted. "I'm going out on a limb and suggesting that whoever owns this one doesn't give a rat's ass about the law."

"Do you think it was spying on Harold Taylor?" Sam asked Reece.

He shrugged. "Hard to say. Harold was into some degenerate past times. My sense is that he was paranoid."

"Disgusting douche-bag," Danny growled.

Reece turned to Eli. "If I wanted my drone to follow someone when I couldn't see the subject myself, how would I do that?"

"The Vanguard has photogrammetry and mapping," Eli said. "You pre-define the flight grid. After it is launched, the internal software takes over." He thought for a minute. "If I had access to your smartphone's GPS, I could program the drone to read and follow the coordinates."

"So, you'd have to hack your subject's phone," Sam said. "Wouldn't an anti-virus stop you?"

Danny snorted. "People are so naive."

"Then educate me," Sam said in an even tone that she hoped hid her exasperation.

"I bump into you somewhere and use a small radio frequency identification tool," Danny said. "It pushes a credential to your phone so it trusts my Bluetooth." She grinned. "That's it—I'm in. I can do anything, like upload a remote access tool or a spy app."

"But if I've disabled the GPS, I'd see if you enabled it," Reece said.

"Look at you, thinking you're a technophile." Danny laughed with genuine glee. "I can do *anything* I want and you mainstreamers won't know dick. All social media apps track your phone's GPS, genius. Even a novice hacker can use your social media apps to find out exactly where you are." Danny grinned maliciously. "Someone like me? I can read your email, see your text messages, and activate your phone's microphone to eavesdrop on you. The next time you connect to your computer, I'll take that over, too. Then I can spy on you through your webcam."

"Enough already. You've made your point." Reece groaned and ran his fingers through his thick black hair. "I'm speaking with Annalise's friend tomorrow. Maybe she'll know something about the drone Annalise complained about." He turned to Sam. "How was your day with Emily Armstrong?"

Sam told them about meeting Dr. Mathias Beauregard and disliking him on sight, which had heightened her indecision over the internship. Then she explained how she'd accidentally instigated a negative exchange with Emily.

Reece sipped his scotch. "If you won't be working with Dr. Beauregard, eliminate him from your decision tree. What did you disagree with Emily about?"

"She asked me to meet Fadiya's mother and her brother, Aazar. Mrs. Basha—"

"You met Aazar Basha?" Danny's eyes widened.

"Yeah. Who is he?" Sam asked.

"Just the most brilliant scientist of our time." Danny typed something on the laptop's keyboard and then turned the monitor to face Sam. "Last year, he won a Gairdner Award for advancing medical research. He's a prodigy. He had a medical degree and PhDs in physics *and* molecular biology before he was even twenty-one. He's my hero."

Sam had never seen Danny so animated. "I knew I recognized the name." She leaned over to read the young man's bio, which was appended to an article in a scientific journal.

"He developed advanced nanotechnology and created a new cancer drug," Danny went on, and then launched into a highly technical explanation of Aazar Basha's accomplishments.

Sam held up her hand to halt the assault of scientific data. "Can we have the *Nanotechnology for Dummies* version?"

Danny thought for a second. "In layperson's terms, Aazar's nanoparticles transport his drug molecules across the blood, targeting and killing cancer cells with no adverse effects on healthy cells. In preliminary tests, the process shrank tumours eighty percent more effectively than chemotherapy and radiation. If experts obtain the predicted results in human trials, Aazar's discoveries have the potential of eradicating cancer."

Aazar Basha was a genius who held the key to curing cancer. No wonder Emily had been surprised that Sam didn't know who he was. She felt like an ignoramus.

"Do you know why he needs a transplant?" she asked Danny.

"That's the tragic part," Danny said. "Aazar was diagnosed with acute myeloid leukemia in childhood. It went into remission but returned in his late teens and is affecting his organs. Oncologists don't expect him to live long enough to complete his work. He has a rare blood type, but I also read something a while back about an abnormality in his antigens that makes tissue matching difficult. They must have found a donor, though. Transplants have saved him a couple of times."

Sam wondered why they didn't use that person for the lung lobe transplant. "When was that?"

Danny typed for a few seconds. "It started seventeen years ago, when an umbilical cord stem cell transplant put the disease into remission."

"It must have been Fadiya's stem cells," Sam said.

"Sure, if that's his only sibling," Danny said. "Over the years, he's had bone marrow, kidney, and liver section transplants."

"All from his sister?" Sam asked.

"Given the difficulty in finding a match, I'd assume so." Danny frowned. "That's a lot of donor surgery for a child."

"Aazar now needs a lung lobe transplant. That was the basis of the disagreement I had with Dr. Armstrong," Sam said. "The family wants the clinic to petition the court to overturn Fadiya's incapacity ruling so she can give surgical consent."

The colour drained from Eli's face. "They are using her as spare parts to keep her genius brother alive." He began to pace, growing more agitated. "Someone is raping her *and* they are harvesting her."

"We don't know that," Sam said.

Reece patted Eli's shoulder gently but firmly, which Sam recognized as an attempt to keep Eli calm.

"She didn't get pregnant by herself," Reece said.

Eli's gaze fluttered around the ceiling. He lifted his hand, tapping his middle finger in the air, and his expression tightened with anxiety. "We must protect her. Fadiya is in danger. They are harvesting her. Stealing parts of her body. Putting her at risk. It is disgusting." He marched around in a tight circle, his arms glued to his sides and his fingers twitching.

"She must have provided consent for the previous living donor transplants," Reece said calmly. "There's no evidence to suggest she had a change of heart and would deny her brother a lung lobe after all the other procedures."

"What's the matter with you?" Danny snapped. "How about this for evidence—the kid ran away and joined Bueton."

"A cult where her parents couldn't reach her," Sam said hesitantly. "A sanctuary where Fadiya believed she'd be safe."

CHAPTER TEN

REECE

"ARE YOU SURE it's supposed to be inside out?" Sam grumbled.

"Positive," Reece said with false confidence. "We turn it right side out after we attach the clips to hold the duvet in place." It had looked much easier on the video he'd watched after he bought the duvet donuts.

"I have new respect for hospitality workers," Sam muttered. "Changing linens on a California King is the worst job in the world."

He grinned at her. "Really? Even worse than hunting rats in the New York sewers?"

He knew Sam had a rat phobia. She had to turn off the television every time one showed up in a program.

"We should visit the Bird Kingdom in Niagara Falls," she said sweetly. "It's the world's largest free-flying, indoor aviary. Doesn't that sound fun?"

Reece shudder at the thought of birds flying around him and threw a pillow at her, which she caught with a laugh.

He checked his watch. "Can you finish?" he asked sheepishly. "Annalise's friend Denise wasn't keen about talking with me, and I don't want to risk being late."

"Sure. It's just pillow cases," she said.

He hurried down the stairs before she realized they hadn't put the sheets on the bed yet. That fitted sheet was a bitch. He'd cook lasagna for dinner—her favourite—to make up for ducking out on her.

On his way to the door, Reece crouched to rub Pepin's bat ears. "Did Mommy give you a nice breakfast and a walk? Yes, she did, didn't she?"

This morning, Sam had offered to feed and walk the little French bulldog while Reece took a shower. Her willingness to care for the puppy was a positive step, which relieved him. Over the past month, her inexplicable negativity toward the puppy had begun to worry Reece.

He grabbed his keys and phone from the church altar. Pepin stayed at his feet gazing up at him with sad brown eyes.

"Go find your elephant." He pointed at the built-in crate in the kitchen.

Pepin trotted over to the crate, scratched at the side of the waterfall countertop, and whined. Reece exhaled in frustration. Sam had securely locked the wrought iron gate, keeping Pepin out and his elephant trapped inside. He unlatched the door with a scowl of annoyance. The puppy ran inside, flopped onto his cozy new bed, and chewed happily on the elephant's trunk.

Reece was late and couldn't address the issue now, but he needed to talk to Sam. Sneaking down and locking the puppy out of the crate was cruel, and it was so out of character for her that Reece didn't know how to initiate an open dialogue. In the five years they'd been together, he'd never known her to be passive aggressive. He understood that she'd had the luxury crate custom built for Brandy, but if Sam disagreed with his decision to move the puppy into it, why hadn't she talked to him?

He went out to his car and continued to think about it as he drove across Queen Street to University Avenue. Three months ago, when they'd brought the puppy home, Sam had been disappointed that the built-in crate was too big. They'd bought a smaller puppy crate, but she'd quickly begun griping about how difficult the latch was to operate, and had said many times that she couldn't wait for Pepin to outgrow it. What had changed? All this was completely unlike her.

As he hunted for street parking, it occurred to him that maybe Sam herself didn't understand what was troubling her. Perhaps she was as confused about her feelings as he was so she was hiding her pain and trying to work it out alone. Whatever the reasons, he knew a supportive talk was definitely in order.

He found parking off Grenville Street and walked to a café near Women's College Hospital where he saw a blonde woman in her early twenties sitting alone at a counter by the front window. Reece recognized Denise from her pictures on social media. She wasn't as tall or as glamorous as her online photos had suggested. In real life, Denise was maybe five feet tall and a bit chubby with bleached hair that hung in waves to her waist. Her eyes were an unnatural shade of bright blue, probably thanks to tinted contact lenses, and her eyeliner was too dark for her complexion. Her beige skirt was a bit too tight and a bit too short. The heels of her flesh-toned sandals were high enough for Reece to wonder how she managed to walk in them. She struck him as a woman uncomfortable in her own skin.

Reece entered the air-conditioned restaurant and smiled. "Denise? I'm Reece Hash. Thanks for meeting me." He held out his hand. She stared at it for a moment before offering her own for a moist, limp shake. "Can I grab you a coffee?" he asked.

She shook her head with a sullen expression. The coffee smelled wonderful and he'd have loved a cup, but his instinct told him that Denise would bolt if he turned his back. He sat on a counter stool beside her.

"I have to be at work in fifteen minutes," she said. "My boss can't get a glass of water by himself. He'll phone if I'm not at my desk by eight fifteen." She fidgeted on her seat, avoiding his eyes. "I talked to the cops three months ago when Annalise died. How come I have to talk to you?"

"I'm just tying up some loose ends," Reece said pleasantly. "You went out with Annalise Huang the night she died, correct?"

Denise picked nervously at the cuff of her white blouse. "Yeah."

Maybe he could put her at ease with a few general questions. "How did you two meet?"

"She was my roommate in university. The residence put us together. We didn't get to pick," Denise mumbled.

Not the enthusiastic response he'd hoped for. Perhaps they hadn't been such great friends, but she'd told police they were close. It struck Reece as an odd thing to lie about.

"In your statement, you said Annalise was depressed," he said. "Any idea why?"

She chewed on a long pointy fingernail covered in tiny pink rhinestones. "A breakup."

"Her mother told police that her daughter's ex stole some money from her," he said.

Her head snapped up. Colour flooded her cheeks. "He didn't *steal* anything," she retorted. "It was his money." There was a genuine spark of anger behind her passionate response.

"Why would Annalise accuse him of emptying her bank accounts and maxing out her credit cards?" he asked.

Denise laughed bitterly. "Because nobody left Annalise. When you figured out her true face, it was too late to get out in one piece. She treated Ronnie awfully. When he left her, she flipped out and told terrible lies about him." Her eyes were intense as she folded her arms protectively over her chest. "You should have seen the garbage she put on social media about him. That was her game, you know. If you pissed her off, she destroyed you."

Reece watched her closely. "They were engaged and he cheated on her, right?"

Denise dropped her eyes and sucked on her bottom lip. "I guess."

"With you," Reece stated amicably.

Her eyes flew to his face. "How did you know?"

Because you wear your guilt like a shroud, Reece thought.

He deflected her question with one of his own. "Did Annalise know?"

Tears filled her eyes. "I was going to tell her, I swear, but after she attacked that woman in the bistro I couldn't."

"What did she do?" Reece asked gently.

"I don't want to say bad things about Annalise," Denise said. "She's dead. I don't want to be a total bitch."

"I just want you to tell me the truth," he said. "What happened?"

She sighed. "Annalise said this random woman was Ronnie's new girlfriend, but that wasn't the reason for what she did. She wasn't a nice person, you know?"

"I don't. Tell me."

"She, like, used to go to this bistro and say mean things about the people who worked there." Denise licked her lips in nervous little flicks. "She'd do it at malls, too. She'd sit on a bench and make nasty comments in a loud voice. Like how fat or ugly someone was. She'd berate homeless people for fun. But the things she said to that server were beyond mean. Annalise called her a 'gimp' and a 'cripple'. She made the woman cry." Denise lowered her head. "Customers were staring. I felt like a monster because I was with her and I didn't stop it."

"If it wasn't about her ex, why did she do it?" Reece asked.

Denise shrugged. "Because the woman's leg was gone below the knee. Annalise was super nasty to people with mental or physical differences." She gnawed on her lower lip and smears of blood streaked her bottom teeth. "She believed civility was wasted on the weak, at least that's how she put it. She referred to people as 'deformed' and 'retarded'. Anyone who didn't fit her standards was a target."

"Why were you friends?" Reece asked.

"She wasn't my friend. She used me because my folks have money. If I'd tried to ghost her, Annalise would have turned on me. She bullied a girl at university until she dropped out of school." A fat tear rolled down her cheek. "Annalise was brutal and she preyed on the weak."

An alarm bell went off in Reece's head: that was how Susan Taylor had described her husband. It couldn't be a coincidence that both these purported suicide victims had been cruel bullies.

"Annalise told her mother that a drone was following her," Reece said. "She believed it was her ex. Do you know anything about that?"

Denise pursed her lips in disgust. "More bullshit drama. If there was a drone—and that's a big *if*—Ronnie didn't have anything to do with it. The police talked to him after she died. They found out he didn't have a Canadian permanent resident card, so immigration sent him back to the US." She wiped her eyes, smearing black mascara across her cheek. "Wherever she is now, I bet Annalise is laughing her ass off. If there's any justice, she's roasting in hell. I know how that sounds, but she was an awful person."

"What's the name of the bistro where she harassed the server?" Reece asked.

"Cardoon," she said. "It's on Queen Street West, east of Jameson Avenue."

That was in the Parkdale district, where Susan Taylor lived.

"The food's amazing," Denise said wistfully. "I'll never be able to show my face in there again. Guilt by association, you know."

"You could talk to the woman," Reece said. "You can acknowledge her feelings without taking the blame for what Annalise did."

Denise shook her head glumly and looked at her feet. "I just stood there. Doing nothing is just as bad as bullying." She picked up her oversized pink bag and climbed off the high stool. "I gotta go. I don't want my boss to flip out on me." She took a step, and then turned back to Reece. "If you talk to the woman at the bistro," she said softly, "can you tell her the ugly fat girl is sorry?"

Reece got to his feet and held open the door for her. "You're neither ugly nor fat, Denise," he said sincerely. "Thanks for talking to me."

They stepped out into the sunshine together, and she turned to look up at him. "I lied to police about Annalise being depressed."

"She wasn't?"

Denise shook her head. "Annalise was an entitled bitch. People like her don't kill themselves, Mr. Hash. They have too much fun torturing other people." She walked away, teetering on her sky-high heels.

Reece watched her disappear into the morning crowd. It seemed he had evidence of a victim connection—entitled cruelty. He pulled out his phone and called Susan Taylor.

"I was going to phone to thank you," she said cheerfully. "A polite young man who helped clean Harold's palace wants to rent the outbuilding. He brought over his wife and two-year-old twins to meet me. For a discount in the rent, he's going to repair all the problems with my house."

"I hope you set a fair rent," Reece said, worried that this 'polite young man' was preparing to take advantage of a vulnerable old woman.

"Well, I guess I didn't, because he insisted on paying more. Brought over some rental listings for places in the area to show me what a two-bedroom apartment rents for," she said.

Reece smiled, relieved. "That's great news."

"I guess if your job is to clean places where people died, you don't worry about ghosts, eh?"

He chuckled. "I suppose not. Susan, do you remember the name of the restaurant Harold used to go to?"

"Oh, the place he met the thug who sold him the gun." She thought for a moment in silence. "It's named after a prickly plant. Harold went on about the name one time because he said the people they hired were useless thorns choking out the flowers of society."

Cardoons were late fall vegetables, alternatively referred to as artichoke thistles. Reece had cooked them a few times. You had to be careful of the small thorns.

"Cardoon," he said.

"That's it."

"Listen, Susan, I'm sure your new tenant is an honest man, but I'd feel better if my PI agency ran a background check," he said.

The woman had suffered enough in her life. Reece wanted to make certain that her new tenant wasn't planning to cook meth in her backyard.

Thanking him profusely, Susan gave him the man's name. After they said their goodbyes, Reece stood on the bustling sidewalk in the morning sunshine. Pedestrians scurried to work, focused on their own agendas and oblivious to those around them. Was it entitlement or a lack of situational awareness, he wondered, that made a woman blind to a man with a cane whom she jostled out of her way? Hectic lives, crushing schedules, and a society that communicated through technology seemed to be stripping people of basic courtesy. Watching the self-absorbed masses, with their eyes glued to their phones, Reece wondered when society had become so rude. In his mind, a shadowy victim profile materialized and a sinister motive took shape.

He knew what to look for in the sudden-death files, and a chilling premonition warned him he'd find more homicides.

CHAPTER ELEVEN

The Journal

THREE MONTHS AFTER the brutal attack on Pearl, we received word that my father was stateside. An IED in Kunar Province had claimed his leg. He served no further purpose to his country, so the military discharged him with a cheap prosthetic and an insatiable craving for morphine.

Any hope of a career in medicine vanished along with his pride. He did carpentry jobs around the parish and made furniture, earning just enough for essentials, and his persona reflected serenity. But occasionally I'd find him in the work shed, frozen on a stool with his left hand resting on his stump and surgical tools positioned neatly on a blue-lined tray. Immersed in the smouldering ashes of his dreams, he wouldn't notice my intrusion and I'd furtively observe him from the shadow of the doorway. Without the mask he placed between himself and the outside world, his gaze was vacuous and my heart would ache. As he caressed each instrument, I would be acutely aware of everything he'd sacrificed for our country.

Pearl had withdrawn into a secret world of order and predictability. She would spend hours sorting every object in our house into sets of matching colours and shapes, counting and recounting as the afterglow of the sun bathed the white walls in tones of pink and orange. Late at night, she would stand motionless in the river, the hem of her white nightgown floating like an open lily on the stagnant water. Her long platinum hair, a sheet of iridescent silver in the moonlight, would lift in the breeze and her fingers would flick to the beat of the cicadas' songs. Effervescent fireflies would pierce the darkness with motes of brilliance as they twirled to the vibrating croaks of the frogs' symphony.

I'd gaze at her from the shadow of our cypress tree and time would slow into lethargic increments. Grief, so potent that my breath would catch in my throat, would transmute the space between us to a gaping chasm I could not cross. We would stand, frozen in time, until the hollow slap of a gator's tail or an owl's hoot would break the spell that nestled Pearl in the bayou's arms and she'd come to me. As I led her back to bed, I would weep over my inability to mend what had broken within her.

My father had not blamed me for the wickedness perpetrated against Pearl, but he mourned the loss of our childhoods and my mother's unadulterated love could not restore the light to his eyes. She would perch on his lap, with her supple body contoured to his, and he would sing to her in his dulcet baritone. But a resounding sadness had leached the joy from the harmonious lyrics and his eyes would spontaneously fill with tears that would trickle slowly down his gaunt face.

Even my mother's utopia of sprawling plantations could not banish our dismal reality. Pearl's assailant had broken our spirits and left us bleeding in the river's mire.

In May, my father agreed to take Pearl and me to the Breaux Bridge Crawfish Festival. She had longed to go, and neither of us could deny her. I craved the simplicity of the past with a painful intensity, aching to witness my sister's childlike wonder and to hear her laugh again. My father longed to restore a semblance of normalcy to our dismal reality. Yet, in our hearts, we both knew that our lives had been irreversibly changed and happiness was now an unattainable dream.

Pearl's swollen belly was an inexorable reminder that moored us to the bleakness of our inescapable nightmare. Her beautiful face had grown pale and pinched as the alien inside her greedily slurped the nutrients she struggled to consume. Above her flip-flops, her ankles had bloated to elephantine proportions, and rarely did a day pass without her suffering excruciating headaches. She had stopped sorting and counting and visiting the bayou. She spent hours sleeping, waking only when the pain became unbearable.

My father and I had taken her to the free clinic, but the doctor had dismissed our medical concerns and focused on Pearl's cognitive impairments. When we refused to discuss the baby's father, the doctor had studied us with stony contempt, oblique accusation hardening his eyes. He'd scoffed at my father's medical expertise and refused him the prescription he requested to lessen Pearl's suffering until the baby was born. We couldn't pay for the doctor's recommended tests, so he'd dismissed us as unworthy of his attention. We had skulked away, burdened with undeserved shame and without the medication that would ease Pearl's misery.

On the day we took my sister to the festival, my mother couldn't accompany us. We couldn't risk the public's negative reaction to her fantasy-prone behaviour. Too many people attended the celebration now, and people were the enemy. As long as my mother remained sheltered in the bayou, we could protect her from authorities' meddling interference.

We arrived in the early afternoon, and Zydeco music rose from the festival grounds and hundreds of people swarmed around us. The cloying odours of fried crawfish, boudin pies, and jambalaya permeated the muggy air. Within an hour, rivers of sweat poured down my father's face and he hobbled in pain from the chronic ulcers that bubbled on his stump above the cheap prosthetic. His scuffed loafers and khaki shorts drew attention to the mechanical rods and it shamed me to wish he'd worn long trousers. A melee of drunken attendees jostled us on their staggering way to the band stages. The rasping scrape of a vest frottoir grated against my ears, and my eyes stung from the greasy smoke that wafted from the cooking booths.

As the afternoon wore on, Pearl became more and more upset by the chaos. She stopped abruptly in the middle of a crowded path, staring wide-eyed at a tourist booth. She clutched her hands against her ears and rocked her body. The hordes parted to pass her and their snickers fuelled a rage inside me so pure I could taste acid on my tongue.

A man suddenly leaned in and stroked Pearl's arm, his long fingers lingering against the paleness of her flesh before he stepped away with a gentle smile. Beside him, his companion's swinish eyes fell to my father's unsightly prosthetic and then rose again to Pearl's distended abdomen. He laughed outright and began to hurl insults at the 'gimp' and the 'preggo retard'. My body tensed and I took a step toward him, but my father snatched my hand.

"Let it be, child. They're Basile Landry's sons," my father muttered.

I followed his eyes to where Basile Landry stood with another man under a tree beside the tourist booth. Landry's hand rose in greeting but mine remained curled into fists as his sons and their friends lumbered across the parking lot to herd into a black Hummer. I knew the youngest, Virgile, but I didn't know his brother—the man who had stroked Pearl's arm as gently as one would pat a newborn kitten.

In the parking lot, the boys climbed into the Hummer and rolled the windows down. Ear-piercing heavy metal music blared from the car's speakers. Virgile's older brother paused outside the truck, glancing over his shoulder at us. His expression was shame-faced as he mouthed a silent apology.

The Landrys were one of the wealthiest families in the parish. The elder son was eight years my senior, and I could not recall his name. I'd heard he was a sensitive man who danced on the end of a puppet's strings, vying for approval from a father who would always find him wanting. Virgile had a darkness in him that Mr. Landry viewed as masculinity, a necessary trait for any son of his. What he did not see was the emptiness in Virgile's eyes that revealed an appetite for cruelty. People gossiped that he often vented his wrath on his older brother, who refused to fight back.

I had also heard that Mr. Landry had financially abandoned his 'effeminate' elder son, and had forced the sensitive young man to join the military to finish medical school. If he had complied to win his macho father's approval, his plan failed miserably. The boy had graduated at the top of his class but this had not warmed his father's black heart.

The crowd around us thickened, and Pearl tapped her fingers in the air. Her aqua eyes were bloodshot and wide, seeing something visible only to her.

"W831780," she yelled and her eyes twitched across the marshmallow clouds inlaid in the periwinkle sky. "W for why, why, why. 831780."

The concentration of bodies around us increased. Too many people were touching her—some with concern and others with spite.

"It's okay, *chère*. We'll go on home now." I gently took her hand and tugged her toward the parking lot, but she tore her hand from mine and refused to budge.

"087138 W for why, why, why. 831780." Her voice rose and her foot stamped out the tempo of her voice. "C, C, C! 831780."

People in our immediate vicinity formed a wide circle around us, as if Pearl's misery was an improv comedy skit. Insensitive onlookers with camcorders eagerly lifted them above the crowd to immortalize Pearl's suffering. Laughter swirled around us like water striders skittering on the surface of the swamp. Pearl's bottom lip trembled uncontrollably, and she flicked her arm violently as if afflicted with palsy.

Anger began to ferment in the pit of my stomach and I shouted at the claustrophobic crowd to move along and leave us in peace. The mob sensed drama, and the cluster of bodies tightened. Molten rage blurred my vision and a microscopic hum filled my head.

A man in a shabby porkpie hat and stained undershirt exited the tacky tourist booth catty-corner to us. His beady eyes drilled into my father like a pair of smouldering coals.

"You get on outta here. I don't need no crazy retard outside my store. Get on, now!" He waved his hand as if he were swatting a mosquito.

I moved in front of Pearl. "*Chère*, how many carrots in the garden?"

"Six rows of sixteen. Ninety-six. Ninety-six carrots."

"They want you to come home."

"W831780." Tears streamed down her pale cheeks. "C, C, C. W as in why. 831780. C, C, C."

"C..." My sluggish brain synapses fired a vital electronic signal. I turned to my father. "It's not a letter," I told him. "She means *see*. She wants us to see something."

"Get the freak outta my door!" the pudgy shopkeeper yelled again. "I got a business to run." He grabbed my dad's arm. The sudden movement unbalanced my father and he teetered. His prosthetic gave way. He fell with a grunt.

I clenched my fists and swung around to face the slob with the roll of flab sagging over his plaid shorts, but my father grabbed my arm in an ironclad grip.

"Let it be, Blu," he ordered. "Help me up." His face was crimson with humiliation, and pain had dilated his eyes to black agates.

Confusion quashed my anger. I could not understand why my father would remain silent in the face of such disrespect. It was his responsibility to protect his blood, yet he stood passively with downcast eyes, accepting the scorn of an inferior man.

"It was an accident," the man said to the crowd, jutting his chin out self-righteously. "Y'all saw." He looked at me without a hint of regret. "Go on now, get them on outta here." He turned his broad back and sauntered back into his booth.

Refusing to meet the eyes of the chortling crowd, I took my sister's hand. "Please, *chère*. Let's go home."

Her shoulders sagged and her hand turned limp in mine. The jeers of the apathetic multitude followed us as we limped to the truck. I scanned their faces as we moved through the crowd, but I could not fathom what Pearl had so desperately needed me to see.

Four months later, I understood.

CHAPTER TWELVE

SAM

SAM HAD HOPED to avoid Ophelia and have security contact Emily directly to escort her to meet Fadiya. No such luck. The gossipy nurse was hovering in the lobby, wearing Mickey Mouse scrubs, better suited to a pediatric unit than a psychiatric facility. Her dark hair was in pigtails, tied with childish pink bobbles. She was chitchatting to an exasperated-looking security guard who kept trying without success to walk away. Relief flooded his face when he spotted Sam. He physically turned Ophelia's broad shoulders and pointed. The nurse waved and trotted over.

"Did I miss the email on casual Thursday?" she quipped, and tucked a file she held under her arm so she could straighten one of her pigtails.

Sam stared at Ophelia's get-up and wondered when Mickey Mouse and pigtails had morphed into symbols of professionalism. She didn't feel the need to justify her presentable jeans and blue silk blouse, but she did anyway. "It's easier to connect with teenagers if you're not in business attire," she replied and forced a smile.

Ophelia wagged her index finger. "Don't let Dr. Beauregard see you. He insists that we adhere to a strict dress code." Her condescending smile complemented her chiding tone.

It was common for nurses to exert power over student doctors, and Sam didn't blame them. The daily care they provided motivated patients to work toward recovery. But she suspected there was more behind Ophelia's overbearing personality. An insecure woman probably cowered beneath the bossy exterior. If Sam could find common ground, it would be a step toward developing a positive relationship.

"How long have you worked here?" she asked.

"Since before we opened. I worked with all the contractors and decorated." She paused to call the elevator.

Sam jumped in before Ophelia nattered in long-winded detail about her décor choices. "How did you hear about the clinic?"

"Dr. Beauregard recruited me." She pressed her lips together and didn't elaborate, which was odd, Sam thought, given her loquacious nature.

An elevator arrived and Ophelia ignored it. A few people got on and Sam watched, curious over why Ophelia had chosen not to ride it. A second later, the one they stood in front of opened. Ophelia waved Sam in, held her keycard to a pad, and stabbed at the button for the third floor.

"Had you and Dr. Beauregard worked together before?" Sam prompted.

"No." Ophelia quickly changed the subject. "Fadiya's family is arriving a little later, so you won't have much time with her today. Speaking of her family, what do you make of that getup Mrs. Basha wears? It's sickening that Islamic men—"

Sam interrupted, which she'd already deduced was her only option if she wanted to get a word in edgewise. "It's a religious option that many Muslim women recognize. They deserve the right to choose," she said patiently, hoping to end the distasteful conversation, and wishing that the elevator would ascend more quickly. "So, why did Dr. Beauregard recruit you if you hadn't worked together?"

"You'd have to ask him." She handed Sam the folder she held. "Record the time, date, and summary of your visit with Fadiya," Ophelia said. "I hope you have legible handwriting."

Sam groaned inwardly. She'd hoped that the clinic recorded session notes electronically. She had terrible handwriting and much preferred to be able to edit her thoughts. She opened the folder. The handwriting was exquisite—it almost looked like calligraphy. Sam flipped to the end and saw Ophelia's signature.

The elevator opened and an alarm rang, making Sam jump. Hoping it wasn't warning passengers that the car was about to plummet to the basement, she quickly exited. A nurse hurried out of a patient's room and peered down the hall at them. The woman waved at Ophelia and disappeared back inside the room. Ah, now it made sense: because the lockdown unit was up here, the alarm was a security measure to alert staff that someone had entered the floor.

Ophelia turned right and then made a quick left and Sam trailed along behind her. She noted that there were multiple nurses, doctors, orderlies, and cleaning staff in the hallways. There would be less people around at night, but the probability of staff not noticing an intruder on this floor seemed low to Sam. They past a nurses' station and she spotted a set of glass doors at the end of the hallway. She assumed they opened into the lockdown unit.

A nurse looked up from the station and greeted Ophelia, who stopped to chat with him. She didn't bother introducing Sam.

Since she hadn't accepted the internship, Sam supposed she couldn't blame her. She stood off to the side as they talked and thought about the job offer. One concern was the insufferable Mathias Beauregard. If she learned a bit about his background, maybe his impressive achievements would make up for his unpleasant personality.

Ophelia joined her again and Sam followed her down the corridor. "Do you know where Dr. Beauregard worked before coming here?" she asked.

Ophelia stopped abruptly and turned to face Sam. Her expression was hard, and there was a coldness in her mismatched eyes that Sam hadn't witnessed before.

"How should I know," she retorted aggressively, planting her feet apart and thrusting her fists against her waist. "I barely know the man, and I mind my own business, which is an example you should follow. Are you even accepting the clinical practicum?"

Taken aback, Sam bit her tongue on a sharp response. Maybe jealousy had motivated the woman's insulting reaction to her innocent question. Ophelia could have a crush on her boss and viewed Sam as a potential rival for his affections. A disgusting thought given the man's arrogant personality, but unrequited love fit with Sam's impression that Ophelia struggled with insecurity. A touch of flattery might defuse the negative vibe.

"If I believe I can help Fadiya, I'd love to join your team." Sam smiled. "I know I'll learn a lot from you."

Ophelia continued to glare at her, hostility oozing from every pore. Then, abruptly, she turned and continued down the hall, her rubber-soled shoes squeaking as she walked. At the sliding glass doors, Ophelia held a card against a reader. The doors slid open revealing a corridor whose cement walls were painted a shade of seafoam green. Sam glanced up and saw two overhead cameras monitoring the entrance—one on either side of the door—and four in the unit's corridor that covered the ten patient doors. The CCTV surveillance for the last patient room on the left must have a wide enough arc to cover the fire door that opened into the stairwell.

If a rapist were sneaking onto the unit, it would be easier to creep up the stairwell than to enter the way they'd just come. It would be tough to exit an elevator with an alarm, trek past a nurses' station, and make it all the way to the lockdown unit doors unseen. Even if an intruder made it without anyone catching him, he'd have to possess a keycard with security clearance to open the doors to the lockdown unit.

"Is that stairwell door locked?" Sam asked, pointing.

"You do understand the meaning of 'lockdown' don't you?" Ophelia drawled sarcastically, as if Sam were the village idiot.

Gritting her teeth, Sam asked, "Can staff use that exit without the fire alarm going off?"

"Authorized staff can and we usually do during the day. Otherwise, the elevator alarm would drive the floor nurses nuts. At night, we're supposed to use the elevator," she said.

"Why?" Sam asked.

"Security protocol because there is less staff on the floor." She stopped outside a door adjacent to the fire exit. "This is Fadiya's room." She held up her access card and shoved the door open.

Sam put her arm across the doorway, blocking the nurse's access to the room. "I'd like to speak to her alone."

Ophelia frowned. "It's policy for authorized staff to remain with visitors."

"I understand," Sam said agreeably. "But if I accept the internship, I'll be alone with Fadiya. Can you call Dr. Armstrong for permission?"

"I don't need to call anyone for *permission*," Ophelia snapped. "As head nurse, I have the authority to make the judgment call."

No matter what Sam said, she ended up offending the hypersensitive woman. It was frustrating and her patience was wearing thin.

Ophelia glanced at her watch. "Her mother and brother are coming shortly so I'll allow it." She stepped aside. "You have ten minutes."

"Thanks."

Ophelia laid her hand on Sam's forearm. "I hope you can help Fadiya," she said. "She needs to go home." There was a sudden odd intensity in the nurse's eyes.

"Why's that?" Sam asked.

Just as quickly, a mask of indifference hid the deep compassion Sam was certain she'd seen.

"No one should live like this." Ophelia turned her back and strode toward the exit.

"You are one strange woman," Sam said to herself and stepped into a pleasant room filled with morning sun.

A colourful bed quilt matched the pale green bed linens, and a large area carpet in hues of blue, green, and yellow softened the institutional setting. In the corner of the space, there was a private bathroom with a shower. The only indications that the room was in a psychiatric facility were the decorative bars on the large window and the absence of anything a patient could use to self-harm.

Even though daylight flooded the room, the overhead lights and table lamps were on, which didn't surprise Sam. At Bueton, Mussani had forbid members from extinguishing lights. The punishment for disobedience was swift and merciless. People had adjusted to sleeping in bright illumination or suffered sleep deprivation. The latter had been Mussani's preference. Exhaustion had been a tool in his indoctrination arsenal.

Fadiya sat in a teal armchair, gazing out the window at a pretty courtyard below. "The dahlias and hydrangeas are in bloom," she said without turning from the window. "We grow them at home and the sisters sell them at our store in Uthisca."

"Did you make the soy candles they sold?" Sam asked.

Fadiya turned with a startled expression. "I thought you were Emily," she said.

"I'm Sam. May I sit?" She gestured to the matching armchair on the other side of a white acrylic table, the legs of which were screwed into the floor to prevent a patient from moving it.

Fadiya nodded, warily watching Sam. The teenager had huge eyes the colour of milk chocolate. Highly arched eyebrows accentuated the innocence in her face. She wore her long dark hair parted in the middle, which highlighted her symmetrical facial features. Her complexion was flawless and her skin was the shade of warm caramel.

Fadiya studied her intensely. A smile gradually formed on her full lips.

"I know you," she exclaimed. "You were at Bueton."

As a clinician, Sam needed to establish a trusting and supportive relationship. As an investigator, she needed Fadiya to talk about her 'affair' with Mussani. Bueton was the perfect segue to achieve both goals.

"I was at the sanctuary for a short time," Sam said.

Fadiya reached across the table and clasped Sam's hand. "I am so pleased to see you. Has Mussani sent you?" She glanced around, as if expecting the deceased cult leader to pop out of the bathroom. "Can I go home to Bueton now?"

Sam squeezed Fadiya's hand. "Not today."

Confusion shadowed the girl's eyes. "Mussani said if I satisfied him he'd take me home." She bowed her head. "Did I displease him?"

Sam sidestepped the question by asking, "Does Mussani wear his ceremonial robe when he visits?"

"He wears the coarse shrouds that the brothers wear. I can feel it." Tears pooled in Fadiya's eyes. "The maroon velvet robe with the braided gold edging is only for the worthy."

If the visits were an erotomanic delusion, Fadiya should describe Mussani in his ceremonial robe. That cloak had spiritual importance to cult members. It represented their Messiah's love and devotion. Alternatively, Fadiya's mind could have substituted her rapist for her Messiah as a defence mechanism to deal with the trauma. If so, perhaps her subconscious had protected the sanctity of the consecrated robe. Sam supposed that made clinical sense. What didn't was why Fadiya hadn't described Mussani in jeans and a crisp white shirt, which is what he wore outside the ceremonies and sexual rituals. Sam found it difficult to believe that a cult member would ever envision her Messiah in lowly hemp. Only

Mussani's minions had dressed in hemp, which was a key symbol of their obedience.

She thought about it. The public believed everyone at the cult had worn the robes in the photographs the media had published. It made sense that an impostor would mimic what he knew from the newspapers, oblivious to the significance of his mistake.

It wasn't ironclad evidence that her hunch was right and a rapist was impersonating the cult leader, but it was a good start.

"Tell me about Mussani," she said conversationally. "Do you find his looks have changed from the days we lived at Bueton?"

"I don't see Father," Fadiya replied sadly. "A brother blindfolds me before he enters the room." She leaned across the table and lowered her voice. "The brother turns out the lights." Her eyes suddenly widened. "Is that why Father is displeased? Does he think I shut off the lights?"

Inserting the mention of a brother into her delusion wasn't strange, Sam knew. Mussani never went anywhere without guards. What made no sense was Fadiya's assertion that the brother turned out the lights and blindfolded her. Not hiding your essence behind false modesty had been a stringent rule.

"How many brothers does he bring with him when he visits?" Sam asked.

"There is only one," Fadiya said with confusion. "Is that not also odd, Sister Sam?"

Her bewilderment was understandable. Three guards had always protected Mussani, even behind the gates. A devote follower wouldn't imagine him with only one.

"There is something else strange," Fadiya whispered. "The brother speaks to me." Her eyes narrowed with disbelief. "He gives me instructions on how to please Father, and he warns me to be silent."

This 'delusion' disturbed Sam. A brother wouldn't dare speak for Mussani, especially not a guard. Guards had been carefully chosen, their positions conferring prestige and power, and all had taken a vow of silence. The logical explanation was that someone with security clearance was impersonating a brother in order to escort the man into Fadiya's room. They could be looking for an accomplice, as well as a rapist.

"The brother who brings him—is it always the same one?" Sam asked.

Fadiya nodded. "I don't understand why he's still in service. Mussani hears him speak. Why wasn't there a public reckoning and banishment?"

At the compound, 'banishment' had been a euphemism for murder, although only Mussani's inner circle had known the truth. Had a guard dared to speak, Mussani would have held a punishment ceremony, where the offender would receive forty lashes minus one. After that, Mussani would privately execute him and grind the meat from the corpse to feed the dogs.

The next question was tricky, and Sam paused to think how to phrase it. "During the, ah, ceremony, does Mussani act differently than you recall from Bueton?"

She lowered her head. "He doesn't say he loves me now." Tears dripped down her cheeks and splashed onto the acrylic table. "Sometimes, he says cruel things and calls me terrible names. Sometimes he hurts me." She lifted her skirt.

An ugly green bruise with swirls of yellowy brown marred her smooth thigh. Based on the discolouration, Sam gauged it to be about a week old. Higher, closer to the curve of Fadiya's hipbone, was a fresh reddish bruise. It looked like a thumbprint.

There would be no reason for Fadiya to self-inflict the injuries to support her delusion. Mussani had prohibited battery assault during his sexual ceremonies. He hadn't engaged in direct violence, at least not until he was bored with the woman. Whenever a woman disappeared, he held a grand event and proclaimed that God had deemed her worthy to transcend. In reality, Mussani would have tortured his victim for weeks, inflicting as much pain as possible, before discarding her corpse in a shallow grave in the woods.

Sam didn't know enough about Fadiya's case to rule out self-harming, but the girl's allegiance to the cult suggested differently. Members had considered their physical bodies to be temples for their Messiah's enjoyment. Health and fitness were as important to them as their twisted spiritual journeys.

"I want to transcend, Sister," Fadiya whispered. "But Father refuses to recite the Creed. When I beg he grows angry."

Sam wasn't surprised—an impostor wouldn't know the words. Without a manifesto, cult experts had only been able to speculate on the meaning behind Bueton's secret creed.

She sat back in her chair, thinking. She was convinced that a rapist was imitating Mussani, and now she suspected that he had an accomplice employed by the clinic—the 'brother' who escorted him to Fadiya. This was all conjecture unless Fadiya identified her assailant and a DNA test proved he'd fathered her baby. Sam wasn't sure she had the clinical qualifications to help Fadiya reach that goal.

The girl's indoctrination was disturbingly resilient after years outside Bueton's gates. In every word Fadiya uttered, Sam recognized Mussani's proselytization techniques. It would take skill to lead her into abandoning her allegiance—skill that Sam wasn't convinced she had. On the other hand, a therapist needed specific knowledge of the rules and sacraments in order to break the cult's hold on Fadiya's cognitive processes. Sam was the only one left alive who understood them. Maybe she could help this poor girl, but first she needed to learn more about the impostor. She considered various strategies and remembered that Mussani's South African accent had mesmerized many of the cult members. She was curious to see if the impostor mimicked it.

"Is Mussani's accent still soothing?" Sam asked.

"His accent is gone," Fadiya said. "Now, he has many voices and many shapes. Sometimes he's tall and thin, other times he's stout and fat," she replied calmly. "It confuses me but he's the Messiah."

Sam's blood ran cold.

Oh my God, she thought in horror. *It isn't a single assailant.*

Eli was right. They were hunting something much more sinister—the phoney brother who ushered the men to Fadiya could be a depraved sex trader, catering to a fetish market.

Aware that her time was running out, Sam asked, "Is it okay if I visit you again?"

"I'd like that, Sister Sam. Will you tell Mussani I miss him?"

The door slid open and Ophelia popped her head in. "Knock, knock! Look who I brought for a visit!" She stepped aside.

Aazar Basha and his mother stood behind the nurse in the corridor. Aazar stared at Ophelia with something akin to disgust. "My sister is not five. Nor is she blind."

Fadiya reached out her hands, and her brother hurried past the nurse and over to his sister's chair. He knelt, and spoke to her in a language that Sam assumed was Farsi.

Sam stood to greet Mrs. Basha, who handed her a decorative tin.

"*Awb e dundawn*—pistachio biscuits, to thank you for helping my daughter," Mrs. Basha said. "May we speak in private for a moment, Doctor?"

"Just Sam, please. I haven't got my PhD yet."

"A technicality," Mrs. Basha said. "After you, please."

Sam led the way into the corridor and Mrs. Basha closed the door behind them, walking a few feet from Fadiya's room.

"How can I help you?" Sam asked.

"I wear the traditional burka because I choose to, not because I am forced to," Mrs. Basha stated. "My mother does not wear it, nor does she choose to wear any form of head covering. I am liberated, my husband is enlightened, and we do not condone female oppression."

"I apologize if I gave you the impression that I held an opinion," Sam said.

Mrs. Basha waved her hand dismissively. "You misunderstand. I tell you this because I watched you last time we met. I saw that the living-donor transplant upsets you. Do you believe we devalue Fadiya's life because she is female?"

"My concern lies in your daughter's mental capacity to make an informed decision regarding a potentially life-threatening surgery," Sam said.

"As does mine," Mrs. Basha agreed. "Fadiya loves her brother and greatly values his work. If it is Allah's desire, Aazar will save millions of lives. Fadiya would do anything to aid him in achieving that goal. If you can help my daughter, you will learn this for yourself."

"Thank you for speaking with me about your concerns," Sam said. She smiled and held up the tin. "And thank you for the cookies. They look delicious."

The woman nodded and walked back to her daughter's room.

Sam continued down the hall to the exit doors, where a security guard glanced up from a desk positioned on the other side of the glass doors. Sam held up her Temp Staff badge and he buzzed her through.

On the other side, she asked him, "Is there always security on this floor?"

"Nah, we don't have the budget," he said pleasantly. "Originally, that was the plan, though. A guard was supposed to monitor the elevator. I'm only up here now because Dr. Beauregard ordered it." The man grinned. "There's a dog and pony show every time Mrs. Basha and her son are here."

"So the lockdown unit is typically unattended?" She wondered if that was normal practise in private hospitals.

The guard shook his head with a laugh. "No. Staff is in and out of the unit all day. Overnight, there are two nurses on this floor, and one is assigned to lockdown. Plus, we monitor the unit and stairwell cameras from the security office twenty-four-seven."

"Why isn't there a camera in Fadiya's room?" Sam asked.

"We only have video surveillance in at-risk rooms, for patients under suicide watch," he said. "Dr. Beauregard strongly advocated against cameras. What he wants, he gets."

She'd read plenty of professional articles that argued against patient surveillance, claiming it negatively affected a therapeutic setting where developing trust was paramount to treatment. That might be Dr. Beauregard's reasoning but it seemed counterintuitive to Sam. Emily had said her partner was aware of Fadiya's mysterious pregnancy. That should have been grounds to add surveillance inside the girl's room.

The guard stood. "The elevator on this floor requires security clearance. I'd like to stretch my legs, so I'm happy to take you."

She held out her hand. "I'm Sam McNamara, Dr. Armstrong's practicum student." Until the words had left her mouth, she hadn't realized she'd decided to accept the internship.

He shook her hand with another grin. "I know. I recognized you because we set up your Temp Badge. Saul Koen, head of security."

They walked toward the elevator and Saul chatted amicably about the clinic and the social committee that he spearheaded. When they reached the elevator, he flashed his keycard on the reader and pressed the down button.

The alarm rang again—announcing the arrival of the elevator—and the doors slid open. Sam stepped inside and pressed her floor number. The doors remained open and the floor number didn't light up. Confused, she hit it again. Nothing.

"This is the only elevator that stops at this floor," Saul explained. "You need authorization to use it." He leaned around her, tapped his card on an inside reader and hit the button for the ground floor.

"I'm going up to see Dr. Armstrong," Sam said.

"Sorry, no can do." He pointed at her badge. "You don't have clearance yet. When you talk with Dr. Armstrong, ask her to make that a priority. The downstairs guard will call her for you. Welcome to Serenity, Sam. Good to know you." The doors slid closed.

She rode down, reviewing what she'd learned about the security. Whoever was escorting men to Fadiya's room was using the stairwell and he had security clearance to access the lockdown unit.

They needed the missing camera footage.

CHAPTER THIRTEEN

REECE

REECE WAITED AS his boss, Gretchen Dumont, reviewed the file on his investigation into the sudden-death cases. She flipped through the pages slowly. Her neutral expression gave nothing away. She was probably a hell of a poker player.

Sitting across from her, with her large desk a barrier of authority between them, was like languishing in the principal's office with his cocky brother. Ray had always perpetrated the mischief, but he and Reece were identical twins. The school administration was never certain which Hash brother had done the deed. Drugs, girls, petty crime—Ray had been into all of it during high school. But Reece had been the one who'd ended up disappointing their father the most, by dropping out of law school to join the provincial police. The ensuing argument had been so brutal that Reece had refused to go with his family to a wedding in Chicago. That pointless disagreement was the last time he saw them. They'd died in a car crash on the I-94 just outside Battle Creek. The transport driver that caused the accident had been drunk, but for reasons Reece still didn't understand, Michigan authorities hadn't laid charges in connection to his family's deaths. As far as Reece knew, the drunk driver was still hauling cereal across the US and Canada.

He had buried his entire family a week before his twenty-fifth birthday. The devastating grief and anger he'd suffered had ultimately fuelled his passion to defend the innocent. Every family of every victim deserved justice, regardless of the cost, and Reece was willing to put his reputation on the line to reopen the cases he suspected were homicides.

He crossed his legs and folded his hands in his lap. It shouldn't be taking this long for Gretchen to evaluate his findings. He'd identified anomalies in at least five cases so far. Granted, he'd based his hypothesis on conjecture, but he stood by his recommendation that the Chief Coroner and Chief of Police should reopen those cases.

Gretchen stacked the sheets and closed the folder. "So, these are homicides. The tip is accurate."

"I'm positive there are more," he said. "What can you tell me about the informant who gave you the tip?"

She ignored his question. "Your theory is that the same perpetrator is responsible."

"Yes."

"And the only victim connection is that they were rude people," she said incredulously.

To her credit, she didn't outright laugh. But her disbelief was obvious in the arch of her one eyebrow and the faint sneer on her full lips. Reece merely nodded.

"In your opinion," she continued, "a serial killer is targeting people across the Greater Toronto Area who exhibit discourteous behaviour."

Aware of how outlandish it sounded, he remained silent.

Gretchen continued to stare at him. "Hundreds of thousands of Torontonians fit your profile."

Reece leaned across the desk. "I believe the killer has a specific code of conduct," he said. "If he witnesses a random act that violates it, he stalks his potential victim using drone surveillance. If the victim continues to exhibit behaviour contradictory to the killer's code, he executes the offender and stages the crime as a suicide or an accidental mishap."

"These crimes require planning, purpose, and organization to conceal them as explainable sudden deaths," she said. "If it's not a crime of passion or opportunity, you're talking about a psychopath. Nothing in the kill pattern supports that conclusion. These deaths lack extreme violence or sexuality that would gratify abnormal pathology."

Remembering what Sam had said, Reece replied, "Police making an erroneous judgment on the cause of death could be the killer's gratification. But I don't think we're dealing with a psychopath. I believe it's a vigilante."

"Someone correcting a social injustice?" Gretchen asked.

"All five of these victims were not just ill-mannered; they were bullies with skewed ideologies about society," Reece said. "They had radical right-wing philosophies and preyed on those they viewed as possessing unfavourable traits."

"So, the killer sees something unpleasant and does what? Gives them a second chance and stalks them with a drone? Only two of these cases reported a drone," Gretchen argued.

"That we know of," Reece countered.

"What about Annalise Huang's ex-boyfriend?" She rummaged through the file folder. "Robbie Cormier. Did police bother to interview him, or was that too much trouble?"

Her negative opinion of Toronto Police Services had always bothered Reece, but as usual, he chose to ignore her insinuation. "He was with his new girlfriend at the time of the murder. He'd met her at the bar after Annalise left. There were multiple witnesses."

"What did you uncover about this drone? Did you identify the manufacturer? Do you know which retail outlets sell them? Have you followed up to get a list of people who bought one?" She fired the questions at him. "Have you done anything productive to support your theory? You used to be a cop." She stated *cop* in a disgusted tone of voice.

He took a deep breath. Gretchen had never been shy about sharing her opinion that officers were incompetent and lazy.

"The task you assigned me was to audit police due diligence in sudden-death rulings." Reece pointed at the closed folder on the desk. "My report recommends that those cases be reopened."

"Because the officers in charge are guilty of gross dereliction of responsibility." She looked immensely satisfied by the conclusion.

"I didn't say that," Reece retorted. "Different divisions handled these cases, Gretchen. There was no failure on the part of any of the investigating officers. Individually, nothing stood out as requiring further investigation."

"Really?" she replied mockingly. "Harold Taylor had created an investigation board, complete with photographs of a drone. Are you suggesting that not one of the first responders noticed it?" She whipped open the file and shoved the photograph he'd taken of the white board across the desk. "Death by an illegal firearm requires a detective to take a look. Are you saying a *detective* didn't notice this giant white board?" she asked sarcastically. "If they had bothered to investigate the bloody drone, people would still be alive. Poor policing is responsible." She spit out the declaration.

Her anger was puzzling. The Crown attorney's office and the police department worked together. They shared a collaborative mandate to protect the public. Reece couldn't understand why she was so determined to sully Toronto Police Services' reputation. He watched her tuck her wavy chestnut hair behind her ears and straighten her skirt across her long tanned legs. When he'd met her, Reece had considered Gretchen attractive. Not anymore. Funny how your perception of beauty changed once a woman's ugly personality surfaced.

"What's really going on here?" he asked.

"When I received the tip three months ago, I requested that the lead investigator on Ms. Huang's suicide take a second look," she said tersely. "Detective Martina informed me that it was indisputably a suicide." Gretchen pointed at the file. "Which you're disputing," she added triumphantly.

Talking to her was exhausting. Leading her back to the discussion on the cases, he said, "One connection is a bistro in Parkdale. They hire employees with disabilities. Two victims..." Reece couldn't find the right word to describe their loathsome behaviour. "Well, they bullied employees with special needs. Annalise Huang allegedly made a barista cry."

"And you think the killer witnessed the incident." Gretchen thought in silence for a second. "The behaviour you're describing could fit the profile of a vigilante," she conceded. "Did you follow-up with the barista?"

"Turn it over to Toronto Police Services," Reece said.

Her lips thinned. "If I publically demand the Chief Coroner re-opens a slew of cases, think of the consequences."

Criminal attorneys in the city could use the media frenzy to their clients' benefits. The detectives and officers who investigated the cases that the city reopened would have to defend every piece of evidence on every prior conviction associated with them. That was a serious problem, Reece agreed, but his gut told him there was more to her resistance.

She tapped the folder with a blunt fingernail. "If you're right, and a vigilante is roaming our streets, bring me evidence. Do it without directly involving this office."

"How do I investigate without official authorization?" Reece asked in frustration.

"You're a partner in one of the city's best-known private investigation agencies," she replied.

"You want me to lie to cops I've worked with and pretend someone hired Sam and me?" he asked with disbelief. "Gretchen, it's a well-known fact that I'm your articling student. They won't believe it's a private case."

Gretchen stood and put on her jacket, pulling her long hair over the collar. "Then allow a killer to run rampant." She straightened her skirt across her thin hips. "Is that a conundrum for someone who used to serve and protect?" She smiled without a hint of warmth. "Having been a decorated police inspector, I'm sure you'll err on the side of civic duty."

He followed her out of the office. The elevator opened and she stepped in. Reece stood immobile. He didn't want to ride down with the insufferable woman, he was too angry that she'd put the onus on him to compromise his integrity.

"Find me evidence. Then I'll take it to the powers that be." She held her hand against the doors to prevent them from closing. "If you turn over any material associated to this investigation to anyone at Toronto Police Services, you will be in direct violation of your non-disclosure and confidentiality agreements." Her expression was foreboding. "Your employment will be terminated and criminal charges will be laid in accordance to the law." She dropped her hand and the elevator door slid closed.

Reece might not understand her endgame but he clearly understood her ultimatum. His choice was to betray men and women he respected or to ignore a potential threat to public safety. If he followed his moral compass and took his findings to the head of Toronto's homicide squad, it would end his law career and conceivably lead to prison.

Gretchen had him pinned between a boulder and a mountain.

CHAPTER FOURTEEN

THE JOURNAL

THREE WEEKS AFTER Katrina had devastated southeastern Louisiana, we braced for the arrival of Hurricane Rita. On September 20th, the president issued a federal state of emergency and shoreline parishes began evacuation.

The coast was an hour south of us, and the hurricane would rapidly weaken over land as the storm moved north from the Gulf. My father said even a twenty-five-foot storm surge, pushing seawater inland, would not compromise us. The levees on the Atchafalaya River would hold, he said. Dad had built our house on ten-foot steel pilings, engineered by a soldier in the corps. If the Bayou Teche flooded, we were well above the water rise. Hurricane ties had been wrapped over the large truss hangers, anchoring the roof system to the walls, and the roof pitch deflected wind lift. Our house was as close as possible to being hurricane resistant.

What he did not say, but what I understood, was that we had no option but to stay. There was no safe haven for my mother outside our oasis on the bayou.

The days of her passing as a fantasy-prone eccentric were gone. Her mind had crumbled after Pearl's pregnancy became obvious.

Mom had vanished into the mystical universe of plantations with stone balustrades and mint juleps sipped at elegant garden parties. It was a world in which my sister also found solace. After the horror of the Crawfish Festival, Pearl had tumbled down the rabbit hole to reside with my mother in gracious Old Savannah. They spent their days beneath the cypress tree, watching life unfold on the bayou. Mom would comb coconut oil through Pearl's long platinum hair until it shone in the brilliance of the afternoon sun. The echo of their childlike laughter would ripple across my skin like gentle caresses, and my heart would fill once more with the nectar of untarnished love. Time would freeze as I immersed myself in the sweet rhythm of their unadulterated happiness. For a moment, I'd long to follow them into the comfort of madness.

The day before Rita made landfall, Dad and I dragged our mud boat under the house, secured it to auger-style anchors, and weighed it down with bags of sand we soaked with water. As we worked in comfortable silence, my eyes strayed to the bald cypress tree that had long ago ceased to be a landmark and had become a living character in our life story. It held our secrets and our dreams nestled safe within the embrace of its gnarled branches. I could not bear for Rita to tear it from the ground and discard it, mortally wounded, in the tempestuous water. My helplessness to protect the people and things I loved from ruin was a profound ache in my soul.

Just before noon, I left my father fastening shutters and took our pickup into town to buy extra batteries. A garish black Hummer hogged three parking spaces outside the hardware store. I wedged my truck into the last remaining spot, circled the Hummer, and peeked through the wide-panel sunroof. A wisp of envy unfurled as I gazed at a leather steering wheel, a Bose sound system, and wood trim on a dashboard that looked serious enough to launch a missile. Discarded on the brown leather passenger seat was a Ka-Bar knife with its wicked serrated blade open. It was a lot of knife for an entitled asshole who had never needed to hunt or fish to feed his family.

"Like what you see?"

I spun around and heat crept up my cheeks. "Hey, Virgile. Nice ride."

He leaned against the Hummer, crowding into my personal space with a whiff of unearned arrogance. "Yeah it is."

"Hard on gas." I turned to go, and he moved to block my path.

"Well, I don't have to worry about that," he said with a snide grin. "Shouldn't you be on the swamp hunkering down for Rita? Y'all gotta take care of your crazy ma, retard sis, and gimpy pa," he said with an exaggerated drawl. "I heard State is offering you a basketball scholarship. Imagine that—an opportunity to wash off the stink of the bayou and broaden your horizons. And I hear you're aspiring to be a doctor. Following in your pappy's footsteps." He laughed. "Oops, *footstep*. Maybe you won't fuck up your life by marrying crazy and breeding retards."

"Step off, Virgile," I said and held his beady, serpentine eyes.

He put his hands in the air in mock surrender. "Or what, you'll move me? Now, that I'd like to see." He snickered and moved in closer, his rancid breath polluting the air between us. "Your sister is one hot piece of meat, Blu. I'm surprised you don't want to stick around. Once she pops that kid out, she'll be ripe again. Rumour has it that your daddy helps himself. Not like she knows enough to care about some good old coonass incest."

"Shut up and get in the car, boy!"

At the sound of his father's voice, Virgile's head swivelled ninety degrees and his neck cracked. The fear in his bulging eyes was more satisfying than the blood that would have gushed from his nose if I'd hit him. His father rounded the front end of the Hummer, and Virgile goose-stepped to the passenger side.

"Blu, caught the game last week. You did real well," Mr. Landry said and stowed two bags in the backseat. "Your fade-away jump is damn impressive. You better believe that State scout was paying attention. My old alma mater—did you know?" He winked and opened the driver's door, glancing up at the gathering clouds. "Goddamn Rita's destined to wipe out the southwestern Louisiana coast. No way will the levees hold, and the Teche will take the brunt of it. Y'all stay safe."

As he drove away with Virgile sulking beside him, I glanced after the Hummer and my eyes widened. A churning whirlpool of confusion sucked the air from my lungs. I sprinted after the retreating truck, unable to believe what I'd seen on the bumper.

The rain began fast, soaking me within seconds, and the gusting wind shook the street signs. The Hummer turned onto St. Phillip Street, sheets of water pouring across the back grill and concealing the rear of the SUV. My knees turned to jelly and I lurched sideways, into the traffic on South Main Street. Horns honked and irate drivers swerved around me. The scorching heat of the truth turned to red-hot lava in my churning stomach. I stopped, turned, and staggered back to my truck, with my hands clenched into powerless fists at my side. My hand shook, and I struggled to get the key into the ignition, unable to see through a thickening black mist that pulsed and ebbed across my eyes. The engine finally caught and the tires squealed as I pulled into a U-turn, cutting off two cars. I drove home in a semi-fugue state, memory reflex my only navigation through the blinding rain.

My father was filling buckets from the hose, the overhanging porch protecting him from the worst of the rain and wind. He turned as I sped into the yard, the truck tires spinning gravel and water. I jumped out, leaving the door gaping open, and took the porch steps two at a time. He caught me as I stumbled over the top riser.

"What's wrong? What happened?"

I clung to his shoulders. "Virgile Landry raped Pearl."

The colour drained from his face. "What? How can you know that?"

"She recognized him at the Crawfish Festival. She told us."

"No. She didn't, Blu. She saw him but she never said he laid hands on her," he insisted.

I shook him, harder than I intended. "She did! C, C, C—W831780! It wasn't a letter—she needed us to *see*."

"See what? You aren't making any sense!"

"The licence plate on Virgile's Hummer is W831780. There was a Ka-Bar serrated knife on his passenger seat—the same type of blade that cut Pearl. Virgile Landry raped Pearl. She saw him before she became upset at the festival. Pearl saw him getting into the Hummer. The licence plate number was how she tried to tell us."

My father took a step back and steadied himself with one hand on a closed shutter. "But... he's Basile Landry's son."

An ugly seed of shame took root in my belly. "He's the son of a rich man, so that makes it okay?" I yelled. "He can rape your own daughter and you'll kowtow?"

My father reached for me and I stepped out of his range.

He dropped his arms to his side. "Blu, that's not what I meant and you know it. We don't have proof. You think the Breaux Bridge Police Department is going to investigate the Landry family based on this?"

"*We* take care of this." I pounded my chest with my fist. "*We* get justice for Pearl."

My father lowered his eyes and shook his head. "If you're right, then after the baby comes, a paternity test will prove Virgile's the father. We wait. We follow the law."

"Before you deployed, you told me not to take Pearl to the hospital." I fought to keep my voice steady. "Because I obeyed you, there's no record of how her hair was torn from her scalp, of the wounds I had to stitch, no semen samples from him plowing into her, no evidence of how he shredded her insides." Tears mixed with the rain that pelted my face. "He'll say it was consensual. Cops will interrogate Pearl and Landry's lawyer will blame her. Authorities will want to institutionalize her. People are the enemy, Dad—you taught me that. The damn doctor at the free clinic and the assholes at the Crawfish Festival proved that. *We* take care of this. *We* protect our blood."

"Listen to me," my father said. "Virgile could have loaned his Hummer to a buddy. There was a group of them at the festival. You can't prove that Pearl was trying to identify Virgile, only that she recognized the Hummer." He folded his arms over his chest. "We don't have enough evidence."

I stood slack-jawed and repulsed, incapable of ascertaining whether he was simply naive or whether he was too cowardly to stand against the wealthy. I remembered how he'd stood meek and voiceless as my grandfather had insulted my mother's honour and dismissed me as unworthy. If my father hadn't left me alone to care for my family while he was overseas, I wouldn't have been hunting swamp rats to feed us. Pearl wouldn't have followed me to the bayou. Virgile would never have had an opportunity to violate her. My father's craven inability to secure protection for his family had set the stage for violence to befall us during his deployment. Then a worse thought surfaced, an ugly supposition that my blistering temper put into words.

"You're refusing to do the honourable thing for your daughter because of money." The contempt in my voice shocked me but I couldn't stop. "You're willing to hold out your hand to a rapist's father in exchange for keeping quiet."

My head whipped to the left and my ears rang. Stinging needles of pain spread across my face.

My father stared in abject horror at his hand. The palm was crimson from the force of its impact against my cheek.

Abruptly, his black eyes became empty. I had witnessed that thousand-yard stare once or twice since his return from Afghanistan and I knew that, right now, he was no longer standing on our porch during the terrifying genesis of a hurricane. The rain, hammering against the roof, had transmuted into a cannonade of gunfire. My father was once again a frightened soldier huddled in the sand amongst the dead, trying to stanch the torrential outpouring of blood from all that was left of his leg.

I could so easily forgive him for striking me, but he'd never forgive himself. By raising a hand against his own child, he had broken a sacred vow that meant more to him than his life did. In a moment of senseless rage, I had minimized my father's self-worth. With a sickening wave of insight, I understood that my accusation would incubate until the poison of my words splintered our relationship. This man had been my hero, and I had walked with pride in his shadow. Now I stood alone, the soul protector of my beloved sister.

I picked up two of the water buckets and left my father in the torrential downpour. Pearl looked up from sorting our battery supply and her joyful smile melted the searing self-contempt that numbed me. Pearl was my *raison d'être*. I would avenge the sins perpetrated against her. If my father offered Virgile Landry clemency, then the duty of judge and executioner fell to me.

There could be no mercy.

CHAPTER FIFTEEN

SAM

SAM JOGGED UP the hospital stairwell, pausing at the fire door that accessed the lockdown unit. She swiped her new employee keycard against the reader and heard a faint click. The steel knob turned when she tried it. Emily had won yesterday's battle, apparently.

Dr. Beauregard had adamantly argued against granting Sam top clearance. Emily had presented her case with calm logic, explaining that Sam required unrestricted access to investigate Fadiya's rape. Her reasoning had infuriated him, and he'd grown cantankerous and belligerent. His objections surrounding the clinical practicum mirrored Sam's ethical concerns, but his belittling conduct was maddening.

The second point of contention concerned Sam's insistence that they install a CCTV camera in Fadiya's room. Mathias had again argued, stating that in-room cameras invaded patient privacy and created an unsafe therapy environment. They wouldn't compromise another established policy to mollify a private detective with a psychology hobby. During Emily's attempts to convince the insulting man that Fadiya required protection more than privacy, Mathias's active defiance, short-temper, and spiteful attacks shocked Sam. By the end of the two-hour meeting, she'd begun to fear the man was a malignant narcissist.

Now she had to attend a weekly staff meeting with the self-aggrandizing ass—so much for Emily's assertion that she wouldn't have to suffer Dr. Beauregard's company.

Sam continued up the stairwell, exited at the top floor, and followed the corridor to the boardroom. At the end of the hall, the door to Dr. Beauregard's enormous corner office stood open. Curious, Sam peeked inside. It was a blatant contrast to Emily's modest office. A mammoth ebony wood desk with sloping sides carved in a reed design sat at centre stage. Polished nickel detailing on the edges emphasized the curved silhouette of the custom piece. Sam had never seen anything like it. The artisanship was exquisite. Two leather Arne Jacobsen egg chairs with matching footstools nestled intimately beside a wall of lake-facing windows. Sam tiptoed into the office and squatted to examine the cylinder base of one of the chairs. The sticker read *Made in Denmark by Fritz Hansen*. They were originals. Her mother had a set in her solarium and had paid over twenty-thousand dollars apiece.

Sam got to her feet and turned back to the door. On her way out, a hung lithograph caught her eye. Pablo Picasso had signed and dated the piece. When Ophelia had told her that Mathias Beauregard enjoyed nice things, she hadn't exaggerated. His office was an opulent tribute to his own ostentatious elitism. It made her wonder why Emily claimed he had no funds to invest in Serenity Clinic. If he sold half the lavish furnishings, the money would cover the mould and coal dust remediation in the old cellar. Sam scurried out before someone caught her snooping, a transgression that would give Mathias the grounds he needed to terminate her placement.

In the boardroom, a sideboard displayed a variety of bagels and pastries. A delicious aroma of coffee wafted from a large urn on a drink bar in the corner. She'd skipped breakfast to squeeze in a quick workout before the meeting, and her mouth watered as she eyed the array of delectable pastries. She selected a flaky cheese croissant and took her treat over to the coffee bar. A group was queued at the station, chatting as they waited their turn. Too hungry to hold off eating, she bit into her buttery croissant.

From behind her, Ophelia said, "Looks like you have your hands full. Want me to pour your coffee?"

Sam nodded and wiped crumbs off the front of her blouse. "Milk no sugar. Thanks."

Ophelia handed her a white china mug. "That cheese pastry looks yummy. Breakfast is the only good thing about these staff meetings," she said glumly. "My shift is over and we had a heck of a night, let me tell you. No time for breaks. I'm exhausted and starved."

Sam followed her to the deserted sideboard, popped the last of her croissant into her mouth, and grabbed a bagel, surprised that no one else in the room was eating other than her and Ophelia.

"Something happen last night?" she asked.

Ophelia examined the pastries. "One of the rehab patients left. A girl called Serena. Didn't bother telling anyone, even the girl she was close friends with."

Sam remembered Emily telling her that another girl had left a few days earlier. "Any idea why they're running?"

Ophelia shrugged. "A lot of them are here because of interventions. You can't help someone who doesn't believe she has a problem. But she was enjoying the sculpting therapy. It was helping her develop a sense of self." She frowned. "And her friend, a girl called Bethany, was doing great, but last night she was ranting about foxes in the withdrawal unit. Delirium tremens, again. Her urine sample was positive for drugs. I've no idea who brought them to her."

"Is there anything I can do to help?" Sam asked.

Ophelia studied her over the rim of her coffee mug. "Yeah. Can you pop in and speak with her? Doug Sullivan is her therapist, but she dislikes him. Maybe she'll relate better to a woman."

Before she could answer, Sam sensed a presence behind her. She moved aside to allow the person access to the food, and turned to see Mathias Beauregard scowling at her. He strolled purposefully to the head of the board table.

"If you gluttonous piglets are through gobbling the free food, perhaps we could get to work," he said to the gathered staff, who shifted uneasily.

Ophelia's hand froze a centimetre from a strawberry Danish.

"Can you pull yourself away from the trough and join us, *Ophelia*?" He spoke the nurse's name with contempt. "We have a responsibility to set a good example to our patients by exhibiting healthy life choices. Now is as good a time as ever to start making wise decisions"

Sam's eyebrows rose in amazement. Calling attention to a person's weight was an unforgivable personal attack, and it solidified her negative impression of the insufferable man. Ophelia was a tall, large-boned woman, but she wasn't over-weight. If anything, she was muscular.

Ophelia retracted her empty hand, picked up her mug of black coffee, and walked stiffly to an open seat at the table. Either rage or humiliation—Sam couldn't tell which—seeped from the woman like a black aura.

As soon as she sat down, people around the table subtly distanced themselves by turning away from her. The man beside her scooted his chair closer to the person on his right, creating physical space between himself and Ophelia.

Herd mentality, Sam thought.

No one wanted to associate with the weak link that the boss was targeting. Well, Mathias Beauregard didn't intimidate her. Sam grabbed the strawberry Danish and marched to the vacant seat on the other side of Ophelia. She placed the pastry on a napkin, slid it in front of Ophelia, and bit into her own bagel, her expression daring Mathias to try to find a derogatory comment about her own physical fitness.

Emily flew into the room, causing heads to turn to the door. A stack of folders slipped from her hands and she stooped to pick them up. "I apologize for being late," she said. "I hope you started without me."

"We were discussing how to set a positive model of behaviour for our patients," Mathias said smoothly, and sneered at Ophelia.

"Oh, yes. Well that's a good start. Lead by example, I suppose." Emily gathered the folders into her arms and plopped into a seat beside her partner. She looked around, smiling. "Did everyone get some breakfast?"

There were murmurs of thanks as people shifted in their seats. Oblivious to the group's discomfort, Emily introduced Sam, announcing that she'd be working with Fadiya due to her expertise in thought reform consulting. The lie increased Sam's discomfort over the ethics of accepting the practicum, but she smiled gamely at the faces around the table.

"Expertise... Well, I guess that's one perspective," Mathias drawled. "Ms. McNamara was a member of the Bueton cult." He chuckled. "Let's hope her allegiance to its leader and his beliefs isn't reignited while she's in the company of a zealous supporter."

Sam grinned, playing off his insult as a mutual joke. "I'll try to resist the urge."

"Interesting case, Bueton," another man piped up. "I'd love to talk to you about it, Sam. Collective consciousness is fascinating, as is the method he used to seduce all those young girls." He rubbed his hand across a scraggly red beard.

"Doug, really, collective consciousness has little to do with why people like Sam join a cult," Mathias said. "It's social and affective vulnerability. Cult members suffer a high prevalence of psychiatric and addictive disorders. I'll send you some research."

"You mean *Fadiya*," Emily corrected him coldly. "You accidentally said *Sam*." She stared at him, unblinking, for a few seconds, then turned to address the table. "Sam went to Bueton to rescue a child. Her inside knowledge of the cult's sacraments will be valuable in leading Fadiya to question her irrational belief system." She opened her tablet and nibbled on the end of her stylus. "Now, let's go around the table and have everyone update us on their primary cases."

The meeting droned on, with Mathias injecting negative feedback on every case. When Emily finally opened the discussion on investors, he majestically raised his hand to prevent her from continuing.

"Non-essential personnel may excuse themselves," he said.

Assuming he was referencing her, a lowly student, Sam stood. Eager to make her escape, she bid farewell to the room at large with a bright smile and trotted to the door, resisting the urge to grab another pastry on her way by the sideboard.

"Anytime, people," Mathias drawled.

Sam glanced over her shoulder, wondering who the other student was, but Mathias was staring at Ophelia with a smug smile. The facility's head psychiatric nurse was anything but non-essential. Sam expected Emily to defend Ophelia. Instead, the doctor busied herself on her tablet, feigning sudden deafness. Sam's respect for her mentor plummeted.

With a thin-lipped frown, Ophelia stood and crossed the room to join Sam at the door.

Mathias now aimed his stony glare at the red-bearded man who had exhibited interest on collective consciousness. "Anytime now, Doug."

Doug's pale cheeks flushed a soft shade of red that matched his curly hair. He gathered his papers and pushed back his chair. The room fell silent, waiting for the three rejects to leave. The trio stepped out into the hall and Sam closed the door behind them, happy to escape Mathias Beauregard. Without a word, Ophelia marched down the hallway to the elevators.

"She and Dr. Beauregard have, ah, well, a complicated relationship," Doug said. "A word to the wise; stay out of it."

"Are you a practicum student?" she asked.

Doug shoved his wire-framed glasses up the bridge of his long, slightly upturned nose. "Yeah, from Western in London. Money has always been an issue, so I took a few years off between my master and doctorate degrees. You're University of Toronto, right?"

She nodded, pitying the poor sod for being stuck with Mathias Beauregard as a mentor. "What's your specialty?"

"Post-traumatic stress disorder, with a focus on veterans and victims of violent crimes," he said. "You?"

"Early detection of psychiatric disorders in puberty and adolescence. How do you find working with Dr. Beauregard?" She wondered what motivated anyone to suffer the man's unpleasant personality.

Doug's close-set eyes shifted to his hands and he fidgeted with a folder he held. "He's a brilliant diagnostician. He was an army physician and saw action in Afghanistan." He cleared his throat. "Have you read any of his research?"

"No."

Doug pursed his lips and gave her a hard stare. Oh God... had she offended him, too? She rushed to add, "I thought his primary role was fundraising and that he didn't treat patients."

Doug nodded. "Yeah, it is, but he still writes and publishes papers. I'm responsible for overseeing his qualitative research, and I treat patients in the withdrawal unit."

"Right. Ophelia asked me to pop in on one. Bethany. Is that okay with you?" she asked.

He blinked like an owl, an exaggerated and slow closure of his eyelids. "I'd rather you didn't." A knotted vein bulged and beat under the thin skin at his temple.

His refusal confused her. Medicine was a collaborative field and it was peculiar for a psychologist to be possessive of a patient. Practicum students received grades from their placement, so Doug's resistance must be insecurity about his internship. With Beauregard as his lead, Sam sympathized.

"This is a bit awkward," she said. "Ophelia specifically asked me to speak with Bethany." Sam didn't want to repeat that Ophelia had said Doug's patient disliked him. Rather than challenging his therapeutic relationship, she said, "Sometimes female patients relate better to a woman therapist."

His face had frozen into a strained expression while she had spoken. He'd pressed his lips into a thin line and the vein in his temple continued to throb. "It seems the decision is made, regardless of my opinion," he said indignantly. "Bethany suffers from night terrors and has a difficult time differentiating between reality and her nightmares." He sighed and relaxed his shoulders. "She doesn't make sense most of the time."

"Thanks. I'll keep that in mind." Hoping to defuse the tension Sam asked, "When did you join the staff?"

"I started my five hundred hours in May," he said. "It surprised me that you started outside the usual placement schedules."

She shrugged. "It worked for Emily and I was flexible."

"You're a private investigator, aren't you?" His expression was guarded.

"I'm a doctoral student," she replied with a laugh.

"Okay, I get it."

"Get what?" she asked.

"I read the papers. I know who you are, but if you don't want to talk about it, that's fine."

His tone was irritable, so Sam switched topics. "How is Dr. Beauregard as a mentor?"

"He's a brilliant visionary." Behind his glasses, Doug's beady eyes studied her, as if challenging her to contradict him.

Sam smiled politely. "It's lucky you have the opportunity to work with him. I'm off to the lockdown unit, so I'll take the stairs."

"You have all-access security clearance?"

She quickly shook her head and lied. "No. I mean I can access the lockdown unit, but I can only open Fadiya's door on that floor."

He owl-blinked again. It was either a physical condition or an unconscious tic. "Aren't you special," he said mockingly. He turned his back on her and walked to the elevator.

Puzzled, Sam watched him angrily jam his finger on the elevator call button. One day in and she was already arousing suspicion and making enemies. With a sigh, she opened the door to the stairwell and trotted down to the lower floor.

At the fire door, she swiped her card, noting that there wasn't an alarm bell here to warn the unit nurse that someone had entered through the stairwell. Perhaps it rang at the nurses' station. She made a mental note to check with security.

Rather than unlocking Fadiya's door and entering, Sam knocked. The unlatched door swung open. The floor nurse must be in the room and had neglected to lock the door. Not wanting to interrupt, Sam poked in her head and stepped back in surprise. In a split second, she took in the scene. Fadiya lay supine on the bed.

Her thin cotton nightgown had ridden up her naked thighs. Her feet thrashed and her body bucked as she fought a man who pushed her against the mattress with his shoulder. Fadiya clawed at the back of the man's head and cried out in pain. He was gripping her right arm, struggling to hold her down while he fumbled around the crook of her arm with his other hand.

Sam flew into the room, grabbed him by his shirt collar, and hurled him off Fadiya. He fell to the floor with a grunt of pain. Sam rolled him onto his stomach and twisted his wrist. A syringe of blood fell from his hand. She wrenched him to his feet and threw him into a chair.

Aazar Basha stared at her. "I can explain." His face was grey. Puffy, bruise-coloured moons circled his sunken eyes. He was breathing in shallow pants. "I was drawing blood."

"Stay in the chair," Sam said.

She went over to the bed to examine Fadiya. Blood dribbled down the girl's forearm. Beads of perspiration covered her flushed skin and her pupils were severely dilated.

"What did you give her?" Sam demanded.

"Didn't. Wanted blood. Someone's drugging her." He spoke slowly, fighting for breath between each word. He stumbled to his feet and fell to the floor beside a black jacket that lay beside the chair.

Ignoring him momentarily, Sam checked Fadiya's arms and legs for puncture wounds. Other than the crook of her arm, there weren't any needle marks, but Sam didn't have time to check for obscured injection sights. She straightened the girl's nightgown, tucked the blankets around her, and spun around to face Aazar. He lay on the floor, sucking on an inhaler and reaching for a liquid oxygen backpack that had slid under the bed. She knelt and retrieved the black leather satchel, found the nose buds, shoved them into Aazar's nostrils, and turned on the tank. Slowly, his colour improved.

"Can you talk?" she asked.

He nodded and tucked the plastic tubes around his ears, securing the nose buds against his face.

"Then start. You have five minutes before I call security."

He stood carefully, using the side of the bed to support his weight. Sam hooked her arm around his frail waist and helped him back to the chair. She sat across from him.

"I've suspected for the past three months that someone is giving my sister a hallucinogenic drug," he said. "It would explain her deluded state and physical symptoms."

"Why would anyone do that?"

He shrugged his emaciated shoulders. "To keep her mentally incapacitated in order to prevent her consenting to the transplant. Or maybe to stop my research, or maybe it's a means to extort money from my father. I don't know the reason." He paused to catch his breath. "I'm a medical doctor, Ms. McNamara, as well as a scientist. Dr. Armstrong assures me that she hasn't prescribed Fadiya medication, but my sister is under the influence of psychotropic drugs."

"How did you get onto the unit?" Sam asked.

"I have an RFID keycard," he said sheepishly.

"How?"

"I used a high frequency antenna and a mini computer to capture the hexadecimal stream of Ophelia's ID card," he said. "I cloned it."

"Give it to me."

Sam would have to check with Danny, but the process sounded ominously familiar. The use of a small radio frequency identification tool was how Danny had described accessing people's smartphones.

She motioned to the door. "I'll see you out."

There wasn't any point in talking to security, she knew. She remembered Saul telling her that Dr. Beauregard always put on a dog and pony show to impress the wealthy Basha family. Telling on Aazar wouldn't accomplish anything and could give Mathias grounds to have her pulled from Fadiya's case. She couldn't risk it. Whatever was going on at Serenity Clinic, Sam intended to get to the bottom of it. To do that, she needed unrestricted access to the clinic.

Aazar studied her. "You believe me. You also suspect they are drugging her. Do you know why?"

Sam held his gaze without acknowledging his question.

He stood, slinging the strap of his backpack over one shoulder. "I know who you are, Ms. McNamara. You're a private detective. I think you're here to protect my sister. For that I thank you."

She glanced around the floor, and then knelt to look under the bed. She picked up the needle by the plastic holder. The vacuum tube was missing. "Where's the blood sample?"

He removed it from his pocket. "I picked it up when you were getting my oxygen. If I test the blood, we'll know if her delusions are due to drugs," he told her.

She narrowed her eyes, thinking. If she let him test the sample, he might discover Fadiya's pregnancy. Sam didn't agree with

Emily's refusal to disclose the pregnancy to the family, but it wasn't her place to question the doctor's decision.

"Something is going on in here." Aazar held out the tube containing his sister's blood. "This could tell us what it is. Please help me."

She didn't have the authority to allow him to take the sample but her gut told her to trust Aazar. She took out a card and handed it to him.

"Those are my cell and office numbers. Call me with the test results. Tell no one but me, understand?" she said.

He nodded. "Do you know what's happening in this clinic?"

"No." She escorted him into the hallway. "But I'm going to find out. I promise you that."

CHAPTER SIXTEEN

REECE

REECE HAD BEEN loitering on the corner across from Cardoon Bistro for ten minutes, waiting on Eli who had texted to say he was on the Queen West streetcar stuck behind a fender-bender. Frustrated by the wait, he decided to have yet another discussion with Eli about getting a driver's licence. He'd taken him to the written test, which Eli had passed with flying colours, but whenever Reece had offered to teach him the ropes, Eli had refused to get behind the wheel. Thinking it worried him to drive his boss's car, Reece had enrolled him in driving school. Again, he'd passed with flying colours. All he needed to advance to the next level of Ontario's graduated licensing system was to take the road test. Not being able to drive interfered with his ability to do his job, yet Eli consistently refused to take the damn test. Reece was sick of trying to work around the problem when there was such a simple solution.

He finally spied a spiky-haired head bobbing through the crowd on the opposite side of the street. The crosswalk was a block down. Reece saw an opening in traffic and jogged across the street, quashing his guilt over jaywalking. A second later, Eli rushed over to him, short of breath and frazzled.

"I got off and walked," he said, stating the obvious. "It is very hot out. There are lots of pedestrians. Traffic is bad. I could not cross at Jameson Avenue. Drivers would not give pedestrians at the crosswalk the right of way. People are very rude." With jerky motions, he swiped away the sweat that dribbled down his forehead.

"It's not a problem," Reece said quickly, hoping to stave off a stress-related meltdown. "Take a minute and we'll go inside."

"I am good. I am fine. I am ready to go." Eli marched in place with his arms glued to his sides. He clearly was not good, fine, or ready to go.

Reece spied a table and chairs outside a store, set out by the store's owner to encourage neighbours to congregate. Seated at it were an older woman with a shopping trolley and a young man who was showing her a stunning abstract painting. The man noticed Reece and Eli and stood, waving them to take the table.

"Let's sit for a minute," Reece said to Eli.

Eli flopped onto a chair. His leg jiggled, his foot kicked the table leg in a two-four beat, and his eyes flitted across the sky, never settling on one focal point.

In a moment of clarity, Reece understood perfectly why Eli didn't want to take his road test. Asperger's didn't just compromise his communication skills: it hindered his capacity to manage stress. Sitting beside a stern-faced examiner, while unable to interpret the person's facial and body cues, would be torture. Navigating a world where over half of all human communication was construed from nonverbal elements must be outright painful. Eli did such a good job managing his Asperger's that Reece often forgot how challenging it must be on a daily basis. He silently swore he'd back off about the driver's licence. They could find a way around it.

After a minute, Eli unhooked a water bottle from his ever-present laptop bag and took a long drink. From his peripheral vision, Reece observed him. Eli's nervous twitching gradually calmed and his eyes settled. He attached the metal water bottle back onto a carabiner and repositioned his satchel across his shoulder.

Reece stood. "That fresh bread smells amazing. I wonder what else they make." He strolled the few metres down to Cardoon and held open the door for Eli.

Inside, art covered every centimetre of exposed brick. Along the back wall was a long wood bar topped with an antique domed-glass case. One half held trays of roasted vegetables, wheels of gourmet cheeses, and heaping piles of smoked meat. The other side displayed loaves of artisan breads, cakes, scones, cookies, and squares. Behind the bar, a gorgeous polished copper and brass Elektra espresso machine and matching grinder twinkled under soft, recessed lighting. The drawers of a vintage apothecary cabinet listed a variety of coffee beans for sale.

There was retro charm in the unfinished oak floors, eclectic accent chairs with vibrant printed seats, and bohemian sofas in jewel toned velvet. Josephine Baker's haunting voice resounded from discreetly placed speakers, and the emotional strains of 'Pretty Little Baby' added to the sense of stepping into a Paris café in the 1920s.

Although it was mid-morning on a weekday, people occupied more than half of the seating. An older man with long grey hair, a tie-dyed shirt, and a fringed suede vest moved between the tables, chatting with the patrons. Reece motioned to him, and the man joined them at the bar.

"Help you?" he asked.

"This place is great," Reece said. "Are you the owner?"

"Yup. Me and the wife." He held out his hand. "Francis Chaudire. First time here?"

"It won't be the last." Reece shook his hand. "My fiancée works around the corner. I think we just found our new go-to place for lunch. Those custom sandwiches look amazing."

Francis beamed. "You should taste the specials. My wife trained at Le Cordon Bleu in Paris. Today is stuffed pig's trotters and morels."

Reece's mouth watered. When they finished their interview, he decided, he'd treat Eli to lunch. He automatically reached for his Crown attorney's office id. With a sharp bite of shame he flicked open his wallet and displayed his Ontario private investigative licence. "I'm Reece Hash and this is my partner, Eli Watson. Mind if we ask a few questions about an unpleasant incident that happened to one of your staff three months ago?"

Francis studied the picture identification and then gestured to a table. "Sure. Can I get you a coffee?"

"An espresso would be great," Reece said, resisting the urge to ask for a plate of pig's trotters.

Francis looked over at Eli.

"Just water," Eli said stiffly.

Francis called to a woman behind the bar. "Lydia, an espresso and a bottle of water, please."

Once they were seated, Reece opened a picture of Annalise Huang on his phone and passed it to Francis. "Do you remember this woman?"

The man nodded. "We get all kinds in here. Sadly, some aren't too enlightened." He tapped the picture. "That woman made me doubt the human condition."

"I understand she verbally abused one of your servers," Reece said.

"Lydia." Francis looked up at the woman operating the espresso machine.

"Do you know what happened?" Reece asked.

Francis shook his head. "We had a packed house that night. I was in the kitchen when I heard the commotion." He held Reece's phone and stared at Annalise's picture. Sadness shadowed his eyes. "The way I heard it, she stood in the centre of the room, screaming vile things at Lydia. A couple of customers tried to intervene but she verbally attacked them, too. By the time I came in, it was over." He passed the phone back to Reece. "I don't know what was said, Lydia won't tell me, but she hasn't worn a skirt since. After cancer took her leg, she worked hard to accept her prosthetic. Now she's ashamed again, hides behind the bar as much as possible. People's cruelty has no limit at times."

"Can we speak with Lydia?" Reece asked.

"You can try," Francis said. "She'll be over in a minute with your coffee."

Reece scrolled through his phone and held out the photo of Harold Taylor. "What can you tell me about this man?"

Francis peered at the picture. "Harold Taylor. I banned him about six months ago. Hated to do it, but it couldn't be helped."

"What was his story?" Reece asked.

Francis shrugged. "Older folks sometimes cling to antiquated prejudices. Harold was one. He disliked anyone with a special need, but he took a special dislike to Billy, another one of my employees. He has Downs. Back in Harold's day, those kids were institutionalized." He crossed his legs with a deep frown. "Downs and autistic children were considered uneducable, and lots of parents refused to acknowledge them. That was Harold's mindset."

"Do you hire people with disabilities because you can pay them less?" Eli asked bluntly.

If the question offended Francis, he hid it well. "No. We pay above minimum wage, offer benefits, and we don't accept government bursaries." He looked around at his servers. "Everyone who works here is a blessing to us. They're the reason Cardoon exists. My wife and I wanted a place where people could celebrate community. That's what this used to be."

"It isn't now?" Reece asked.

"Yes and no. For the past few years, Parkdale Village has been battling the gentrification beast. Urbanites who want to live closer to the city core are changing the dynamics of the area," Francis said. "Indifference and desensitization are a plague that's causing more causalities than people admit."

"Your business is thriving," Reece said, watching the bustling clientele.

"We owe it to an influential food blogger and a great review from the *Globe and Mail* food critic." Francis sighed. "I'm not complaining, but I miss the neighbourhood spirit we used to have."

Reece showed him the pictures of the other three victims he suspected were linked to Harold and Annalise.

Francis studied them carefully but shook his head each time. "Can't say I remember them. What's this all about?"

"Annalise Huang committed suicide three months ago. We've been hired to follow-up on her movements prior to her death."

"What do the other folks have to do with it?" Francis asked.

"We're trying to determine if these five people knew Annalise," Reece said. "Do you recall a regular customer who was in the restaurant when Annalise and Harold were here?"

"Like I said, the reviews attract people. If you'd asked me a year ago, I could have named more than half of the people in here." Francis glanced around the restaurant. "It's different now."

"You have a security camera," Eli stated. "How long do you store footage?"

"No clue. One of the line cooks takes care of it for me. He's good with technology."

"I would like to copy it," Eli said, opening his satchel and removing his laptop and a portable hard drive.

"That's fine by me," Francis said.

Lydia came to the table, put down their drinks, and tucked the tray under her arm.

"This is Reece and Eli," Francis said to her. "They're PIs and would like to speak to you about the woman who harassed you back in April."

"Okay, I guess. I mean, if you want me to," she said hesitantly. She tugged nervously at the fabric of her right pant leg.

Her slacks were baggy and unflattering. They didn't match the bold style of her peacock-emblazoned T-shirt, turquoise belt buckle, and feather earrings. It angered Reece that Annalise Huang's hateful behaviour had made this cancer survivor insecure over something that should have been an inspirational badge of courage.

Francis stood and addressed Eli. "I'll show you where the security equipment is."

Lydia perched awkwardly on the edge of the seat Francis had vacated. Short blonde hair framed a full face with huge blue eyes. She flicked her pink-streaked bangs out of her eyes and studied Reece with apprehension.

"Do you know why Annalise verbally attacked you?" he asked.

She spun a wedding ring around her finger. "I saw her a few nights earlier. My husband and I were at a martini bar in the Entertainment District. She had an altercation with a man sitting beside me." She cleared her throat and yanked at the leg of her trousers.

"Did something happen in the bar?" Reece asked.

"The woman threw a ring in the guy's face. It fell on the ground and I tried to pick it up. I moved my leg wrong and lost my balance." Lydia looked up at him. "I wasn't going to take the ring. I was grabbing it before someone kicked it under the bar."

"Did she think you were trying to take it?"

"I don't know. She yelled at me about stealing what wasn't mine," Lydia said. "But I don't know if she was talking about the ring or her boyfriend. She said nasty stuff about my ugly prosthetic." Her eyes filled with tears. "The guy got up and dragged her out before my husband came back from the washroom."

"How did Annalise end up here?" Reece asked.

"She came in with another woman," Lydia said. "I served them at the counter. When I took the order over to their table, they saw my prosthetic." She tugged so hard on her pant leg that Reece heard fabric tear. "I was wearing a skirt." Her nose crinkled in disgust. "I know better, now."

"What happened?"

"I guess she recognized me from the bar." She swiped her eyes and looked away. "Maybe it had something to do with the guy she was yelling at that night. I don't know. She went ballistic, screaming about how I was hideous and deformed." She lowered her head and chewed on her lower lip. "I don't want to repeat what she said."

"I'm sorry that happened to you. Did anyone intervene?" Reece asked.

"A few tried, but the woman was a total psycho. It was scary." She sighed. "Besides, let's face it, people love to watch humiliation. Some even took out their phones and videotaped it." Lydia lowered her eyes in shame. "The people who posted the video raged online over what happened, but they still put it out there without my permission. My husband and I are private people. We had to shut down all our accounts."

"Do you recall if there was anyone in the restaurant who's here frequently?" Reece asked.

Lydia shrugged. "A few, I guess. Why?"

"Do you know their names?" Reece asked.

"Not off hand. Francis might. There's a really nice nurse who comes in a lot, I think she works at St. Joseph's Withdrawal Management." She looked around. "She was here a minute ago with a man, but I don't see her now."

"Can you think of anyone else who might have witnessed it?" Reece asked.

Lydia thought for a minute. "It was late, so someone from the food bank could have been here. Francis donates our overages."

"I'd like to speak to some of your regulars. Can you give me a list?" Reece asked.

Lydia's back stiffened and her lips thinned. "Why? Are you working for her and trying to prove I deserved to be humiliated? I knew I shouldn't have spoken to a PI," she stated heatedly. "Detective Martina, from the *real* police, talked to me in the spring after it happened. He said it was a hate crime."

This was exactly why Reece hadn't wanted to interview her under the guise of a PI. Had he been able to use his Crown attorney credentials—an office that protected victims—she wouldn't have jumped to conclusions about his motive.

"I'm not suggesting you did anything wrong," Reece said quickly, but she was too angry to hear him.

"Leave me alone or I'll call Detective Martina." Lydia grabbed the tray from the table, her face flushed with anger. She stomped back behind the bar, slamming the flap behind her.

Eli returned from the kitchen, holding a paper bag at arm's length. He handed it to Reece with a grimace. "This is the special from Chef Chaudire." He rubbed his hands against his jeans and leaned in to whisper. "It has hooves in it. I saw them. They were disgusting."

"How did you make out with the security footage?" Reece asked.

"Most businesses keep a maximum of ninety days of footage," Eli said as they made their way through the crowd to the door. "This set-up downloads the camera footage to a sixteen-terabit external hard drive," he said. "When it is full, they switch it to a secondary hard drive. Talk about over-kill. Anyway, they had not erased the first. I gave them two of mine and took both of theirs."

Reece held open the door and scorching heat smacked him in the face. "Meaning?"

"There are over eight thousand hours of footage on the full one. There are six thousand hours on the second one." Eli turned and faced him, his expression grim. "We have to go through a year and a half of video."

Reece's heart sank. They had a snowball's chance in hell of identifying one person near all of their suspected victims.

CHAPTER SEVENTEEN

THE JOURNAL

A VIGOROUS SHAKE pulled me from an unsettled sleep. The harsh beam of a tactical flashlight blinded me. Bewildered, I raised my hand to block the piercing light. The screaming wind that rattled our house sounded unnervingly human, and steady rain lay down a backdrop of white noise that rose in volume and intensity. I bolted upright in my bed. Confusion and dread merged into raw fear.

Hurricane Rita had made landfall. Her manic fury was slaughtering everything in her path.

"Get up," my father ordered. "It's Pearl." He disappeared into the gloom and his uneven footsteps faded away down the loft stairs.

The fear churning in my stomach crystallized to ice-cold terror. The high, ululating screams were not the wind—it was Pearl. I groped to find the flashlight I'd left on my bedside table and flew downstairs.

My mother stood motionless in the corner of the room, her eyes glazed with horror and her mouth moving silently. Six propane lanterns highlighted Pearl, writhing on white sheets drenched in blood.

"There's too much intrapartum hemorrhaging," my father told me. He threw a blood-soaked cloth to the floor. "Start an IV, hang saline, and get her vitals."

I grabbed a bag of saline and a needle, panic swirling around me like the hurricane winds outside. "Is it placenta praevia? That's what you feared, based on her pregnancy difficulties, right? Do we have to do a C-section?" I fired the questions at him, yelling over the screeching wind that hammered against the metal shutters on the windows.

"Blu, calm down. I need your help," he said. "Hang the saline."

The tremor in his voice scared me more than the copious amount of blood that saturated the sheets beneath my beloved sister.

Pearl's agonized howls echoed against the bedroom walls, and my hands shook as I doused them with alcohol-based sanitizer. I grasped her upper arm and wrapped a rubber tourniquet around it, but I couldn't see a vein. I was hurting her and she didn't understand. She stared beseechingly at me and the expression of betrayal in her aqua eyes wounded me deep within my soul.

"I need to help you," I said. "Let me help you, *chère*."

Her wails of agony faded to strangled whimpers of anguish as her strength waned. Her wide eyes mutely begged me to stop the pain, to hold and protect her. Instead, I was torturing her because I was too inept to find a vein.

I mentally reviewed everything I'd read about inserting an intravenous catheter. I slipped a blood pressure cuff over the rubber strap to act as a venous tourniquet. Even with it inflated, I felt nothing. Her blood pressure was too low.

Choking back tears, I said to my father, "I can't start the IV."

"Use a winged infusion set," Dad said without raising his eyes.

I found the butterfly needle and snapped my forefinger over the site to stimulate the vein. The constant thud of hurricane rain was an ominous reminder of our isolation. During my repeated failures, Pearl lost consciousness, her expression of forgiveness before her eyes fluttered closed accentuating my sense of incompetence.

Panicked, I screamed at my father, "You have to do it!"

"She'll bleed out if I move. You can do this, Blu. Breathe and concentrate," he said.

I tried again and again, to no avail. Finally, I closed my eyes, breathed out, and felt a soft flutter beneath my fingertips. My eyes snapped open and I anchored the skin over the vein by pulling it with my left thumb so it wouldn't roll. With my right hand, I carefully inserted the catheter tip and guided it into the lumen of the vein. Weeping with relief, I taped it down and hooked the saline bag over the top of the bedpost.

"Get me a scalpel," my father said grimly. "I have to get the baby out."

My mother uttered a terrible yowl and flew at my father. "Don't you cut my angel!" she shrieked. Gone was the harmless, deluded woman who drawled dreamily about southern plantations and simpler days. She was a raving lunatic now, a dangerous animal protecting her young.

Outside, I heard a gunshot crack as a branch broke under Rita's wrath. From somewhere in the house, glass shattered. I grabbed the sterilized surgical kit and tore open the blue paper.

Mom howled like a jackal, pounced on my father's back, and beat her fists against his head. This crazed woman who furiously attacked Pearl's only hope of survival was unrecognizable to me. I stood paralyzed, watching in horror as she bit down on his ear, shaking her head like a pit bull.

Dad bellowed in pain as his blood dripped from my mother's locked jaws. His arms flailed and a propane lantern fell with a clatter. Adrenalin flooded my system with electrified strength. I threw the instruments on the bed, gripped my mother's shoulders, and wrenched her off him. I shoved her so hard she flew across the room and bounced against the wall. She lay dazed and snivelling on the floor.

"Pearl will not die because of you." I pointed an unsteady finger at my father. "He's the only hope we have."

I thrust a scalpel into my father's trembling hand as he stared in astonishment at the slobbering beast his wife had become.

I clutched his chin in my hand, the blood from his earlobe slick against my fingers. "Pearl can't die," I told him. "I believe in you."

His eyes cleared. "Do you remember what to do?"

I nodded. The steps he'd taught me after the clinic's idiot doctor had dismissed us were razor sharp in my mind's eye.

Dad made an incision in Pearl's lower abdomen with a swift movement that resulted in minimal bleeding. Underlying yellow fat burst out, which I had anticipated, but theoretical study hadn't prepared me for the emotional trauma of operating on my sister. I took a step back, feeling lightheaded and dizzy.

"Blu, detach and perform the steps."

My father's calm voice centred me and the encroaching black dots that twirled around me receded.

Fighting the urge to gag, I stuck my fingers into the incision and shoved the gelatinous fat out of his sightline. Deftly, he executed a series of cuts and nicked an opening through a shiny, fibrous layer. Swallowing a mouthful of bile, I handed him the scissors and stood ready to part the abdominal muscles at his cue.

Hunched in the corner, crone-like, my mother uttered an explosive shriek. The vileness of her piercing, inhuman growls caused the hair on my arms to rise. I watched her with a wary eye, wishing I had taken the time to restrain her.

When I glanced away from Mom, my father was opening Pearl's womb. I quickly suctioned the amniotic fluid and my father stuck in his hands, manoeuvring the baby back and forth until it was born.

It was a boy. He was dead, far beyond resuscitation. My father silently placed the tiny body on the bed, reached into Pearl's body once more and removed the placenta, and then began to repair her uterus.

I stared at this thing that had ravaged Pearl's young body, greedily perpetuating the unspeakable violence she'd endured at the evil hands of a rapist. Even through the blood, the infant's striking resemblance to Virgile Landry was undeniable. Rage blossomed in my chest.

"Check your sister," my father said. "She lost a lot of blood."

I put my fingers against Pearl's wrist. Her pulse was rapid and her breathing was shallow. The only speck of colour in her sheet-white face was her blue lips.

"She's in hypovolemic shock," I said softly.

"He murdered my angel." My mother guffawed like a hyena, a hysterical sound that belonged in an asylum. She slumped into the corner, her mind fractured beyond repair, no longer capable of recognizing the man she had loved unconditionally for two decades.

As my father worked, I lay beside Pearl, stroking her cheek and wiping the clammy sweat from her brow. My tears soaked into the sodden pillowcase beneath her head. When I found the strength to look up, my father's hollow expression confirmed what I feared. His work was without fault, but we hadn't performed the caesarian section in time. The expanding pool of blood beneath Pearl dripped steadily from the sheets to the floor, and we had no drugs to stop it. Hurricane Rita raged outside, cutting us off from any hope of obtaining help.

My father refused to give up. He held his fist inside my sister, applying pressure while he massaged her abdomen with his other hand. He was making a high-pitched keening noise as blood ran down his forearm.

In a moment of hypervigilance, a revelation hit me—a chance to save Pearl.

"I have the same blood type. Do a direct transfusion." I knelt beside the combat kits to look for the equipment. "We can keep her alive until the uterus contracts." I heard the frenzied hope in my voice.

My father's shoulders slumped and he removed his gloves. "It's too late."

"No! We pump my blood into her until she stops bleeding." Tears streamed down my face. "Help me!"

He turned and grabbed my hand. "Blu, she's lost too much to sustain organ function."

I shoved him off me. "Take *all* my blood. Let me die. Save Pearl." I tightened a rubber tourniquet with my teeth and jammed a needle into the crook of my arm, fumbling to attach a hose as precious blood spurted into the air. "Help me," I yelled.

My father tore the needle out of my flesh and pressed gauze against my inner arm. "It won't work, and I can't lose you, too. Be with her, now. That's all you can do." Tears dripped down his face, mixing with the blood that flowed from his torn earlobe.

I fell beside Pearl and buried my face in her soft hair, inhaling the tropical scent of coconut oil. I could not let her go. I had to bring her back to me.

"Six rows of sixteen. Ninety-six. Ninety-six carrots in the garden," I whispered through my tears. "They want you to come on home now, *chère*. Please, fly o'er the bayou to me."

In my mind, I saw her dancing under the old cypress tree in the mellow pink light from the setting sun, smiling her radiant, innocent smile, her fingers tapping out the rhythm of the frogs' requiem. I held her tight and sang our Cajun lullaby, praying for her to murmur the chorus.

Her ivory skin grew cold under my touch. I hugged her tighter, willing the heat of my body to enter hers. Pearl drew a shallow breath that released in a rusty wheeze. It was then that I sensed her physical pain as acutely as if it were my own. I could not bear her suffering, and I knew in my heart that she was clinging to life because of me. She was suffering because I didn't have the courage to let her go.

"I failed you, but I'll make things right," I promised. "Let go now, *chère*."

I kept my arms locked around her until she took a final rasping breath and lay still in my arms.

"I'll find you, someday," I whispered through my tears. "We'll be together again, I promise."

CHAPTER EIGHTEEN

SAM

SAM LIKED HER home uncluttered, obsessively organized, and fresh smelling. She could live with a bit of dirt, but she couldn't live in smelly chaos. Disarray didn't begin to describe what greeted her when she entered the loft: pandemonium came closer. The floor was littered with dog toys and fawn-coloured fur. Pepin was running in manic circles, barking in ear-piercing yelps that supplemented the cacophony of blasting heavy metal music that thumped from Eli's Bluetooth speaker. Danny had shoved all the living room furniture against the southern wall of windows and rolled up the area carpet, which she'd tossed onto the Italian leather sofa. A long, ugly table faced Sam's eighty-inch flat screen. Cords snaked from numerous monitors on the white folding table. A thick coaxial cable ran across the floor and up the wall to the television, which was apparently serving as a computer monitor. Eli's laptop, a second monitor, and an array of unidentifiable computer gadgets were strewn across the dining room table, along with the pocketknife Eli always carried. Beside a mouse pad, a gooey ring stained the weathered wood tabletop. Half a dozen cans of Mountain Dew and greasy, scrunched-up paper towels littered the Carrera marble counters in the kitchen. Something smelled weird. Her eyes fell on a plastic container that squatted on the kitchen counter. Sam put her armful of textbooks on the stovetop, the only clear space, and peeked under the takeout lid. With a gasp, she stepped back and held her hand against her nose.

"What is that?"

Eli glanced up. "A cloven hoof."

"Stuffed pig's totters with morels," Reece yelled over the blaring music. He removed the lid, holding it out for her inspection. "Compliments of Chef Chaudire from Cardoon Bistro."

Jammed into a beige mound of some gelatinous substance were slivers of greyish honeycomb that resembled an old sponge. Beside the lump was a greasy brown tube. On the end were two distinct toes with pointy bones that reminded her of toenails. Burgundy gravy, which looked disturbingly like blood, dribbled across the hoof.

"It's a difficult recipe, even for Michelin Star chefs," Reece shouted. "I saved it so we could share."

Sam swallowed a mouthful of bile. "That's okay. You can have it." It was enough to turn a person into a vegetarian. "Put it in the fridge. Make sure you close the lid securely." Hopefully it wouldn't taint the leftover lasagna.

"How was your day?" Reece hollered, snapping on the lid and tucking the container into the fridge.

"Eli, turn off the music," she bellowed.

He said something she didn't catch. Based on his surly expression, it was a protest, but he complied and she took a moment to delight in the merciful silence. A minute was all she got. Pepin filled the audio void by barking and pouncing on a stuffed elephant.

Sam glared at the little demon as he vigorously shook the elephant clamped between his jaws.

"Can you do something about that dog?" she exclaimed, completely frustrated by the bedlam.

"He is not a dog," Eli stated with a sour expression.

"What do you think he is?" She was pretty sure the hellhound Cerberus wasn't going to be Eli's response.

"He is a *puppy*. You need to play with him. He is bored." He tugged the elephant out of Pepin's locked jaws and hurled it across the room. Pepin ran after it, slid across the glossy floor finish, and careened into the windows.

Sam winced as his solid little body bounced off the glass. She ran over and scooped him into her arms. He might aggravate her, but she didn't want him smashing through the glass to plummet ten metres to the sidewalk.

"Don't forget we have dinner with your mom and stepfather tonight," Reece said, stepping over to her and rubbing the top of Pepin's round head.

"Mother called me six times," she said. "It's not dinner. It's a tasting menu for the champagne brunch. Did you know we were getting married at dawn?"

He laughed. "We'll discuss that. Brunch sounds better than a six-course sit-down dinner with five hundred of their closest society friends."

He had a point, but she wasn't in the mood to nibble on frou-frou appetizers. It was a Big Mac and double order of French fries type of day.

"Based on your frown, I take it things didn't go well at the clinic," Reece said with a sympathetic smile.

That was an understatement. After catching Aazar in Fadiya's room, Sam had tried to talk with Bethany in the withdrawal unit. It hadn't gone well. Ophelia had said Bethany was detoxing, but Sam didn't think drugs came close to explaining the girl's problems. She'd found Bethany in the garden, stirring mushy cereal around in a bowl of milk and ranting about a fox forcing Special K into her. She waved a tiny cereal box around her head as if she were swatting invisible bugs. It wasn't even Special K; it was Corn Pops. When Sam had offered to get her something else to eat, Bethany had become irate, claiming the fox had sent Sam to poison her. She brandished a spoon at her in quick, stabbing motions and screamed that Sam was trying to take her to the fox's den. Security had rushed over, restrained the girl, and escorted Sam out of the courtyard garden.

It was humiliating and had left her feeling completely incompetent.

Sam took Pepin into the kitchen and gave him a chicken strip. He trotted into Brandy's old crate with his treat clamped between his teeth. It hurt to see the puppy in Brandy's bed; there was something traitorous about allowing him to use it. Brandy had been her rock for twelve years. They'd done everything together. Sometimes at night, Sam still woke to a phantom echo of Brandy's toenails clicking across the living room floor. Sometimes, she'd make it all the way downstairs before the truth punched her in the face. Brandy was dead. She'd sit on the stairs and quietly sob alone in the dark. Nestled tight beside her grief was shame that she lacked the emotional strength to bridge the cavernous void in her heart.

Choking back tears, Sam tucked Pepin's elephant beside him. The crate was too big for the French bulldog, but Reece had made it cozy with colourful blankets and an array of toys. Pepin looked adorable, curled into a ball with his treat propped between his paws, and his bat ears twitching as he chewed. She blinked rapidly to prevent her tears from spilling. What was wrong with her? Why couldn't she love him?

"Want to talk about it?" Reece asked, wrapping his arms around her and pressing his body against her back.

"Aazar had a cloned keycard to the lockdown unit," Sam said, pretending he was asking about her bad day. "I caught him drawing Fadiya's blood."

"Did he say why?" Reece asked.

"He claims someone at Serenity is giving his sister hallucinogens." She had her sappy emotions under control now, so she turned to face him. "He wants to test the blood to prove it. I'm not sure what to think."

"Well, we found something that may help." Reece went over to the makeshift workstation in the living room. "Danny, can you pull up the file?"

"This is one of the obstructed video files on the clinic's security camera that I recovered," Danny said to Sam.

Sam watched silently as the video clip played on her television screen. A thin person with a backpack crept through the stairwell door. The figure wore a dark windbreaker and a baseball cap, the brim of which shadowed the face. The person sidestepped to Fadiya's door, keeping their back to the camera. Fadiya's door opened and the figure disappeared inside the room.

"In about an hour, at about two a.m., the person comes out of the room and leaves through the fire exit," Danny said. "It looks like a woman's build. Do you know who it is?"

"It's Aazar Basha," Sam said. "I recognize the backpack. It's a medical unit designed to carry portable oxygen. He had it with him today when I caught him in his sister's room."

"What's he doing in there in the middle of the night?" Reece asked.

"Nothing good," Sam said. "Otherwise he wouldn't be creeping around and tampering with the camera."

"The sophistication of the encryption on these files is crazy. That's why it's taking me longer to break it," Danny said. "Aazar is a scientific genius. This would be a cakewalk for someone like him."

Sam felt the blood rush from her head. She had bought Aazar's story about drug testing and had let an incestuous rapist walk out of the clinic. The lapse of judgment made her physically ill.

"He was my hero." Danny sounded like she was about to cry. "But now I find out he's just another disgusting douche-bag."

"Maybe there is an explanation," Eli said, patting her back.

"He's a rapist," Danny snapped. "Look at him, skulking around like the douche-bag he is."

Suddenly, the pieces clicked into place. Sam couldn't believe she'd been so stupid. Drawing Fadiya's blood had nothing to do with testing for alleged drugs.

"The clinic hasn't disclosed the pregnancy to the family," she said. "Aazar's a medical doctor, and I think he's suspected it. A blood test would confirm it."

"And he'd know that a DNA test on the baby could prove incest," Danny said. "There will be multiple runs of homozygosity—parts that are the same on both parent donated chromosomes."

"I don't know what you're talking about," Sam said, embarrassed by how shrill and nasty she sounded. This wasn't Danny's fault. They were lucky to have her geeky, scientific mind working for them.

"Simply put, Aazar needs to terminate the pregnancy," Danny retorted. "If they run a DNA test, a clinical geneticist could probably prove that a sibling fathered the baby. Aazar's her only brother. Get it?"

"Is there a non-surgical way of aborting the fetus near the end of the first trimester?" Sam asked.

"Mifepristone and misoprostol pills would induce a miscarriage," Danny said grimly. "Easy-breezy."

"What if he is correct and someone is drugging his sister?" Eli asked. "Maybe he was in her room to protect her."

"What happened to the blood sample?" Reece asked.

"I let him take it," Sam admitted. "He said he'd call me with the results." She felt like a complete idiot.

"How long will it take him to test the blood?" Reece asked Danny.

"A toxicology screen is fast," she said. "But if you don't know what drug you're looking for, I think it takes a bit of time to identify it." She swallowed hard and blinked rapidly. "You should never admire anyone," she said. "They'll let you down every time." Her hands shook and she gnawed on her lower lip as she turned back to her keyboard and pressed a key. "I can't watch this any longer."

"If you haven't heard from Aazar by tomorrow, we'll confront him." Reece put his arm around Sam's waist. "Your instincts are good. Trust them."

She didn't trust anything anymore. She'd thought her empathy and intuition would make her a good clinical psychologist, but after the debacle with Bethany, and now this, she had serious doubts about her abilities. She stared at the pile of textbooks on the stovetop, all related to working with ex-cult members. She still had no idea how to break Mussani's hold over Fadiya. At over thirty, the idea of another botched career made her lightheaded. She'd failed as a cop and now she was failing as a psychologist, before she'd even achieved her PhD.

She glanced up at the television. The recovered footage from Serenity's security camera had been replaced by a shot of a restaurant's interior.

"What is that?" Sam asked.

"Cardoon Bistro," Danny said. "I'm setting up an algorithm python to search for Reece's sudden-death victims."

"We're trying to determine if any of the other possible victims visited the restaurant," Reece explained.

"Once we extrapolate the footage, we can look for someone near each of the victims," Eli said. "Close enough to tag their phones."

"Pause it there," Sam told Danny. She moved closer to the screen on the wall. "Zoom in on the table in the back left corner."

Danny froze the picture, closed in on the table, and brought the faces of the two diners into focus.

"That's Ophelia, the head nurse at the clinic," Sam said.

"That is from today, just before we arrived," Eli said. "Who is she with?"

"Dr. Mathias Beauregard."

Sam wondered why Ophelia would meet Beauregard a few hours after the humiliating staff meeting. She'd worked a twelve-hour night shift and had told Sam she was exhausted. There was something strange about the interaction between the two figures, but Sam couldn't put her finger on what was bothering her.

"Move it forward in slow motion," she said, and leaned in to study the close-up video play. Ophelia's body language was assertive. Her facial expression was stern as she addressed Mathias. Authoritative was the best description that came to Sam's mind. And instead of his usual smug attitude, Mathias seemed vulnerable, even intimidated. Given their professional positions and the demeaning way he treated Ophelia, neither her aggression nor his reaction made sense.

Sam watched as Ophelia stood and left the bistro. Mathias sat alone for a minute. Then, he crushed his paper coffee cup in his fist, pushed back his chair, and stormed out, knocking aside a woman with a stroller.

On the day she'd visited the lockdown unit for the first time, Ophelia had turned hostile when Sam had questioned her about Mathias Beauregard. She'd claimed she barely knew the man. From what Sam could gleam from the footage, they had a personal relationship outside work.

Ophelia had lied to her.

CHAPTER NINETEEN

REECE

REECE TURNED ONTO the Bridle Path and drove through an upscale residential area known as Millionaires' Row. At an ornate, wrought iron gate, he punched in a code and the gate swung open. He continued down a long, brick-paved road to a circular entrance in front of a stunning French château-style mansion. Although it was less than twenty minutes to the heart of downtown Toronto, the thirty-million-dollar home sat on four acres of mature trees and meticulously landscaped grounds. He parked beside a hedge-trimmed water fountain and admired the lush green lawns, spectacular gardens, and peaceful seclusion of the property.

Sam hated her mother's opulent lifestyle, but Reece admired the woman's impeccable taste. The thirty-thousand-square-foot home was stunning. He'd seen the back of the property on a previous visit and loved the double set of stone stairways that led from the elevated patio deck to the dazzling gardened acreage. Holding the wedding ceremony here would be perfect. He just had to convince Grace to pare down the pomp and pageantry so Sam could see beyond the extravagance to the natural beauty of the parkland setting.

Having not said a word during the entire ride, his cranky fian-cée sat sulking in the passenger's seat. Reece got out of the driver's side and circled the car. "Ready?" he asked through the open passenger window.

She thrust the door open with a grunt, climbed out, and slammed it shut behind her.

He reached for her hand. "Want to stroll around the grounds before we go in?" His plan was to wax poetically about the scen-ery, in the hope it inspired her to imagine their wedding the way he did.

"No. Let's get this over with," she grumbled and marched to the front door.

He trailed along behind, dreading the evening, and hoping that their wedding wasn't going to cause more conflict between Sam and her mother. Sam had hero-worshiped her detective father, who a drunk driver had killed ten years ago. Harvey, a wealthy philanthropist, had been her father's best friend and her mother had married him a year or so after her first husband's death. Sam adored her stepfather, who was a homely man, with a grass-roots approach to life, but even Harvey—a brilliant negotiator—hadn't been able to heal the estrangement between his wife and step-daughter. At least they were civil to each other now, which was a start. Reece had learned to celebrate the small wins.

Sam ignored the doorbell and hammered on the front door with her fist instead. A maid in a loose black dress with a white bibbed apron answered the door. "They're waiting in the front room," she said.

"Thanks." Sam stomped across the marble foyer and turned right at the base of a sweeping staircase. Reece followed her into a luxurious room with coffered ceilings, exquisite wood mouldings, and multiple French doors that opened onto lush gardens.

"She redid the room *again*," Sam muttered under her breath. "Look at that chandelier." She snickered. "She probably snagged it from the Palace of Versailles."

Reece's temper rose. "Can you be nice, please?"

She shrugged. "Just being honest."

"Well don't. Let's enjoy the tasting." As an enthusiastic gourmet, he was excited to taste the food. Sam's testiness was ruining it for him.

She squeezed his hand. "You're right. Sorry." She leaned in and kissed him softly on the lips. "The chandelier is pretty gross, though."

Reece had to agree; the thing was a crystal monstrosity. Beneath it was an elegant pedestal table, four tapestry wing chairs, and an antique tea trolley with trays of delectable hors d'oeuvres.

Harvey was standing next to a bar in front of a fireplace large enough to roast a hog. "There they are." He engulfed Sam in a bear hug.

Reece went over to Grace, who sat straight-backed in one of the tapestry armchairs, and pecked her cheek. "You're looking well, Grace." He eagerly inspected the array of appetizers. "Thank you so much for arranging all this."

Caviar tartlets sat beside maple-caramelized figs with smoky bacon. Silky ricotta topped with shredded Brussels sprouts, raisins, and pine nuts covered toast points. Lobster and avocado terrine shared that tray. There was foie gras with pickled grapes, endive cups with beets and feta, and potato blinis with smoked salmon.

Sam stared at the selection, frowning. "Mother, these are too fancy."

"But Reece is a gourmet," Grace said. "I wanted your event to celebrate his love of food."

"Oh, well, that's thoughtful," Sam said. "But can we celebrate a bit more plainly?" She held up a Waterford crystal shot glass filled with crab salad. "I don't want my friends to have to sell their cars to pay for something they broke."

"Good point," Harvey said and shoved his thick-framed glasses up his bulbous nose. "Let's have a taste." Hitching his trousers over his protruding belly, he sat awkwardly on an antique chair. "Cocktail food always looks fancy, even if it's beans on toast." With a wide smile, he put his elbows on the table and rubbed his hands together. "Dig in, everyone."

Reece didn't need to be asked twice. He loaded his plate with samples of everything and chatted amicably to Grace about seasonal ingredients and presentation. Harvey suggested lobster rolls rather than serving it as a terrine, which cheered Sam. They voted down the endive, and tweaked one or two other things until everyone, including Grace and Sam, was happy.

"I'll just nip out and powder my nose," Grace announced, with a smile. "Excuse me a moment."

Harvey patted Sam's hand as he watched his wife walk away. "Thank you," he said quietly. "Your mother couldn't be happier."

"How's her treatment going?" Sam asked. "She doesn't seem as confused as she did before you went to Sweden."

"The Alzheimer's specialist changed her medication," he said. "They're cautiously optimistic that it's slowing the progression of the disease. Since we came home, we take things day by day. She gets confused when she's tired, but having the wedding to focus on is the best medicine."

Sam sighed. "Look, I don't want to be difficult, but everything she's planning is too elaborate."

"Leave it with me and don't worry," Harvey said. "Now, tell me all about the clinical practicum."

Grace returned and sat beside Reece. She ran long fingers through her perfectly groomed black hair and arranged her skirt neatly across her knees. She was an attractive woman in her early sixties, tall and willowy with huge brown eyes and high cheekbones. Reece imagined she had been a knockout in her youth. Sam had inherited her gorgeous strawberry blonde curls, green eyes, and fierce loyalty from her Irish father. But her stubborn nature was all her mother. Reece listened with half an ear as Sam and Grace and Harvey chatted; it was nice to visit without the two women volleying critical remarks back and forth all evening.

"He's an arse," Grace suddenly exclaimed.

Reece hadn't been following the conversation and feared they were on the cusp of a nasty disagreement again.

Sam only looked surprised when she asked, "You know him?"

"Of course," Grace replied. "The man is unbearable, I tell you." She turned to her husband. "What's your opinion, dear?"

"If he weren't a neighbour, I'd have nothing to do with the twit," Harvey said.

"Mathias Beauregard lives on Millionaires' Row?" Sam asked, clearly bewildered.

"That's right." Harvey went to the bar, grabbed an open bottle of red wine, and brought it back to the table.

"But Emily Armstrong told me he hasn't any money to invest in the clinic," Sam said.

"Malarkey," Harvey replied with a snort of laughter. "He could have lost it all in some lowbrow venture, but he still lives in the house." He ran a hand across his bald crown. "Perhaps it's mortgaged to the hilt. What a cheerful thought."

"It wasn't his money," Grace added. "His wife inherited a massive trust fund from her late grandfather."

"I didn't know he was married," Sam said.

"To Adaline Beauregard of the Charleston Beauregards," Grace said. "Adaline died about five years ago. I don't recall the details. Do you, dear?"

"There was some sort of scandal." Harvey paused once more. "Drowned in their swimming pool, I believe, and it seems to me there were drugs involved and whispers of suicide."

"Beauregard is his wife's last name?" Sam asked.

Grace laughed. "He had little option but to adopt it, unless he wanted to marry a disinherited debutante, which was certainly not his intention."

"Didn't Mathias have some connection to the family?" Harvey asked Grace. "Grew up in the South, didn't he?"

"I don't know where he comes from," Grace said. "His medical degree is from Harvard." She wrinkled her nose. "He reminds us every time our paths cross at social events. We're supposed to be impressed." She turned to her daughter. "The man's an alley cat, watch yourself around him."

"No worries," Sam said with a smile. "He loathes me."

Grace turned to Reece. "How are you finding the Crown attorney's office?"

Reece explained his task, but his distaste must have shown on his face because Harvey patted his back.

"Your colleagues at Toronto Police Services won't hold it against you," Harvey said. "Even legacy officers miss things."

"Then why am I researching Judas's positive traits?" Reece asked bitterly.

Harvey laughed. "You aren't betraying coppers by digging into a few closed cases. They'll understand."

"Trust me, they don't," Reece said.

Detective Martina had been assigned the hate crime against Lydia, and he'd subsequently caught Annalise Huang's suicide case. Martina had quickly put the pieces together when he'd heard that Gretchen Dumont's articling student—who happened to be an ex-police inspector—had questioned Lydia at Cardoon. Reece suspected that Lydia had called Detective Martina herself. Based on how upset she was at the end of their chat, he should have reached out to Martina himself. Now, however, it appeared he was furtively snooping around, which was exactly what he'd feared when Gretchen had set this mess into motion.

"What do you think?" Harvey asked Sam. "Could Toronto be dealing with a vigilante?"

"Maybe," she said. "Social control vigilantes believe they're remedying a structural flaw in society," Sam said. "They rationalize the inflicting of punishment as social defence. So, there's opportunity—the killer can sit anonymously at a table in Cardoon Bistro to guard the special needs employees and stakeout targets."

"There's also means," Reece said. "Vigilantes stalk potential victims prior to allotting justice, which ties in with the drone."

"So, the transgression in the social order is the motive," Harvey concluded.

Reece nodded. "I want to turn my suspicions over to Toronto Police Services but my hands are tied. Identifying a crime pattern and apprehending a potential killer doesn't seem to be Gretchen's main objective."

Grace's eyes widened. "Gretchen Dumont is your articling principal?"

Reece nodded.

She turned to look at Sam. "What a coincidence. Gretchen Dumont is Mathias Beauregard's secret lover, although it's not so secret in our circle. They've been carrying on for years, which fed the scandal after Adaline's death."

Harvey was staring at Reece with a strange expression. "I didn't know you worked for Gretchen Dumont. That's unfortunate."

"Why?" Reece asked nervously.

"There's chatter on the political grapevine that the newly appointed deputy attorney general is investigating her," Harvey said grimly.

"Do you know why?" Reece asked him.

"Conflict of interest, breach of trust, and misuse of office. There may also be criminal charges forthcoming," Harvey said. "I hear she has a vendetta against Toronto Police Services."

That's why she'd told him to gather evidence under the shield of his PI agency. She could care less about a vigilante: she wanted to prove officer incompetency in the closed cases.

"Aren't the police and Crown attorney's office on the same side?" Grace asked.

Harvey rocked his hand in a *so-so* gesture. "Usually, but there was a federal inquest after the Frozen Statues fiasco and it was nasty. Both sides pointed fingers over where the negligence lay on the issue of Incubus's cabin."

"Who's Incubus?" Grace asked innocently.

The shocking question reminded Reece how insidious Alzheimer's was. Sam's sister, Joyce, had been one of the serial killer's victims. Due to the horror of the event and Grace's disease, she often forgot that Incubus had savagely murdered her elder daughter. When Grace was confused and asked where Joyce was, Harvey and Sam told her Joyce was holidaying in Europe.

Sam's clinical opinion was that stepping into her mother's reality with therapeutic fibbing was kinder than forcing her to experience the grief over and over again. So, Reece was not surprised now when Sam carried on the conversation without missing a beat.

"Incubus is an incarcerated serial killer," Sam said simply. "Five years ago—during Incubus's court case—his lawyer alleged that Toronto Police Services set a fire that destroyed his client's cabin," Sam explained, reaching for the bottle of wine. "Last winter, a copycat killed multiple university students and authorities missed an important link, because they believed the cabin had burned to the ground."

Sam offered Reece the bottle and he shook his head, but Grace lifted her glass. Sam sucked her lower lip, clearly conflicted over whether to give her mother more alcohol. Grace waved her glass impatiently, and Sam poured her half a glass.

"Since Gretchen Dumont was the prosecutor on Incubus's case five years ago, his lawyer briefed her about the pending civil suit over the alleged fire," Harvey continued. "The lawyer never filed his client's claim with the court, so Gretchen never verified what happened to the cabin."

"But Toronto Police Services were the plaintiffs in the threatened law suit," Reece said. "It was their responsibility to investigate. I don't see an issue."

"The chief of police claims Gretchen never told anyone about the law suit," Harvey said.

"But she swore under oath at the inquest that she disclosed the threat to him," Reece argued.

"Therein lies the problem," Harvey said.

Officials believed Gretchen had committed perjury. Reece felt ill. As an officer of the court, if Gretchen had lied under oath at the inquest, what else was she capable of?

"She's been on a mission to prove police misconduct and humiliate the chief of police ever since," Harvey concluded. "The chief is equally as driven to remove her from her position. Now he has the support of the deputy attorney general, it's going to get ugly."

"What will happen to Reece if they prosecute her?" Sam asked. "It's not going to look good that he's been snooping into a slew of closed cases behind the cops' backs."

"Well, he did it by order of his principal." Harvey's worried expression didn't support his encouraging words.

Gretchen would try to shift the blame onto him and assert she knew nothing about his investigation. Reece would have to *prove* he was following the direction of his myopic principal. There were no emails or witnesses to support his claim that she had ordered him to audit the cases for police due diligence. If she denied it, it would be his word against hers.

He'd disagreed with the unofficial approach of Gretchen's inquiry from the start. He should have outlined his concerns in an email so he had a paper trail. Instead, he'd focused on gathering evidence any way he could. Even if the deputy attorney general and chief of police believed she'd ordered the investigation, Reece hadn't been transparent with Toronto Police Services. He'd gone behind their backs and used his PI agency as a cover. The implication would be that he'd colluded with Gretchen in her quest to dishonour the police department. The optics would be that he'd betrayed the blue brethren to curry favour with a Crown attorney and advance his law career.

"Turn everything over to Bryce Mansfield." Sam told him and turned to Harvey. "Bryce is the inspector in charge of the homicide squad."

"If Reece shares confidential documents, he's in breach of his non-disclosure and confidentiality agreements," Harvey said. "Truthfully, he shouldn't be discussing it with us but nothing we speak about will leave this room."

"He has to do something," Sam insisted. "Presumed complicity in this vendetta will destroy his law career."

As the significance of the situation settled onto Reece's shoulders, he realized it was too late. He couldn't prove he wasn't a key player in a corrupt official's game.

Gretchen Dumont was going to ruin him and hand a prolific vigilante a licence to kill.

CHAPTER TWENTY

The Journal

MY FATHER WOULD not allow me to report Pearl's death. He grew increasingly irrational, ranting about indifferent strangers touching her, authorities investigating, and pathologists dissecting her. Outsiders would not pollute Pearl's final resting place with their prejudicial judgments and interference. Her interment would be private, conducted and attended by the people who had loved and understood her. As we had protected her in life, we would protect her in death. It was my filial duty, he said. I could not find the spirit or the words to disabuse him of the notion.

He handcrafted Pearl's casket from wild persimmon, polishing the wood until it gleamed. He toiled in solitude, refusing my offers of companionship and assistance. Furtively, I would observe him from the shadows outside his workshop, and inchoate pity would engulf me. Looking wan and much too thin in his tattered jeans, he laboured with hands that weren't quite steady. He was poised on the brink of a precipice, clinging to a scintilla of control, his only salvation this grisly labour of love. The drone of a radio delineated the catastrophic damage wrought by Hurricane Rita, but our grief was too raw for empathy.

Together, we tore down a section of the limestone wall that marked the lane to our property, and we built a small crypt to protect our beloved. We sealed her casket inside her tomb of stone beneath the ancient bald cypress she had loved.

I would not allow the murderous demon, conceived from the violence of rape, to rest beside Pearl for eternity. I swaddled the small body tight in white linen and ran with it along the banks of the Teche until I spotted the dark olive scales and yellow eyes of a floating gator. My hands trembled as I dangled my gruesome package over the water but I could not bring myself to drop it. This instrument of death that had purloined my sister's life deserved no better, yet a shred of humanity still existed within my withered heart. I faltered at the water's edge, clutching the baby to my chest, and sobbed as rain beat down. How I hated it for taking Pearl's life and how I hated myself for what it had driven me to become. Daggers of white lightning lit the horizon as I stumbled home and lurched into my father's workshop to thrust the shrouded corpse at him. He laid it gently in a box of cypress wood he'd crafted as its casket, refusing to meet my eyes.

Without Pearl, my mother surrendered to madness. She sat silently in her dead daughter's room, her eyes vacant, and her small white teeth gnawing mercilessly at the peeled and infected skin around her ragged cuticles. Tears of blood would surface against her shredded skin and dribble down her fingers to dapple her hands in crimson blossoms. When twilight ebbed, I would drape an eyelet comforter across her shoulders and sit quietly at her feet, watching her blood soak into the cuffs of her ivory nightgown.

Without my mother's love, my father reacquainted himself with the escapism of morphine. He'd disappear into the bayou, to the man he had so often warned me to avoid, returning with a hunger in his eyes and the poison clutched in his fist. He'd sit on the front porch in a rocker that faced the cypress tree that sheltered Pearl's crypt. Within seconds, sweet oblivion would eradicate the deep furrows of grief from his face. Yet occasionally, I could still glimpse a flicker of the man he used to be—a diaphanous shadow I chased but could not catch.

I planted a ring of bluehearts, Louisiana iris, and Queen Anne's lace around Pearl's eternal bed. On oppressive, starless nights, I'd lie beside her and imagine the sweet melody of her laughter. I'd envision our parents when they were whole, their bodies intimately coiled around each other as they waltzed. I'd imagine Pearl's white skirt floating on the water, her fingers tapping the rhythm of her words, her hair a radiant halo. I'd torture myself with a vivid montage, driving my mind to the brink of collapse, but I could not vanish into the warmth of madness as my mother had. Emotion would gather like black clouds above me and I'd stoke my blistering wrath until it choked my grief. Anger was my only reprieve from the incessant pain, and so I clutched it tight, vowing I would avenge my sister's murder.

The day I destroyed what was left of my family, my father was nodding in the rocker on the front porch, a bead of blood oozing from the crook of his arm. I rifled through his pockets and found a chain with a key to the lockbox he kept in the shed. It caught in the seam of his jeans. My hand slipped and knocked his chest. I waited, breath held, for him to jerk awake. If he had, I would have confessed my intention so he could persuade me to abandon the plan I had no true wish to execute. His head merely lolled against his shoulder and a string of drool dribbled off his chin. On a gentle breeze, I smelled a phantom fragrance of coconut oil and accepted that the task ahead of me was preordained.

In the shed, I took my father's .45 semi-automatic from the strongbox, loaded the weapon, and tucked it in the waistband of my jeans. My hands shook and doubt weakened my resolve, but I told myself that Basile Landry's money and reputation protected his son from justice. It was foolhardy to believe Virgile would not brutalize another innocent girl and ruin another innocent family.

I told myself that this was murder for the greater good.

Virgile brazenly updated his Facebook with every detail of his vile life, and I had stalked his timeline, waiting for an opportunity. Today, he had boasted about attending an illegal dogfight on a private section of the Bayou Teche. *Only by exclusive invitation,* he had written, as if inclusion at a blood sport was a symbol of merit.

It was a well-known fact that owners frequently shot their losing dogs, leaving the battered corpses for the gators. The despicable masses who sought entertainment in maltreated animals battling to the death would ignore a gunshot. Their only care was the dollars they'd bet on the grisly fight. If I was to kill Virgile Landry it had to be tonight, but misgivings again filled my heart. I ached for a sign from Pearl that she sanctioned my quest.

The sun dipped behind the cypress tree and the sunset hues of orange and gold rippled across the still water. A sultry breeze stroked my cheek, perfumed with the aroma of wildflowers from Pearl's grave. I glanced over my shoulder at our house. My eyes lingered wistfully on the silhouette of my father slumped in the porch rocker. At only sixteen, I was too young to shoulder this act of vengeance alone, yet honour compelled me to fulfill the death-bed promise I'd sworn to Pearl.

I followed the Teche for an hour until I spotted lights and heard bloodthirsty squeals of delight. A ghastly stench of blood and feces wafted on the breeze, and the pitiful yelps of the wounded animals made my stomach clench with rage. A circle of spectators three deep surrounded what I assumed was the fighting pit. Camcorders waggled above heads and fists pumped the air. A preteen girl crawled up the back of a middle-aged man to perch on his shoulders. He massaged her buttocks as she lifted her shirt to expose budding breasts.

I froze at the rear of the crowd, unable to move forward to see the dogs' terror and the betrayal in their woeful eyes as they fought to survive. I could not bear to stand witness to the atrocities perpetrated against these blameless animals.

A feral screech echoed from the pit, and the crowd howled and cheered. Bile filled my throat and gooseflesh prickled my arms. I staggered to the bushes and vomited burning acid, struggling to block out the rasping death knells of the beaten dog.

It took a moment for me to comprehend that there were people milling around me. The losers in the crowd had dispersed, while the winners collected their ill-gotten gains. Excited chatter drifted over me as the crowd clamoured for the next round, and I had to fight the urge to open fire and rid society of these dregs of humanity.

I mingled inconspicuously with the crowd and sauntered to a cluster of parked vehicles. I saw Virgile's black Hummer under a copse of oak trees. A quick reconnaissance of the area exposed a thicket of brush where I could lie in wait. I headed to my hiding spot but jerked to a stop when a voice called my name. Fortifying my nerve, I turned to face my prey.

"Hey, Virgile," I said.

"Well, well, well. Wonders never cease." He leaned close to my face, his breath reeking of bourbon and cigarettes. "Are you crashing our little party, Blu?"

Refusing to step back, I held his eyes. "I was out for a walk and heard the noise. Wanted to see what the excitement was about."

"How's that gorgeous retard sister of yours? Haven't seen her around town. Your pa keeping her on her back?" He laughed.

"She's dead," I stated. "So is your son."

He took a step back and his lips spread into a smile. "Y'all accusing me of something?"

"I know everything."

"Really? Brought the sheriff, did you?" He glanced around mockingly. "How about you and I have a chat?" He strolled toward the water, away from the sightlines of any stragglers leaving the dogfight.

My fingers grazed the butt of the gun in the small of my back and my heart jackhammered in my chest. Virgile led us further from the lights and commotion of the pit, unaware that every step brought him closer to death. His arrogance was boundless, a cloak of false protection that he wore with supercilious entitlement.

As I trudged behind him, fresh doubt suddenly rose unbidden in my mind. I saw the haunted expression in my father's eyes when he returned from Afghanistan. I heard him screaming from the nightmares that plagued him, his conscience unable to reconcile the lives he'd taken for his flag. I saw him in his shed, caressing his surgical instruments and pining for all he'd sacrificed.

A clairvoyant image of my future flashed across my mind. There would be no basketball scholarship, no university, and no medical school. There would only ever be cold darkness, wrought with more loneliness than I currently suffered. If I killed Virgile, I would not escape unscathed. Lying dormant inside me was my mother's insanity gene and my father's penchant for drugs. I understood now, with painful clarity, Pearl was showing me the truth. If I went through with this savage act, I would not survive the psychological aftermath. She didn't want me to sacrifice my life to avenge her death. She embodied love.

Pearl was begging me to find the strength to forgive.

Virgile leaned against the trunk of a cottonwood and folded his arms over his chest. "I've been watching y'all for years," he said in a conversational tone. "Watching how you took care of your crazy mother and sister. I used to sneak out at night and spy on you, see." He wagged his finger at me. "Naughty kid, in cahoots with a soldier for the mob." He smiled and lit a cigarette. "Cyril works for the New Orleans mob, but I guess you know that. He supplies your pa with his *medicine*." He wrapped the word in air quotes.

I turned to go. "See you later, Virgile."

"Wait, now—we're having a conversation," he said. "I think you'll be interested in what I'm going to tell you."

I ignored Pearl's beseeching voice in my head that begged me to walk away. I turned back to face him.

"How old were you when you were selling those nutria tails to Cyril?" Virgile asked in a pleasant tone. "Fifteen? You're a good shot, Blu. You know your way around a Remington." He flicked his cigarette into the water. "Let's play truth or dare. I'll go first. Pick your pleasure."

"Truth," I said and wished I had the strength to leave.

"I was hoping for that one." A cheerful smile lit his face and he swiped a lock of brown hair off his eye with a graceful finger. "One night, we spotted your sister outside. She was wearing a white nightgown and standing in the water, looking for you, I guess. The moon was shining down on her, and you could see *everything* through the sheer fabric. What a show for a horny young buck." He exhaled through pursed lips and waggled his eyebrows salaciously. "She came out almost every night. Instead of following you, we started watching her."

Blood pounded in my head in a wave of white noise. *Almost every night...* Why hadn't I anticipated her natural curiosity and desire to be with me? Why hadn't I locked her in her room on the nights I went hunting?

"I intended to wear a rubber but she fought, see. I hadn't expected her to." He shrugged. "I figured I could sweet-talk her and she'd submit. It's perfectly logical to expect a retard to go along but your sister screamed. That's when things took a nasty turn." He took the serrated hunting knife out of his pocket, flicking it open and closed, then open again.

Grief paralyzed me as moonlight glinted off the silver blade. The night Virgile raped Pearl had also been a full moon. Had she watched paralyzed, as I did now, while light shimmered against the deadly knife that slashed her flawless skin?

"The deeper I cut, the less she fought. She just lay there making these stupid little whimpers." He mimicked slashing, thrusting the knife across the air in front of him. "Not so much fun, see. So, I wrapped her nightgown around her neck. Then she bucked and writhed underneath me." He chuckled and rubbed the crotch of his jeans. "Looking into those huge eyes, all wet with tears, and feeling her blood all over my hands was such a rush." Virgile snickered. "I wrapped my fist around her hair and pulled." He reached into his pocket and held something out to me.

I stepped forward and froze. Grasped between his thumb and forefinger was a lock of long platinum hair, tied with a pink satin ribbon. My mind flashed to the bloody clump of hair that had lain on Pearl's naked shoulder when I found her. I remembered that the pink ribbon in the bodice of her nightgown had been missing.

"A little souvenir to remember our special night," Virgile said serenely. "Too bad we won't get an encore." He winked.

I leaned over and vomited across his shoes, the sick bathing my mouth in acid. Virgile jumped back, squealing in disgust.

My eyes felt hot and dry in the cloying humidity and a cold sweat chilled my arms. I moaned deep in my throat, unable to stop my mind from conjuring filmic images of Pearl's angst.

Virgile dipped the toes of his shoe in the Tech, one after the other, swirling them around to wash off my vomit. He was muttering something. For a panicked moment, I thought he was talking to someone before I realized he was mumbling to himself. This thing in front of me wasn't human. It was an abomination—a creature devoid of emotion or conscience.

From the direction of the dogfight, there was a high-pitched yowl and a gunshot.

A second shot rang out. A rosebud bloomed where Virgile's left eye had once been. His body pitched backward and he fell into the water.

My ears rang, and my arm fell to my side under the weight of the weapon I grasped. Confused, I stared at the gun in my trembling hand, bewildered by how it had gotten there, and unable to recall retrieving it or pulling the trigger. A sour taste of vomit coated my tongue and the humidity was stifling. I gasped to inhale the water-drenched air, feeling lightheaded and dizzy. Virgile's one sightless eye gaped up at the moon.

Like the dogs in the pit, a primitive survival instinct consumed me. Slowly, I clicked on the safety and tucked the gun into my belt. I circled Virgile's prone body, reached down, and grabbed his wrists. In jerking motions, I dragged him into the water. Once he began to float, I shoved his feet, propelling him further into the flowing Teche. He bobbed along the surface and I prayed to see the snapping jaws of a gator or hear the slap of a scaled tail. The only sounds were the hoots and hollers from the dogfight pit.

When Virgile's body vanished from my sightline, I turned and ran for home, avoiding the crowd and ensuring that I stayed hidden in the shadows of the trees along the banks of the Teche. My mind raced as I sprinted for the safety of home. Virgile's father would eventually report his monstrous son missing. If the gators smelled blood in the water and took the body, there would be no reason for the sheriff to suspect murder. I hadn't recognized anyone milling around, ergo no one had recognized me. My name was not amongst the invited. No one had witnessed me talking to Virgile, of that I was certain, so I had no need to fear anyone would offer a description to the police.

By the time I reached home, I had convinced myself that I was safe. I crawled into bed and closed my eyes, eager for the sanctuary of sleep. I felt no satisfaction, no guilt, and no regret. I felt nothing but the gentle kiss of a breeze through the open window. And then

I detected the whisper of Pearl's sweet voice from beneath the cypress tree, and I knew everything would be all right.

I drifted off to sleep as she sang me our Cajun lullaby.

CHAPTER TWENTY-ONE

SAM

SAM REMEMBERED CARDOON Bistro from the day of her interview at Serenity Clinic. When she'd bought the veteran a coffee and a sandwich, she'd been too anxious about her interview to pay attention to the restaurant's interior. She took a minute to look around, immediately understanding why the eatery intrigued Reece.

The bohemian style was charming and the aroma of rich coffee made her mouth water. Stunning prints—abstract, cubist, and surrealist—decorated every wall. Wildly coloured chairs, vintage light fixtures, and soft jazz music accented a carefree boho ambience. A chalkboard offered a selection of foodie delights, including a daily special of smoked-sturgeon cheesecake with caviar. It sounded disgusting to Sam, but Reece would salivate over it.

She spotted Aazar at a table for two and walked over to join him. She wasn't discounting him as an incestuous rapist, but he'd kept his word by contacting her to discuss his sister's blood results. The real test of his honesty, and perhaps his innocence, would be if he disclosed Fadiya's pregnancy.

A woman with a pronounced limp approached them and put a plate of multi-coloured macarons in the centre of the table. She removed a white china coffee pot from her tray and set two mugs, a pitcher of heavy cream, and a bowl of coloured sugar cubes beside the coffee pot.

Aazar waited until the server had left before he spoke. "Thank you for meeting me." He was wheezing softly, but seemed able to handle communication without too much physical distress. "I'd prefer no one at Serenity knew we were speaking."

"Why's that?" Sam asked, reaching for a purple macaron.

He slid a sheet of paper across the table.

She shoved the second half of her macaron into her mouth and glanced at the paper. "What am I looking at?"

"Fadiya's blood results," he said. "It's positive for ketamine, a drug primarily used during anesthesia. It induces a trance-like state and memory loss." He paused to catch his breath. "It's a psychoactive agent that can cause hallucinations and perceptual anomalies."

"Delusions," Sam said, pouring a mug of aromatic coffee for each of them.

"At first, I believed they were drugging her to prevent the lung lobe transplant," he said. "Cancer drugs cost patients tens of thousands of dollars a year. If I live long enough to complete my research, the pharmaceutical industry will suffer significant losses."

Sam had read that the top cancer medications generated annual revenues that exceeded two billion dollars. That was after the cost of research to develop the drugs. The global population would benefit from Aazar's scientific genius, but capitalistic pharmaceutical companies would not.

"You think Fadiya is a victim of mind-altering drugs as a plot to ensure your death?" Sam asked.

"I did, but now I fear it's much darker than that," he said.

"How so?"

"Fadiya is pregnant," he said. "I ran a quantitative beta HCG. Based on the levels, she's over eight weeks. You knew, didn't you?"

"I did." She put down her coffee mug. "There's missing CCTV footage from the camera outside her room. We're in the process of recovering the data." She paused, holding his level gaze. "When we do, we'll identify the rapist."

Aazar waved his hand dismissively. "She wasn't raped," he said. "Do you know about my illness and the living-donor transplants Fadiya has gifted to me?"

Sam nodded, curious where he was going.

"Human leukocyte antigens are proteins on the cells in the body," he said. "Out of one hundred different antigens, six are essential in organ transplantation. People inherit three from each parent. With the exception of identical twins, there's just a twenty-five percent chance of siblings being a six-antigen match." He adjusted his oxygen flow.

"So, it's lucky your sister is compatible." Sam reached for a pink macaron.

"Luck had nothing to do with it," he said grimly. "Fadiya was not conceived naturally. Genetic modification created a perfect DNA match."

She dropped the macaron onto her plate. "I don't understand."

"A geneticist edited the DNA of the germline and altered the contradictory hereditary factors to create a perfect match to me," Aazar explained. "They transferred the genetically engineered embryo into my mother. The stem cell transplant from Fadiya's umbilical cord blood put my disease into remission. The process also ensured they'd have access to a perfectly matched organ donor."

Sam understood where he was going. "You think a geneticist replicated the process and impregnated Fadiya with the embryo."

"Yes, because Fadiya has outlived her usefulness."

What he was suggesting entailed such gross medical malfeasance that it didn't warrant serious consideration.

"Human gene editing is illegal in Canada," Sam said. "You're talking about a conspiracy that would involve multiple highly skilled scientific experts. Why would these people risk their medical licences and prison?"

"Utilitarianism theory—the greatest amount of good for the greatest number," Aazar replied. "My work has the potential to eradicate cancer. Imagine what that means for millions of people."

"But why take this monumental risk when Fadiya's lung lobe can save you?" Sam argued.

"Every day that passes reduces my odds of surviving the surgery," he said. "Stem cells are the best chance for my disease."

"Then why not use a surrogate to carry the scientifically designed match?" Sam argued, unwilling to believe any doctor would use a mentally incompetent seventeen-year-old as an incubator.

"There are scientific reasons Fadiya is a perfect host, but if we're right, they need to minimize collusion," he said. "A surrogate might someday speak out. A raped, deluded patient minimizes risk of exposure."

"Someone at Serenity Clinic would have to be involved," Sam said. "It would be the only way to access Fadiya to administer the fertility medications, harvest her eggs, and implant the embryo."

"I have suspected for some time that something malevolent is going on in that clinic," he said. "My sister never suffered from delusional disorder, not until she arrived at Serenity."

"The court ruled her incompetent *before* your parents admitted her to Serenity," Sam said. "Why did the psychiatrist at the hospital testify that she was deluded?"

"Because I taught her how to fake her symptoms," Aazar said calmly.

His admission shocked her. "Why?"

"Fadiya had undergone multiple living donor operations by the time she was twelve," Aazar said. "A few days after authorities found her alive at Bueton, my parents consented to another transplant. I love my sister very much so I devised a plan to prevent further harvesting. I taught her to fake her mental illness so the court would revoke her right to consent."

"I agree that Fadiya has good days but the others are bad," Sam said. "She can't fake what I've witnessed."

"I agree," he said. "Someone at Serenity Clinic is drugging her with hallucinogens to mimic delusional disorder."

"Fadiya's allegiance to Mussani and Bueton is very real," she said patiently. "Your sister suffered complex trauma from her experiences in the cult. Her mental health issues are real, Aazar."

He leaned across the table. "Don't you see? Someone is using that trauma to control her. Whoever it is pretends to be Mussani. So long as Fadiya believes a dead man visits her, she'll never be free to make her own life choices," he stated with passion.

"I also believe that someone is impersonating Mussani," Sam said gently. "But the reason for the hallucinogens is that your sister is a victim of sexual assault. The drug keeps her docile during the attack and works to discredit her in the event she reports the assault."

Sam didn't disclose her suspicion that someone was selling his sister to multiple men, profiting from the sick fetishes of deranged predators.

"Before the pregnancy confirmation, I also feared that someone was violating Fadiya," he said. "I took measures to protect her."

"That's why you were sneaking into her room at night," Sam stated. "Did you tamper with the security camera outside her room?"

"You don't understand," he said in frustration. "I *wanted* them to know someone was in her room."

"Why?"

"To see if anyone would investigate. They didn't. I sat up there for an hour twice a week for over a month." He held her eyes and there was anger boiling in his. "Do you see?"

She did. Security monitored a live feed from the cameras. The night guard would have seen a stranger going into Fadiya's room. The guard protected the intruder by ensuring uninterrupted access to a vulnerable patient. Then the corrupt security officer removed any trace of the man's visit from the camera.

"The bribed guard witnessed you entering the lockdown unit and assumed you were connected with the person who pays him," Sam said.

"Because the co-conspirator believed I was with the medical team." Aazar's hand shook as he sipped from his coffee mug. "My sister is being used as a human incubator."

Sam didn't know what to think. If his theory was accurate, it didn't account for the bruises on Fadiya's body or her description of Mussani's visits.

"Wouldn't ketamine harm the baby?" she asked.

"Lengthy use of the drug could have a negative effect on brain development." He put down his coffee mug. "If they genetically engineered a child merely to sustain my life, do you think they'd care?"

"But how would they ensure Fadiya would carry the baby to term?" Sam asked. "When pregnancy follows a violent crime, abortion is many people's choice."

"So long as the court deems Fadiya incompetent, it won't be her decision," he said bitterly.

"I realize that, but your mother is her guardian and power of care. Won't she demand termination?"

"Muslim scholars hold that the child of rape is a legitimate child. That will be her excuse," he said with anger. "After the baby is born, my mother will assume guardianship of the child—a child she will use to sustain my life, the way she used Fadiya."

Sam felt her eyes widen. "You can't be suggesting that your parents are behind this?"

"Do you know what the name *Fadiya* means?" he asked.

Sam shook her head.

"Sacrificing saviour," Aazar said. "Why do you think my parents chose that name?"

Sam had considered it possible that Aazar's parents valued their son's life over their daughter's due to cultural and religious beliefs, but this was unspeakably evil.

"A great deal of money has exchanged hands to make this possible," Aazar said. "My father travelled unexpectedly to the Middle East in the spring. I believe it was to liquid international assets and wire-transfer the associated fees to off-shore accounts."

Sam was having a difficult time believing Fadiya's mysterious pregnancy was an elaborate plot orchestrated by corrupt scientists. Aazar's rationale was persuasive, but his immense intellect was ignoring the higher probability of rape—a terrible crime Sam had investigated too often when she'd been a cop. If Aazar had convinced Fadiya to fake delusional disorder, his guilt over putting her at risk must be crushing. Perhaps it was easier for him to fabricate wild theories than to accept that his sister was a victim of rape.

"You hold Dr. Armstrong in great esteem," Aazar said. "Is your resistance due to your admiration?"

"I've been an investigator for a long time," Sam said. "The simplest explanation is usually the right explanation. Evidence currently points to sexual assault, not an elaborate medical scheme."

Aazar picked up the blood report. "Ask Dr. Armstrong to test Fadiya's urine for ketamine," he said. "It can only be detected in blood for a few days, but it stays in the urine for over a week. If Dr. Armstrong denies its presence, will you consider my theory?"

"Fine," Sam said. "Give me the blood report."

He held it out. "My condition and treatment renders me impotent and sterile." He swallowed hard, and an expression of unmitigated revulsion twisted his features. "If you believe I violated my own sister, I will consent to a medical procedure to extract sperm. A seminogram will prove I'm infertile."

"That won't be necessary." Sam plucked the blood report from his hand and tucked it into her pocket.

She believed him. If he were guilty of incest, his reaction to her questions would have been much different. Everyone had a 'tell' when they lied—an unconscious and uncontrollable tic or body motion. Sam had spent years honing her skills to become a human lie detector. Either Aazar was a stone-cold psychopath or he was telling the truth.

"Thank you for hearing me." He stood, walked to the door, and exited the restaurant. A black SUV pulled up outside the door and a driver helped Aazar into the back seat.

Ugly conspiracy theories circled like vultures in Sam's mind. The medical and scientific industry needed Aazar Basha. They didn't need his sister.

If Aazar were right, after the baby's birth, Fadiya would be a serious liability.

CHAPTER TWENTY-TWO

Reece

REECE HAD BEEN awake most of the night, agonizing over what to do. His future father-in-law would only have shared the impending political nightmare if he were certain that his information was accurate. Reece had to accept the inevitable—Gretchen Dumont was about to be exposed for unprofessional, amoral, and possibly criminal conduct. Her vendetta against Toronto Police Services would taint Reece's investigation into a vigilante killer with unfounded bias and render his findings immaterial.

He had to get his investigation into the right hands. If he didn't, a killer would continue to hunt. He could accept any number of consequences, but he couldn't live with that.

His only option was to follow Sam's advice and reach out to Bryce Mansfield. Reece trusted the head of the homicide unit implicitly, but Bryce had excellent political contacts. He would have heard about Gretchen's quest to humiliate Toronto Police Services. Reece wasn't sure how Bryce would react to a speculative declaration from her articling student that a serial vigilante was hiding homicides as sudden deaths. Reece had to convince Bryce without impugning the officers who caught those cases.

Assuming he could persuade Bryce to take over the investigation, Reece would own his actions and confess his betrayal to Gretchen. She would fire him. He'd heard of a few articling students being canned by their principals. To the best of his knowledge, it had destroyed their future law careers. He supposed that was the least of his troubles. Breaching confidentiality could mean criminal charges. Ex-cops didn't fare well in prison but he saw no option. When he'd been with the provincial police, he'd made an oath to faithfully and impartially preserve the peace and prevent offences. His responsibility was clear, regardless of the personal consequences.

By seven o'clock in the morning, he'd made his decision and reached out to Bryce. It had taken a bit of persuading, and the promise of a Fancy Franks Coney Island dog, but Bryce agreed to meet him at noon.

Reece arrived at Sugar Beach Park fifteen minutes early. The two-acre urban park was busy. Parents and young children frolicked in the granite maple-leaf-splash pad, and sunbathers enjoyed the Muskoka beach chairs and bright pink umbrellas along the shores of Lake Ontario. Reece walked the promenade by the water's edge until he found an unoccupied bench. He sat and texted Bryce his location.

It was warm, with a nice breeze from the water, and the bright blue sky was freckled with cottony clouds. Mariners piloted giant yachts, slick sailboats, and small recreational crafts around the still waters of the lake. The ferry glided toward Toronto Island from the foot of Queen's Quay on the mainland. It was a beautiful summer day. Reece wished he could enjoy it rather than anticipating the implosion of his career.

A few minutes before noon, Bryce flopped onto the bench beside him. He stretched out his long legs and tugged at his tie. Streaks of grey highlighted his closely cropped dark hair, and his face had deeper lines than Reece remembered. Bryce wiped at the sweat on his forehead with the back of his hand.

"Want to tell me what I'm doing out here roasting my nuts in the middle of a work day?" he asked gruffly.

Reece handed him a greasy paper sack.

"You walk this puppy through the garden?" Bryce asked with a grin.

"And bought it a ring," Reece said.

Bryce took a giant bite of his hotdog and moaned. "Alice has me on a hippy, plant-based diet." He dug into the bag for an onion ring. "Never marry a woman half your age. The liabilities outnumber the benefits. How's Sam doing?"

"Good. She's working on her clinical practicum at Serenity Clinic over in Parkdale." Reece bit into his hotdog.

"Once she has that PhD, I hope she reconsiders her options. She'd make a hell of a great criminal analyst." Bryce shoved the second half of his hot dog into his mouth.

"Resigning from Toronto Police Services wouldn't be a great recommendation," Reece said.

"Water under the bridge," Bryce mumbled through a full mouth. "The work you guys did on the Frozen Statues case was stellar." His upper lip lifted into a sneer as he chewed. "Too bad your boss didn't have the common sense to check the status of that cabin. It would have resulted in fewer deaths." Bryce jammed his last four onion rings into his mouth.

Reece's lunch suddenly tasted like sawdust. He dropped his leftovers into the bag with the garbage.

"If you're throwing out half a Fancy Franks dog, whatever's going on must be earth shattering," Bryce said.

Reece reached for a file on the other side of the bench. He passed over the folder.

Bryce licked his fingers and took it from Reece's hand. "What's this?"

"Gretchen Dumont asked me to look into closed sudden-death cases," Reece said. "She was auditing police due diligence."

Bryce wiped his mouth and crushed his napkin in his fist. "That sounds like her."

"My sense is that she has a grudge against Toronto Police Services," Reece said, unwilling to bring Harvey into the discussion. "I don't know why."

"She's still trying to get out from under that cabin debacle by blaming us." Bryce waved the folder at Reece. "So, I ask again, what's this?" There was suspicion in his dark eyes.

"I found something that would be easy to miss," Reece said tactfully. "Different divisions caught the five suicide cases I'm looking at. You remember Danny, Eli Watson's sister?"

"Yeah. The computer genius. What about her?" Bryce opened the folder.

"She set up an algorithm of some sort. It found a weird commonality between at least five of the sudden-death cases," Reece explained. "I did a bit of legwork and have a theory. I want your opinion."

Bryce read in silence for a few minutes, then closed the folder and placed it on the bench. "You think a vigilante stalked these folks with a drone and executed them."

"Yes."

"You're saying these are homicides." Bryce stared across the lake, his body tense. "And every investigator involved missed it."

"They landed at different divisions. They appeared to be legitimate suicides," Reece said. "If I'd been the lead on any one of them, I wouldn't have made a connection either. It's when you look at them together that you see a pattern." He paused. "I'm positive there are more. Not just suicides, but accidental mishaps."

"And what does Ms. Dumont say about it?" Bryce asked tersely.

"Here's the thing, Bryce." Reece turned on the bench so he could speak directly to him. "I took an oath of office when I joined the provincial police. I still live by that vow." He pointed at the file between them. "These cases need to be reopened. It's the right thing to do for the victims and their families. I refuse to let politics get in the way of the public service promise I made years ago. I'm taking a leap of faith by involving you."

Bryce sighed and removed his sunglasses. "I'm assuming your boss told you to drop it. That's why I'm here."

"She told me to use our PI agency as a cover to gather evidence," he said.

"Evidence that would discredit the officers who handled these cases," Bryce said bitterly. "So, the rumours are true. She's fabricating misconduct and dereliction of duty charges against respected officers."

"I don't know what she's doing," Reece said truthfully. "But these cases need a second look. Your homicide unit has the skill and manpower."

"Reece, you have rigid principles. Some might even call you sanctimonious. Your fixation with the moral high ground is blinding you to the personal consequences." He held up the folder. "This isn't just insubordination; it could be construed as breach of confidentiality. That's an indictable offence. If the Crown attorney's office presses charges and can prove you liable, you're looking at prison time."

"I know." The magnitude of what faced him was daunting, but Reece straightened his back. "It's worth it if you can stop a killer."

"You're that certain these cases are homicides?" Bryce asked. "You're willing to throw yourself in the lion's den over this?"

"Someone has deemed himself judge and executioner and has committed multiple murders," Reece said passionately. "The killer has to be stopped and brought to justice before more people die."

"Contemptible, abusive people who are guilty of gross indignities against society," Bryce countered.

Reece understood he was playing devil's advocate, but it still angered him. "You know as well as I do that no one, under any circumstances, deserves to be murdered. Are you going to reopen these cases? Are you going to find this damn vigilante or not?"

Bryce sat quietly for a minute, gazing across the still water. He sighed and turned to face Reece. "Here's what we'll do. I'll run with this, but I'll keep it on the down-low and off the deputy attorney general's radar. In the event he finds out, or Gretchen Dumont guesses, I won't involve you. I'll say I ordered an audit of random closed cases and we found a possible connection."

Reece shook his head. "I won't be responsible for you lying."

His dad had been a Supreme Court judge, and Reece had learned his ethics at his knee. The measure of every man's character was his integrity and commitment to duty. Reece had breached his boss's trust and violated a non-disclosure and confidentiality agreement for the sake of justice. He would face the consequences, knowing his father's spirit would stand proudly by his side.

Bryce stood, tucking the file under his arm. "Our flawed legal system only survives because the noble stand to fight another day," he said. "I don't agree with you throwing yourself on your sword. That bitch will destroy you and possibly save herself in the process."

If Reece were lucky, the deputy attorney general would fire Gretchen before that happened, but he knew it was a pipe dream. Gretchen already suspected that the vultures were circling. She was a malicious and vindictive woman. She'd ruin him before she fell and hope his stained reputation cushioned her fall.

"Doing the right thing often comes at a high cost," Reece said.

As they walked to the parking lot, Bryce asked, "What are your plans?"

"I'll talk to Gretchen and then go to the law school." He was dreading both conversations. "My advisor might see a way to salvage my legal career."

At his car, Bryce held out his hand. "Thanks for the invitation to your wedding," he said. "Alice is chirping about seeing the famous Pietre estate on Millionaires' Row."

Reece shook his hand and forced a smile. "It'll be a wonderful day." Assuming he wasn't in jail.

Bryce removed his sunglasses and held out the folder. "You're sure about this? If what I hear is true, they're closing in on her. I can forget we talked, you know."

"This vigilante has been watching, judging, and executing for years," Reece said. "I feel it in my gut. The longer he stays hidden in the shadows, the greater the risk of escalation."

"When the shit hits the fan, Reece, if there's anything I can do to help, you know where to find me," Bryce said.

"Find this killer and it'll be worth whatever is coming my way." Reece got in his car before he changed his mind.

CHAPTER TWENTY-THREE

The Journal

LIFE SELDOM UNRAVELS the way we hope or plan. There are so many little details that we fail to grasp in the heat of battle. Looking back, I see with perfect clarity that my first mistake with Virgile was that I lacked a methodical and skillful execution style. Back then, I held the capacity to appreciate the finality of my conduct and to feel moral doubt. Without cold-blooded detachment, one makes mistakes.

The gators did not take Virgile's body. I hadn't pushed him far enough into the Teche. He drifted less than ten yards downstream before coming to rest in a nest of cypress tree roots. A bayou tour guide found the body the next day. Within a week, the media reported that the coroner's ruling in Virgile Landry's death was homicide by gunshot.

I had meticulously cleaned the gun and returned it to the shed, but I feared forensics could match the bullet. I had to dispose of the weapon. Should the sheriff trace licenced .45 semi-automatics in the parish, my father could honestly say he didn't know what happened to his gun. The last he'd seen it was the night of Hurricane Rita, the night before he fell off the wagon and had succumbed to the blissful oblivion of morphine.

My father had painstakingly climbed back on that miserable wagon and was now shrugging the monkey from his back again with fierce resolve. He claimed he had the flu—a determined bug, he said with a smile when I voiced concern. His complexion was sallow and his bloodshot eyes rheumy as he continually snuffled into a damp tissue. Perspiration coated his forehead and neck, but even in his customary long-sleeved shirts, his arms trembled with chills. I recognized the symptoms of withdrawal from the previous time he had gone cold turkey. I could do nothing to minimize his physical pain and depression. Only time would ease his suffering.

For a reason I didn't understand at the time, my father tore off the southeast-facing wall of the shed and rebuilt it. There was no opportunity to fetch the weapon I desperately needed to dispose of. He worked long into the night and I cared alone for my mother the best I could.

Every night, I'd lie beside Pearl's tomb, sleep an elusive craving, and fear would seep into my heart. My certainty that no one had seen me with Virgile began to wane. In lucid dreams, my semi-conscious mind would narrate in Virgile's rasping drawl his vile tale of rape and violence. I would jerk awake with an uneasy feeling that I had missed something, but I couldn't grasp the threat my subconscious mind insisted was there.

Until Pearl whispered the truth.

One night, we *spotted your sister outside.*

I had disregarded the pronoun at the time, consumed by the horror of Virgile's satisfied confession.

Too bad we *won't get an encore,* he had said in response to learning of her death.

Someone had accompanied Virgile on his midnight expeditions to our bayou oasis. Someone had been with him the night he raped Pearl. That person knew I had a motive to kill Virgile, and I had no way to protect myself from this faceless stranger.

A week into his 'flu', my father woke me early and suggested we sink some crawfish traps. He had a hankering for étouffée, he said. He was a shadow of his former self, yet a ray of hope flickered in my heart. It was the first time since Pearl's death that he'd exhibited an interest in anything other than the poison he religiously pumped into his veins.

He treated the infection in my mother's fingers from her compulsive gnawing and wrapped snowy gauze around them in thick mittens to prevent her from tearing at the swollen skin. He dressed her in a blue shift and brushed coconut oil into her long hair until it shone silver in the morning light. As he tucked her into the mud boat and pushed it through the shallow water, my tiny ray of hope blossomed into a warm sunbeam. Without Pearl, our family would never be whole again, but I naively believed on that beautiful day that we might rise like phoenixes from the ashes of our misery.

Late that afternoon, I was heating oil in a pot to fry hush puppies when a sheriff's car drove into the dirt yard. My father paused in stirring a simmering pot of crawfish étouffée and wiped his hands on a dishrag. Basile Landry climbed from the passenger side, circled the cruiser, and joined a uniformed sheriff at the base of our front steps. My father's expression was difficult to decipher, but I sensed acceptance and a coiled readiness that escaped my understanding.

"Stay with your mother," he told me, and walked to the door, his prosthetic clumping unnaturally on the wood floor.

SHADOW TAG, PERDITION GAMES

As the two men climbed the steep steps, my father stood waiting on the wraparound porch. I dawdled by the open window, hovering in the deep shadows out of sight. Basile's complexion was pale, as if bleached by sunlight, and grief had aged him unkindly. He was fat as a prize hog, and dark perspiration stained the pits of his short-sleeved white shirt.

My father shook his hand. "I was shocked to hear about your son," he said. "Deepest condolences to your family, Basile."

The man's lip curled into a snarl of contempt and he grunted a few incomprehensible syllables.

"Remy, you look unwell," the sheriff said, removing his hat. "I apologize if we caught you at a bad time."

My father brushed aside his concern. "We have the flu in the house. Been running its course." He tugged down his long sleeves and wiped his nose with the knuckle of his forefinger.

"Lord, but it's hot for this time of year. How's the wife?" the sheriff asked politely.

"No complaints. She and Pearl are—"

"We're here about my boy," Basile interrupted. "You own a .45 semi-automatic, right?"

My father nodded. "Did. Don't anymore."

Basile's smirk was incredulous. "You saying someone stole it?" He turned to the sheriff. "Stolen gun requires reporting, doesn't it?"

My father held up his hand. "Rita took it, along with half my work shed and pretty much everything inside."

My father knows what I did, I thought from behind the safety of the window glass. *He got clean and set about manufacturing a plan to protect me*. I had no idea how he had discovered my crime or why he hadn't confronted me. White-hot panic flooded over me as I continued to eavesdrop.

The sheriff mopped his sweating face with a grubby handkerchief. "Well, that howling bitch Rita took a chunk of St. Martin Parish with her. But why didn't you let me know?" he asked in a bemused tone.

My father shrugged. "Figured y'all had enough to worry about. Lots of folks suffered worse. What's this all about?"

Basile blew air through his puckered lips. It was a gesture so similar to his deceased son's mannerism on the night I'd killed him that my heart skipped a beat.

"Someone shot my Virgile with a .45 semi-automatic, and it's pretty convenient yours is missing," Basile declared. "Is Blu at home?"

My father ignored him and spoke to the sheriff. "You can't be suggesting I shot Virgile. Why would I?"

The sheriff shuffled his feet. "Well, it seems the afternoon before Rita made landfall, Virgile and Blu had words outside the hardware store. Witnesses say it got ugly. I'd appreciate a word with Blu just to ease Mr. Landry's mind."

My father called my name and I took a steadying breath before joining them on the porch. From ground level, Pearl's crypt under the cypress tree looked like an odd but innocuous garden decoration. From the high porch, though, it looked exactly like a tomb. If either of them glanced behind them, there would be more questions to answer.

"Go ahead and tell the sheriff what happened with my boy back in September," Basile ordered me. He puffed out his chest and planted his fists on his thick waist. "Before you get to lying, you remember I was there."

"Nothing odd happened," I replied passively. "I don't want to speak poorly about your son, but what you overheard him saying to me was nothing out of the ordinary. Virgile was a straight-up bully."

From my peripheral vision, I glimpsed a slight nod of agreement from the sheriff.

Basile's piggy eyes narrowed until they all but disappeared into the rolls of fat on his face. "You were at that dogfight. You gonna deny that fact?"

"What dogfight?"

"The one my Virgile attended on the night he was murdered!" Basile yelled. "It was just over yonder from here. Folks say they saw you." His chin tilted slightly and the tip of his tongue flicked over the corner of his lips.

My biology teacher had claimed that the human brain contains a reptilian throwback gene that enables us to decipher imperceptible nuances in body language when survival instinct heightens our senses. I believed I had indisputable evidence to prove that hypothesis, because I was certain Basile was lying. I hadn't recognized anyone. Ergo, no one had recognized me. It was such a childish conclusion to reach, I realize now, as if I could close my eyes and become invisible.

"I'm not into blood sports, and I've got no interest in associating with people who get off watching them," I retorted.

"Blu," my father murmured, and put a hand on my shoulder. "Basile, I can't express how sorry I am about your boy. No parent should suffer the loss of a child." His voice was thick with emotion and he swiped at his eyes. "Especially not to violence."

"I want to see that shed you claim Rita took," Basile stated.

My father nodded. "My leg is acting up some, but you help yourself. You'll see I had to rebuild two walls."

"I'll meet you down there," the sheriff said, patting Basile on his wide back. "I'd like a private word with Remy and Blu."

Basile marched down the stairs, throwing a scathing look over his shoulder. From the ground, he shouted up to me, "I know you killed my boy." He pointed a sausage finger at me. "Mark my words, you and your family will pay for what you did. I'll see to it."

The sheriff sighed. "Blu, you sure you weren't around that dog-fight? Maybe heard the ruckus and went to see what was going on?"

I shook my head. My tongue was thick and dry with fear.

"Virgile's brother claims you accused him of raping Pearl," the sheriff said with another sigh. "What you said about Virgile being a nasty piece of work is true. Did that miserable son-of-a-bitch touch Pearl? I know she's expecting. Saw her at the Breaux Bridge Crawfish Festival back in the spring." His eyes drilled into mine and I saw not an ounce of compassion toward my sister, regardless of the slight he'd made against Virgile's character.

My father clenched my shoulder and I remained silent.

"It was a boy from Savannah," my father said briskly. "The wife took Pearl for a visit. My daughter became smitten by a young man at the hotel. There was nothing sordid about it. Pearl told Blu all about her romance, so Landry's accusation doesn't make sense."

"Mind if I have a word with Pearl?" the sheriff asked.

The pressure on my shoulder tightened. "I do," my dad said evenly. "Pearl lost the baby—a third trimester miscarriage. She's had a difficult time. I don't want her upset."

The sheriff studied us silently for what felt like a full minute. "Remy, I'll respect your wishes as Pearl's father. For now," he added ominously. He wiped the sweat from the brim of his hat and replaced it over his coarse black hair. "They have folks over at the Department of Children and Family Services who have experience with autism. If we need to pursue this to satisfy Basile, I'll arrange for a specialist to talk with Pearl."

"If it comes to that, they're welcome to try," my father said. "But I'm asking you to keep my daughter out of this nonsense. I understand Basile's grieving, but I fought for our freedoms and know my rights. There are laws against bearing false witness. Money doesn't change that fact."

The sheriff nodded. "I hear that." He stared through the screen door, twisting his neck to get a better look inside the house. "Something sure smells good."

"Étouffée and hush puppies," I said, moving to block his view.

When neither my father nor I invited him in for a quick taste, he looked pointedly at my father's ugly prosthetic. "Remy, I've been meaning to thank you for your service to our country. I know things haven't been easy for you since your return." His eyes roamed meaningfully over my father's long-sleeved shirt.

My father nodded in acknowledgement but didn't respond.

"Good luck with the flu, Remy." He patted my father's shoulder. "Ride it out and keep the faith," he said with a wink. "Y'all have a good day, and enjoy your dinner."

We watched in silence from the high porch as the two men poked around the rebuilt shed, Basile Landry becoming irate and agitated. Finally, the sheriff turned and sauntered to his cruiser with Landry stomping along behind him. The sheriff gazed up at us for a moment and then lifted his hand in a mock salute. My father waved back, but my arm stayed frozen by my side.

"Who saw me?" I asked quietly.

"Cyril." My father continued to stare at the cloud of dirt that rose from the back of the sheriff's retreating car. "At least he's the one who told me."

"He runs the dogfights," I said, cursing my stupidity.

Anything illegal and immoral in the parish fell under Cyril's purview. He would have recognized me from the days when I'd sold him the nutria tails.

"I didn't accuse Virgile until that night," I said. "His brother's lying."

"It's more likely Basile who's lying. His elder son doesn't have the backbone to stand up to his father. He'll swear a statement if Basile orders him to," my father replied with no expression. "There's no coming back from this. Not for any of us." He turned his back on me and the screen door slammed behind him.

I had brought the authorities to our doorstep. They would return and find Pearl. That discovery would explode the tenuous shards that remained of our lives.

The only thing that would ever rise from the ashes of my family's destruction was a killer, and I accepted that had always been my destiny.

CHAPTER TWENTY-FOUR

Sam

EMILY SAT MUTE and expressionless while Sam explained Aazar's allegations and his theory on Fadiya's pregnancy. After the debriefing, Emily lowered her head and fiddled with her Montblanc fountain pen, twirling it between her fingers like a mini baton. Sam waited for her mentor to express outrage or to ask questions—anything that would fray the uncomfortable veil of silence that hung between them. Emily dropped the blood report on the table with a grimace and rubbed her hand across her tan slacks, as if desperate to cleanse it of something vile.

Unable to withstand the silence any longer, Sam asked, "Can you think of a therapeutic reason Fadiya would be given ketamine?"

"No."

"Do you have any reason to believe she had a pre-existing drug problem?" Sam asked.

"No."

The response didn't surprise Sam. Fadiya's parents had institutionalized her directly after her rescue from Bueton. Mussani hadn't permit the use of unsanctioned drugs and the compound dogs had ensured that his followers abided by the rule. If the dogs detected drugs on a cult member, Mussani's punishment had been merciless.

"Do you keep ketamine here in the clinic?" Sam asked.

"No."

"Did you know Mrs. Basha underwent IVF to genetically engineer a DNA match to Aazar?"

A muscle above Emily's eye twitched. "Yes."

Sam tried to keep her tone neutral. "Is it possible it happened again, except Fadiya is the host this time?"

"No."

"Why's that?" Sam asked, annoyed by the monosyllable responses.

Emily held up her hands to emphasis the absurdity of the suggestion. "Harvesting eggs is a surgical procedure, one that we aren't equipped to undertake here."

"I've read about egg retrieval," Sam said. "All they'd need is sedation and a portable ultrasound machine. Egg aspiration only takes about ten minutes."

"You're talking about a delicate technique executed by a highly trained specialist." Emily shook her head in denial. "Fadiya is a mentally incapacitated teenager, legally unable to provide consent. Not to mention that human gene editing is illegal in this country. No doctor would risk his medical licence and a prison sentence in a desperate attempt to save a scientific prodigy. It's a ridiculous notion that doesn't warrant discussion."

Sam decided to take a different approach. "How do you explain ketamine in her blood?"

"I don't know if that report is real." Emily pointed a trembling finger at the sheet of paper on the table. "Even if it is legitimate, there's no guarantee that it was Fadiya's blood."

"Will you do a urine test?" Sam asked.

Emily's shoulders tightened. "Fine." She crossed her arms over her chest. "I'll ask a nurse to collect urine."

The doctor's hostile behaviour bewildered Sam. "Since Aazar knows about the pregnancy, we have to disclose it to Fadiya's parents," she said.

"Her father is in the Middle East on business," Emily said tersely. "I was waiting for his return but Mrs. Basha told me he plans to remain for another month. I had every intention of telling her today."

"I'd like to be there when you speak to her," Sam said.

"Why?" Emily stood and paced the small office. "So you can tell her that someone in this clinic conspired with outside forces to illegally impregnate her daughter with a genetically modified embryo?" She jammed her hands into the pockets of her lab coat. "We have no evidence. All you have is the paranoid rantings of a young man who is fighting a terminal disease."

"I understand that this is—"

"Are you going to tell Mrs. Basha that someone in this clinic is using mind-altering drugs to rape her daughter? Or, maybe it's your theory on sex trafficking you plan to share." Emily turned her back and strode across the office to her desk. "Innuendoes—that's all you have." She turned and faced Sam once more, with her desk a protective barricade between them. "An outrageous supposition like this will spiral into an unfounded scandal that will destroy my life's work."

"Emily, I'm not the bad guy here," Sam said calmly. "Fadiya is pregnant. Discovering the truth is the only way to ensure that the female patients at this clinic are safe. I know that's your main objective too."

"This is an unmitigated disaster that will close my clinic and blemish the integrity of all my years of research—research that has developed innovative and successful treatment options," Emily said bitterly. "A sex trafficking ring—operating under my nose and most likely perpetrated by someone I hired—or gross medical negligence." She laughed humourlessly. "I can't get my head around which is more loathsome."

"The only way to limit the damage to your reputation is to uncover the truth," Sam said.

"Mathias warned me not to dig into this," Emily said, her voice quivering. "He begged me to deal with the problem discreetly. I should have listened to him."

Sam slumped against her chair in shock. "Are you saying he wanted you to secretly abort the pregnancy?"

"Wouldn't that have been best for everyone?"

"You can't believe that," Sam said, shaking her head. "You're talking about covering up a crime."

"You could still investigate and identify the rapist." Emily licked her lips rapidly. "We'd save Fadiya and her family unnecessary angst. No one needs to know about the pregnancy."

"I'm not obstructing justice," Sam said coolly. "Aazar knows about the pregnancy, and others may as well because they made a monumental effort at high risk to guarantee it." She breathed deeply to reign in her anger. "Look, based on Mrs. Basha's reaction to the news, we may be able to uncover the truth."

Emily stared at her with her mouth agape. "You can't possibly think that Mrs. Basha is the mastermind behind this gene editing scheme?"

Sam shrugged. "It would take money to accomplish. She's put her son's health ahead of her daughter's welfare many times. Living donor transplants are complex surgeries with significant risks to the donor. Surgeons preformed multiple procedures before Fadiya had even hit adolescence." She held Emily's eyes. "What does that say about her mother's love?"

Emily crossed the room and collapsed onto the sofa. She put her face in her hands.

Sam moved from her chair to sit beside her. "Did you really consider following Mathias's advice and aborting the pregnancy?"

"Of course not," Emily said. "The suggestion disgusted me." She looked up and took Sam's hand. "I am so sorry. This isn't your fault and I've been awful to you. I'm exhausted, but that's no excuse for my terrible behaviour." Tears filled her large hazel eyes. "I'd like it very much if you'd be with me when I tell Mrs. Basha."

Emily was facing a gruelling government inquiry, a public shaming, and the destruction of her reputation. The Canadian Medical Association could potentially strip her of her licence to practice. It was little wonder, Sam realized, that the celebrated doctor's first reaction was to scramble to find a way to save her life's work.

Sam squeezed her fingers. "I understand. We'll get to the truth, I promise."

"How is Fadiya?" Emily asked, wiping her eyes with a tissue.

"During our session this morning, she was lucid again. She continued to discuss Mussani visiting her at night." Sam paused to organize her thoughts. "Her story of a single, cloaked brother accompanying him and the series of events leading to Mussani's visits are consistent. She hasn't deviated from her version or altered a single fact."

"Deluded patients often stick to the same story," Emily said.

Sam shook her head. "But Fadiya is questioning the omitted sacraments, which are details only a Bueton member would know. That doesn't fit with delusional disorder."

"It doesn't," Emily agreed with a frown. "When you challenge a delusion, the patient typically embellishes it to justify the point you disputed."

"Fadiya is challenging it herself," Sam said. "The missing elements confuse her but the details of Mussani's visit never waver. Someone brings men to her room."

"And they can't replicate the sexual ceremony because they don't know the secret rituals." For the first time, Emily sounded as if she believed what Sam had been trying to tell her. "But I'm struggling to believe Fadiya faked her symptoms," Emily said. "I would have picked up on it."

"Fadiya wasn't in your care when the courts ruled her incompetent," Sam said. "Her parents transferred her from the hospital after the diagnosis was in place."

Emily vigorously shook her head. "I reassessed her. I'm telling you, she met the criteria for delusional disorder."

"I don't doubt that," Sam said. "Fadiya suffered complex trauma in the cult. I was undercover there for only a short time, and it took me months to deal with what I endured in that compound." She swallowed hard, quickly stuffing the emerging memories to the back of her mind. "Regardless of what Aazar taught her and the ketamine, Fadiya isn't stable."

"PTSD would account for some of the clinical aspects of psychosis I witnessed," Emily said. "Combine that with the adverse effects of periodical ketamine drugging, and it's possible I made a diagnostic error."

Sam respected her willingness to consider that she made a mistake. Must doctors of her caliber were too arrogant to entertain the idea.

"What do you know about ketamine?" Sam asked. "Why choose that drug?"

Emily thought for a minute, again twirling the pen she held. "It's fast acting and the trance-like state and memory loss last for less than an hour. As the drug wears off, a patient can present with psychological signs like confusion and hallucinations."

"And that would have led you to believe she was deluded, which would discredit any allegation she might make," Sam concluded.

Emily nodded. "The after-effects of the drug differ between patients, but they can present like delusional disorder." She stared out the window. "If they're administering the drug sporadically, it explains why she's lucid a lot of the time. Based on her symptoms, they're still giving it to her."

"Someone should be with Fadiya at night," Sam said.

"I agree." Emily's expression darkened. "I don't know who we can trust. What about Ophelia? I can ask her to switch to night shift and sit with Fadiya."

"Can you think of a plausible excuse as to why you want her in the room?" Sam asked.

"I'll say Mrs. Basha requested it," Emily said. "They were discussing private nursing a while ago."

"It's best not to tell Dr. Beauregard what we've discussed today," Sam said.

"You can't think he's behind any of this." The shock on Emily's face was genuine.

"Did you know he lives on the Bridle Path?" Sam asked.

"No."

"Did you know he was married?" Sam asked.

Emily nodded. "Widowed. His wife died about five years ago. Why?"

"Adaline Beauregard was exceptionally wealthy. Mathias inherited her estate," Sam said.

The news appeared to trouble Emily. "He's always been tight with a dollar, but it disturbs me that he lied about his inability to invest in our clinic."

"I don't know what his financial situation is currently, but I'm looking into it," Sam said.

"He more than makes up for his personal lack of investment," Emily said, perhaps reading disquietude in Sam's face. "Mathias is able to connect with potential investors on a personal level. He's gifted at persuading them to see our vision."

Emily seemed oblivious to the fact she'd just described a con artist. They succeeded because of their ability to appeal to their marks. They were calculated, cunning people who exuded confidence. Just like Mathias Beauregard. Sam didn't view manipulation as a redeeming quality.

"It worries me that he wanted to terminate the pregnancy and cover it up," Sam said, watching Emily's reaction.

"It was a knee-jerk reaction to a crisis," she replied dismissively. "Mathias wouldn't have followed through with it any more than I would have allowed him to."

"He was very determined not to put a camera in Fadiya's room," Sam said.

Emily shrugged. "He stands by his principles and strongly believes that in-room cameras breach the patient's trust," she said. "When it comes to our patients, he's very dedicated and refuses to sway from his medical values."

Sam had witnessed that bullheaded arrogance herself but her gut told her that Mathias's values served him first and foremost. After speaking with her stepfather, who saw the good in everyone, Sam's opinion of Mathias Beauregard had dropped even further. It was possible that her personal bias against the odious little man was tainting her objectivity but she intended to trust her gut.

"Please don't discuss this with him," Sam insisted. "The fewer people who know what we're investigating, the better."

"Benjamin Franklin: *Three can keep a secret, if two of them are dead.*" Emily reached to answer her phone. She listened for a moment, then thanked the caller and stood. "Mrs. Basha and Aazar are waiting in the board room." She held her hand out to Sam. "Again, I'm so sorry for my unprofessional and emotional reaction. Are we okay?"

There were thin lines on Emily's face that hadn't been there a week ago. Her skin was dry, with small scaly patches around the corners of her lips. Red streaks tinged the whites of her eyes, and the skin beneath was discoloured and puffy. Her trousers hung loosely against her hips, and beneath her white silk blouse, her collarbones were pronounced. Emily was under tremendous stress, and Sam wasn't going to hold a lapse of judgment against the exhausted woman.

"We're fine," she said sincerely.

Emily blew out her breath with a weak smile and straightened her back. "Let's do this."

They walked to the end of a long corridor and entered the boardroom, where Aazar sat across from his mother. Emily chose a chair at the head of the long table, flanked by the family. Sam sat beside Aazar so she could watch Mrs. Basha, not that she'd discern much. The pale blue shuttlecock burka would make it impossible to judge the woman's reaction to the news of her daughter's pregnancy.

"I'm afraid we have bad news to share," Emily said directly.

Mrs. Basha turned her body so the mesh of her head covering faced the doctor.

"Fadiya is pregnant, nine weeks now," Emily said. "At this time, we're unable to verify how it happened. There is missing CCTV footage from the lockdown unit. We believe the perpetrator came up the stairwell and through the fire door, thus avoiding the nurses' station and the alarms on the elevator."

Mrs. Basha sat frozen and silent. Sam couldn't tell if it was shock or some other emotion that rendered her paralyzed and speechless.

"Did you know?" Aazar asked his mother.

Her head swivelled in his direction. "Know? How would I know?" Her voice sounded choked and there was a hint of hysteria in its high-pitched tone.

"Did you pay a geneticist to create a DNA match to me?" He fired the question at his mother, his voice rising. "Did you implant the embryo in my sister's womb?"

"Allah has commanded you to treat your parents with utmost respect, no matter the situation." Mrs. Basha's voice caught before she softly added, "Paradise lies under the feet of the mother."

"Don't quote the Prophet Muhammad to me." Aazar lowered his voice. "Please, *Tāyi*, answer the question."

"I did not do this awful thing you accuse me of," she murmured.

"Islamic jurisprudence does not encourage abortion, but there is no direct biblical prohibition," Aazar said to Emily. He directed his next comment to his mother. "We will proceed with an abortion, yes?"

"Islamic law recognizes a fetus in the womb as a human life," Mrs. Basha stated.

"One hundred and twenty days have not lapsed," Aazar responded. "Many scholars allow victims of rape to abort before ensoulment occurs."

"No," Mrs. Basha said. "The child of rape is a legitimate child."

"Rape is a violation of divine law," Aazar argued. "Fadiya will have an abortion."

"No," Mrs. Basha repeated. "I have spoken and you will obey my decision." She turned her attention to Emily. "Aazar's specialist will perform a test to ascertain whether the fetus is a match for stem cell transplant. We will pay all costs associated with transporting Fadiya to Princess Margaret Cancer Unit for the procedure."

The colour drained from Aazar's already pale face. "You can't do this." His breathing was shallow, and he was wheezing from the exertion that it took to speak. "You will bring shame to her in our community. It will prevent Fadiya from marrying." Aazar suddenly smacked his palm against the table, causing his mother to jump. "Fadiya will have an abortion now, before Islamic law prohibits it."

"No. You must survive long enough to conclude your research," his mother said. "Allah has sent us this child, a child who may hold the power to save your life. Allah sent you to end cancer, Aazar."

"If it were Allah's intent for me to eradicate cancer, Allah wouldn't have given me leukemia," Aazar argued. "Please, put Fadiya's life ahead of mine."

"Allah sent Fadiya to save you," she said stubbornly. "This is what your sister would want."

"You cannot believe Allah sent a rapist to violate Fadiya," Aazar shouted.

"The blood sampling may not support stem cell transplant," Emily said reasonably. "How soon can you arrange it?"

"I will contact our specialist immediately," Mrs. Basha said.

Aazar struggled to his feet, looping the strap of his oxygen backpack over one thin shoulder. "I will not consent to any medical procedure that uses any part of that child."

"Aazar, I—"

He held up a shaking palm to silence his mother. "If I'm meant to finish my research, I will survive long enough to do so. I will not allow Fadiya or this child to be used as spare parts," he said bitterly.

Sam watched him exit the boardroom. The depth of his love for his sister and the sacrifice he was making to protect Fadiya awed her. She realized that Fadiya might feel the same way about her brother. Court ruling aside, the girl had the right to choose.

They needed to tell her the truth. About everything.

CHAPTER TWENTY-FIVE

REECE

REECE DROPPED HIS heavy bags on the kitchen island and crouched down to unclip Pepin's leash. The puppy scooted to his water fountain and eagerly lapped the cold water before collapsing onto the cooling pad in his crate.

"Sorry, boy," Reece said. "Too vigorous a walk on such a hot day."

He'd hoped that exercise would have sweated away the dismal sense of impending doom that shrouded him. It hadn't worked. Maybe he should have hit the gym, but he wasn't in the mood to suffer anyone's company. He took his phone from his pocket and stashed it on the antique church altar by the front door.

Out of sight, out of mind.

But he could still see it, sitting on the sloping top of the lectern like a black slug. He had to fight an intense desire to hurl it against the exposed brick wall.

For a long time after his family died, he had used anger as a barrier to protect him from tumbling into the beckoning pit of depression. It had taken a lot of therapy to move through the stages of grief, but anger had continued to be there as a warm shelter whenever his life spiralled out of control. Reece had learned anger management tools, though, and the beast rarely pounced from its iron cage. Most people didn't have a clue that he battled it more often than he'd like to admit. Today was one of those days.

He'd expected Gretchen to be angry. What he hadn't bargained for was the unprofessional personal attack that she'd launched at him with precise aim. The entire office had listened in as she'd browbeaten and insulted him. Reece had stood humiliated and furious at her offensive tyranny. The snarling black dog of rage had hunkered beside him, straining at its lead. It shamed Reece to admit that if security hadn't arrived to escort him from the building when they did, he would have lost control of the beast. He would have made things a hundred times worse, and they were already bad enough.

Reece unpacked his prep ingredients and neatly folded the cloth bags, tucking them under the sink. He breathed deeply, aching to talk with Sam. It had been a long time since he'd felt so unsettled.

Word of his termination had spread rapidly throughout the courthouse, and the rumour mill was spinning with exaggerated versions of his assumed transgression. His phone had already begun to ring off the hook with curious 'friends' keen to hear the grisly details of his fall from grace. He'd finally had the common sense to text Sam that he had to turn off his phone.

I'm coming home, she'd responded. *We'll figure it out together.*

Inexplicably, his eyes filled with tears. His emotional state was an aftershock of the adrenalin crash and exhaustion, he knew, but it infuriated him that he was this upset. He told himself again that he'd done the right thing, even though he'd known it would result in his immediate termination. If the Crown attorney's office pressed charges, it could cost him his freedom. He'd leaked confidential material. Right this minute, Gretchen was meticulously preparing paperwork to have him charged. At the ensuing press conference, she would refuse to disclose to whom he'd given the information or why. The inference would be that he'd leaked it to felons to aid in their defence. The media would run with a juicy story of treason. The papers would allege that he had betrayed the blue brethren with whom he'd once stood. The court of public opinion would prosecute him.

If Toronto's frontline officers believed Gretchen's trumped up charges and her lies, even Inspector Bryce Mansfield's loyalty wouldn't stop the thin blue line from turning their backs on him. Losing that allegiance was what hurt the most, and Gretchen had known that. She'd stuck her knife into the most vulnerable part of his heart and twisted. Everything Bryce had warned him about was coming to fruition, and Reece had only his unyielding principles to blame.

Since exercise hadn't helped settle his mind, maybe cooking would. He measured out his West Indian spices and dropped them into a cast iron pan to toast. As the kitchen filled with the heady fragrance of allspice and coriander, Reece felt a bit of weight lift. The black dog was skulking back to its iron cage. He ground the warm spices and dumped the powder into a glass jar. Next, he prepared his puff pastry. As the dough rested and the ground beef sizzled, he diced onions and scotch bonnet peppers. The filling for the Jamaican patties simmered, flooding the sunlit kitchen with scrumptious aromas. He felt the smothering caul of depression lift a little bit more as he worked. Maybe he was over-reacting and things weren't as catastrophic as he feared. Maybe Gretchen would cool down and reconsider.

Manic pounding struck the front door.

Reece froze and his heart dropped to the pit of his stomach. His legs felt weak and his pulse galloped in his neck, causing white noise to fill his head.

Pepin yelped and jumped out of his crate. He skidded across the floor, scrambled to regain his footing, and raced over to Reece. Whimpering, he leaped against Reece's leg in search of protection.

The pictures on the wall shuddered under another assault against the door, more aggressive than the first.

They'd come to arrest him.

In stiff, robotic movements, Reece put the pastry in the fridge and turned off the heat under the meat filling. His mouth was bone dry and his hands shook.

The relentless hammering continued nonstop against the heavy metal door. Pepin whined and cowered beside Reece's feet.

Careful not to accidentally kick the puppy, Reece picked up his wallet and his phone from the church altar, fumbling to turn on his cell. He needed to text Sam. He wouldn't get another chance once they'd cuffed him. It could take hours before they'd let him contact anyone. The cell phone slowly rebooted, the icon swirling in a lazy sweep across the screen. He grabbed his suit jacket from the back of the chair. Stupid, but he'd feel more in control if he had it on when they took him. He should crate Pepin. He couldn't remember if he'd turned off the stove. A hundred frantic thoughts spun through his head and he turned in a circle, trying to figure out what he should do first. He couldn't concentrate with the violent pounding.

He yanked open the door.

Sam flew into his arms. "I took an Uber. I forgot my keys. Are you okay? You're shaking."

He hugged her close, inhaling the scent of her lemon shampoo. "You hate Ubers," he murmured into her soft curls. "You think half of the drivers are predators in disguise."

"Yeah, well, I pity any man stupid enough to tangle with me," she said, and pulled out of his arms. "Why do you have your suit coat on?"

He let out a shaky laugh. "You still have your cop knock down to a fine art. I thought I was headed to the slammer."

Her face paled and her freckles were stark against her ivory skin. "I didn't think. Come on, sit down. You look wrecked." She led him to the living room sofa. "I'll get wine. You start talking."

As she opened and poured their wine, Reece told her about his meeting with Bryce. She listened without comment, waiting for him to get to the bad part. After he finished telling her what happened with Gretchen, she put her glass on the side table and hugged him.

"I'm so proud of you," she said.

"Giving Bryce the file was the right thing to do," he said without conviction.

"Not that." A brilliant smile lit her face. "I'm proud of you for not smacking that bitch."

He laughed, and it felt great. "Well, I came close when she called me a snivelling swine and an embarrassment to law enforcement."

Sam rolled her eyes. "Oh boy. There's something seriously wrong with that woman. Did you speak with anyone at the university?"

"I met with my ethics professor," Reece said. "Since Gretchen kept her inquiry off the official channels, he thinks a case could be made that the information in the file I gave to Bryce belonged to our PI agency."

"I was wondering about that," Sam said. "Eli's our employee and Danny is our consultant. Neither has any affiliation with the Crown attorney's office. You interviewed Lydia at Cardoon Bistro using your PI licence, not your office credentials."

"Right, but I talked to Susan Taylor as a Crown attorney employee," he said.

"Okay," Sam said slowly. "Would she remember? Our agency did the background check on her new tenant. Eli followed-up with her. Isn't it possible she'll associate you with McNamara Hash Investigations?"

"You want me to ask her to lie?" Reece asked incredulously.

"No, I want to rely on subliminal perception," she said. "We go see her again, maybe to check in on the new tenant, and we show her our PI licences. We talk about how McNamara Hash Investigations is liaising with homicide to reopen her husband's case."

Reece saw where she was going and his first instinct was to veto it out of principle. Maybe Bryce was right and his inflexible ethics would be his demise.

"It will influence her to remember that she only saw the PI identification," Reece said, swallowing his distaste. "If asked, she'll say I interviewed her as a private investigator rather than a civil servant employee."

Sam shrugged. "Calling into question the validity of the claim that you surrendered confidential material," she said. "It's worth a shot. Danny can testify that she was operating in her consultant role when she wrote the algorithm that found the commonalities in the sudden-death cases. By the way, that algorithm is her intellectual property." She paused in thought and sipped her wine. "Eli can testify that we were looking into Annalise Huang's case because it didn't sit right with us."

Rigid morals aside, it shocked Reece that Sam was calmly suggesting that Eli lie to authorities. Reece quashed a sharp retort to the suggestion. He rubbed his temple in a feeble attempt to mitigate a wicked headache that was burrowing into his skull.

Sam squeezed his hand. "I honestly don't think we'll need to testify. But if Gretchen comes after you with a vengeance, we'll circle our wagons around you."

Meaning they'd lie under oath. They'd commit perjury. Reece's stomach roiled. How did doing the right thing result in people he cared about plotting the most effective way to break the law? He should have given it more thought before he'd righteously galloped toward justice, with a sword in one hand and a balance scale in the other.

"The piece you're missing is that Gretchen gave me the files. Our agency wouldn't have had access to them," he said. "She'll probably accuse me of stealing them with the intent of leaking confidential material."

"They're closing in on Gretchen," Sam said with confidence. "She has bigger problems than manufacturing charges against you."

Reece shook his head doubtfully. "Between personal insults, Gretchen was clear that she would exercise every ounce of her power to cause a scandal 'from which you'll never recover' as she put it," he said with a grimace.

Sam's green eyes darkened to emerald stones. "Let her try. We've survived worse. Besides, I think the deputy attorney general will clip her wings before it goes too far," she said. "We'll plan for the worst but hope for the best. What about your law degree?"

He shrugged. "I spoke with the Law Society of Ontario. There have been cases where a principal fired an articling student and the person went on to write the bar exam."

Regardless, it was inconceivable to him how a fired articling student could have a successful law career. The only thing worse than being terminated with cause, was having the law firm press criminal charges. Even the most gifted resume consultant couldn't polish that turd.

His headache slithered under his left eye, shooting barbs of agony into his cranium. "It's my responsibility to find another placement to complete the term." Reece braced for her response.

"Jim Stipelli," she said immediately. "He's a senior partner in one of the biggest firms in Ontario, and he's Toronto's most renowned defence attorney."

It was what he'd expected her to say, and she was trying to be optimistic and helpful, so Reece forced a smile. "Sure. That's a great idea."

It was a terrible idea. He didn't want her best friend's husband to be his principal. He didn't want to article with a defence attorney at all. His dream was to be on the prosecution side of the table, arguing for the people. Studying law was about supporting a justice system he believed in, not aiding criminals in weaseling out of serving time.

"Jim's firm has an impressive pro bono division." Sam's green eyes drilled into his. "Our legal system needs good people on both sides of the table to defend the downtrodden."

She was right, but it still wasn't how he'd envisioned his future. It would be awkward and humiliating to be a friend's subordinate.

When he remained silent, Sam asked, "Will you think about it?"

"Sure. I'll give Jim a call," he said with feigned enthusiasm. "Eli and Danny are coming for dinner. I've got a few more things to do before they arrive." He stood and headed for the safety of the kitchen. He didn't want to talk about it anymore and needed to be alone to sort out his thoughts.

She jumped off the sofa and followed him. "What can I do to help?"

"Nothing," he said a bit too quickly. "I downloaded that movie you wanted to see. Why don't you and Pepin snuggle and watch it?"

She looked hurt by his rejection, but smiled weakly. "Okay. Holler if you need a clumsy sous chef." She picked up the puppy and settled onto the sofa.

Reece felt like a total dick. He followed her and picked up the remote to organize her movie. Once it was queued, he passed her the remote and leaned down to kiss her. "I love you. Thanks for being my rock."

"We'll get through this," she said. "I promise."

Reece turned away before she saw the torment on his face. He regretted not heeding Bryce's advice. He should have left well enough alone. He shouldn't have put the apprehension of a face-less vigilante over his career.

His selfish hypocrisy tasted bitter.

CHAPTER TWENTY-SIX

The Journal

IN THE WEEKS that followed the sheriff's visit, Basile Landry tried my family in the court of public opinion. The verdict was absolute.

He defamed my sister's reputation until she became the whore of Babylon, a wanton simpleton who preyed on unsuspecting boys. Not a soul would believe Virgile had raped Pearl. Basile cast aspersions on my character as well, portraying me as a violent and unstable delinquent. His alma mater rescinded my basketball scholarship with no explanation. Basile then went on to malign my father's military career, establishing doubt over his patriotism by insinuating he had fraternized with Taliban supporters during his deployment. The furniture he designed with exquisite care went unsold.

With an election forthcoming, the sheriff would eventually concede and launch a full investigation into our family. When that happened, they would arrest me for murder, find Pearl's body, and charge my father with concealment of death. With no family to care for her, authorities would take my mother from our home and institutionalize her. Without the seclusion of the bayou to comfort her with false memories of a genteel past, she would die a slow and mentally agonizing death alone.

My father understood the risks to our family as well as I did. Although we never discussed the future, I watched helplessly as his depression grew and he aged decades before my eyes. He made no further effort to instill an iota of normalcy to our lives. He didn't brush my mother's long platinum hair or sing her Cajun folk songs. He cared for her with clinical efficiency but surrendered to the darkness of our living nightmare.

I once again hunted and fished to feed our family, relying on the bayou to sustain our lives. The three of us would sit at the table in oppressive silence as twilight ebbed over the Teche, the pinkish light flashing through the high branches of the cypress tree. Like a helpless baby bird, my mother would open her mouth each time my father pressed a spoonful of food against her lips, her face void of expression and her eyes mercifully vacant.

The inequity of what was happening to my victimized family leached the vibrancy from the colours around me. I could no longer hear the music in the bayou's night sounds. An evening breeze no longer felt like a gentle kiss from Pearl against my neck. Because of me, we existed in purgatory, waiting for the authorities we feared to drag us into perdition.

A month after the sheriff's first visit, my father asked to speak with me. We sat in matching rockers on the front porch and he handed me a thick manila envelope.

"Do you remember how to find Cyril?" he asked. "His compound is where it was when you sold him the nutria tails."

I stared in silence at the envelope that lay on my lap like a ticking bomb.

"Basile won't give up, Blu. Nor will his surviving son." Dad's eyes lingered wistfully on the high branches of the cypress tree. "You have to run. I can buy you time and plant doubt. Cyril will get you documents. I sold the truck. There's enough money there to pay him." He nodded to the envelope.

"Where will I go?" I asked.

"North. Get across the border," he said. "Pick a city large enough to swallow you—Toronto, Montreal, Vancouver. Make a life. Do it for Pearl."

Tears welled in my eyes. "They'll find her when they come."

"The angels have Pearl, child." He reached over and placed his warm hand on my chest. "Her spirit is infinite. Pearl lives in your heart for eternity. She is your shadow now and will always be with you."

"I can't leave her," I said.

"You can and you will." He handed me a leather-bound notebook. "Remember us, Blu. Write our story. Someday, you'll find someone who will understand what we had to do. With understanding comes forgiveness. Don't come back, not ever." His eyes were dark and intense. "Understand? Do not come back here, child."

"I'm sorry," I whispered through my tears.

He clasped my hand in both of his. "No, *I'm* sorry. I failed my blood and that's my greatest regret. You have to survive, Blu. You're all that's left of us." He stood. "Take the boat. When your documents are ready, Cyril will take you as far as Houston." He squeezed my shoulder. "Always remember I love you. Everything I'm doing is to protect you, not to punish you."

Without another word, he stood, stepped inside the house, and abandoned me to my dreary future. The door to my childhood home closed firmly behind him.

I descended the stairs with nothing but this leather-bound journal and the manila envelope of money. I slipped the envelope into my breast pocket. The bleakness of a life without my family loomed miserably before me. Yet, I could muster no remorse for having executed Virgile Landry. My only regret was my inability to identify his accomplice.

Halfway to Cyril's camp, I cut the engine and let the boat drift along the still water. An overwhelming sense of having missed something vital consumed me. I sat quietly, emptying my mind and focusing on the birds' rhapsody. The water lapped gently in a two-four beat against the sides of the mud boat. My father's haggard face rose in my mind. I saw his eyes locked onto a ladder leaning against the cypress tree. I heard the serenity in his voice that had been absent for months. I saw the button-down shirt he had been wearing and the corner of a folded piece of white paper that had peeked from the breast pocket.

A bustle of egret wings broke the spell. I watched as the elegant white birds lifted majestically into the sky. Their long necks were extended in graceful curves as they soared above me.

I understood what my father planned to do.

He would make the ultimate sacrifice to protect me, if only long enough for me to escape Basile Landry's reach.

The engine caught on my second try, and I frantically turned the boat around and pushed the throttle to maximum speed. The boat bounced across the water and the old engine screeched in protest. I had been gone too long, and as each moment ticked past, my despair tightened.

I rounded the bend to our house and saw him. Tears mixed with the beads of moisture from the bow wave splashing against my face. The engine sputtered and died and the boat drifted toward the bank.

The ladder still leaned against the leathery trunk of the cypress tree. Lying neatly at the base of the ladder was my father's prosthetic.

He'd attached a thick-coiled rope to an aged branch that would hold his weight. His single foot hung two feet from the top of Pearl's stone crypt. He twirled with a macabre elegance in the soft wind.

Staggering to shore, I dug a knife from my pocket and clamped it between my teeth as I climbed the ladder. My father's black eyes bulged from their sockets and bands of red tainted the whites. His grey, bloated tongue lolled from blue lips. Streaks of blood from his shredded fingertips stained the coarse fibres of the rope around his neck. He'd choked to death, primal instinct driving him to claw at the rope that strangled him.

As the last filament of rope surrendered under the sharp blade of my knife, his body fell on the top of the stone crypt. I scrambled down the ladder, pulled him gently to the ground, and cradled him in my arms, weeping over what I had driven him to do.

It had begun under this cypress tree, when my parents had danced to music only they could hear on the night before my father deployed to Afghanistan. Virgile had watched Pearl from the cover of this cypress tree, coveting her beauty and then pilfering what he viewed as his entitlement. The ancient tree protected my beloved Pearl, and now, its gnarled branches had taken my father's life.

There was one thing left to complete the fiery ring of destruction that had besieged my family so many years ago when my grandfather had denied his kin.

I found my father's bogus confession in the pocket of his shirt. The gun I'd used to execute Virgile Landry was in a holster attached to his belt, a damning piece of evidence that would corroborate his guilt. I pocketed the weapon and tore the letter into tiny pieces of wedding confetti that I scattered across the water.

I swathed my father in a white linen sheet, buried him beside Pearl's tomb, and laid a blanket over the freshly turned soil.

In the house, I clothed my mother in her favourite seafoam silk dress with the yards of billowing chiffon. I quietly wept as I recalled our trip to Savannah when I was ten. She sat still and blissfully unaware as I brushed her platinum hair until it was a glittering sheet down her back. I led her to the porch and took her hand. Together we descended the grand staircase my father had constructed for her. She passively followed me to the white blanket I had laid beneath our cypress tree. She sat and tucked her legs under her dress. As she gazed across the bayou, a radiant smile lit her face. She reached up and clasped my hand in hers. I knelt beside her and held her waifish body against me. I loved her with a frightening intensity and had one gift left to bestow upon her.

"There is a Georgian jewel with antebellum architecture on East Gaston Street in Savannah," I whispered. "Old Savannah's finest are arriving for a ball hosted for the most sought-after debutante in the Confederate. There isn't a man in the world impervious to your beauty and charm." My tears darkened the silk of her dress and I reached up to caress the warmth of her face.

People had always been our greatest enemy. They had never understood my fantasy-prone mother's eccentricities. Without understanding, I knew that cruelty would always reign. When the authorities came, they would institutionalize her in a bleak box where her fear and confusion would extinguish her essence. There was only one way to protect her.

Gently, I pressed the gun to her temple and pulled the trigger. Her head jerked sideways, and her warm blood sprayed across my face and chest, spattering the envelope that contained the money my father had given me. I moved her limp hand from my thigh and stepped into the still water of the Teche, screaming as her blood ran from my skin in narrow ribbons of diluted pink. The last of my humanity crumbled and floated across the top of the algae-covered water.

Everything I cherished was gone, everything except the ancient bald cypress tree.

CHAPTER TWENTY-SEVEN

Sam

SAM MOVED A snoring Pepin off her lap and reached for the remote to stop the movie. Twisting around, she grabbed her buzzing phone from the table behind her. She read the text and sat immobile, trying to reconcile Emily's message. Her cheeks felt flushed and her stomach roiled. There had to be an explanation, other than the obvious. Sam had witnessed Aazar take Fadiya's blood. He had no motive to substitute it in his lab or to forge the test results. Ketamine remained in the urine for over a week. Fadiya's sample should have tested positive, yet Emily's text claimed it was negative. It didn't make sense.

Reece glanced up from stirring something on the stove. "What's wrong? Who was that?"

"Emily," she said. "Fadiya's urine tested negative for ketamine."

He frowned. "But it was less than a week ago that Aazar took his blood sample."

She swallowed, the residual wine on her tongue tasting sour. "I know."

"Who drew the sample?" he asked.

"Ophelia... I think," she said slowly. "I know where you're going with this, but why would she switch samples?"

"Did Ophelia take it to the lab, or did she give it to someone to deliver?" he asked.

"I don't know." A graphic image of Emily, flushing the original sample and replacing it with one of her own, flashed across Sam's mind.

"Maybe the lab made a mistake," Reece said. "They could have mislabeled Fadiya's sample."

"I suppose," Sam said hesitantly.

He studied her from across the room. "You don't think that's what happened."

The conversation she'd had with Emily two days ago replayed in her head. The doctor had been concerned about her professional standing. Sam wanted to believe the lab had screwed up, but she wasn't sure how far Emily would go to protect her clinic and her life's work.

"Labs do mess up," she said, trying to give her mentor the benefit of the doubt. "I mean it's possible, right?"

"Get your own sample tomorrow and have an independent lab test it." Reece put down the wooden spoon he was holding and grabbed a teaspoon from the cutlery drawer. "Come and taste my filling."

She trudged to the kitchen with heavy steps, her thoughts spinning with nasty suspicions. She couldn't shake the sense that Emily had switched samples to protect her clinic from yet another scandal. The idea made Sam ill. Could she have misjudged her mentor so badly? She took a deep breath. Before she jumped to conclusions, she'd get a sample from Fadiya and have it tested. If it were positive, she'd confront Emily.

Sam dipped the teaspoon into the spiced ground beef and pea mixture. "It's good," she said. "What is it?"

With a flamboyant flick of his wrist, Reece lifted a moist tea towel off a baking sheet. Two dozen half-moon bundles with artistically crimped edges nestled on the tray.

"Jamaican patties for Eli," he said with a big grin. "I learned how to make them to surprise him. I even made peach chutney."

"Oh, well, they look delicious," she said tentatively.

Confusion crossed Reece's face. "What's wrong?"

Eli was a picky eater, probably somewhat due to his Asperger's. He avoided certain textures, such as meat. Sam was cognizant of his proclivities and typically picked a pizza joint for lunch. If they shared a pie, it had to have sauce, caramelized onions, and cheese. Nothing else, or Eli would only nibble at the crust. He liked the boxed Jamaican patties because the meat was heavily processed, almost pureed, and the dough wasn't flaky. Reece had thought he was doing a kindness and Sam wasn't sure how to prepare him for the inevitable.

Rather than dancing around the issue, she took a page from Eli's book and spoke directly. "He won't eat them," she said bluntly. "The filling in the boxed ones is mushy. The processed pastry is a denser texture. It doesn't have peas."

"What a waste of time." Reece threw the wooden spoon in the sink.

He was still upset over the ugly confrontation with Gretchen and his ominous future in law, Sam realized. She got that, but his adolescent hissy fit didn't sit well with her. Reece was spoiling for a disagreement, so Sam ignored it, deciding they could talk after Eli and Danny left.

"Danny and I will devour them," she said eagerly and dug her spoon into the leftover filling. "I love West Indian food—you know that."

"Does it need more curry?" he asked, somewhat mollified by her enthusiasm.

Sam glanced at the tray of assembled turnovers. It was too late to suggest a tad more curry so she smiled and shook her head. "Nope, the spice is perfect. Super yummy."

"What's Eli going to eat?" Reece asked peevishly.

She opened the sub-zero freezer and pointed at a box of frozen patties.

Reece sneered at them. "You've got to be kidding me."

Her own temper was fraying now and it was a struggle to keep up her cheerful tone. "Don't take it personally," she said with a stiff smile. "It's an Asperger's thing. It isn't Eli's fault."

Reece muttered something under his breath and poured syrupy chutney into a bowl. "Can you set the table?"

Sam was placing the last napkin when the doorbell rang. She shooed Pepin aside and opened the door for Eli and Danny. The puppy hurled his solid body at Eli's legs. He scooped up the French bulldog and laughed as Pepin slobbered all over his cheek.

"Did you miss me? Yes, you did, and I missed you." Eli looked over at Sam. "I would like to borrow Pepin. May I take him home tonight?"

"What for?" Sam asked.

"He wants to teach him to swim," Danny said, dumping her laptop bag by the door. "He bought him a lifejacket." Her snarly expression suggested she didn't endorse the idea of Pepin doggy-paddling around their immaculately maintained saltwater pool.

"I guess it's alright with me." Sam caught Danny's eye. "Reece made Jamaican patties."

"You can smell the curry all the way down the stairwell." Danny peered over Reece's shoulder at the tray of turnovers. "Eli won't eat them."

"I know."

Reece shoved the tray into the oven and closed the door harder than necessary. He threw open the freezer and hurled a box of frozen patties onto the marble counter, causing Danny to flinch and jump back.

She held up her hands in an angry gesture. "Whoa! What's your problem, dude?"

"Sorry," Reece mumbled.

Danny shoved by him and took a can of Mountain Dew and a beer out of the fridge, glaring at him as she walked by. She handed her brother the soda and opened her beer.

"I found out some stuff about that doctor's financial situation," she said and flopped onto the leather recliner in the living room.

Sam followed her and sat on the corner of the sofa, reaching for her glass of wine. "Anything out of the ordinary?"

"Well, your mom was right. Adaline Beauregard's grandfather established a trust in her name," Danny said. "The old man died over a decade ago. The trust was in a South Carolina bank."

"Makes sense," Sam said, remembering that her mother had told them Adaline was from Charleston.

"Yeah, but things got weird five years ago," Danny continued. "Money moved out of the trust through a web of complex transactions. Almost thirty-million dollars vanished."

"Adaline died five years ago." Reece sat down beside Sam, placing his hand on her knee. He mouthed *Sorry* with a weak smile.

She laid her hand over the back of his, silently signalling her forgiveness for his bad temper. "Mathias probably inherited the trust," she said. "He must have liquidated it."

"I don't think he removed the money," Danny said. "I think the family clawed it back."

"Are you sure?" Sam asked.

"No, but the dude is broke or close to it," Danny said. "He's carrying a hefty line of credit at the Royal Bank and has over a quarter of a million dollars in commercial debt on various credit cards."

Reece whistled. "That would keep me up at night. Grace told us that Adaline's family didn't approve of the marriage and there were rumours around her death," he said. "Maybe they had some way of preventing the trust from falling into his hands."

"Does Mathias pay income tax?" Sam asked Danny.

She got up, fetched her laptop from where she'd dumped it by the front door, and took a minute to look up something. "Every year before the due date," she replied, studying her computer. "Beauregard's net income last year was just shy of two hundred grand. He filed partnership income from Serenity Clinic and investment income."

"Is the house on Bridle Path in his name?" Sam asked.

Danny nodded. "And I didn't find anything levied against the house."

Even without a mortgage, Mathias's annual income was barely enough to sustain his multimillion-dollar home.

"Mom and Harvey spend over seventy-five-thousand a year on property tax," Sam said. "Hydro, water, and gas are close to five grand a month. Then there's maintenance on the house and property, which I don't even want to guess at."

"So the man needs money and a lot of it," Reece said.

"If he's involved in some medical conspiracy to implant a genetically engineered fetus in Fadiya or he's a sex trader, there should be a money trail," Sam said.

"I'm not a financial forensic analyst," Danny said. "If you want to track illegal money, you need to involve someone better qualified."

"If it is not related to computers, bioinformatics, or genetics, Danny is not interested." Eli tossed Pepin's elephant across the room and the puppy scrambled gleefully after it.

"So, Mathias didn't lie to Emily about his financial situation," Sam said.

"He's living a conspicuous consumption lifestyle in a mansion he can't afford," Reece said.

The doorbell rang and Reece went to answer it. "I've never understood why people think the appearance of money makes them superior."

Sam wasn't sure if she felt relieved or disappointed that Mathias wasn't a corrupt doctor on the take. She would have garnered a great deal of satisfaction from exposing the arrogant man as a criminal. Hearing voices at the door, Sam went over and peeked around Reece's shoulder.

"Aazar," she said in surprise. "What are you doing here?"

"I'm sorry to intrude. I wonder if I can speak with you."

"Sure. This is my business partner and fiancé, Reece Hash."

Reece offered his hand. "Nice to meet you," he said and closed the door after Aazar.

His colour was bad, a sort of bluish grey. Fearing he'd pass out before they got him to the living room, Sam pulled out a dining room chair for him. She waited until he had sat and adjusted his oxygen flow before she took the chair across from him.

Danny stood beside the table with a dazed expression. "You're Aazar Basha," she squeaked. "You won the Gairdner Award last year for advancing humanity. You're rumoured to be a sure winner for the Nobel Prize in physiology and medicine."

"If my research has the desired outcome, perhaps they will consider me," he replied modestly. "They've yet to name me as a candidate."

"You're my hero," Danny blurted, and a deep blush coloured her full cheeks. "I mean, your work is brilliant. I've read everything you've ever written." She tucked her short hair behind her ears in a preening fashion Sam had never witnessed.

"Are you a doctor?" Aazar asked politely, but his tone and expression showed little interest.

"My sister has her PhD in computer engineering and a master's in computer science," Eli said proudly. "She is only twenty-five and is one of Canada's youngest women to earn such high academic achievements. She is very smart. Now she is studying genetics at Harvard."

"This is Eli Watson," Sam said. "He works for us and Danny often consults."

"My current focus is bioinformatics," Danny said to Aazar, sitting on the ladder back chair beside him. "I only do online courses at Harvard."

"I will invite you to my lab," Aazar replied, and fussed with his oxygen.

"You will or you are?" Danny asked.

Aazar finally looked at her. "Tenacious. I admire that trait in a scientist." He rummaged in a pocket of his portable oxygen bag and handed her a card. "That's my private number. Text me your availability."

Danny blushed again and took the card, staring at it with reverence.

"You are Fadiya's brother." Eli squashed a chair in between his sister and Aazar, forcing both to shift their own chairs to make room for him. "Has something happened to her?" Anger flickered in Eli's eyes and he turned to glare at Sam. "You said she would never be alone. You said she was safe."

Sam ignored him. "What's going on?" she asked Aazar.

"I saw my sister today. She has a large hematoma on the inside of her left thigh. The bruise is a hand print." Aazar's frown deepened. "She said that the 'brother' who brought Mussani last night carried a small black box. He moved the instrument slowly and methodically around her room. Then, he turned out all the lights and again circled the room."

Danny leaned around her brother to speak to Aazar. "The box sounds like a radio frequency detector."

"He was sweeping her room for cameras and bugs," Sam said. "LED lights on cameras blink in low light. That's why he turned off the lights."

Eli abruptly stood, knocking over his chair in the process. He marched in a tight circle, his eyes darting across the ceiling. "You said a nurse would be with Fadiya every night." He tapped the words against the air in front of his face, becoming more agitated with each syllable. "You said she would be safe. Someone is selling her for sex. She is being raped. We must do something. She is not safe. You lied." His voice rose with each sentence.

"Eli—" Sam began.

"He's right," Aazar interrupted. "My sister is in grave danger in that clinic. Dr. Armstrong lied about the results of the urine test."

"The lab could have made a mistake," Sam said. "I'll have another sample tested at an independent lab."

"Pointless!" Aazar's shout startled her. His frustration was clear in his sharp tone and the way he physically closed off his body by crossing his arms and legs. "Assuming Dr. Armstrong isn't behind what is happening to my sister, she'll dispute the results. Her only focus is to protect her precious clinic."

"Emily Armstrong promised that a nurse would be with Fadiya overnight." Eli continued to pace in a tight circle. "That was a lie. Emily Armstrong is a liar."

"We don't know that," Sam said sharply. "Aazar, was Ophelia in your sister's room last night?"

"Not that I'm aware, but something strange did happen yesterday," he said. "My specialist performed the cordocentesis to test the umbilical cord stem cells. When Fadiya returned to the clinic, a patient accosted her in the lobby and screamed at her not to take candy from the wolf. It scared my sister."

Something about the statement tugged at Sam's memory. It hovered just beyond her consciousness, but she couldn't grasp it.

"I've noticed that my sister is more herself lately," Aazar said. "I believe that's why she remembered the man searching her room before 'Mussani' arrived." His lips thinned with contempt.

Sam had also noticed Fadiya's increased lucidity. Sadly, it hadn't helped her get through to the girl. She'd shown her pictures of Eli's horse ranch for kids with Asperger's, which was situated on the old Bueton land, hoping it would help her to accept that the cult was gone. This had only angered the girl, who then claimed a brother had warned her that Sam would lie to keep Mussani to herself. Sam had planned to appeal to Emily tomorrow for permission to take Fadiya to the camp. Allowing Fadiya to see the changes for herself could be a monumental step in her recovery. But that was before Emily had denied the presence of ketamine in the girl's urine and neglected to assign Ophelia to Fadiya's room overnight. Right now, protecting the girl—possibly from her primary physician—had to take precedence over therapy.

"What did your sister say about the bruise on her thigh?" Sam asked.

"She said 'Mussani' was rough. He hurt her." Aazar held a handkerchief against his mouth with a shaking hand. "The bruises, the ketamine, the pregnancy—" He spat out the word and choked, pausing to catch his breath. "Her confusion over Mussani is because he is not one man." He twisted the white handkerchief in his hands and dropped his eyes to his lap. "He is many men in the same disguise." He lifted his eyes and held her gaze. "I still believe the baby could be a product of human gene editing, but I also agree with Eli. Fadiya is a victim of forced prostitution and it's my fault."

"None of this is your fault," Sam said gently, reaching for his hand.

"It is." His expression was blank. "I took my sister to Bueton. I gave her to Mussani."

CHAPTER TWENTY-EIGHT

REECE

SHOCK SLACKENED DANNY'S face. She jerked her chair away from Aazar, creating physical distance between herself and her fallen hero. Eli abruptly stopped pacing and stared at the back of Aazar's head. Sam's hand froze a centimetre from Aazar's hand.

"Everything I did was to protect and honour Fadiya," he said softly. "Everything I did destroyed her life."

"You took your twelve-year-old sister to a cult and left her there." It was a supreme struggle for Reece to keep his voice impassive. "Why?"

"I didn't know it was a cult," Aazar said, wringing his handkerchief in his hands. "I thought it was a religious retreat where people lived closer to God. I wanted to free my sister."

"From what?" Reece asked.

"The harvesting," Aazar said quietly. "If they couldn't find her, they couldn't force her to be a living donor."

"Why didn't you refuse to undergo the procedures like you did today?" There was a razor-sharp edge to Sam's tone.

"Back then, my mother was my substitute decision-maker," Aazar said. "I didn't have the legal power to refuse."

"You can't expect us to believe that authorities deemed a scientific prodigy incapable of making his own medical decisions," Reece said incredulously.

Sam sighed and folded her hands against the top of the table. "Consent is complicated in chronic conditions," she explained. "Physicians have the legal and ethical right to assess capacity on case-specific circumstances. Aazar, is that what—"

"Bullshit." Danny's face flushed with anger and she jumped to her feet, knocking aside her chair. "Five years ago, *he* was testing his nanotechnology research." She pointed an accusing finger at Aazar. "No judge would deem him incapable. He had a medical degree and PhDs in physics *and* molecular biology before he was even twenty-one."

Aazar flinched. "You don't understand. Islamic law prohibits me from dishonouring my parents."

"But it doesn't *prohibit* you from giving your sister—an inferior female—to a sociopath," Danny shouted. "And now that some man has raped her, you can *free* her through death!" She took a threatening step toward Aazar, who cringed against the back of his chair. "Muslims condone honour killing." Danny's face was puce, and a thick vein throbbed in her forehead. "In your twisted culture it's okeydokey to murder and dehumanize women because—"

"Danny, enough," Reece yelled over her tyranny. "Go for a walk." He got up and tossed her Pepin's leash, which she angrily caught in one hand, spinning around to glare at Aazar once more. For a horrible second, Reece feared she was going to whip him with the leather leash.

Eli took it from her hand. "My sister is passionately opposed to the Taliban's oppression and mistreatment of women and girls," he said stiltedly.

"We are Afghan, not Taliban," Aazar replied.

"Giving your sister to a sexual deviant for his enjoyment sounds like something a Taliban would do," Eli stated.

Danny's eyes blazed with fury as she stared Aazar down. Before her temporary inability to speak manifested into physical violence, Reece physically backed her toward the front door. He left Eli inside to fetch Pepin, herded Danny into the hallway, and then shut the door behind him. Rather than confronting her over her behaviour, Reece took a minute to cool off himself.

He didn't agree with her insulting conduct, but he understood what had triggered it. Because of the physical and sexual abuse in their childhoods, Danny and Eli viewed Fadiya as a kindred spirit. Once Sam had cleared Aazar from the suspicion of incest, Danny had returned him to the pedestal she'd constructed for the scientific prodigy. She had believed that Aazar protected Fadiya in the same way Eli protected her. Instead, her hero, a genius whom she admired for his vast intellectual prowess and humanitarianism, had perpetrated the ultimate betrayal. Aazar had abandoned his pubescent sister to a stone-cold sociopath, just as Danny's mother had sold her to a human trafficker.

Eli opened the door and stepped out into the hallway with the puppy trotting beside him. He closed the door behind him and avoided Reece's eye. Rather than acknowledging his sister, Eli walked to the base of the staircase that led to the front lobby. He paused without turning. Danny marched to the staircase, edged past him, and jogged down the stairs two at a time.

Eli turned to Reece with no expression. "She is fine now." He followed his sister, Pepin at his side.

Reece blew out his breath in exasperation. He had seen no indication that Danny was *fine*. He silently watched them through the large stairwell window. They exited the building and strolled down Queen Street.

They shared an unsettling, codependent relationship that had always made Reece uneasy. They lived on the fringes of society, entombed by tragic childhood memories. Their past governed their present and would eventually destroy their future. Worse, Danny chose to live in self-imposed isolation—employing tactless brusqueness to deter anyone who tried to penetrate her armour— and Eli enabled his foster sister's reclusive behaviour, believing he was protecting her. It was dysfunctional, to say the least.

As he stood alone in the quiet hallway, a sudden memory flashed across Reece's mind. He remembered being fifteen, and he'd been lecturing his twin brother about his poor life choices.

"*It must be complicated to be you,*" Ray had said with his iconic half-smile. "*Don't you ever get tired of being so judgmental? You're the moral majority, bro, and living up to your lofty standards is exhausting. I pity the woman who ends up with you.*"

Reece felt heat rise in his face now, and he experienced a rush of shame over how he'd always policed his twin brother's actions. Was he doing the same thing by judging Danny and Eli's relationship? When had he turned into such a pedantic and superior man?

His headache had returned with zeal and pain throbbed behind his left eye. He wanted to curl up in bed and try to forget this day had ever happened. Instead, he had to go back inside and listen to Aazar justify why he'd delivered his twelve-year-old sister to a cult.

When Reece grudgingly entered the loft, Aazar was saying to Sam, "That's when I found a cottage in Uthisca for rent and asked my parents for a holiday."

Half-listening, Reece went into the kitchen and selected a bottle of wine. Probably not a great idea with a migraine brewing, but Sam looked as if she could use a glass. He took three clean glasses and the wine to the table. Aazar shook his head when Reece offered him a glass.

"Fadiya and I went into town one afternoon," Aazar continued. "I went to the store the Bueton member on campus had told me about."

"Mussani had people on the university and college campuses across the Greater Toronto Area," Sam explained to Reece. "While attending University of Toronto, Aazar heard about a cloistered paradise in Uthisca."

"Bueton Sanctuary." Reece sipped the full-bodied, ruby red Shiraz.

"I didn't know it was a cult," Aazar said miserably.

"I was the Inspector of the provincial police detachment in Uthisca," Reece said. "We didn't know what it was, either." The admission was bitter, souring the sweet blueberry undertones of the wine. How naive he'd been to view Bueton as a harmless commune.

"There were girls in the store, some of them the same age as my sister," Aazar said. "Fadiya had never had friends. My mother home-schooled her because of how much time she spent in hospital." He looked into the distance, his brown eyes wistful. "She was so excited to spend time with girls her own age. They were all so nice to her."

Sam lowered her eyes with a strained expression. "Mussani trained the children carefully. Their job was to befriend a potential member's kid. It's easier for children to convince other children." She scrubbed at her lips with the back of her hand, a gesture of anxiety Reece recognized.

"Fadiya wanted to go back to the compound to help the girls make candles," Aazar said. "I wanted to meet Mussani." He hung his head. "I wanted to ask him to take my sister."

"Did you meet him?" Reece asked.

Aazar nodded. "I explained my medical situation and Mussani was sympathetic, saying that no child of God stood above another. He promised that Fadiya would be safe at Bueton," he said. "I spent the day with Mussani and his council. I'm ashamed to admit that I liked him."

"You aren't alone. Mussani was very charming," Reece said. "His amiability tricked almost everyone in Uthisca."

"Thank you for saying that," Aazar said. "I've replayed that day over and over in my head, trying to understand how I failed to recognize him as a monster."

"He hid it well," Reece said. "He was an extremely intuitive person and a gifted manipulator."

"He saw what Fadiya needed—companionship—and he played to her desires," Aazar said. "She wanted to stay. I thought I was saving her."

"What did you tell your parents?" Reece asked.

"That I'd put Fadiya on a train to Hamilton to visit our auntie," he said. "But no matter how hard I tried to convince them to let me die, they refused. They claimed that Allah had bestowed the gift of intelligence on me, and I was duty bound to help humanity."

He removed a bottle of water from his backpack. "Allah commands impeccable respect toward parents. I couldn't stand against them because severing family relations is an act of *fasad*—corruption—and is a great sin."

"But they must have realized Fadiya wasn't with her aunt," Reece said.

"They did, and I admitted that I hid her," Aazar said. "Eight months later, I read about the massacre at Bueton and believed my sister was dead." His hand shook as he sipped from his water bottle.

"What happened when authorities found Fadiya alive?" Reece asked.

"My mother took her directly to Princess Margaret Hospital, where my oncologist extracted some of her bone marrow to save my life," Aazar said. "Fadiya was mentally unwell and didn't understand the pain." His voice caught and a tear ran slowly down his gaunt cheek. "Before our parents could subject Fadiya to more suffering, I convinced a psychiatrist to demand a competency hearing."

"And the Ontario court ruled in favour, preventing any further operations," Sam said with a sigh. "That's when your parents transferred Fadiya to Serenity Clinic."

"Where someone is drugging and raping her. My little sister, who I have a duty to protect," Aazar said through his tears. "Fadiya is a victim of forced prostitution. I believe you now."

"I dealt with some human trafficking with the provincial police," Reece said. "Just one girl forced into servitude produces over one hundred thousand dollars a year."

"It could be more, if you're catering to a fetish market, where a client rapes a patient in a lockdown facility," Sam said. "In addition to other deviant gratification, there's the adrenaline junkie fix."

"And if they're selling my sister, they're probably enslaving other girls as well," Aazar said. "Did you know that five young girls have disappeared from the withdrawal unit this month?"

Sam frowned. "I know about three. There's no proof anything sinister happened in those cases, though."

"I don't believe they left of their own accord," Aazar said defiantly. "I believe they were taken and sold into slavery." His eyes hardened. "I would kill to avenge my sister's honour. Some people are not worthy of life."

The front door banged open and Eli marched to the table. "Danny is admitting me into a psychiatric hospital on an involuntary hold," he announced.

"What?" Reece stared with disbelief at Danny, who was calmly unclipping Pepin's leash.

"His Asperger's has become uncontrollable," Danny said without expression. "I'm his power of attorney. Eli is a danger to himself and others."

Reece opened his mouth and then closed it again, stunned. Danny had cracked. That was the only explanation. He looked at Sam, expecting her to intervene, but she merely sipped her wine and raised an eyebrow.

"Let me guess," Sam said at length, turning in her chair to look at Danny. "You're taking him to Serenity Clinic."

"Where they will put me in lockdown." Eli smiled. "I will protect Fadiya until Aazar can get her out."

CHAPTER TWENTY-NINE

The Journal

I SPENT A week in Cyril's camp, lonely and despondent. Away from the bayou, I could no longer feel Pearl's essence. Without her light, I existed in a cavern of darkness where my senses became numb and the memories of my beloved family dwindled. Amid the chaos of the camp, I slept for long hours and dreamed of a lane flanked by towering oak trees that led to a brick mansion, its verandah ringed with urns spilling over with sweet olive.

Cyril graced me with his company on just one occasion. He sat at a rickety camp table that might once have held Robert E. Lee's plans for the Battle of Chancellorsville. On its gouged wooden top, he placed a birth certificate from somewhere called Lethbridge, Alberta, an Ontario driver's licence, and a Canadian passport. He handed me a sheaf of papers: high school transcripts. I leafed through them. The marks were my own, which I had earned in Louisiana, and the highest were in math and science.

"Your *père* was a good man with a bad habit," Cyril said in a thick Cajun accent. He dropped a stained envelope on the table between us.

I shoved it back to him, cringing as my fingertips grazed my mother's spattered blood. "He said to give it to you when I arrived.

It's payment for this." I gathered the identification and stuffed it into my jacket.

Cyril pushed back the envelope of money. "I owed him," he said. "Now the debt is paid."

"The morphine you gave him paid the debt," I said gruffly. "You did enough."

Cyril's cold eyes drilled into mine. "Some demons are beyond mortal man's ability to conquer. It don't change the goodness in a man's heart. Your *père* was a good man."

Curiosity got the better of me. "Why did you owe him?"

Cyril opened his shirt. Across the upper left quadrant of his chest was a puckered, circular scar. "He saved my life. He saved the lives of two of my soldiers."

I slid the money back across the table. "I need three things from you. Take the cost from this."

I told him what I wanted and why. He sat silently for a few moments. "The first two ain't a problem," he said. "The other one is. Could be a couple of days."

"Tonight," I insisted. "Get it from a veterinary clinic. I need a syringe and rope, too."

"What you need is to get out of Louisiana," he said. "Blu, I promised your *père* I'd do right by you. College is different up north. The government helps pay." He pointed at the transcript I held. "You earned them marks for true. You could be a doctor. Make your *père* proud."

"He's dead. That was his choice. I'm going to Lafayette." I thought about the inferior man who resided in the palatial estate, entitled and heartless toward his kin. I'd made a vow a long time ago, and I meant to see it through.

Cyril stood. "You'll get you what you ask." He studied me in the dim light. "Virgile Landry, he was a piece of shit and y'all done the world a favour. Back on the bayou, you done the right thing to protect your *mère*. You do what you're planning, that's different."

"I'm not asking your permission or your blessing," I retorted. "Get what I ask and you'll never see me again. I promise you that."

His expression hardened. "Wait here. Someone will come for you. I owe you nothing now."

Even with his parting comment, I believed he'd keep my new identity secret. After everything I had done, and everything I planned to do, I still clung to a whisper of adolescent idealism. I truly believed Cyril would keep his promise to my father and do right by me. I believed he would never betray me. It was a mistake that cost me dearly in the end.

At a little after midnight, a man with a sub-machine gun strapped across his chest handed me a car key, a thick coil of rope, a vial of succinylcholine chloride, a syringe, a package the size of a box of tissue, and a cell phone. "Press three to detonate. Range is sixty yards. There's a two-minute delay. Truck's behind the mess hall." He walked away.

The truck was an old brown Ford pickup. One of a million in Louisiana. Sitting in the driver's seat, I loaded the syringe and capped it. I followed 90 East and reached Lafayette without arousing attention. Outside the city, I drove to an oak-lined lane that led to a looming brick mansion. I switched off the headlights and coasted down a slight decline to the back entrance. The house was dark, and the only sound was the oscillating warbles of cicadas and the occasional call of a great horned owl. A good half acre from the back of the estate was a scattering of utilitarian cabins. My father had rarely spoken of his childhood home, but he'd told me that the servants lived on my grandfather's land, in lodgings reminiscent of slave quarters. They would be safe in those run-down shanties.

I tucked the rope over my shoulder, shoved the package into the deep pocket of my long black coat, and walked to the back entrance. My father had once told me that my grandfather viewed home security systems as a sign of weakness for cowardly men unable to protect their property. It seemed the old man's opinion hadn't changed over the years, because only a deadbolt lock secured the kitchen door. It took me longer than I thought it would to pick it, but eventually I was able to jimmy the pins until I could turn the lock with my tension wrench.

I crept through an elaborate gourmet kitchen and around to the front of the dark house. A massive vestibule with a thirty-foot ceiling showcased an imperial staircase with gilded rails and polished mahogany banisters. Ten steps up from the foyer was a large marble landing. Two symmetrical flights of stairs rose from the landing to the second floor, which circled the two-story staircase. I climbed the stairs and my hatred toward my grandfather intensified with each step. He had lived in all this opulence and wealth, while Pearl and I had eaten swamp rats to survive.

At the top of the stairs, moonlight from a glass cathedral ceiling above the vestibule provided sufficient light for me to detect a set of ornate double doors on the far side of the circular corridor. The other doors were single, so I walked toward the double doors, assuming they opened into the master suite. My sneakers squeaked against the marble floor and the long cotton coat rustled against my jeans. At the engraved mahogany doors, I grasped a crystal doorknob. It turned easily, and I gently pushed the heavy door, which opened into a sitting room with floor-to-ceiling bookshelves, a wheeled book trolley, and a massive stone fireplace. Two doors led from the sitting room. The first I tried was a bathroom. The second was his bedroom.

He lay on his back in a high four-poster bed with his head perched on a mountain of white pillows. Stiff with spray, his coiffured grey hair was a helmet around his wrinkled face. His gnarled hands rested on a maroon silk bedspread. Diminutive snores emanated from his wizened mouth.

I backed out of the room, gently closing his bedroom door behind me.

Outside the suite's double doors, I shrugged the rope off my shoulder and tied a noose on one end. I attached the other end to the railing that surrounded the high circular corridor. I peered over the long drop to an antique foyer table on the main level. A peaceful surge of righteousness fluttered in my stomach.

Retracing my steps, I entered the parlour and took hold of the brass handle on the book trolley. It rolled silently over a vintage oriental rug. Inside the old man's bedroom once more, I parked the cart alongside the bed and put up the hood of my coat.

He woke when I stabbed his jugular vein with the syringe.

He squinted at me through the gloom, trying to discern my facial features from beneath the hood. "Remy?" he croaked.

In less than sixty seconds, the short-term paralysis would take full effect and he would begin to suffocate. I had to move quickly. I wanted him to anticipate his death and feel the same fear Pearl had.

"Not Remy," I whispered. "I'm the urchin his Yankee whore spawned."

I rolled his limp body onto the trolley and wheeled it hastily across the parlour and through the double doors. He gurgled as I slipped the noose around his neck. I leaned over his face, vindicated to witness fear darkening his wide eyes.

"You denied your kin. You left your grandchildren starving while your only son fought for your country. You're a worthless man." I lowered the hood of my jacket and stared into his eyes.

His mouth opened and closed like a flopping catfish gulping for air.

"I am the omnipotent judge of the unworthy," I told him. "I am your shadow and see inside the darkest part of you. For the atrocities you committed against the innocent, I sentence you to death."

I rolled him off the trolley. His body plummeted over the railing. Gravity tightened the rope's slack until he dangled helplessly, suspended by the noose around his stretched chicken neck. His callused feet swung above the elegant centre table, the price of which would have fed us for the entirety of my father's tour of duty.

I descended the stairs, never bothering to look back at my grandfather. His heartless superiority had orchestrated the desecration of everyone I loved. The only regret I had was that his execution had been fast.

I placed the bomb on top of a six-foot-long gas range and exited through the back door. Mindful not to exceed the sixty-yard range, I drove up the incline to the lane. I pushed the number three on the cell phone and continued to drive to the main road. A minute later, I stopped and got out of the truck. The cicadas serenaded me as I waited. The C-4 explosive must have ignited the oven's gas lines, because the explosion and resulting fireball were exquisite.

I had kept the vow I'd made to myself when my grandfather had shamed my father two years earlier. As the grand old house burned, I felt a warm sense of rectitude. What my mother had begun by destroying a Fabergé egg the old man had valued over his son, I had finally ended. Our family saga had come full circle.

I got into the truck and drove the three hours from Lafayette to Houston in quiet reflection. I shut my mind to Pearl's tempting siren song that beckoned me home, where I could be with her and my parents for eternity. As I took the exit to the Houston airport, the sun rose behind me in a ball of fire that burned my youth to ashes and scattered the last speck of my soul into the indigo light.

I relinquished Blu to the bayou, as an ethereal shadow beneath a cypress tree strung with Spanish moss. But I could not cast aside the memory of my mother's humiliation on East Gaston Street when I was ten. I could not leave behind Pearl's suffering at the Crawfish Festival or the flicker of shame in my father's eyes when mindless people stared at his unsightly prosthetic. The only way to avenge society's indignities against all the other innocent and struggling people was to break free from Blu's chrysalis and emerge as someone new.

For six months, I resided in my new birthplace of Lethbridge, Alberta, in Canada, studying the cultural nuances of the north, and learning to conquer my southern accent in solitude. I emerged from my cocoon as the perfect impostor, able to blend in amid the masses as an unremarkable and forgettable person. Then, I travelled to Toronto and hid amongst the two-point-seven million people in Canada's largest city, while Blu lived anonymously in my shadow.

Until Cyril betrayed me to Virgile's brother and he came for his revenge.

CHAPTER THIRTY

SAM

SAM WALKED THROUGH the hospital to the garden exit, juggling her phone, a large coffee, and a cranberry muffin. Outside, the late afternoon sun shone down from a cloudless blue sky. A calming fragrance of lavender wafted from the landscaping along the meandering stone walkways. From a high branch of an ornamental pear tree, two blue jays serenaded the patients and employees who congregated at bistro tables on the pink flagstone patio. Ophelia sat alone at a table for two and Sam strolled over.

"Hi. Mind if I sit?" she asked.

Ophelia looked up from her tablet, her mouth set in a straight line and her eyes hidden by mirrored sunglasses. She snatched the tablet off the cast iron tabletop and jammed it into an ugly brown leather bag.

"Sure, sit." Neither her tone nor her expression suggested it pleased her to have Sam's company, but she moved aside an empty plate and coffee mug from the centre of the table.

Sam sat, lifting her face to the glorious sun. "It's nice to have a break from the smothering humidity."

The nurse laughed but Sam had no clue what she'd found so humorous.

"Oh, a muffin from Cardoon," Ophelia said. "They're so yummy. I would have gone over there, but I overslept. These twelve-hour night shifts are brutal."

Sam pulled her muffin in two and offered half. "Do you know what the spice is? It's good with the cranberry."

"Star anise, I think." Ophelia nibbled on the half Sam had given her. "Or maybe cardamom. I always get them confused. The chef is super experimental. Her cooking is sublime."

Seeing an opening, Sam said casually, "I saw you at the bistro the other day."

Ophelia dropped the remainder of her muffin onto the table and wiped her hands on a paper napkin. "Cardoon is Toronto's undiscovered gem. A lot of people who work and live in the vicinity eat there."

"It was a couple of hours after the staff meeting last week," Sam said. "I was surprised to see you out and about. You'd just finished a grueling night shift, remember?" Her distorted reflection stared back at her from Ophelia's silver sunglasses.

"I live in the neighbourhood." The skin across her cheekbones tightened and her shoulders tensed. "I don't sleep well during the day. I probably went for comfort food."

Sam took the lid off her coffee, thinking about the security footage she'd seen of Mathias and Ophelia. "You were with Dr. Beauregard. The conversation looked intense. After how rude he was at the staff meeting, I wanted to make sure you were okay."

Ophelia wagged her finger in Sam's face. "You should have made your presence known, rather than eavesdropping and spying," she said in a teasing tone that didn't soften the hard edge in her voice.

Refusing to back down, Sam said cheerfully, "So you do remember."

Ophelia jutted her chin forward. "If you must know, we had a difference of opinion on a patient. It doesn't concern you." She scrunched the rest of her muffin into the paper napkin, causing crumbs to scatter across the table and fall through its ornate wrought iron. "Speaking of patients, how are you making out with Fadiya? It strikes me as odd that Dr. Armstrong would assign you to an important patient when you have such limited experience," she said with a tight smile. "Perhaps you're out of your depth."

Sam ignored the insult, using the question to segue to one of her own. "Did Dr. Armstrong ask you to stay with Fadiya overnight?"

"Why?"

"Aazar was looking for you two nights ago and you weren't in Fadiya's room," Sam said, sipping her coffee. "I wondered if the plan had changed."

"Maybe I was in the bathroom. Am I allowed to go pee?" she asked caustically.

Sam sighed inwardly and held her tongue. Ophelia's sarcastic responses and recalcitrant attitude made it difficult to socialize with her and near impossible to carry on a professional conversation. This wasn't the first time Sam had witnessed the nurse's toxic personality, but she suddenly had the sense that Ophelia was doing it on purpose now to drive her away.

"Aazar waited nearly an hour. You never showed up," Sam said.

"At a little past midnight, I received a call to help in the withdrawal unit. He should have paged me." She frowned. "I hope he wasn't complaining. I've got enough to worry about right now."

It couldn't be a coincidence that someone had called Ophelia away while men entered Fadiya's room.

"Who called you?" she asked.

Ophelia pulled down her sunglasses, scrutinizing Sam over the tops of the wire frames. "Security, I think, or maybe it was Doug Sullivan, the other practicum student." She thought in silence for a few seconds. "It could have been Dr. Beauregard. I don't remember. Why?"

"What was the problem?" Sam persisted.

"Bethany was having issues. Earlier, there had been an incident in the lobby when they brought Fadiya back from her hospital procedure," Ophelia said.

She must be referring to the incident Aazar had told them about. Sam was curious if Ophelia had any more information. "What happened?" she asked.

Ophelia shrugged. "I wasn't there. When I arrived for my shift, Doug told me Bethany attacked Fadiya for no reason. He wanted her kept under sedation and transferred to lockdown."

"Is she up there now?" Sam asked.

Ophelia laughed. "He doesn't have the authority to make that decision. Besides, security had a different take on what happened. Bethany was just talking to Fadiya." She blew her breath out in a sigh. "I don't know why Doug made such a big deal out of it."

"So Bethany was the reason you weren't in Fadiya's room last night?" Sam asked.

Ophelia removed her sunglasses and peered intensely at Sam with her mismatched eyes. "What was Aazar doing here in the middle of the night?"

"Fadiya told him what happened," Sam said quickly. "He wanted to discuss it but you hadn't started your shift. He came back to find you."

Ophelia studied her with a worried expression. "I didn't abandon my post," she insisted. "Is that what Aazar's alleging?"

"Did Dr. Beauregard call you downstairs?" Sam asked.

"I told you, I don't recall if it was him," Ophelia said impatiently. "It could just as easily have been his know-it-all student."

"If Doug was with Bethany, why did he need you?" Sam asked.

Ophelia scowled and replaced her sunglasses, shoving them up the bridge of her nose. "They had to call him too, I think. *Lord Doug* showed up about forty-minutes later." She folded her arms over her chest. "I had just managed to settle Bethany when he strutted in and set her off again."

Since Ophelia couldn't remember who had asked her to go downstairs, continuing to question her was pointless.

"I hope Bethany is okay," Sam said sincerely, remembering her awful encounter with the unstable girl.

Ophelia gathered her garbage from the table. "I don't know. I worry about the night terrors and the significance of the wild animal she sees."

"When I talked to her after the staff meeting, she told me about a fox in the withdrawal unit at night," Sam said.

Ophelia stood and picked up her dishes. "I remember. That was the morning after someone had given her drugs."

"Could her night terrors be manifesting into psychotic depression?" Sam asked.

"I don't know," Ophelia admitted. "Her symptoms are consistent with the residual effects of long-term Special K abuse, so I hope that's the problem."

"Special K?"

"Ketamine," Ophelia replied. "It's a dissociative anesthetic similar to PCP. The street name is Special K."

Bethany hadn't told Fadiya not to take candy from the wolf. She'd told her not to take cereal from the fox. Bethany knew who was giving Fadiya the ketamine. The same person had given it to her when her friend had disappeared from the withdrawal unit.

Sam stood and gathered her things. "I need to speak with her."

"You have to get Doug's permission," Ophelia said.

"Where is he?"

"I don't know." She walked into the cafeteria and put her dirty dishes in a plastic bin on a dish trolley.

Sam followed and took her arm to get her attention. "Ophelia, I think Bethany knows why the girls have been disappearing from the withdrawal unit."

Ophelia tucked her sunglasses into her oversized brown bag. "What are you talking about?"

"It's possible her friend didn't leave by choice," Sam said.

"Serena left on her own accord. Addicts make bad decisions all the time. It's sad, but it's life." Ophelia wended her way through the labyrinth of tables and chairs, heading for the cafeteria exit that led into the hospital.

Sam followed on her heels. "Bethany told me that a fox gave her Special K that she didn't want."

Ophelia abruptly turned to stare at her.

Before Sam could tell her what she knew, a security guard rushed over. "Ophelia, you're needed at the ambulance bay. They just brought in a patient on an involuntary hold. Dr. Beauregard wants you to handle intake while he talks with the sister."

She blew her breath out again in another exaggerated sigh. "My shift doesn't start for half an hour. Find someone else."

"Doc said it has to be you. Looks like it could be a VIP," the guard said. "Some rich game designer."

"What's wrong with him?" Ophelia asked irritably.

"Asperger's," the guard said. "His sister says he's a danger to himself and others."

Ophelia put her hands on her hip. "Asperger's is on the autism spectrum. It's not a mental health condition." Her eyes narrowed and there was edginess in the aggressive way she stood.

The guard held up his hand to stop her from speaking. "Look, I don't know anything about it. The ambulance just brought him in, and Dr. Beauregard wants you downstairs now."

"I'll go," Sam offered.

"No, I'll take care of it." Ophelia smoothed the pink fabric of her smock across her thighs. "Someone needs to give his sister a reality check." She pushed by the guard and strode toward the ambulance bay.

Sam followed, feeling uneasy about the rage in Ophelia's eyes. They reached the ambulance bay doors, where Eli was slouched in a wheelchair with Danny standing stiffly beside it. A leather duffel bag sat on Eli's lap. Sam had his phone—complete with an indoor positioning app Danny had written—and a cloned all-access keycard Aazar had given them. She'd drop both off after Ophelia processed Eli and he was alone in his room.

"She gave her brother six milligrams of Ativan prior to calling us," the paramedic said and lifted his eyebrow, in either disapproval or skepticism.

Ophelia knelt and studied Eli's face. "This man does not appear sedated. With that much Ativan on board, he should be asleep."

"He has a high tolerance," Danny said.

Ophelia turned to her, a flash of anger in her eyes. "Can you explain why you're admitting a man with Asperger's to a psychiatric facility? And why does he have a high tolerance for a sedative that should only be given on an intermittent basis?"

Danny matched Ophelia's hard stare. "I discussed all this with Dr. Beauregard prior to calling the ambulance." She looked over Ophelia's shoulder. "Here he is now."

"Danny, I'm so sorry we have to meet under these trying circumstances," Dr. Beauregard gushed. "Our head nurse will get Eli settled, while you and I chat in my office and discuss next steps." He reached out to shake Danny's hand.

Danny frowned and looked at his hand for a second before reluctantly offering her own. "Eli doesn't handle other people well and needs his own room. Spare no expense."

"Of course. Just as we discussed over the phone." The doctor turned to Ophelia. "Take Eli up to 317."

"You're putting him in the lockdown unit?" she asked incredulously. "Don't be ridiculous. He has Asperger's."

"Take him up to 317," he repeated firmly, and brushed by her. With mawkish deference, he escorted Danny through the ambulance bay doors and ushered her to the elevators.

Dr. Beauregard's obsequious behaviour was exactly what Sam had hoped for, and she released a breath of relief. During Danny's initial contact, she'd emphasized how wealthy her brother was, completing her web of seduction by sharing the address of their multimillion-dollar Harbourfront penthouse. Predictably, the man now kowtowed to Danny in the same way he did with the wealthy Basha family.

The paramedics closed the ambulance doors and climbed back into their vehicle, leaving Eli seated beside Ophelia and Sam in his wheelchair. Ophelia stared after the departing ambulance, her rage almost a palpable entity.

Sam regarded her cautiously. Ophelia's anger was unwarranted and Sam was hesitant to leave Eli alone with her. The plan they'd made two nights ago had been for Danny to pretend she'd sedated her brother prior to bringing him to Serenity Clinic, thus preventing anyone at the hospital from administering additional drugs. Ophelia was already suspicious and Sam wasn't certain Eli could keep up the charade. More worrisome, however, was the abrupt shift in Ophelia's expression and her stance. She struck Sam as unstable and she felt wary of the woman.

"I'd like to watch the intake process," Sam told her. "Good learning experience."

Ophelia grasped the wheelchair handles and rolled Eli through the doors and into the hospital. She continued to ignore Sam as they waited for an elevator. The doors opened and Ophelia turned and backed the chair into it, smoothly blocking Sam's access. She laid her hand possessively on Eli's shoulder and stared at Sam with her mismatched eyes.

"I'm the only one who can help him now," she said and the doors slid shut.

CHAPTER THIRTY-ONE

ELI

THE NURSE ROLLED the wheelchair out of the elevator and Eli jumped when an alarm rang. A radio played softly from somewhere on the floor, and Eli heard anguished sobs from behind one of the closed doors that lined the wide corridor. Along with the muffled cries of misery, the harsh odour of disinfectant was freaking him out. A shiver of dread scampered up Eli's spine. The awful certainty that he'd made a dire mistake engulfed him. He gritted his teeth and squeezed his eyes shut. Being a valuable member of the investigative team required moving out of his comfort zone, he reminded himself. Sam and Reece never complained about his eccentricities and social ineptitude, but Eli desperately wanted to prove that he had what it took to be a kick-ass detective. So, here he was pretending to be mentally ill and already feeling trepidation over his reckless decision.

His escort spoke to a grouchy-looking nurse who had come out of a room. "This is Eli Watson. He'll be in room 317. Check on Diana, please. Dr. Armstrong changed the dose on her quetiapine."

She wheeled Eli down the corridor, turned right, and then left. She nodded to another nurse behind a reception desk. Once they were about a metre from the nurses' station, she stopped and applied the wheelchair brakes again.

"My name is Ophelia," she said. "You can walk from here."

He was supposed to be doped up on sedatives. Eli had never taken tranquilizers, but he assumed he wouldn't be able to walk. He sat motionless—his nerves strung as tight as piano strings—and tried to figure out what to do.

Ophelia smiled. "You can cut the act, Eli. I know you aren't on Ativan. Up you get."

His stomach gurgled as panic swelled in his chest. If he confessed he hadn't taken the tranquilizers, she might give him drugs. If she gave him an injection, he wouldn't be able to vomit it out of his system. He'd be helpless and imprisoned in a psychiatric lockdown unit. Eli snapped the elastic around his wrist, hoping the sharp sting would redirect his brain activity and stabilize his rapidly growing anxiety. Reece was right. He couldn't do this. It was idiotic to believe he had sufficient acting skill to accomplish such a risky venture.

As if she had telepathy, Ophelia said, "Eli, I'm not going to drug you. Did you spit out the pills your sister gave you?"

Unable to trust what would come out of his mouth, he merely nodded.

"Come on, let's go." She left him in the wheelchair and strolled to a set of heavy glass doors.

Seeing no option, Eli stood and clutched his duffel bag with a shaking hand. He followed her, his heart careering in his chest, and wondered what had possessed him to volunteer to do this. Danny should have been the one they sent inside the facility. She would rock a task like this. Instead, he was already crippled by anxiety, which aggravated his physical tics. His free hand twitched and jerked beside his thigh as he strode robotically through the heavy glass doors. They slid closed behind him with a petrifying clunk.

They walked the length of the corridor. Perspiration pooled under Eli's arms, gluing the fabric of his long-sleeved T-shirt to his armpits. Ophelia stopped in front of a door. The original blueprint of the old building and the hospital's renovation blueprint that Danny had found flashed in front of Eli's eyes. He discarded the image of the original and focused on the renovation blueprint. It rotated in his mind until it took on a 3D shape, the lines a shimmering blue, as if displayed on a transparent OLED screen. Knowing exactly where he was in the hospital—and how to escape, should it come to that—reduced a bit of his panic. He was about two metres from Fadiya's room on the opposite side of the hallway. Adjacent to her door was the stairwell that descended to a street exit. Once Sam dropped off his phone and a security card, he could nudge open his door and have a decent view of Fadiya's room. If he full out freaked, he could escape down the stairwell. Eli blinked and the rotating blueprint dispersed like dust motes until the specks evaporated from his inner eye.

Ophelia held open the door to his room and Eli marched in with his arms pasted to his side and his leather bag thumping against his shin. He dropped the duffel bag on the bed and reluctantly turned toward her. His eyes darted around the ceiling. Keeping secrets was tough for him, which Reece had pointed out multiple times in an attempt to persuade him to abandon the plan. Rather than taking the criticism personally and arguing, Eli wished he'd listened to his boss's sensible concerns. Now he was here, he felt frightened and overwhelmed. The idea of being alone in the cramped room was terrifying.

Ophelia sat down in one of two armchairs by a window that overlooked a busy street. The window had bars. Shuddering, Eli took the chair on the opposite side of a circular table, noting that thick screws bolted the table to the floor.

"What's the best part of Asperger's?" she asked.

The question baffled him. No one had ever suggested there was anything remotely positive about his condition.

"The best part?" he echoed stupidly, his voice cracking like an adolescent boy's.

She nodded.

He considered her question. "I have an eidetic memory," he said. "But only for things that interest me. That is usually facts and data. I do not know if it is because of Asperger's, but it can be very useful." He cleared his throat and snapped the elastic against his skin to prevent his sudden urge to ramble about his photographic memory.

"I've read about declarative memory being associated with high-functioning autism," Ophelia said. "Do you find it useful for memorizing guided conversation to help you navigate social situations?"

Eli wished he had his phone. He felt naked without a device, exposed even. That rectangular screen was his comforting baby blanket. Without his phone to fiddle with, he didn't know what to do with his hands. He shoved his long-sleeves up his forearms.

"I have never used it for that." Against his will, his arm lifted and his fingers tapped the air as he spoke. "The eidetic memory enables me to repeat a conversation verbatim. Danny, my sister, translates subtext and innuendoes for me." He tried folding his hands on the table. "She is very good at reading people. She points out what I missed during the original conversation. I guess that is useful." Danny's insights into all the subtleties he missed usually made him aware that he had been a victim of ridicule. He decided to keep that to himself.

"What was your favourite subject in school?" Ophelia asked, staring at his naked forearm.

"Math." He tugged down his sleeve to cover the cigarette burns his biological father had seared into his flesh when he was four. "You have an accent."

She raised an eyebrow. "You can hear it?"

"A little, on certain words." Curious, he asked, "Why do you try to hide it?"

"I worked hard to overcome it," she said. "What was your least favourite subject in school?"

"English," he answered, wondering why she was so interested in his academic background. These questions weren't anything like the intake process Sam had rehearsed with him. "I do not understand symbolism and metaphors."

"Literature is very subjective," Ophelia said. "Nonliteral language is difficult for anyone on the spectrum."

"You know a lot about it," Eli said.

"My sister had autism," she said. "Pearl and I grew up on the bayou in Louisiana."

Eli didn't relish the thought of being alone, and he found he was becoming more at ease with Ophelia. He wasn't suffering the usual stress associated with having to analyse every phrase he uttered, constantly trying to assess whether he'd offended his audience. Maybe he could get her to stay for a bit, just until he felt more settled. He sorted through his minimal understanding of social nuances. Danny had taught him that asking a personal question helped to bridge relationships. He'd try that strategy.

"Is it nice in Louisiana?" he began. But maybe a *yes* or *no* question wouldn't work. "What is it like there?" he quickly added, giving his elastic another hearty snap.

"We lived on an isolated property on the Bayou Teche, outside Breaux Bridge," she said. "My dad and I would bait crawfish traps every morning, and my mother would tell us stories of her childhood in Savannah." A resounding sadness in her eyes was so apparent that even Eli recognized it. "In the evenings, Pearl and I would take our mud boat into the bayou and watch the sun set. The water was very still, and the sun would cover it in brilliant streaks of gold and fuchsia."

"Do Pearl and your parents still live there?" he asked.

She wrapped her arms around her waist and gazed out the window with a faraway look in her eyes. "They're waiting for me beneath an ancient bald cypress tree draped in lacy Spanish moss," she said wistfully. "On humid summer afternoons, Pearl and I would sit beneath that cypress tree. She had long platinum hair, and I'd comb coconut oil through it until it shone silver in the sun. Her fingers would tap the rhythm of the birds' songs, and her laughter would soothe my soul. We were happy then."

Her obvious melancholy unnerved Eli. She appeared about to cry, and he hoped she didn't. He was not good at comforting people.

"Go home and visit them," he said clumsily.

"Someday I'll fly o'er the bayou to my beloved Pearl," she said. "I still need to make the world a better place for people like you, who live with a special need. Imagine a world where the entitled are the ones who are marginalized, the ones who live in fear of scorn." She bowed her head. "You shouldn't be here, Eli. I wish your sister hadn't brought you here."

Eli worried that she was judging Danny harshly. "Danny and I are like you and Pearl. She understands me and keeps me safe." Realizing he was nervously tapping his fingers in the air again, he sat on his hands. "Just like you understand Pearl and keep her safe."

An expression of deep sorrow crossed Ophelia's face, so intense that, again, Eli could read it. "You remind me so much of her. Pearl would have liked you," she said. "I failed her, but you'll be okay, Eli. I'll protect you."

He felt a fusion of fear and apprehension. "Protect me from what?"

"There's something very wrong in here, and I only know a small part of it." She studied him earnestly. "Trust only the woman who was with me when we met. Her name is Sam McNamara. If I can't protect you, she can."

Eli's mind whirled at warp speed. Before he could sort out his next question, Ophelia stood and went to the door.

With her back to him, she said softly, "Wealthy patients get worse in here, Eli." She held her keycard to the reader and a green light flashed. She opened the door and stepped through it. There was a soft click as it closed again behind her.

Now it was on. He was locked in and trapped. Panic swelled in Eli's chest. It was suddenly hard to breathe and he lurched over to the window, knowing it wouldn't open but trying anyway. He took a deep breath through his nose and released it slowly through his mouth.

"This is bad. This is not good. This is very bad," he muttered.

His duffel bag sat like a giant cockroach on the fancy quilt that covered the bed. It irritated him that Ophelia hadn't searched it or made him change out of his street clothes like Sam had warned. He could have brought his phone with him, rather than waiting for Sam to deliver it. It was lucky, however, that Ophelia hadn't searched his clothes. He'd disobeyed Sam and Reece and had brought his pocketknife with him. His foster father had given it to him for his eighteenth birthday, and he never went anywhere without it.

The air seemed close, and the stench of disinfectant was making him nauseous. He went into the bathroom to splash cold water on his face. There was no stopper for the sink. Above the vanity was a large mirror. He rapped it with his knuckles. It wasn't glass, maybe acrylic or some other unbreakable material.

Eli wandered back into the bedroom, and looked up at the grill of the air vent in the ceiling.

"There is lots of air," he muttered, but his body wasn't listening to his voice of reason. His lungs felt tight and butterflies were convulsing in his stomach.

There was a call button for the nurse by the side of the bed. He wanted to press it and demand to see Danny so she could get him out. Was less than two hours in a locked room going to be his downfall?

Well, yes. Yes it was.

Just as he was reaching a trembling finger toward the call button, the door clicked open. Eli jerked back and spun around.

Sam slid into the room, closing the door quickly behind her.

"Where have you been?" Eli squeaked. "I am totally freaking out." He held out a quivering hand for his security blanket. "Give me my phone!"

She handed it over and he quickly swiped in his password. A wave of calm engulfed him as the screen lit up, connecting him to the outside world. He cradled the phone in his open palm, and its solid weight soothed his nerves.

"I've been trying to find a rehab patient," Sam explained. "Someone gave her ketamine. Bethany claims this 'fox' took the missing girls."

"Whoever it is must also be giving Fadiya ketamine," Eli said. "It must be the man who pretends to be a brother and brings the perverts to Fadiya's room. Bethany could identify him."

"And now she's missing," Sam said grimly and handed him a blank white keycard. "Aazar said he cloned it from Dr. Armstrong's card. It opens all the clinic's doors."

Eli snatched the card out of her hand and marched to the door to test it. The reader light glowed green and he heard the lock click open. The claustrophobia that had plagued him since his arrival in the room vanished.

He quickly told Sam about Ophelia's southern accent and then repeated what she'd said, repeating every word verbatim.

"So, she knows something's wrong in here," Sam said. "Did she elaborate on what exactly she knows?"

He shook his head.

"I never noticed an accent. It's weird that she hides it," Sam said. "The conversation you described doesn't sound anything like Ophelia."

Eli shrugged. "Why does she wear one coloured contact lens?" he asked.

Sam frowned. "She does?"

"The brown one. The lens moved when she looked out the window," he said, curious about why someone would want to have different-coloured eyes.

Sam thought quietly. "It's a brilliant way to alter your appearance," she said at last. "Pretty much all you notice about Ophelia is the heterochromia."

"I like her. She is nice," Eli said.

"She is?" Sam asked.

He nodded. "I think her sister is dead."

"What makes you say that?"

"Ophelia said she had failed Pearl, and she used past-tense verbs while talking about her sister." He couldn't read subtext in language, but he had no trouble with direct statements. He often thought life would be easier—probably for everyone—if people spoke frankly. "She said 'Pearl *would* have liked you,'" he repeated. "So, I think Pearl is dead." For some odd reason, it troubled Eli that Pearl was no longer listening to birds singing in the high branches of the ancient cypress tree. "I think something bad happened to her." He couldn't explain why he thought that, so he didn't bother trying to justify his feeling.

"Listen, I need to go and see if anyone has found Bethany. Then I'll go home and check in with Reece and Danny. Are you going to be okay?"

He nodded, hoping he wasn't going to flip out the second he was alone again.

Sam partially opened the door and poked out her head to glance furtively into the hallway. "It's only nine o'clock, but you better grab a nap. It could be a long night," she said quietly and softly latched the door behind her.

Right, like he would be napping in a locked room in a psychiatric hospital.

CHAPTER THIRTY-TWO

ELI

ELI JERKED AWAKE. Darkness surrounded him. He blinked rapidly, uncertain where he was. A cloying scent of disinfectant hit him.

Right, he was in Serenity Clinic in a private room on the lock-down unit.

The digital clock on the nightstand read one-twenty-eight in the morning. He couldn't believe he'd fallen asleep. This was his first undercover mission and he was acting like an amateur. No wonder Reece had opposed the idea of sending him to protect Fadiya.

Filled with self-disgust, Eli scrubbed his face with his hands, feeling the familiar scratch of his neatly trimmed goatee against his palms. He grabbed his phone and sent Danny a text. Before he'd fallen asleep, he'd sent numerous messages until she'd ordered him to leave her alone unless it was important. Telling her everything was fine wasn't important but he felt less isolated by reaching out.

He lay in the darkness, dreading the next few hours. The time between two and four in the morning freaked him out. These were the witching hours—a time when demons were most powerful. When he was nine, a bully at one of the group homes had shared that nugget of unwanted information. It had stuck in his head more than the beatings and ridicule had.

He thought he heard something and sat up, straining to identify the noise. He eased off the bed and tiptoed to the door, pressing his ear against the heavy metal. There were muffled voices in the hallway, close to Fadiya's room. He couldn't distinguish words, but he definitely heard the cadence of speech. A whispered argument, maybe. Probably just nurses, but Eli didn't like that they were outside Fadiya's room. Unlocking his door to peek was too big a risk. If the people were standing close to his door, they'd hear the click when the lock released. He waited anxiously, wondering what he should do.

After a minute, a door slammed. The noise was too loud for a room door. It must have come from the self-closing fire door that accessed the stairwell. Eli counted slowly to thirty and heard nothing more from the hallway. Holding his breath, he tapped the white plastic card against the reader. The click of the lock sounded deafening in the silence. He nervously turned the knob, opened the door a couple of centimetres, and peered into the lit corridor. About two metres from his room, on the opposite side of the hallway, a figure in a long beige robe stood outside Fadiya's room door. A hood concealed the person's face and Eli couldn't get a sense of gender because of the loose fabric of the garment. As he watched, the person walked to the fire door, opened it, and disappeared into the stairwell.

Here was his opportunity to prove his investigative prowess to Sam and Reece. Eli eagerly typed a text to Danny.

Someone in a hemp robe outside Fadiya's room. Went down the stairs. In pursuit.

He silenced his phone, tucked it into the back pocket of his jeans, and dashed to the stairwell door. He jammed his keycard against the reader, hoping Aazar was right and the cloned card accessed all the doors. The box flashed green and the door clicked. Relieved, Eli slipped into the stairwell and eased the door shut. There were footfalls on the stairs below him. He snuck a look over the banister and caught a flash of beige. The person was moving fast. Eli descended the stairs, pausing at the second-floor landing to listen for the sound of a door closing below him. He continued to the first floor and his anxiety rose. Still no echo from a latching door. Then it hit him; they were escaping through the basement level. There must be a connection to the underground parking garage. If the robed figure made it to a car in the garage, Eli wouldn't be able to follow.

Apprehension churned in his stomach as he dashed down to the last landing. To the left of the door, the staircase continued down. A sign screwed into the cement wall read Restricted Access. Below him, he finally heard a door slam. The stairs must lead to a floor below the basement, but Eli hadn't seen a sub-basement in the renovation plans.

The blueprint of the hospital renovation rose in his mind. He studied the rotating 3D schematic of the clinic and overlaid it across an image of the circa-1900 blueprints. There was a cellar in the original building. It wasn't part of Serenity's renovation plan, which was how he'd missed it.

Ignoring the Restricted Access sign, Eli sprinted down the stairs. At the bottom was a heavy grey door. Ribbons of rust ran through deep scratches and dents in the old paint. Affixed to the centre was a large white sign with red letters that spelled *Danger.*

Below the sign was a D-1 symbol, a circled graphic of a skull and crossbones.

Eli hesitated, with his right hand on the door handle and his left holding the security keycard. A class D-1 symbol meant that beyond the door were toxic materials. But this was a psychiatric hospital. Whatever danger lay behind the door couldn't be that bad. Maybe Serenity Clinic had posted a higher warning than necessary to discourage employees from entering an unsafe area. Given the age of the building, it made sense that a Victorian-era cellar would be a health hazard. Coal had been the primary heat source in Toronto during that time and the building's sub-basement had probably housed the old boilers. Coal dust was a physical toxicant, so that must be the reason for the symbol, he told himself. He wouldn't be down there long enough to cause a health issue.

Eli flicked his card against the reader and it flashed green. He shoved the door open a crack and peered into the darkness, waiting for his eyes to adjust. The only light was from a few low wattage bulbs that hung from frayed cords. Toward the back of the vast space, a light bobbed along what looked like a wide corridor. Eli slipped through the door and eased it closed behind him. The cavernous area smelt dank and musty. The massive, antiquated boilers cast eerie shadows in the dim light. Rusted pipes ascended from the heavy machinery to the ceiling. Beneath his feet, crumbling sandstone and bricks littered the packed-dirt floor.

Eli tugged out his cell phone. No service. He fiddled with the settings to no avail. The thick sandstone and brick walls, plus the fact he was underground, created a dead zone. Danny's location-positioning app wouldn't be able to find his phone. He hesitated by the door, snapping the elastic against his wrist to quell his rising unease. His law enforcement training screamed at him to leave, find service, and alert Danny to his location. He could wait outside the door and identify the person when they exited the sub-basement.

But the person had to have a reason for coming down here. There had to be something in this desolate space. He stood motionless, chewing on his lower lip as he studied the giant boilers. It took a lot of fuel to run them. Back in the day, how did they transport tons of coal to a sub-basement? Then a light went off— some of these old buildings had tunnels with rail links to connect the boiler room to a surface area where wagons delivered the coal. While he was standing around like a loser, his perpetrator could be escaping through a tunnel. No way was Eli going to blow his chance at proving his value to Sam and Reece by letting the person escape.

Decision made, he dimmed the brightness on his cellphone flashlight so he could make out where he was going without exposing his location. He inched down the dimly lit corridor between the boilers, stepping over the occasional chunk of bituminous coal that had escaped a sweeper's eye. He snuck forward, circled a vintage coal cart, and abruptly froze. A light was bouncing toward him. The person was returning to the hospital exit. Eli frantically looked around for a hiding spot. There were no crevices around the colossal boilers large enough to conceal him. His eyes fell on the rusted coal cart. If he sat on his shins and tucked his head against his knees, it should be deep enough to hide him. His black shirt would add extra camouflage in the shadowy darkness. Eli quickly climbed in, cringing as ancient coal residue coated his hands. He pulled the neck of his black T-shirt over his nose and breathed shallowly through his mouth. Footsteps drew closer and stopped about a metre from his hiding spot.

"Pick up in an hour," said a male voice. There was a pause. "She's fifteen, but looks thirteen. You'll get a good price on auction." There was another, longer pause. "No one cares about this one so they won't look for her."

The man was talking about a girl. Eli's heart galloped in his chest. He tried to memorize the man's voice so he could identify it later.

"It's too risky. The family hired round-the-clock nursing. You shouldn't have sent me that regular tonight. I had to send him packing."

He had to be talking about Fadiya. Eli clenched his fists, digging his nails into his palms. Some asshole had expected to rape Fadiya tonight. That must have been the argument Eli had overheard.

"Make it work. I need this girl out of here tonight."

Another pause.

"I have to check in upstairs but I'll meet you in the room in exactly one hour. I want the full payment or you don't take her."

He grunted in response to something, and then continued speaking. "This is the last one. That detective bitch is asking too many questions."

The man began walking again. His footsteps faded and a door closed.

Eli climbed out of the coal cart and brightened his phone light, scanning the beam down the aisle toward the back of the cellar.

This was huge. If he aided in shutting down a human trafficking ring, he'd earn validation. No one would ever doubt his investigative abilities again.

He hurried down the wide aisle to the rear of the sub-basement. In a corner was a walled alcove with two wooden doors. The dirt floor around the doors was black with coal dust. Beneath the caked grime were metal tracks inlaid into the packed dirt. This must be the old coal room. The men would shovel the coal into a cart and run it along the tracks to get it to the boilers. If he were right, then a chute or a tunnel would lead to the surface to accommodate the coal delivery. That was the way the sex traders removed the abducted girls from the hospital and escorted in the degenerates who paid to rape Fadiya.

Between the thick wood handles on the door was a chain with a heavy padlock. Eli hunted around the base of the mammoth boiler and found a chunk of iron pipe. He ran back to the doors, jimmied the pipe between the chains, and pulled. They held fast, the thick iron links refusing to budge. He jammed his foot against the door to gain extra leverage. After a couple of failed attempts, there was a loud crack. One of the door handles was loosening. Eli repositioned the pipe closer to the weakened handle, braced his foot against the door, and applied his full body weight to pull down the pipe. His biceps burned under the strain. He repositioned his hands, steadied his feet, and threw his upper body against the pipe. The top half of the handle pulled away from the door with a snap. He lifted the chain over the broken handle. It hit the wooden door with a clang. He cautiously opened the doors and shone his light around the confined space. A tiny blonde girl sat on the floor in the corner, tied and gagged. Eli rushed in, dropped the iron pipe beside her, and placed his fingers on her dirt-encased neck. Her eyes flickered open; the pupils were enormous in her bloodshot eyes.

"I am here to help you," he said. "I am going to get you out." He gently removed the gag and she gurgled something incomprehensible.

He took the pocketknife from his jeans and carefully sawed through the thick plastic restrains on her wrists. Her arms dropped lifelessly to her side and her head lolled against her shoulder.

"Are you hurt?" He couldn't see any sign of injury. Drugs would be his best guess.

He placed the knife on the ground beside him. She was shivering and he rubbed his hands along her upper arms. "Who did this to you?"

She whispered something that sounded like *fox*. He stood and thought for a moment. Based on her physical and mental condition, she wouldn't be able to walk. He had to get her out before the man returned from upstairs.

Eli shone his light around the room, tracing the old metal rails leading away from the door. They led to a wood-framed black hole in the back wall. Someone had piled newer bricks and large chunks of cement against the walls. Years earlier, they must have sealed the tunnel entrance, but someone—probably the sex trader or someone who worked for him—had broken through.

The girl's eyes followed the light. She made a strangled noise deep in her throat and reached up to grab his hand.

He crouched down again. "It is okay," he assured her. "We will leave together. I promise. My name is Eli."

"Bethany," she whispered. "Help me. The fox is coming."

"Who is the *fox*?" he asked, but her eyes were drifting closed.

He dropped his knife and clutched both her shoulders to prevent her from toppling over. He gently laid her on the ground and pressed his fingers on her neck again. Her pulse was a weak and rapid flutter against his fingers. He knew he had to move fast and get her out.

Eli jumped up and accidentally kicked his knife into the rubble surrounding the mouth of the tunnel. He shone his light around but couldn't see where the knife had disappeared. He hunted vainly for a few seconds, while his gut screamed at him to get Bethany to safety.

Abandoning his search for the pocketknife, Eli directed his light at the hole in the wall. The tunnel slanted upwards; it was a little over two metres high and bridged with ancient logs on the walls and ceiling. The thick logs were black with coal dust, wood rot, and mould, but they appeared secure.

The building's original blueprint rose again in Eli's mind. He located the sub-basement tunnel and traced the upward trajectory to ground level. From what he could discern, it was about ten metres to the surface—maybe thirty-two feet. He checked the time on his phone. Fifteen minutes had elapsed since the robed man's telephone call. Whoever was picking up the girl wouldn't arrive for over half an hour yet, but Eli didn't know when the robed man would return.

He remembered a seminar at university where a retired police chief had told Eli's criminology class never—under any circumstances—to enter a confined space without backup. Eli didn't relish the thought of travelling through a dark tunnel without knowing for sure if there was an exit at the end, but he didn't see any option. Bethany's abductor had said on the phone that he would wait with her, so he was clearly coming back. The risk of encountering him before they made it to the hospital exit and safely up the stairwell was too high. The tunnel was their best chance of escaping.

He squatted down to lift her. Her eyes focused above his head and a strangled whimper escaped from between her dry lips. She cringed against the wall, covering her soot-covered face with her forearms. Eli's heart jackhammered against his rib cage as he sensed eyes on his back and realized what was happening. He'd wasted too much time figuring out what to do. The fox was in the room.

With his back still towards the intruder, and without physically reacting to the man's presence, Eli slowly reached for the iron pipe, leaning slightly so his body blocked his arm's movement. He had only one shot at this, he knew: he had to spin around and strike the man's shins hard enough to take him down.

His fingers grasped cold metal. He rotated his toe, preparing to swing with all his strength. Blinding pain filled his head. His body pitched forward. As if from a distance, he heard Bethany screaming. Wind whistled in his ear as the weapon lashed down on him a second time. A brilliant starburst erupted across his eyes.

Then nothing but darkness and the echoes of a girl's screams.

CHAPTER THIRTY-THREE

The Journal

OVER A DECADE had passed since Pearl and I marvelled at the speckled rays of sun pirouetting across the mirrored surface of the Teche. Blu had long since vanished into the ethereal mist, abandoning Ophelia with a posy of rue.

I found solace in my dreams, where I watched Pearl's skirt float around her lithe body as she danced in the still water at dusk. I would hear my father's dulcet baritone drifting on a midnight breeze, feel the gentle touch of my mother's caress, and smell the fragrant coconut oil from her iridescent hair. I existed within this shadowy realm, caught between the living and the dead, where Pearl's innocent spirit blessed me with peace.

With only my dreams to connect me to my bayou home, I had no way of knowing that Cyril had broken the vow he'd sworn to my father, a man who had saved his worthless life. For thirty pieces of silver, Cyril had betrayed his saviour's daughter, and Virgile's brother had come to Toronto for his revenge.

I hadn't known the elder Landry son well, for he was eight years my senior. During most of my childhood in Louisiana, he was away at the finest schools money could buy. When I encountered him in Toronto, he was using a different surname and his physical features didn't resemble his porcine father or brother, but his cruel persona was what truly deceived me.

Basile Landry had all but disowned his elder son because of the young man's gentle manner, which was nothing but a soulless mask he donned with artful ease. Over the years, I've seen the effortless way Mathias Beauregard switches on insincere magnetism and transforms into the sensitive young man I recall from childhood. He hides his limitless greed beneath a veneer of professional empathy that seduces wealthy families into sparing no expense to save their loved ones. He bleeds those desperate souls until their fragile wings of hope disintegrate to dust.

Mathias's presence in my life has vanquished the absolution Pearl had gifted me through my dreams. Now at night, I stare blindly through the darkness of my lonely bedroom, haunted by my failure to recognize his true face. Across the blank canvas of the white spackled ceiling, a grotesque montage plays on an endless loop. I relive Pearl's defilement and anguish beneath our ancient cypress tree, and I see what I had missed: Virgile's brother stands in the moonlit shadows cast by the gnarled branches.

Mathias had stroked Pearl's arm at the Crawfish Festival. When he'd laid his hand on her, it was then that Pearl had fallen apart. My failure to understand what she had tried so desperately to communicate has damned me to suffer the resounding echoes of her dying screams for eternity.

In a macabre twist of fate, Mathias now holds the string that rules my destiny. In Louisiana, there is a standing warrant for my arrest, charging me with four counts of first-degree murder in the deaths of Virgile, my parents, and my grandfather. If Mathias identifies me, Canadian authorities will extradite me and I will stand before my accused. Basile Landry and his surviving son will ruthlessly advocate for the death penalty and they will win.

And so, I live on borrowed time, contorted by a puppet master's strings, ruing the day I walked into his insidious trap.

I didn't know Dr. Mathias Beauregard when Serenity Clinic opened, and his unsolicited job offer came as a pleasant surprise. The private hospital was close to a bistro I'd stumbled upon that hired people with special needs. Although the neighbourhood was transforming, a Community Living residence and a Veteran's Affairs facility still operated in the area. I found amity amongst those neglected and discarded people. Gentrification was attracting upwardly mobile millennials to the Parkdale housing market, and the favourable reviews of Cardoon Bistro were enticing a mix of privileged and middle-class visitors. I realised this was the perfect experimental group to watch interacting with those I'd vowed to protect.

By the time I accepted the position of head nurse at the clinic, I had exterminated twenty-two entitled offenders who habitually degraded the weak and downtrodden. I had refined my techniques and had grown skillful in surveillance, judgment, and execution. I chose only the dregs of society, who maligned the blameless with impunity and exuded blatant rudeness.

It's easy to stalk people. I start with a chance meeting in public, which you'll never notice, busy as you are on your phone. That tiny computer you grasp tight in your fist is your lifeline and my covert access to your world. I stand innocuously beside you for the few seconds it takes for my phone to connect to yours and download malware that wirelessly uploads to yours. My little RAT invisibly burrows snug beneath your array of frivolous apps, infiltrating your privacy. I learn everything about you. All those confidential things you share via email, text, and FaceTime, never suspecting that someone is watching.

I am your shadow. I see inside the darkest part of you. I am your omnipotent judge.

If you go anywhere without your phone, you might be safe. From me, at least, but if that miniature computer is rarely out of your clutch, you are prey. I alone will determine if you're worthy of life.

Tagging your phone's GPS is easy. But even if you disable it and think you're safe, you aren't. Social media apps track your phone's location. They want to know where you are. If you fit my profile, so do I.

Linking your phone's GPS coordinates to my sophisticated drone is simple, as is downloading video from the unseen drone stalking you. If, during the weeks of surveillance, I recognize a pattern of prejudicial behaviour that fits my criteria, I'll come for you.

I am an ingenious stalker. Yet I failed to see that someone hunted me.

Mathias had me under surveillance for years before he made his presence known. He discovered I was a vigilante executioner and cunningly imprisoned me within an iron cage that I myself had unwittingly forged. After I terminated Annalise Huang, he told me that he'd witnessed the deed from outside her living room window.

He had no opinion on her death—no moral outrage or victim sympathy, not that she deserved any. He simply told me that Annalise's execution was one of five that he had videotaped. His demands, although sinister, were relatively harmless. In exchange for his silence, I was to administer drugs to specific patients. The wealthy parents would pay exorbitant fees to keep their mentally ill child at the clinic. Mathias would continue embezzling money, right under Emily Armstrong's unsuspecting nose, and I could continue to kill, if it suited me; he didn't care one way or the other.

He assured me, with a counterfeit smile and serpentine eyes, that if anything happened to him, his attorneys would deliver one package of evidence to the Toronto police department and a second to the Louisiana State Police. There would be nowhere to run.

He selects only wealthy patients who have suffered extreme trauma. There is no psychological recovery for these tortured souls. The best they can hope for is to live with their terrifying memories of unspeakable evil without succumbing to madness. Most fail. I've seen them turn to drugs, alcohol, sex, or self-harm to anesthetize themselves. These innocent victims suffer infinitely within a circle of hell beyond our comprehension. Shutting down their minds is a blessing, and so, I do what I must to secure my freedom.

However, what Mathias has asked of me now, I cannot justify.

He ordered me to his office tonight. I closed the door behind Ophelia and turned to face him as Blu. "What do you want?"

He raised his eyebrow. "Check yourself, Blu. I own you." He stacked papers neatly on the glossy surface of his opulent desk. "That new patient will be happy here," he said.

Eli Watson, the Asperger's patient whose obtuse sister had committed him.

"Ensure that his sister has no reason to believe he's making progress," Mathias said. "Try phencyclidine to start. If we're lucky, it will cause aggression." He stood and rubbed sweet-smelling hand cream into his manicured nails.

"PCP could kill him," I said.

"Melodrama doesn't suit you." Disdain dripped from his tone. "I want him violent so his overwrought sister opens the bank vault to get him the best of care."

His casual disregard for Eli's life warranted only one word. "No."

My hand was on the doorknob before he spoke again.

"I understand, Blu," he murmured in a saccharine tone. "Eli reminds you of Pearl. I never did tell you what happened to her after you left." He ambled over like a surefooted lion stalking its prey. "They found her in her limestone tomb, encircled by blue-hearts and Louisiana violets under that old cypress tree."

His breath was hot and rancid against my neck. "After they cut her apart, they threw her in a pine box fit for a whore." He leaned close and whispered intimately into my ear. "My daddy had them burn your crazy ma and coonass pa. Then he slashed open their sacks of ashes and threw them on his compost pile," he said with a chuckle that made my skin crawl. "Now they fertilize our sugarcane crops. Serving their betters, you might say."

I spun around, my hands bunched into fists at my side, but words failed me. To my horror, I felt tears sting my eyes.

A triumphant sneer met my moist gaze. "Drug the kid, Blu, or they'll take you home to the bayou in chains to ride the needle."

"No," I said through clenched teeth.

Mathias removed his cell phone from the pocket of his tailored pants. "One phone call, Blu. If you think your sacrifice will save the kid, think again. I'll drug him myself."

I left his vile presence and stumbled down the corridor to the boardroom. I stood alone in the dark silence and closed my eyes against my tears. A sweet aroma of coconut filled the empty room, and a humid breeze caressed my neck. I opened my eyes.

She stood just beyond my reach, and her platinum hair shimmered in a beam of moonlight from the window. Pearl held open her arms, and I yearned to let the purity of her love soothe my tattered soul, but I couldn't go to her. A flicker of understanding crossed her aqua eyes before her spirit dissipated, leaving only the fragrant scent of coconut behind.

I had failed Pearl. I would not fail Eli Watson.

CHAPTER THIRTY-FOUR

SAM

SAM'S EYES BURNED as she peered at her computer monitor. It was almost one-thirty in the morning and she'd been up for twenty-hours. When she'd suggested they crash for a bit, Danny's horrified expression had kyboshed any hope of sleep.

Eli hadn't contacted them in hours, probably because his inane text messages had heightened Danny's anxiety and she'd told him to stop unless it was about the case. She may not want to chat with her brother, but she kept a strained vigil as she waited for the night to end so she could fetch him home.

"More coffee?" Reece offered, looking remarkably fresh after a quick shower.

Sam shook her head and rubbed her dry eyes. Her massive caffeine consumption over the past few hours had dehydrated her and made her twitchy.

Reece stood behind her, massaging her tense shoulders. "Find anything?"

She shook her head again. For the past three hours, she'd been hunting databases for information on Ophelia. Allegedly born in Lethbridge, Alberta, she'd attended high school there and her marks were high, especially in math and science. Nothing unusual there, but Sam had found a yearbook database and had located an online copy of Ophelia's graduating year. The yearbook didn't list her name among the graduating class.

"Her background check came back clean," Sam said. "I verified that she did graduate from University of Toronto. That's legit, but this high school transcript bugs me."

"Eli just woke up," Danny said, laying her phone back on the table. "He was napping." She rolled her eyes.

"I told him to rest." Sam turned back to her conversation with Reece. "Why did Ophelia tell Eli she grew up in Louisiana?"

Reece shrugged. "She could have moved to Louisiana and returned to Canada for high school. Why is this bothering you so much?"

"The conversation Eli repeated is nothing like Ophelia. She sure doesn't speak in poetic terms. And why hide a southern accent?" Sam paused to consider what was really bugging her. "Sometimes, people talk a lot about nothing, use offensive sarcasm, and become overly intense to repel their audience." She thought about their earlier conversation in the courtyard. "When we chatted at dinner, I had the sense that her off-putting comments were intentional so I'd leave."

"Does it matter if she's developed a technique to avoid social contact?" Reece asked.

"It usually means the person is hiding something. They don't want you asking questions," she said. "That would also explain why she's faking heterochromia. A physical anomaly can make people uncomfortable."

Reece frowned. "You can't think people would avoid her because her eyes are different colours. That's so shallow."

Sam shrugged. "We live in shallow times."

"Ophelia is in Cardoon Bistro a lot," Danny said.

Sam looked up. "So?"

Danny's phone chirped but rather than turning it over to check the new message, her eyes flickered to Reece. "I saw her on the security footage Eli took from Cardoon."

Reece's hands froze against Sam's shoulders. "I told you to drop it."

"I'd already set up the face templates on your suspected victims to run against the Cardoon video files, and it took this long to find—"

Reece interrupted with a hard edge to his voice. "You sent Bryce Mansfield the footage didn't you?"

"Yes. But the algorithms were running against a duplicate file, and you need to know—"

Reece held up a hand to silence her. "I don't need or want to know anything." He stomped to the kitchen and poured a cup of coffee. "The deputy attorney general has ordered me to his office tomorrow. I'll find out if they're pressing charges. I swore that we handed *everything* over to Toronto Police Services." He slammed the metal coffee carafe onto the kitchen island. "For God's sake, Danny, do you know how it'll look if they find out I kept copies and lied to them? Delete all the footage."

Sam swivelled in her chair so she could see Reece. "No one is going to find out Danny kept a copy. Even if they do, they can't hold you accountable for someone else's actions."

He ran his fingers though his thick black hair. A tuft stood up at the back of his head. "I swore we didn't have copies. Make sure we don't."

Sam wasn't in the mood to suffer another heated debate between her straight-laced fiancé and their nonconformist associate.

"We're all tired and worried about Eli," she said. "Was that text from him?"

Danny turned over her phone and frowned as she read the message. She swiped something and her grey eyes widened. The colour blanched from her cheeks until her skin appeared translucent against her jet-black hair.

"He's gone." She stood and backed away from the table, colliding with a chair.

Sam intercepted her and barricaded the front door before Danny could bolt. "You can track him inside the clinic. Right?"

Danny shook her head with a crazed expression, as if she were on the verge of unraveling.

Reece took the phone from her limp hand and read the text. "He saw a robed figure outside Fadiya's room and is in pursuit." He cursed under his breath. "The location-positioning app can't find him. Could his phone be dead?"

"Have you met my brother?" Danny snatched her phone from his hand. "He'd never let the battery die." She tried to shove by Sam to open the door. "We have to go to the clinic. We have to go right now."

"We're going. Hold on." Sam tugged on her sneakers as Reece set the home alarm. They ran down the hallway to the back entrance and sprinted across the parking lot to Reece's grey Toyota. Danny kept her eyes glued to her phone, urging Reece to hurry as he pulled onto Queen Street.

"Does your app show Eli's last known location?" Sam asked.

Danny shook her head. "Once the phone is offline, it's gone."

Reece swung onto the exit for the Don Valley Parkway. "Maybe he's in a dead zone."

"In a hospital?" Danny screamed. "Someone's taken the phone and destroyed it or removed the battery. Hurry up! Go around that transport truck."

"Calm down. We'll find him." A sense of impending peril engulfed Sam. She never should have agreed to Eli's plan. He wasn't ready to take on an undercover assignment. He was too reckless and spontaneous. If anything happened to him, it would be on her head and she'd deserve every ounce of guilt.

Reece sped west on the Gardiner Expressway. "Maybe a staff member found him with his phone and took it," he said. "Eli could be in his room with no way to contact us."

Sam pressed her hand against his knee, grateful for his quick deductive reasoning. "You're right. If security were doing rounds and found a patient in the stairwell, they'd call a nurse who would confiscate the device." An iota of relief washed over her. "That's probably what happened."

Reece took the exit into Parkdale and wound through side streets to reach the back of the hospital.

Before the car had even stopped, Danny had jumped out and was running up to the entrance. They hurried through the ambulance bay to the hospital entrance, and Sam flashed her security card at the door reader. Once through the door, a guard stopped them.

"Who are these people?" he asked Sam.

She recognized him from the day she'd met Fadiya. He'd helped her get off the lockdown unit when her temporary badge wouldn't operate the elevator.

"Saul, I need to check on a patient." She gestured at Reece. "This is Reece Hash a private investigator."

Saul's frown deepened. "I don't care if he's the Prime Minister. He can't be here in the middle of the night. You know that."

Ignoring him, Sam flicked her badge against the elevator call button. "Eli Watson's sister has reason to believe there's a serious issue with her brother. Have you seen him?"

The guard's stern expression shifted to confusion. "The rich kid up on the lockdown unit?"

Sam nodded. "Did one of your team pick him up tonight outside his room?"

He shook his head. "It's been quiet all night."

"You better come with us," Sam said, hoping that by involving him he'd ignore the break in protocol. "If something happens to Eli Watson, Dr. Beauregard will have our heads."

Saul stepped into the elevator, hit the reader with his security card, and pressed the floor number. He turned to Danny. "Why do you think something's wrong with your brother?"

"He called me," she said simply, her eyes glued to the floor readout at the top of the elevator door. Her foot tapped impatiently as they ascended.

"He'd have to leave his room to use a phone," Saul said grimly. "A female patient did the same thing two nights ago. She grabbed the room door before it latched. We've told staff a hundred times to ensure the door locks before they walk away."

The elevator opened and Sam led the way down the hall and around the corner. Danny sprinted past the vacant nurses' station, stopping short at the thick sliding doors that accessed the lockdown unit. Sam dashed after her and opened the doors. The second Danny could squeeze her body through; she rushed down the corridor to her brother's room. She pounded on the door, calling Eli's name.

Fadiya's door opened and Ophelia stepped out, grabbing Sam's arm. "What the hell is going on out here?"

Sam swiped her card against the lock on 317, opened the door, and flicked on the light.

The room was empty.

Ophelia stomped to the bathroom. When she came out, she threw her hands on her waist and stared at the group that crowded into the doorway. "Where is this patient?"

Sam turned to Saul. "Can you lockdown the building?"

"What?"

"Lock all exits and deactivate everyone's security cards so they can't open the exterior doors," Danny said.

"Deactivate… I don't know how to do that," he said.

"Take me to your security system," Danny ordered.

"What?" He turned to Ophelia. "Is the missing patient dangerous? How did he get out of the unit?"

Ophelia stepped between them and glared at Danny. "Why are you here?" She glanced at Reece and her frown deepened. "No one is moving from this room until someone tells me what's going on."

"Eli Watson is an employee of our investigation agency," Sam explained. "He was here undercover. There's a positioning app on his phone. We lost him about forty-minutes ago."

Ophelia looked at Danny with an expression Sam couldn't read. "You mean you didn't commit your brother on an involuntary hold because of his Asperger's?"

"Of course not," Danny growled. "He's protecting Fadiya."

Suspicion narrowed Ophelia's eyes. "From what?"

"It's a long story," Sam said, reluctant to waste time by disclosing what they knew.

"Then you better get explaining, because no one is leaving this room until you do," Ophelia stated.

Reece stepped forward and shot Danny a warning look. She shut her mouth on whatever she was about to say and stood with her arms folded over her chest, her nervous energy a palpable entity that charged the stale air in the room.

"Some unknown perpetrator is selling Fadiya for sex," Reece told Ophelia. "She's pregnant."

Ophelia stood perfectly still with no expression. "Someone raped Fadiya?" Her voice caught.

"Her claim about Mussani visiting her at night isn't a deluded fantasy," Sam said. "Someone *is* bringing men to her room. The trafficker preys on her indoctrination by making the buyers impersonate Mussani."

"What are you saying? She's not suffering from delusional disorder?" The colour drained from Ophelia's face.

"We also believe that the girls who disappeared from the withdrawal unit were abducted and sold into slavery," Sam said. "I think Bethany knows who took them."

Ophelia's complexion was grey. "Human trafficking?" she stuttered.

"Eli was following a man he witnessed outside Fadiya's door just after one thirty," Sam said.

Ophelia shook her head. "That's impossible. I was with Fadiya all night. I didn't hear anything in the hallway." She paused in thought. "Wait. I left Fadiya's room around one-thirty to add a dosage change to a patient's chart. I forgot to record it after I brought Eli upstairs. But I was at the nurses' station for less than ten minutes."

"Are there dead zones in the hospital?" Danny asked. "Anywhere that a cell phone wouldn't work?"

"Not that I'm aware," Ophelia said briskly, her usual air of authority returning. "Saul, lockdown the hospital. No one in, no one out." She moved to the door.

"I don't have the authority or the IT expertise to do that," he said.

"I'm your IT expert," Danny retorted. "Let's go."

"But you need administrator credentials," Saul argued. "We'll have to wait for the head of IT." He reached for the radio on his shoulder.

Danny grabbed his elbow. "Take me to a computer now."

"Emily gave her full access to the security system," Sam explained to Saul. "Alert your staff that there's a missing patient. We'll start searching."

"It'll be faster if we split up," Ophelia said. "You and Reece take the main level. Security will take the executive offices and basement. I'll check the rooms on this floor and the withdrawal unit." She brushed by Danny and went out the open door, turning toward the stairwell exit.

Danny stomped through the doorway and stood in the corridor, waiting impatiently for her escort.

"We need to call the partners," Saul said miserably. "I saw Dr. Armstrong before you arrived. She might still be here." He ran his hand across his bald crown. "Christ, Dr. Beauregard is going to have a meltdown."

"Let's go!" Danny yelled through the open door.

Saul visibly winced and joined her in the corridor.

Reece took Sam's arm before she could follow them.

"Eli has been gone for nearly an hour," he said solemnly. "You know what that means."

Dread and fear coalesced into a wave of physical sickness. She'd known that Eli's determination to do this was because he was insecure. He'd wanted validation that he could do the job. If she'd offered more encouragement and had told him how much she valued him as a friend and an employee, he wouldn't have felt it necessary to put himself in danger to prove his worth.

"We need a forensic team," she whispered.

Reece scrolled through his cell phone and then held it to his ear. He gazed down the hallway while he spoke to Inspector Bryce Mansfield.

Sam didn't need Reece to explain why he'd called the head of the homicide squad. She'd been a cop long enough to know what they were dealing with.

The chances of finding Eli alive were slim.

CHAPTER THIRTY-FIVE

Eli

A DAMP COLDNESS had seeped into Eli's bones. Danny must have turned up the air conditioning again. He tried to reach for his bedside lamp. His arm wouldn't move.

Terror jolted him into consciousness. His vision blurred and excruciating pain sheathed his head. The agony surged in a thudding crescendo. Projectile vomit erupted from his mouth and he choked on acidic bile. His vision receded into shadowy darkness and burst into blinding white light. A high-pitched ringing filled his ears.

Eli toppled over and curled into a fetal position on the dank floor, moaning and rocking as torturous pain assaulted his head. Gradually the agony dulled to a throbbing ache. He felt warm syrup dribble across his cheek and pool against his lips. He flicked out his tongue and tasted the metallic tang of blood.

He lay still and breathed shallowly, trying to remember where he was and what had happened. Behind his closed lids, he saw a tiny girl with long blonde hair and elfin features. She was cowering in a dirt hole.

No. Not a hole. A room below ground.

An oily aroma of rock dust surrounded him, along with a dirty odour that was similar to cigar smoke.

As if from a far distance, Eli heard a gruff voice echo in his head: "*No one cares about this one so they won't look. You'll get a good price at auction.*"

He rolled sluggishly onto his knees and cautiously rose to a kneeling position. The buzzing in his ears intensified. He gritted his teeth and eased open his eyes. Dim yellow light pooled on the floor from a naked bulb that hung from the centre of a rotten wood ceiling. His eyelids closed against his will and his body swayed. He pitched onto his side, and a starburst exploded behind his closed eyes.

He was in a university hall, and a speaker was lecturing about police procedures: "*Never, under any circumstances, enter a confined space without backup.*"

"But I had to," Eli mumbled. "I had to get her out."

He couldn't remember who he was trying to help or why.

In a shadowy picture in his mind, he was holding Danny's hand. Their foster mother was crouched in front of them. Dazzling sunshine ignited the ribbons of gold through her thick chestnut hair.

"*It's perfectly safe, honey. It's a museum now and a guide takes us in. Don't you want to wear a hardhat?*"

Their east coast vacation to the Maritimes.

He had been thirteen and Danny had been eleven. His family had rented a cottage in Toney River, Nova Scotia. They'd taken day excursions, and one had been to visit the Springhill Miner's Museum. The yawning mouth of the mine had terrified him but he'd tried to be brave for Danny.

It was coal he smelled.

As he regained consciousness, asphyxiating panic sucked the breath from his lungs.

He was trapped in a coalmine.

A fuzzy image of an antiquated boiler rose in his mind. Beside the monstrous machine was a rusted cart, stained black with dust.

He wasn't in a mine. He was in a coal room.

His memory flooded back in a rapid series of disjointed images.

He was in an unused boiler room at Serenity Clinic. Wagons used to dump coal down a shaft to this storage room, and men had shovelled it into carts that ran on the rails. Someone had opened the mouth of the tunnel and was using it to abducted girls from the clinic.

Eli forced his eyes open and searched around the cramped space. Where was the girl he'd tried to rescue?

He rolled onto his back and stuck his legs out in front of him. They were bound with thick white zip ties. He couldn't move his hands from behind his back, and he figured the same plastic ties restrained them. He clenched his abdominal muscles and lifted his upper body into a sitting position. Pain erupted in his head. He screamed, the sound of his misery ricocheting against the crumbling walls of the confined space that imprisoned him.

Eli woke to the sound of a door crashing open. Hands were suddenly on him. Someone was dragging him from behind. He thrashed his bound legs and tried to squirm out of the person's iron grip.

"Stop Eli," a female voice ordered. "I need to get you against the wall."

The woman shoved him. His back hit a solid surface.

"You have a serious head injury," she said. "Try not to move."

He opened his eyes and his vision slowly cleared.

She leaned over him and peered into his eyes. "Do you know who I am?" she asked anxiously.

"Ophelia," he mumbled.

"Thank God I found you," she said. "Your sister asked about dead zones in the hospital. This sub-basement was the only place I could think of. I was searching it when I heard you screaming. I haven't anything to cut your restraints."

"Dropped a knife," he muttered. "Kicked it into the rubble."

She got up and hurried to the opening of the tunnel. She dropped to her knees, and Eli watched her rummage around the pile of broken stones and chunks of cement. The high-pitched ringing in his ears increased in volume. His eyes drifted shut.

Suddenly, he heard yelling and a sharp prick in his arm that pinched.

"Wake up, Eli! You can't go to sleep."

He tried to obey the commanding voice without success. He felt as if he were tumbling into a warm bath. The sensation was pleasant—comforting, even—and he experienced a wonderful sense of euphoria.

A hard slap across his face jerked him awake. He blinked and Ophelia's face gradually came into focus.

"Stay still," she ordered sternly.

He felt her fingers probe his head. Sudden, intense pain caused him to yelp and struggle, but she shoved her shoulder against his chest to keep him immobile and continued her examination.

"I think your skull is fractured at the occipital lobe." She tenderly moved his head to the side. "You may also have a temporal fracture. There's blood in your left ear. I need you to move as little as possible." She gently reached behind him.

Something sharp dug into the skin on his wrists and his hands jerked up and down. Eli's lethargic brain tried to make sense of what was happening. His arms thumped against his thighs. She must have found his knife and cut the restraints.

"Who did this to you?" she asked.

"There was a girl," he said slowly. "Her name was Bethany."

Ophelia stood and crossed the room to peer into the mouth of the tunnel. "Bethany attacked you?"

"No, he took her."

"Who took her?"

Eli moaned as shards of glass impaled his brain and roaring white noise filled his head. "The fox," he murmured.

It was then that Eli realized he might not make it. If he died before he shared what he knew, they'd never find Bethany.

"I heard the sex trader on the phone," he muttered through gritted teeth. "He said they would get a good price at auction. He drugs the girls with ketamine and takes them." Speaking was excruciating and he paused to catch his breath.

"Ketamine?" she asked. "Are you sure?"

"That is also how he subdues witnesses to the abductions. Bethany's tolerance to ketamine must be high, because she saw him take her friend. The fox knows Bethany can identify him." He forced the words from his dry lips. "That is why he took her and sold her."

Her eyes widened and she stood, grasping his knife limply in her hand. "He abducts our patients?"

"He sells them to a human trafficking ring," Eli said, wishing she'd free his legs. "He also caters to men's perverted fetishes. The fox uses ketamine to keep Fadiya deluded so he can prostitute her."

"The ketamine is so he can sell Fadiya for sex?" Tears congested Ophelia's voice.

"I would recognize his voice," he said.

She made a strangled sound and backed away from him. "No. It can't be."

Eli slumped against the wall. He knew he had to keep fighting to stay alive. He was the only one who could identify the fox's voice.

"What have I done?" Ophelia moaned. "What did he make me do?"

She screamed and pounded her fist against the wall. Eli cringed as the pressure in his head tightened.

"What the hell is going on?" A tall man in a white lab coat stood in the doorway.

Eli searched his brain to try to place him. He remembered a picture on one of Danny's multiple HD monitors. Ah, this was Dr. Mathias Beauregard, the psychiatrist they had manipulated to check Eli into the lockdown unit.

Mathias stared at Eli and shock slackened his face. His eyes pivoted to Ophelia. "What the hell have you done?"

"You sick piece of shit," she growled. "You're a sex trader."

His brow furrowed and his eyes narrowed with confusion. "What are you talking about?"

With a howl, she charged forward, grabbed the doctor by the throat, and shoved him against the wall. "You made me drug those girls so you could sell them to the highest bidder. You made me a filthy accomplice to rape and slavery."

Mathias threw her off him and staggered back, clutching his throat. "I don't know what you're talking about." He pointed at Eli, who cowered against the wall. "Why is he down here?" Mathias demanded.

Ophelia thrust her hand into the pocket of her sweater. "You made me give Fadiya ketamine so you could sell her to degenerates," she said in a dead voice. "You're contemptible, worse than your abomination of a brother."

Mathias snorted in disdain. "I'm not the criminal here, Blu. You're the one who strung up Annalise Huang. You're the one who shot Harold Taylor." Scorn dripped from every word. "Need I go on about the countless others you executed? You're the murderer." He jabbed his finger into her chest. "And don't forget I have evidence of your crimes here and in Louisiana."

Bit by bit, the truth slowly penetrated the haze of fear and pain that shrouded Eli's mind: Ophelia had killed Annalise Huang and Harold Taylor. She was the vigilante Reece was hunting.

"Y'all are going to ride the needle back home in Louisiana," Mathias drawled. "And when they lift the curtain, I'll have a front row seat to avenge my brother's murder."

"Your brother raped and brutalized Pearl," Ophelia said evenly. "And you watched."

He laughed. "I wasn't there." His tone smoothly melded amusement together with contempt. "I worried what I'd catch."

Unadulterated rage froze Ophelia's face into a hideous mask that made the hair stand up on Eli's arms.

"Pearl saw *you* at the Crawfish Festival. You and your brother murdered my sister." Her calm voice was an eerie juxtaposition to the murderous rage that twisted her facial features.

The corner of Mathias's mouth lifted in amusement. "You still don't get it, Blu. My *father* was Virgile's partner." He leaned into her face. "You should have held out your hand. He would have paid you off, the same as he did for the families of all the other girls. Your sister would have had the best medical care money could buy. Instead, your junkie pa butchered her. That's on you, not my brother."

Ophelia took a step back and bumped into Eli's splayed legs. He pulled them up to his knees, trying to make himself as small and invisible as possible. Could he make it to the chute that led to the surface and escape while they fought? His vision doubled and he saw two dark holes in the back wall.

"Pearl saw you," Ophelia insisted.

The doctor shook his head with a sneer. "She saw my father talking to the man who ran the tourist booth. Remember the guy in the pork pie hat who shoved your pa?" he asked pleasantly. "My father paid him to make a scene before your idiot sister identified him." He laughed. "It was entertaining to watch your retard sister squawking like a lunatic and your one-legged pa splayed useless on his ass."

"You're a vile man," Ophelia whispered.

Mathias dismissed her by turning his back and speaking to Eli. "Let's get you upstairs," he said merrily. "The right cocktail of drugs and you won't remember any of this."

Eli's eyes widened as Ophelia crept up behind the doctor and jammed the knife into the side of his neck. She twisted Mathias's body around to face her and smiled. She drove the knife to the hilt and then slashed it across his neck in a single fluid motion.

Blood shot in an arcing stream from the severed carotid artery and spattered Eli's face. Mathias pressed his hand against his neck and staggered back. He fell to his knees and uttered a hideous gurgling sound deep in his throat. He pitched sideways. His hand fell away from the gaping wound in his neck and glanced off Eli's calf.

Eli scooted back, staring in revulsion as blood pooled around the doctor's head and stained his lab coat maroon.

Ophelia crouched beside Mathias, on the opposite side of the blood. "I failed Pearl a long time ago, but it's over now. We're finally free of your family's evil."

Eli stared into Mathias's dead eyes. His heart hammered in synchronicity to the pounding in his skull.

Ophelia looked up at him. "This was murder for the greater good," she said. "You see that don't you?"

He avoided her eyes and tried to keep his expression agreeable. He must have failed because Ophelia turned away.

"You don't understand." She released a trembling sigh and turned back to face him. "Not yet, but I hope you will." She sat cross-legged on the floor in front of him.

Eli swallowed hard and ran his tongue over his dry lips. His eyes flickered aimlessly around the room.

"Will you listen to Pearl's story?" she asked softly, moving the knife to her left hand and absently wiping the doctor's blood from her right.

Eli's heart lurched into his throat, rendering him mute. He nodded.

"I am not seeking forgiveness," she said. "Judge me harshly, if it pleases you. Decide that only a monster is capable of what I've done." Ophelia folded the bloody knife and handed it to him.

Confused, he took it with a shaking hand and set to work cutting the restrains from his ankles.

"My name is Blu," she said. "I am the omnipotent judge and executioner of the unworthy."

CHAPTER THIRTY-SIX

The Journal

LIFE ALWAYS COMES full circle. Pearl has delivered to me this young man with spiky brown hair, eyes that never settle, and facial scars that bear testament to someone's appalling inhumaneness. Eli's fingers tap the rhythm of his words as he speaks to me. I cherish the gesture. It transports me to a time when the last vestiges of a sunset flickered through the branches of an ancient bald cypress, and Pearl's white skirt twirled as she spun in the fading light.

I have patiently explained to this special young man my *raison d'être*. This entitled society we live in has enabled passive cruelty, I told him. At accidents and crime scenes, the desensitized masses hold phones high to immortalize the suffering of strangers. Everyone is eager to post a video that attracts millions of views, and gruesome misery draws the highest engagement.

What I have done is murder for the greater good.

Eli doesn't condone the acts I've committed. There is judgment and horror undulating beneath his surface veneer of understanding. To him, I am an abomination. Yet, he believes I am innocent of conspiring with Dr. Beauregard to enslave and prostitute our patients.

I am not blameless. The ones Mathias prostituted, such as Fadiya, I administered the mind-altering drugs to. Fadiya could neither defend herself against the sexual assaults nor speak of the atrocities perpetrated against her. Because of the drugs I administered to her. Aazar could not protect his beloved sister. Because of the drugs I administered to her.

I made a pact with the devil, ignorant of Mathias's true motivation, yet my actions make me complicit in rape, kidnapping, and sex slavery. I am those girls' faceless demon. I have paradoxically evolved into the worst of those I hunt. I will never claw free from this mire of shame.

My father believed that one day I would find someone who would understand what I had to do in Louisiana. I've honoured my promise to him. Over the years, I have written my family's story in this leather journal he gave me. Now I'm giving it to you, Sam. Perhaps my father was right and you have the capacity to understand what I had to do.

Your fiancé trusts in the sanctity of our flawed judicial system, and he has built his career within those hallowed halls. Like my father's world, I suspect that Reece's too is black and white. There is right. There is wrong. They never intertwine. What they do not see is that society teeters on a gossamer string suspended between the two. Sometimes, to achieve justice and bend the string closer to the side of humanity, one must have the courage to embrace immorality.

Albert Einstein said: 'The world will not be destroyed by those who do evil, but by those who watch them without doing anything.'

I did something.

I must hurry now because time is running out. Pearl's siren song lures me home to Louisiana, to a time when my father's body was whole, my mother's mind was strong, and our bayou oasis was benign. My family beckons to me from the high porch of our Acadian house. Sunshine glimmers through the lacy Spanish moss that droops from the twisted branches of our bald cypress tree. Pearl's hair gleams in the brilliance of the dappled sunlight, and her fingers rise against the azure heavens to tap the rhythm of her siren song.

My sweet Pearl, we'll lie together in our mud boat with our arms entwined again and drift soundlessly across the placid surface of the Teche. You'll count the fluffy clouds and I'll stroke your silken cheek, until the frogs' requiem lulls us to sleep. We'll be as we were when innocence reigned and happiness fortified our delicate wings of hope. We'll never be broken again.

Watch for me now, *mon chère*. I'm flying o'er the bayou to you.

CHAPTER THIRTY-SEVEN

SAM

SAM HAD LEFT Reece in Eli's room with Inspector Mansfield and a forensic team. In her opinion, it was a waste of time. Eli had texted Danny that he was in pursuit of the intruder, meaning forensics wouldn't find anything useful in the room. Danny was in the security office with Saul, searching for data obstruction that could explain why none of the security cameras had caught Eli traversing the stairwell. The clinic's security team, with the help of a slew of officers, were searching the hospital. So far, no one had found any sign of Eli. Sam's sense of impending doom grew with every minute that passed. The only person who might be able identify the hooded assailant was Bethany. Sam had hunted every nook and cranny of the hospital to no avail. Bethany had vanished.

Sam exited the withdrawal unit after questioning the residents again regarding Bethany's disappearance. The girls' reluctant, monosyllable answers to her question had left her uneasy. She couldn't shake the sense they were terrified that someone would catch them talking with her.

As she loitered in the lobby, fighting exhaustion and trying to figure out next steps, Dr. Beauregard's practicum student, Doug Sullivan, rushed over.

"What's going on in here?" he asked breathlessly. "There are police officers at every exit and they won't let me leave."

"A patient is missing," Sam said.

He blinked slowly, reminding her again of an owl. "But we're staff. Surely we can leave," he complained. "This doesn't make sense."

It made perfect sense to her. The clinic was a crime scene, so everyone—including the staff—was a potential suspect.

Rather than enlightening him on police procedures, she asked, "Have you seen Bethany?"

Doug shoved his wire-framed glasses up the bridge of his up-turned nose and his lips thinned. "No. Why would I?"

"She's your patient."

"Well, no. I haven't seen her." He assessed the melee around him with distaste. "The presence of all these cops is intrusive. It's not good for our patients." He tugged nervously on the tip of his ear. "I have to leave, I have an appointment."

Doug's whiny tone and agitated body language implied he was more concerned about himself than with their patients. An appointment at four o'clock in the morning was a ridiculous excuse, but Sam understood that being forcibly confined upset people.

"When was the last time you saw her?" she asked.

"Who?"

"Bethany," she said impatiently.

Doug folded his arms across his thin chest. "This afternoon at our session. She wanted to leave." He sighed dramatically. "I bet she did. You know, before the cops arrived. The girls in rehab leave all the time." He waved his hand in a dismissive gesture, as if a patient vanishing was a regular occurrence. "Surely they're not here looking for Bethany."

"They aren't here for her," Sam said, disturbed by his lack of empathy toward his patient.

"How long are they going to force us to stay here?" he asked again.

"What are you doing here?" she asked.

Doug's thin lips pursed as he stroked his scraggly beard. "Dr. Beauregard asked me to come in and check on something," he said distractedly. "Look, I really need to leave. As a PI, you must have some clout. Can you talk to them about letting me go?"

Sam heard footsteps behind her and turned to find Danny.

In way of introduction, she said, "This is Danny, a business associate. Doug is a practicum student."

"I need to speak with you. It's important." Danny stared pointedly at Doug.

He slow blinked at her and brushed his hair off his forehead.

"In private," Danny added.

"Doug, talk to security," Sam suggested. "They might have an idea of when we can go."

"This all seems over the top for one patient," he grumbled. "Ophelia probably didn't latch his door properly and the rich kid walked out." He turned with a sulky expression and stomped toward the elevators.

Danny scowled after him. "What a sweetheart," she said, with sarcasm dripping from her words. "He's probably super insecure with those ugly Vulcan ears. He should grow out his hair."

Sam's eyes followed Doug as he strode through the lobby. Something he'd said was bothering her. It lay just beyond her exhaustion. Whatever her subconscious had picked up was putting her cop sense on high alert.

"According to the keycard data, Ophelia accessed the stairwell exit from the lockdown unit just before Eli texted me," Danny said. "But here's the weird part. The data overlaps, putting her in two places at once. It has her opening doors in the stairwell and simultaneously opening Fadiya's room door," she said.

"Someone cloned her card," Sam guessed.

"That's my assumption," Danny agreed. "There's something else. I tried to tell you at the loft but Reece lost his shit before I could."

Sam watched Doug enter the elevator. The floor numbers decreased as the elevator dropped. It stopped at the basement level. The security office was on the fourth floor, near the executive offices. Maybe Doug thought he could bypass the police and sneak out through the underground parking garage.

"Ophelia was beside or near every one of Reece's victims in Cardoon," Danny stated. "The facial recognition algorithm pulled all five of Reece's suspected victims. Ophelia was at Cardoon every single time."

Confused, Sam said, "She lives in Parkdale and eats there a lot."

"You aren't listening," Danny retorted. "She witnessed Annalise shove the barista. When the woman's prosthetic gave out and she fell, there was this murderous look on Ophelia's face. She left a full meal on the table and bumped into Annalise on her way to the exit."

"Okay…" Sam said slowly. "Ophelia can be passive aggressive. Intentionally bumping into a bully was probably retaliation."

Danny growled low in her throat and her body stiffened. "Ophelia was there when Harold Taylor went off on the server with Down syndrome. Again, she had this scary look on her face. She left her coffee and pastry untouched on the table and caught up to Harold just outside the bistro doors."

Sam realized what was bugging her. Doug had said he didn't know who the police were looking for, but then he'd speculated that Ophelia hadn't latched the door and the 'rich kid' had walked out. Doug had nothing to do with the patients in lockdown, and he hadn't even been in the clinic when Eli had been admitted.

"Remember that woman who mowed down the pregnant mother and her toddlers at the grocery store?" Danny was asking.

Sam shifted her attention back to Danny. "Sure, she appealed a ten-year licence suspension because she deemed it too harsh a consequence for killing two kids."

"There's video of Ophelia chatting with her at the counter at Cardoon," Danny said. "If the bistro is the vigilante's hunting grounds, Ophelia is the common denominator with all the victims Reece was investigating," she said with utter certainty. "And she was the last person who saw Eli."

Emily Armstrong rushed over before Sam could respond.

"Sam, this is an unmitigated disaster. Saul told me Bethany is also missing." She wrapped her cardigan protectively across her chest. "I talked with the police but I'm utterly useless and haven't a clue what's going on in here."

Saul and a police officer joined them. "Dr. Armstrong we need access to the sub-basement."

The officer lifted his hand to silence Saul. "First, we need to understand why you have a toxic substance warning on the door."

"Public Health deemed the area unsafe because of mould and coal dust," Emily said. "What's this all about?"

"Security tells us they can't open the door," the officer said.

Emily nodded. "It's on a locking system that we separated from the rest of the security system. No one can open it other than me and my partner, who, by the way, I also can't find."

"What about Ophelia?" Sam asked. "She told me she worked with the contractors and decorated before you opened. Does her keycard access the sub-basement?"

Emily frowned. "Well, it did, but I thought we changed her access after we opened the clinic." She paused and chewed her lower lip. "Maybe we didn't. I can't recall."

"Do we need to bring a bio-hazard team in prior to entering?" the officer asked.

"That isn't necessary." Emily headed to the stairwell. "I wouldn't recommend staying too long without protective equipment, but you can search it."

They followed her down the stairs to a rusted metal door a flight below the basement and underground parking access. Emily flicked her card against the reader.

"We'll take it from here," the officer said, and he reached for the radio on his shoulder.

Danny barrelled into him, jostled him to the side, and raced through the door, screaming Eli's name.

The officer cursed under his breath and chased after her. Emily hesitantly stepped through the door. Something moved in Sam's peripheral vision, and she stepped around Emily to peer into a narrow corridor behind the gigantic boiler.

"What is it?" Emily asked, leaning over to see. She gasped and staggered back with her hands pressed against her mouth.

Halfway down the aisle, a body swayed gently from a noose attached to a ceiling beam. A naked bulb behind the body cast long shadows against the wall. The body spun in a macabre pirouette and came to rest facing Sam.

Ophelia.

Danny screamed for a doctor. Emily jerked away from the gruesome sight of her head nurse and hurried down the wide corridor alongside the front of the boiler. Sam quickly followed.

In a low-ceiling alcove in the old cellar, Danny held Eli in her arms, murmuring to him as she wiped blood from his face.

"I don't think he's breathing," Danny sobbed.

Emily tore her eyes from Mathias's dead body and knelt to check Eli's pulse. She shoved Danny out of the way, flung aside a notebook, and straddled Eli. Her shoulders pumped as she began CPR.

Mathias Beauregard lay in a pool of blood beside Eli's feet, staring sightlessly at the ceiling. Severed ends of muscle tissue were visible through a yawning wound across his neck.

The officer was calmly calling for an ambulance as Reece charged into the cramped space.

"There's a defibrillator and Epinephrine upstairs," Emily said briskly. "He'll die if I don't get supplies."

Reece rushed over and relieved Emily, his face grim as he counted chest compressions.

Sam moved out of the doorway to let Emily by. She spotted the leather-bound notebook that Emily had tossed off Eli's lap. Sam bent down and grabbed it. She turned her back to the room and read a paragraph. It appeared to be a journal, and she recognized Ophelia's neat handwriting from Fadiya's chart. Sam flipped to the last page. The final words made it clear that Ophelia had chosen to take her life, but Sam had no idea why. She turned a page and saw her name. She read the paragraph and realized that Ophelia had recorded her life story. For some reason, she'd wanted Sam to read it.

The journal was evidence and Sam knew she had to turn it over to the police. She glanced over her shoulder at Reece and the officer who was gently restraining Danny. Everyone's attention was focused on Eli, and it seemed that no one had noticed her pick up the notebook.

One line that Ophelia had written stood out in Sam's mind— *sometimes, to achieve justice and bend the string closer to the side of humanity, one must have the courage to embrace immorality.*

Sam had tried but had failed to bridge a relationship with Ophelia. Yet, the woman had entrusted her story to Sam's hands. She'd quickly take photos of the pages and then give the journal to Bryce.

Without weighing the wisdom of her decision, she tucked the leather-bound journal into her waistband and pulled her blouse over her slacks.

Emily returned with a nurse and two orderlies. She charged the defibrillator and Reece stood, coming over to stand beside Sam.

As they worked, the officer gently restrained Danny, telling her that Eli was in good hands. Reece steered Sam out of the doorway to let the paramedics pass.

"He's going to be okay," Reece said.

Sam couldn't speak over the lump in her throat. As she watched the herd of medical personnel working on Eli, tears burned in her eyes. This was all her fault. She never should have agreed to Eli's reckless plan. She should have protected him from himself.

"It looks like severe head trauma." Reece's voice was detached. He'd automatically switched into 'cop' mode during the crisis. "Someone must have struck him from behind. Emily thinks he has a subdural hematoma. The brain bleed could have put him into cardiac arrest."

"We need to help Danny," Sam croaked. "What will happen to her if Eli dies?"

Reece held her close to his side. "He's young and he's strong."

"There could be brain injury," she whispered.

Reece's arm tightened. "Or he could be fine. We have to stay positive."

The paramedics had Eli on a stretcher and they were gathering their equipment. Above the oxygen mask, Eli's eyes opened and a rush of relief turned Sam's legs to jelly.

As they rolled by, Eli fumbled to remove the oxygen mask. His face was grey and his eyes were bloodshot. There was a blue tinge to his lips, but Sam recognized the determined expression on his face.

His fingers weakly reached out to her. She clasped his ice-cold hand between hers.

"It's going to be okay, Eli," she said. "You've got this. Keep fighting."

"It was not him," Eli whispered. "It was not his voice."

She leaned closer. "Who?"

"Dr. Beauregard was not the fox."

"The fox?" Sam echoed.

"I tried to rescue Bethany. Ophelia found me. She thought it was Mathias but he was not the fox."

A paramedic replaced the oxygen mask. "We need to take him."

Sam reluctantly let go of Eli's hand and stepped back. As she stood still in the shadowy light, everything came together in perfect clarity.

She knew who the fox was.

CHAPTER THIRTY-EIGHT

SAM

ELI WAS SITTING in bed with his computer in front of him. The tip of his tongue was poking out from the corner of his lips, and reverberations of gunshots emanated from the computer speakers.

Sam entered the private hospital room with a smile. "That doesn't sound like your game," she said. The video game he'd sold to Microsoft was strategic; Sam had played it once or twice. From the cacophony, it seemed Eli was playing a war game.

He looked up, and grinned. "My game is boring. I know the tricks." He tapped on the keyboard and blessed silence filled the room.

She sat on a chair beside his bed. "Makes sense since you developed all the cheats and Easter eggs. Where are your folks?"

He closed the laptop and shoved the table with his computer to the side of the hospital bed. "They left this morning for Yemen. With the humanitarian crises, they need to help."

His father was a surgeon with Doctors Without Borders. His mother was a social worker who had returned to school for nursing when Eli and Danny were in high school. They were good people, and Sam had enjoyed meeting them.

"Reece is on his way," she said. "He had another meeting with the deputy attorney general."

Gretchen Dumont had stepped down from her position when the noose had tightened. Documents in Mathias Beauregard's office safe proved that he had given Gretchen, his lover, video evidence of Ophelia's crimes, including Annalise Huang's murder. In her eagerness to humiliate Detective Martina, who had caught Annalise's sudden-death case, Gretchen had withheld the evidence. Detective Martina had worked the Frozen Statues case and had testified against Gretchen at the subsequent inquest. Her hatred toward Toronto Police Services, and Martina specifically, had blinded her to anything but revenge.

Gretchen's efforts to sully Reece's reputation had also failed. The Crown attorney's office had received a slew of letters from all ranks of the city's police department that had pled Reece's case. The thin blue line had stood behind him with pride. With five sudden death victims deemed as homicides so far, those families finally had closure. Annalise Hung's mother had cited Reece a hero, and her story had gone viral on social media. Reece wouldn't be welcomed back to finish his articling at the Crown attorney's office, but they weren't pressing charges. That was something, at least.

"I hope Reece brings food," Eli said, pulling her from her reverie. "The doctor has not given me any dietary restrictions, but Danny is being a food Nazi." He blew his breath out in an aggravated sigh.

Eli had suffered an acute subdural hematoma from the multiple blows to his head. A neurosurgeon had operated to relieve pressure on his brain, and Eli appeared to be recovering well. Although doctors would carefully monitor him for the next few months, his surgeon had agreed that he could go home tomorrow. Sam wasn't certain if Eli understood how lucky he was that he hadn't sustained permanent brain injury. His sister did, and Sam sympathized with Danny's need to control as much as she could in Eli's recovery.

Reece popped his head through the open door. "I bring food."

"Jamaican patties?" Eli asked hopefully, kicking aside his blanket.

Reece raised an eyebrow with an exaggerated shudder. "I have no intention of laying eyes on a Jamaican patty again, homemade or otherwise." He tossed a greasy paper bag to Eli. "But I'm learning your culinary preferences. I believe this is one of your favourites." He winked at Sam.

Eli rummaged eagerly in the bag and grinned when he pulled out a Fancy Franks corn dog. He squirted ketchup over it, took a large bite, and cracked open a Mountain Dew.

"Any news on the sex trader?" he asked Reece.

"Police apprehended Doug Sullivan at Pearson International Airport trying to board a flight to Heathrow," Reece said.

Doug's slip about knowing Eli was the patient the police were searching for was the primary reason Sam had suspected him. The frightened reactions of the girls she'd questioned in the withdrawal unit hammered it home. Doug was their primary therapist. When Sam had asked Doug's permission to speak with Bethany after the staff meeting, he'd refused and turned hostile. Ketamine had been Bethany's drug of choice and her threshold was high. He hadn't given her enough, and she'd witnessed him abduct her friend Serena. Doug knew Bethany could identify him, and so he'd taken her.

Sam handed Eli a paper napkin. "One of Saul Koen's security officers had requested straight nights. Saul knew the man had IT chops and a gambling problem," she said. "He told the police and they arrested the guard, who copped a plea in exchange for testifying against Doug."

Reece carried a chair around the bed and placed it beside Sam. "Doug cracked under interrogation and gave them the location of the storage unit that held the girls," he said. "The Human Trafficking Enforcement Team has five men in custody."

"Are the girls okay?" Eli asked through a full mouth.

Reece caught Sam's eye, silently asking her to answer Eli's question. He was trying to be less rigid, but outright lying wasn't in his wheelhouse.

"They kept them drugged on heroin," she said. "The physical side effects and detox will be rough. They'll need extensive therapy to deal with what happened." She hoped her answer satisfied him and he'd drop it.

The truth was that the girls had suffered brutal sexual and physical assaults while awaiting auction. Their captors had denied them water and food. Police found one of the six victims dead. She was fourteen. Serena had died on the way to the hospital. The other three were in critical condition. Bethany—having only been in captivity for twenty-four hours—was recuperating physically. Mentally was a different story. Some people recovered from horrendous trauma and learned to live with appalling memories. Others didn't. For the ones with the capacity to recover, it took a lot of work and support. Bethany's family had abandoned her, and she had a hard road ahead of her.

Bethany's moniker 'the fox' was not only a perfect description of Doug's sly and deplorable behaviour, it was an accurate depiction of his physical characteristics. His sharp features, red hair and beard, and strange eyes were reminiscent of the animal after which Bethany had named him. In Sam's eyes, Bethany was a hero, but she knew the girl's sense of worthlessness would be her greatest obstacle during recovery. Sam hoped that one day a therapist could lead Bethany into seeing herself as the strong and courageous young woman she truly was.

Wanting to change the subject, Sam asked Eli, "Where's Pepin? We went to your place last week to pick him up and Danny said he wasn't there. She wouldn't tell us where he was."

Eli sipped his soft drink. "You are not nice to Pepin," he said.

Sam felt heat rise to her cheeks. "That's not true. I love the little guy." She realized it was true and that she missed Pepin's rambunctious shenanigans.

"Pepin reminds you that Brandy is dead," Eli said frankly. "That is why you are mean to him."

"That's not fair," Sam said.

Eli shrugged. "It is the truth."

Was it?

Sam remembered locking Pepin out of Brandy's crate and being angry with Reece for refitting it for the puppy. She'd never given poor Pepin a chance, busy as she'd been comparing him to Brandy and finding him wanting. Eli was right and shame swelled in her heart.

"I miss him and I want him to come home," she said truthfully.

"He graduates tomorrow," Danny said from the doorway.

Eli quickly jammed the last bite of his corn dog into his mouth and thrust the crushed paper bag at Reece.

Danny rolled her grey eyes at him. "You really think I didn't see you stuffing your face with that processed crap?"

Confused, Sam asked, "Graduates from what?"

"Puppy boot camp," Eli said. "I hired one of the best dog whisperers in Toronto to work with Pepin."

"It's a wedding present," Danny added and sat on the side of her brother's bed, fluffing Eli's pillows as he squirmed and swatted at her hand.

"Pepin is ready to walk down the aisle with the rings at your wedding," Eli announced with a grin.

"Like Brandy did at Lisa and Jim's wedding," Sam said softly, remembering her best friend's ceremony. "That's what bothered me about the wedding you and Mother want," she said to Reece.

He put his arm around her. "Danny figured it out. She showed me a picture of how posh Brandy looked trotting down the aisle with the pillow on her back. As soon as I saw it, I knew she was right."

Tears welled in Sam's eyes and she looked over at Danny. "Thank you."

Colour flushed Danny's round cheeks. "Whatever," she mumbled.

"Are we interrupting?" a voice asked.

Fadiya and Aazar Basha stood in the doorway. Fadiya held a gorgeous bouquet of white hydrangeas, green orchids, and white roses.

Eli's mouth dropped open as he stared at her, and Sam stifled a snicker. The girl was stunning. Her dark hair hung in shiny waves across her slim shoulders and her huge chocolate eyes were clear.

"These are for you," she said and put the vase on the table beside him. "May I sit?"

Eli nodded and Fadiya perched on the side of his bed. "My brother told me everything you did to protect me. I want to extend my gratitude for your bravery."

"Ah ... I did not do anything," Eli stuttered and his face flushed crimson as he sat up straighter.

"You did," Fadiya said. "You all did. You believed Aazar."

"Did Emily discharge you?" Sam asked.

Aazar laid his arm protectively across his sister's shoulders. "Yes, and we'd like to ask a favour."

"What's that?"

Fadiya reached across the bed and took Sam's hand. "It would honour me if you'd agree to be my therapist. With your help, I believe I can leave Bueton behind."

"Dr. Armstrong thinks it's a good fit," Aazar added. "Fadiya can work with you at the clinic on an outpatient basis."

Sam had resigned from the clinical practicum. Dr. Armstrong hadn't chosen her for the position because of her academic achievements or her skills as a therapist. Sam didn't want to gain her hours under the tutelage of a mentor who didn't believe in her. However, Emily had refused to accept the letter of resignation, asking Sam to wait until after her wedding to make a final decision.

Now, Bethany and Fadiya needed her. The decision was easy.

"I'd like that," Sam told Fadiya.

Fadiya looked at Eli. "You bought the land that belonged to Mussani's cult. Is that right?"

He nodded. "It is a horse ranch and a camp for kids with autism and Asperger's." He pressed his lips together and gave the elastic around his wrist an enthusiastic snap. Sam suspected he was worried about nervously rambling on about his charity.

"I'd like to visit," Fadiya said and turned to Sam. "If you think it would help, and you'd agree to go with me."

"We'll talk about it," Sam said, realizing that Fadiya had referred to Bueton as a cult. It was a very positive step toward recovery. "But I think it might be a good idea."

Fadiya placed her hand on her abdomen. "I'm keeping my baby," she announced with a brilliant smile. "An angel has breathed the soul into the fetus and has written down its provisions. If it's Allah's wish, the stem cells will save Aazar," she said. "This life is a blessing and brings me joy."

Sam's gaze flickered to Aazar. She assumed that Fadiya would not be able to donate a lung lobe until after the baby's birth. Aazar didn't look well enough to survive six more months. His best chance would be the umbilical cord stem cells, although there was no guarantee that it would put his disease into remission. The likelihood of Aazar surviving long enough to finish his research seemed slim, but there was an aura of peace around him now that his sister was safe.

The familial love Sam witnessed between them was inspiring. She wondered if she had the capacity to share such unconditional, selfless love. For most of her life, her mother had acted as if Sam's mere existence was a hardship to endure. Once Grace had accepted that she couldn't change her stubborn daughter, she'd avoided

Sam's company. Maybe the elaborate wedding plans were her mother's way of making amends. Maybe extravagance was the way Grace expressed love.

Reece was right, it didn't matter where they got married or what sort of an event it was. Her mother was making an effort. The least Sam could do was to deal with the pomp and ceremony for one day. After all, how bad could it be?

EPILOGUE

SAM

"THIS IS HELL," Sam grumbled to Reece. "Why didn't we elope?" She tugged at the front of her sleeveless, V-neck dress. The simplicity of the silk sheath with its mermaid skirt and cowl back had been elegant and luxurious in the air-conditioned fitting room. She hadn't considered the effect of the clingy material in the stifling August heat. By the time they'd wrapped up a ridiculous amount of photos in her mother's pristine gardens, the afternoon sun was beating down from a cloudless sapphire sky. Perspiration pooled between her breasts, and her inner thighs were slick with sweat. She was miserable and uncomfortable.

Reece's eyes gleamed with admiration. "I can't believe we're finally married. You are so damn beautiful."

"You're only saying that because you know I'm a heart-beat from running upstairs and putting on a pair of shorts and a T-shirt," she grumbled. "God, here comes Mother and she's on a mission."

Grace marched across the grass to where they were hiding by a large maple tree. As she drew closer, Sam noticed with distress that her mother's facial features were scrunched together. It appeared she might cry.

"Samantha, who is that woman standing with the tall dark-haired man?" Grace was short of breath from traversing the yard on her tiptoes, in an effort to save the heels of her Christian Louboutin stilettos.

Sam glanced to where her mother's diamond encircled finger pointed. "The man is Bryce Mansfield. That's his new wife, Alice. Why?"

"I believe she stole one of the Waterford shot glasses," Grace said anxiously. "I saw her eat the crab salad and then the glass vanished."

Sam rolled her eyes. "Bryce is the head of the homicide squad. A police inspector's wife wouldn't steal something right under his nose."

She refrained from pointing out that she'd specifically asked her mother not to serve the fancy cocktail food in over-priced serving vessels. Her eyes skimmed over Eli and Danny. Eli was rolling around getting grass stains all over his Kiton tuxedo. Pepin was happily barking and nipping at the fifty-thousand-dollar pant cuffs. Sam watched Danny scarf down a lobster roll in a single bite and drop the vintage china plate on the grass, an inch from where Eli was about to roll.

Sam stepped to the other side of Reece to block her mother's view. "I'm positive Alice isn't a kleptomaniac," she said to comfort her mother. Sam wasn't positive. She'd only met Alice a few times, which had been enough. All she knew about Bryce's second wife was that she was twenty years his junior and had the intellect of a squirrel.

"I'm certain she stole the glass, and I caught her wandering around inside the house," Grace said, growing more agitated.

"Goodness knows what she took! There's an original Van Gogh painting in the front room." A tear trailed down Grace's cheek.

How Alice would lift a priceless painting, trot out to Bryce's car—a Mini convertible, no less—and manage to hide a giant oil painting was a mystery to Sam.

"Bryce is coming over," Reece said gently. "I'll speak to him about your concerns. Enjoy this fantastic party. You've done so much for us, and we're both very grateful."

Her mother visibly relaxed under Reece's doting attention. "I was certain you'd know exactly how to handle it."

Reece steered Grace in the direction of the stairs to the elevated patio, where guests mingled around multiple bars lined with top-shelf liquor. "Oh no," he said dramatically. "The Ontario Premier has Harvey cornered."

Grace's eyes widened. "Oh good lord! He's fundraising again. Harvey will gift him a substantial donation just to get rid of the insufferable man."

"You better intercept them before Harvey empties the vaults." Reece leaned into Grace's ear and whispered in a conspirator tone, "I'll investigate the case of the stolen Waterford glass."

Much to Sam's amazement, her mother giggled. Grace kissed her new son-in-law's cheek and tottered over to the sweeping staircase that led up to the enormous patio.

"You're embracing therapeutic lying," Sam said to her new husband. "That isn't the Premier. It's my dad's old partner."

Reece laughed. "I know, but now Grace and I have officially bonded as family."

Bryce left his child bride at the stairs that led up to the patio and strolled over to greet them. After he shook Reece's hand and kissed Sam's cheek, his expression turned serious.

"Sam, did you leak Blu's journal?" he asked.

"Of course not."

He nodded. "I didn't think so. Sorry I asked." He shaded his eyes against the sun and peered up at the patio. His face tightened at something he saw and he turned away, pulling on a pair of sunglasses. "We've received a tip that over the next twelve weeks an anonymous online site is publishing the journal in its entirety."

Sam had read Blu's story multiple times and had felt a confusing sense of compassion. As authorities ruled more sudden-death cases as homicide, she'd had to tell herself repeatedly that murder was never excusable. What Blu had done to her grandfather, the victims she'd killed in Toronto, and Mathias Beauregard was inarguably first-degree murder, which made her one of Canada's most prolific serial killers. What troubled Sam was how it started.

Virgile Landry had perpetrated an unspeakable crime against Pearl. He had been a monster, protected by status and wealth. Sam was conflicted over the morality of exacting justice in a broken system that shielded the rich and powerful. People like Pearl were rarely allotted justice in the Deep South, not when they stood against an established family with old money. Yet, Blu had decided against killing Virgile. She'd wanted to walk away at the dogfight. He had been the one who had led her into a secluded area and had brandished the knife he'd used to slash Pearl. If Blu hadn't fired her father's gun, Sam was certain that Virgile and his father—whom Sam believed had been hiding in the bushes—would have raped and killed her. In her opinion, Virgile's death was self-defence and

Sam had no compassion for the vile young man. If she were honest, she didn't have much empathy for the vigilante's heartless victims either.

Reece completely disagreed. In his mind, Ophelia's vigilante murders proved she was a stone-cold killer who had invaded people's privacy and stalked them mercilessly with a drone prior to executing them ruthlessly. Reece was adamant that without a societal-enforced judicial system, anarchy would rein. Regardless of how hard he was working toward tolerance, justice would always be black and white to him.

Sam suddenly realized that Bryce and Reece were watching her with matching expressions that fused concern and disapproval.

To break the uncomfortable silence, she said, "Readers might sympathize with Blu."

Bryce shrugged. "Murder is never for the greater good. People understand that." He looked up at the bustling bar. "Let's get a drink. We're here to celebrate."

"Go ahead," she told them. "I need a minute."

Reece and Bryce waved at Eli and Danny to join them. As the group went up the stairs, Sam gazed at the people on the crowded patio. Any of these strangers could someday feel compelled to exact vigilante justice against a mean and entitled society. That was exactly what Ophelia had warned:

When I dwindle away like the grey mist that hangs above the bayou at dawn, some likeminded soul will materialize from the dissipating vapour. We are the omnipotent judges and executioners of the unworthy.

Sam rubbed the chill from her arms and stood in quiet reflection under the giant old maple tree. For just a second, a fragrant scent of coconut surrounded her. She stared up at the dappled sunlight from the heavy green foliage of the towering tree, and tears stung her eyes.

"Blu, I hope you made it o'er the bayou to Pearl."

THE END

AUTHOR LETTER

PEOPLE OFTEN ASK where I get my ideas. Usually, I can't answer, because something comes to me and the seed grows on its own volition. A fan once wrote in a review that he wondered what goes on my head. I appreciate the fact he didn't add the adjective 'crazy', although I wouldn't have blamed him. You probably don't want to know what goes on in my head, but I can tell you what motivated this story. One day I was shopping, and everywhere I went I encountered rude people. I told myself that their situational awareness was low and they weren't being obnoxious and entitled intentionally. Then, a shopper came barrelling down an aisle and plowed into me with her grocery cart. Rather than apologizing, the woman glanced up from her phone and snarled at me to watch where I was going. As I stood rubbing my wounded shin, I wondered about the apathetic and self-absorbed tendencies of today's society. It didn't take long before I sensed Blu standing beside me.

I was fortunate to live in the southern United States a long time ago. Here in Southwestern Ontario in Canada, I still keep a hurricane kit nestled in our basement, much to the amusement of my family. I visited Louisiana frequently and fell in love with the state, the rich culture, and the amazing people. If you haven't visited the Breaux Bridge Crawfish Festival, I highly recommend it. If you take a tour down the Bayou Teche, you're likely to pass the inspiration for Blu's home, assuming it's still there. I took a bit of literary licence, but I tried to remain authentic to the unique beauty of the area.

Mike Doyle is the graphic designer responsible for the amazing cover. This is the third cover he's done—*Red Rover* and *Frozen*

Statues—and Mike's sheer brilliance in capturing the essence of my stories amazes me. Jennifer McIntyre handled the developmental edit for this novel. The newest addition to my editing team is Erin Hall, and she deserves the biggest shout-out. After a catastrophic mishap with the substantive editing of the final manuscript, Erin stepped up and took over the project with very little notice and a crushing deadline. I'm eternally grateful to her for her professionalism, loyalty, and support. She is a rock star.

Any mistakes are mine. I'm an insecure neurotic who fiddles after the final proofreading. I suppose this illustrates the duel personality trait of a Gemini, because I live in perpetual fear of typos. Regardless of everyone's best efforts, typos slip through occasionally. I'm grateful to any eagle-eyed reader who lets me know. We fix them immediately. I write in Canadian English—which can be a bit confusing for some readers—but if you find any pesky typos, please email me at **lori@lefraser.com.**

Thank you for reading *Shadow Tag, Perdition Games*. I'm requesting a bit more kindness by asking you to write a review on **Amazon** and **Goodreads** to offer your honest opinion. Leaving a review, no matter how short, helps make it possible for me to continue to write for you. And as always, please connect with me on social media to hear about new releases and book promotions or just to say hello.

QPP, your spirit is infinite.

Lori

www.perditiongames.com
Twitter: **@perditiongames**
Facebook: **perditiongamesseries**